Apocalypse Unleashed
Book 1 - And, So It Begins

An Omniverse Series
By ItalianDragon

Contents

Dedication

To my family, friends, and now fans, your support has been amazing. I love you all.

For this book, I wanted to give special thanks to the strong, intelligent, and loving women in my life.

To my mom and aunts, your unconditional love is part of the glue that keeps our family together. All of you encouraged us to be the best versions of ourselves and created a haven from the turbulent storms of life. I was blessed to have aunts who have been more like additional moms that helped me grow as a person.

I must thank my mom for my imagination and creativity! She is full of life, love, and joy and that shall be forever a part of me.

To my Aunt Terri, your heart could melt the coldest of weathers. We may not always tell you how much we appreciate you, but you make life just a bit brighter and warmer. Thank you for being you!

I also wanted to give a special thank you to a Kindle Customer. They didn't leave their name but the headline they gave was "Fantastic escapism". I want you to know that your kind words inspired me. I write to reach people and to help people come together. To know that, even if for a moment, my stories helped you deal with your depression has truly touched my heart. For you and others out there who might feel alone or struggling with depression, know that you are not alone, we are never truly alone.

Many years ago, I learned an old story that mentioned how certain tribes would say "I See You" as a way of greeting someone rather than just saying "hello". To you and all the others who battle depression, feel lost, or unnoticed, I say, "**I See You** my fellow traveler in this journey called life. We are not alone!"

Chapter 1 – How My Imagination Saved Lives

When the wave of energy hit, I felt pain like no other. I did what I do when things get crazy or hard, I used my imagination. I shifted my focus and visualized wielding every magic imaginable. I had always dreamed of being the most powerful warrior wizard.

My mind immediately escaped into my imagination as the pain was unbearable. From using creation magic to create anything I could imagine. I thought about throwing fireballs, or creating crystal clean water, shooting shards of ice, or summoning lightning, soaring through the sky, to creating massive fortresses from solid stone and forging weapons from fantasy metals and crystallized mana itself.

On and on I went. As the pain intensified so did my imagination. I dreamed of using space magic to teleport around everywhere. Thought about moving things with my mind or reaching out and having conversations without speech. From there I desperately visualized traveling to different realms or creating a realm of my own, anything away from this excruciating pain and pure torture. That got me thinking about purity itself and being able to purify or transform anything. Which led my mind to think about dragons and hydras and their ability to regenerate. From there my mind thought about healing myself and all those out there that might be suffering as I was. I wished with all my heart I could resist and heal anything. A part of me always wanted to be a true healer.

From healing to wielding the raw forces of nature to smite my enemies. That made me think about nature itself and animals as I hoped they were not currently suffering as I was, if they were, I wished I could take their pain from them as they didn't deserve whatever hell this was. Thinking about hell made me think about death magic and necromancy, my creativity coming to my salvation once again as I re-doubled my efforts to mentally visualize a different person. I was strong, stronger than the man of steel, I was faster too, wielding weapons I created to defeat my enemies.

Then my mind went to time and using it to speed up or slow things down. I thought about traveling through time to go somewhere before this event occurred or moving forward in time to when it was over. I used time to pause this pain and reverse it. This made me think of my family and the stories of our ability to glimpse insights we shouldn't be able to know.

Finally, as the torture and pain hit a crescendo, I thought about purifying this, turning it into something I could use. I wanted to wield this very power and so I thought about a vast space where I poured all this pain. I imagined the pain in my blood that felt like poison and fire being sucked in this vast void. I mentally pushed and pushed, condensing all of it into a super dense well-spring, an ocean deeper than the Pacific. I pulled and pulled, creating a giant funnel in my mind that would draw everything into it.

I thought about nothing else. I just wanted to draw in the pain, removing it from my body so that I could wield this very power and turn it into whatever I desired. My massive funnel continued to draw in everything into the super-dense well-spring. At the same time, I visualized generating my own unlimited power to match, then exceed the power I was transforming my pain into. This power joined my own mass of galaxies and stars generating unlimited power. For a moment I thought of myself as a universe unto itself.

That thought made me remember all the animals and innocents that I hoped were not suffering as I was. With my last vestiges of mental will I increased the size and gravity of my funnel to desperately try to pull in whatever was causing this pain, making it grow to not just around me but the very planet itself. I did not care about my life any longer if I could sacrifice myself to save everyone else from this pain. That was my last thought before I blacked out.

I awoke or was having a dream, still not sure. All I knew was I was surrounded in pure white light.

"Am I dead?" I spoke out loud.

A jolly laugh that reminded me of St Nick and Christmas greeted me. "Ha, ha, ha, ha! No, not yet. We are between moments."

"Which moments?" I asked.

"Good question. You will need that imaginative and critical mind of yours for what is to come."

"What is to come?"

"Yes. Ages ago your world was shattered into different realms. Magic as you understand it along with the creatures of your fantasy were pulled into those separate realms. Since then, only the smallest trickle of magic has existed in your world beyond faith magic."

"What caused this shattering?"

"Another good question. It was a sacrifice of one who willingly took on the sins of the world. The shattering limited the forces to interfere with the realm of man... that is until now."

"I am guessing this has something to do with the unending and excruciating pain." I stated.

"Yes. The forces of the Dark have finally twisted enough of humanity while those of the Light have asked for salvation. The agreement was made to begin to merge the realms and bring your world back into the fold. As such, your world is about to become a more literal battleground than you know."

"Even in great tragedy there is good that comes from or in it." I said as I recalled my family's mantra.

"Ah yes, you glimpse understanding, yet there is more you must comprehend. This is something many have written about. Your spirit is already saved but you made a choice at the end there to sacrifice yourself to save everyone else. That act has created a choice."

"A choice? You mean some kind of opportunity for these different forces." I hypothesized.

"Ha, ha, ha, ha! Your combination of intuition and critical mind serve you well, hold on to both. Yes, you have presented an opportunity. You are not aware of what you were doing, not fully, so that is why we are speaking. Within all of humanity exists the capacity for good and evil... and I DO MEAN EVERYONE!" The voice boomed the last few words.

"Both sides have agreed you will be given a choice and make a decision."

"What kind of choice and isn't making a choice a decision?"

"Yes. But this choice will impact your salvation and the decision you will make will impact all those on your world."

"My salvation? You said earlier that my spirit was already saved." I asked with some trepidation as I did not like where this was going.

"Yes. This choice will risk much and change that outcome and others. In your final moments you offered yourself as a sacrifice to save others. Do you still stand by this choice?"

I did not even give it a second thought. "I do!"

I heard dark whispers upon giving my answer. Some I could make out, others I could not.

"Pspsh. Pstst."

"He has agreed."

"He rejects salvation!"

"The die is cast."

The voice boomed. "SILENCE! YOU ARE ALLOWED TO WITNESS BUT YOU SHALL NOT INTERFERE OR ATTEMPT TO MANIPULATE HIM!!!"

All at once the growing whispers ceased.

"As they have spoken so shall I. The Dark and the others that move in the void gain much when they turn away someone from their salvation, it denies the Light with another force for good. They also believe if you are turned you can be a weapon like no other to serve their machinations. This is the gravity of your choice."

"I understand what I do for others."

"No, not yet. Perhaps you glimpse it, but you do not fully understand. Others can still choose to turn away and deny, this in their eyes would diminish your sacrifice and make you a fool. However, the Light sees otherwise and so an accord is reached. Instead of immediately joining salvation, you will go back. You will be another path, a choice to save those you can or wish to. This event shall change the very nature of your world. As time progresses more changes will occur."

"Another path? Changes?" I asked.

"You must choose to help those that remain in your world. Many would have died from the event. Your pain was so intense because you held on so long rather than accepting your salvation."

"Oh. So, I caused my own pain, that sounds about right."

"Yes, perhaps you are wiser than you even realize. You have chosen to return to a world that will go through dramatic changes over time. Magic and creatures of fantasy and nightmare will return to your world. Some of the old ones will still not be able to enter but their influence will still be felt."

"Influence?"

"You will know it when you see it. Now that you have made your choice, as a result you shall be granted authority, and it is now time for you to make the decision."

"Authority? What decision?" I asked in confusion.

"You will decide how the humanity will interact and interpret this new world."

I knew I had to understand this situation better, so I spoke up. "Please provide me with more context."

"It has been over two thousand years since your people truly Interacted with the universe and magic itself. There are many ways in which one can exchange and interact with the universe and the inherent magic that will now be within everything. You must choose the way in which humanity with comprehend this new world."

"The way they understand the world itself. Well, we use our eyes and other senses to interpret the world but that doesn't always quantify things as we would prefer. Yet everyone's perceptions also influence our understanding. Hmmm. There are some fundamental truths though that you can try to ignore but that does not change the facts. My thoughts immediately go to a system, like something from one of the many LitRPG books I've read. A system that can quantify the world around us and help us understand the new reality we will be in. Is something like that possible?"

"Anything is possible. To answer your question, what you ask can be done."

"It should be more than that though. We should have the capacity to use our senses, including perhaps a sixth sense to also understand things. Hopefully the combination will help us to thrive."

"Wise to not rely on one thing. Such can be done. Anything else?"

"There should be some penalties for unjustified killing or murder. If that is not possible some way for those of us to counteract those who do such things."

"A balance must be reached. As you will follow a different path, I will grant you an awareness of such things, but the world must be allowed free will, even if it is to destroy itself. That is the accord, the meek must fight to bring about the world they want. IT IS DONE. THE DECISION IS MADE." The voice boomed and echoed the last part.

"It is time for you to return and reap what you have sown. Remember you can pull others to a different path if you so choose. Those left in your world have already denied salvation but that does not mean it is not possible to receive it. Use your creativity, imagination, critical thinking, and intuition. All of those skills will serve you."

Then there was a flash.

Like that I startled awake as my eyes shot open. I did what anyone would do and patted myself down. My eyes, ears, hands, fingers, legs, wiggled my toes, yep toes check. Grabbed my manhood, woo-hoo, check.

"Alright everything seems to be in place. Did I have some junk food induced wild dream about the world ending?"

Just as I said that a screen popped up in my vision!

Greetings! Your world has forever been changed, what was separated shall now begin to return. Magic is real as are the beings you called monsters. Many of you have left your world and reached salvation. Now it is time for you to determine what you will do with the rest of your life on this planet.

This system has been chosen to help you interpret the changes to yourself and the world around you. Think or say "status" should you want to view your character sheet or information regarding your skills and abilities. You can concentrate on an ability or area to gain additional information. If you desire to adjust your notifications or display think "system settings" and your options will appear. These options are limited by person due to a multitude of factors.

After I re-read the notification, I mentally dismissed it. As soon as I did another series of notifications popped up.

Congratulations! You have created a magic core! When creating your core, you must determine its nature. Upon creation that core and its functions are solidified. Growth and some change in functions can change or evolve but those changes must align with the original intent of your core. Size, strength, capacity, and magical type or types all factor in to determine the rarity and purity of the core. Anyone can use magic they are attuned to, but a true magic caster or warrior requires a core to accomplish the miraculous.

Congratulations! You have created an Omni-Core! Omni-Cores are the rarest as all magic types exist and are attuned within this core, as a result, you have 100% chance at wielding any, and all magic types. This also grants you the ability to learn any spell, body movement, or combat form without restriction. Warning you must possess the mana required to use said ability or you could kill yourself in the process.

Congratulations! You have created a magic spiral! Mana and energy can be gathered and regenerated without a spiral but at a slower rate and far less efficient manner. Magic spirals are constructs that help you cultivate the magic around you. Size and speed determine both length of time to grow and evolve your core along with how quickly you regenerate the energy spent. New spirals are fragile constructs, easily shattered, or lost without focused time and attention. Continue to strengthen your spiral to further solidify and grow its capabilities.

Congratulations! You have created a Celestial Spiral! Celestial spirals can gather energy at a cosmic level, across realities. Such spirals are exceptionally rare and require a comprehension of multiple elements and an insatiable hunger for growth and knowledge.

Congratulations! Your Celestial Spiral has strengthened and grown to a gather intensity beyond that of a black hole. How it has not shattered is beyond comprehension. Your core has expanded to accommodate the prodigious growth rate. Your will must be strong, or perhaps you had help, either way, congratulations on not killing yourself!

"Errrrr, hold up! Wait a minute! What?! Congratulations on not killing myself?! You can kill yourself by gathering too much energy?!" I thought about that for a moment.

"Well, if I think about it, I guess that is true in science, too much energy or a big enough catalyst and boom. Ok note to self, try to avoid going boom. For that matter no boom boom right now either." I said before diving back into my notifications.

Your creativity and imagination allowed you to strengthen the visualization of your core. This has let your core rapidly expand and take in multiple magical and energy sources. Taking in energy not aligned with your nature can lead to poisoning your spirit or ultimately result in your death. However, you possess an Omni-Core which has allowed you to take in any magic or energy source and transform it into what you require. Core's capacity has vastly increased.

Congratulations! Your quick thinking and willingness to sacrifice yourself caused you to take in magic across the planet, taking just enough to save many lives. This selfless act has caused your core to gather enough energy to reach the pinnacle stage and forced it to evolve into a Divine Core!

"Was that what the voice was talking about. He said I could save lives." I commented before continuing reading.

Congratulations! Your Divine core and Celestial Spiral have merged and evolved into a Divine Infinitum! A Divine Infinitum has the larger capacity and potency of a divine core, along with the ability to absorb magic and energy across multiple realities. What sets the Divine Infinitum apart is its ability to both transform any energy into what it requires and its ability to generate magic itself! This allows the wielded to not be restricted in environments where mana has been absorbed or devoid of a type of mana desired. Warning if not handled correctly can result in an apocalyptic event if you travel to a world without magic.

"Whaaaat?! I can generate my own magic?! That's so freaking cool! Hmmm, apocalyptic event? I wonder if something like that influenced what happened to Earth? If what the voice told me is true, then most of my family and friends should have been saved. I somehow knew of a few that believed the lie and as such would not have chosen salvation. It was for those and others I did not know that I chose to return. Eh, figure out the whole cause of the apocalyptic event later. Time to see what my status says before I start making plans. Hmmm, let me change my name to one of my gamer handles. There we go."

Name: Shadowalker	Race: In Transition	Level: 1
Strength: 8	Dexterity: 10	Constitution: 10
Intelligence: 21	Wisdom: 26	Charisma:15
Spiritual Attunement: Omni	Core Stage: Divine Infinitum	Spiral Stage: Divine Infinitum
Health, Mana, Stamina Values & Regen Rates per hour (pH)		
HP: 130	MP: 286	SP: 188
HP/pH: 5	MP/pH: 130	SP/pH: 82
Core Capacity: 13	Special: Core Generation	Core Generation: 13

"Interesting. As to be expected my Strength and Dexterity are ok, not great but not bad considering the 'Dad Bod' I have cultivated over the last several years. I am surprised my Constitution is higher than I expected but still not where I would like it to be. I knew I had a sharp mind so no surprise my Intelligence is one of my higher stats. I definitely did not expect my Wisdom to be so high, that is a total trip. Lastly, Charisma is surprisingly decent. This may be real life, but I have played enough games to know you do not ignore Charisma, especially if I plan on trying to help others.

All in all, not a bad start. I had areas to work on regardless of what 'build' I was planning to go with. Heck, I don't even know how I level up or how many stat points I get per level. That's a good question.

"System? How do I increase my stats and or level up?"

Query Accepted.

Another notification popped up in my view.

There are multiple ways to gain permanent stat points. The most common is fighting and killing other beings. When a being dies some of its accumulated magic is released. Part of that magical energy is collected in the form of experience points. If you contributed to the kill in any way, whether directly damaging or providing support to your allies you gain a portion of those experience points. The higher your core and gathering spiral, the more experience you can gain per kill. Gathering enough experience points will cause you to level up.

When you level up, humans will gain 5 attribute points, which are commonly referred to as 'stat points', to distribute into any area you choose. Please note: your Divine Infinitum grants you an additional 8 'stat points' per level...

"Wow, way to go Divine Infinitum!"

Query Accepted

Another notification popped up right in front of what I was reading.

Please Note that creation of a core is exceptionally rare so early on. The creation of the Divine Infinitum at all, let alone at this level... let's just say the probability is so low that to display the number would take up too much text. In your current state it is unwise to let others know you have formed a core. Others may attempt to kill you for your core as attempting to absorb power from cores is another way to attempt to gain additional stat points and help expand your existing core.

Additional note: There are beings out there that can swap their core for a larger one if it is of the same type.

"Good to know! Thank you for the warning, System!" I said before thinking 'Let's not think about how it interjected itself, but maybe it has to do that to help us understand this new reality.'

I went back to reading the stat gain notification.

Additional ways to gain stat points include the following:
• Attempting to absorb cores from other beings.
• Potential stat gains from absorbing concentrated mana sources similar to cores.
• Performing specific magical rituals that can provide both temporary and permanent stat bonuses.
• Stat gains from certain Titles and Achievements
• Crossing a threshold in your magical cultivation can also provide stat bonuses.
 Please note: Additional descriptions are available if required.

I whistled. "Whew! That is a much more expansive list to gain stats than I was thinking! I'm going to file all those away for now, but I will come back to them. For that matter... System is it possible to prompt me when I encounter one of those above sources and provide me additional information at that point?"

Query Accepted

Text appeared in front of me once again.

System Setting Changes Have Been Applied.

"Cool! Thanks System, you rock!"

Just then another thought crossed my mind, so I asked my favorite source.

"Umm System, how do I use magic or gain new spells?"

Query Accepted

Most magical abilities come from the following:
• Gaining a class can automatically grant new abilities and spells.
• Learning to channel your power to a certain part of your body or Experimentation using your creativity and imagination in combination with your power to unlock existing known spells and abilities or create new ones...

I was reading along until my brain caught up with what I read. "Wait, there are classes in this system?"

Query Accepted

Yes. Classes can be unlocked after level 13. Options for available classes are based on a multitude of factors including but not limited to achievements, titles, formation and type of core and spiral, etc.

<u>Please note</u>: *A class does not need to be chosen right away but will grant bonuses per level gained afterwards.*

"Man, that is a big catch 22. Rush to choose a class and you might miss out on something better later. Wait and you miss out on additional bonuses per level that you can't get back. Again, let me add it to the list of things to address later. Back to reading. Where was I, oh right, I can gain spells and abilities through experimentation."

As I returned to the notification describing how to learn magic, I noticed the warning text next to it.

*...Experimentation using your creativity and imagination in combination with your power to unlock existing known spells and abilities or create new ones. **Warning**: Experimentation can lead to crippling injuries or even death if you carelessly try to force through your magical channels or you expend too much power before your body, mind, and spirit are ready.*

"OK so take it slow and cautious when it comes to experimenting." I said to myself before reading the final line with some golden text right after it.

*... Some cores can contain abilities that can be gained upon absorption. Core must align with your magic type, your core must have capacity to absorb the ability, and your body, mind, and spirit must be capable of using said ability. User must spend extra time to attune to the core prior to absorption attempt. **Warning**: Some cores are such an anathema to the user that absorption attempts could result in injury, loss of sanity, or even death if a proper healer is not available. **Please Note: Your Divine Infinitum does not possess these restrictions and is based solely on probably chance. Attunement prior to attempt can increase the chance of success.***

"Now that is freaking awesome! My mind is running wild with possibilities! As long as I take time to sync up with the cores, I'm absorbing I could gain all sorts of cool abilities!"

After getting an initial handle on this new system, I figured it was high time I assess my environment and do some proper situational awareness.

Chapter 2 – The End of the World is Messy

I spoke as I stood up from the floor I somehow was laying on. "When did I fall off the bed?"

That was when I noticed my clothes were totally shredded and I was completely naked.

"Man, I don't have many pants that fit me anymore!" I complained as I grabbed one of my remaining good pairs of jeans from my suitcase and put on a simple T-shirt. I wasn't planning on going outside just yet so figured I could worry about socks and shoes later. Regardless of what I was planning best to protect my important bits and not just have everything dangling out there.

It was just me and my roommate back at my place. I wouldn't call us preppers, but we had plenty of emergency food and water. Sadly, that was several hundred miles away as I had decided to rent this cabin to get away from it all. My original plan was to get some time for myself on my birthday. I loved nature and going hunting, but doing both wasn't really an option in Southern California, hence my current location in the middle of nowhere.

Of course, I still brought my laptop along as the place had satellite internet even though I was in the middle of a forest. I mean come on I'm good at roughing it, but there are limits. Plus, this allowed my friends and I to still have our raid nights.

After unlocking my door, I left my bedroom. There were three bedrooms on the top floor and downstairs held the living/dining room, a kitchen, and doors leading outside. He had an attached garage that was converted into a faraday cage protecting everything inside from any electromagnetic interference. The guy knew how to plan for the end.

I listened for any response to the noise my door opening made. After hearing nothing for a few moments I made my way to check the remaining bedrooms upstairs. Both rooms were clear, so I made my way downstairs to check the doors and Windows.

The man who built this place was smart. Paul was his name, and he was more of a prepper than even my buddy and me. He built this place to last. It was heavily insulated and even though the place was a log cabin that was by external appearance only. The foundation and walls were solid concrete re-enforced with thick steel rebar. Logs were placed across everything to give the appearance of a simple log cabin. Heck, even the windows were thick bulletproof glass with steel shutters that could be closed over the top of them. It had a direct line to an underground well and both backup generators and solar panels with batteries. The waste system even funneled to a greenhouse garden to provide fertilizer. It truly was an impressive construction.

Paul let me use the place periodically after I met him at a gun show in Texas. We hit it off as my cousin and I started talking about archery and hunting. My cousin was a skilled bowman and marksman. The older man offered up the place if we were ever interested. This was the first time I came up here on my own. Of all places to be while in the middle of nowhere, this would work as a decent base.

As I expected the place was secure. I'm pretty sure the place could withstand a bear assault without taking anything but superficial damage. My immediate safety addressed, I decided to fix some food as I was starving. Good thing I stocked up before coming here.

I cooked up some elk steaks as they still are my favorite meat. After I devoured four large cuts, I started to feel better. I knew I was hungry but man that's a lot of meat.

Now that my mind wasn't distracted by my stomach I could start experimenting. If I was going to explore this new reality, I was going to need to have some offensive and defensive spells, for that matter, a few utility spells wouldn't be a bad idea either.

Starting with offense, my go to would naturally be 'Fireball' but probably not the best idea in a forestry area. My next best solution...

———————

ZAP!

"Ha, ha, ha, ha! Success!"

*Congratulations! You have learned the known spell **Lightning Bolt**!*

"Sweet!" I said after reading my notification.

"Well looks like I'm going to have to replace that lamp." I commented as I looked at the results of my **Lightning Bolt** hitting my target.

It had taken me some time to get a feel for, and visualize, what I wanted to do. After a few inquiries to the System, I learned how to manipulate and move the energy within me. This was referred to and allowed me to learn a skill called Mana Manipulation. That gave me a better feeling for how to move the energy around within both in my core and what I learned were mana channels or what Eastern medicine called meridians.

According to the System, **Mana Manipulation** wasn't a required skill for non-casters, instead they could get a skill called **Energy Circulation**, which allowed them to move the energy through their body and begin to develop and strengthen their channels. Magic casters had to learn to move their mana outside their bodies to cause actual effects in the real world. Body enhancement or what some martial artists and cultivation stories focus on is Chi or Ki, which is just learning to draw in and enhance yourself so you can accomplish superhuman effects. Most of those effects are body related but not all. An offshoot of this second set of beliefs was Spiritualists, who were a hybrid of both a caster and body enhancement, but most stories I read typically portrayed this hybrid approach as having great utility but weaker than the other two options.

This reminded me that what we visualized and our focused on drove much of our results. Plus, I refused to believe learning both made you weaker, casters are physically weak and body enhancers are not as smart or can't cast, UTTER NONSENSE! Some could not see past popular beliefs even if those beliefs were flawed or missing information. As I got older, I learned to have a flexible mind to help see different perspectives, critically think about them and compare it to facts, then take the nuggets of truth buried in them and apply it to give me greater understanding of life and how things really were.

That was when I asked the System a question and got an 'AFFIRMATIVE' in response. In most cultivation stories characters could move energy to their fist or foot to deliver a powerful punch or kick. In most magical stories, casting certain spells required specific movements, incantations, or materials to act as catalysts. Most of this was a combination of a mental ritual that focused your mind and magic in such a way that you got the same outcome and using mediums as the body could not always survive acting as a catalyst itself. If I added the aspect of channels, that made even more sense why a caster had to use their hands, their channels were more developed from constantly moving power from within you to your hands, after all we use our hands for everything. I knew I was on the cusp of a greater understanding, but it wasn't completely solidified just yet.

With all of those realizations in mind, I spent time gaining the **Energy Circulation** skill. This helped me gain greater awareness of my channels and I knew I was going to strengthen them to get the type of results I wanted. The challenge was figuring out how. That was when my knowledge of biology and our circulatory system gave me an idea. We have both arteries that move precious blood to every part of the body and then veins that circulate the blood back into the heart and that also helped me recall other systems and other organs that helped purify and remove waste.

With those things in mind, I spent hours creating dual connections to my channels and my core. Each channel would split its connections. One connection allowed energy to flow from my core into the channel. This proved the easiest as an initial connection was created after I gained **Mana Manipulation**. The second connection was to the spiral that was now my core. This would allow me to better draw power not just directly through my spiral but also my whole body. The **Energy Circulation** skill partially helped but my imagination and focus on purifying and transforming the power created a third connection that seemed to surround and infuse my channels and connections. Funny enough this last part along with some related memories for past D&D campaigns I was in had gained me a new ability called '**PURITY!!!**' What an odd name for an ability, it was all caps and emphasized too. Funny how the imagination works.

That is when the System prompted a new notification that was literally glowing with golden white script and borders.

*Congratulations! Your creativity, imagination, and critical thinking have allowed your Divine Infinitum to create a new ability. Abilities are greater than skills as your mental space, physical body, or spiritual signature also changes. You have created a new ability called '**PURITY!!!**'*

*Congratulations! You have gained the achievement: **Ability Creator!** This achievement grants you the Title of Creator or enhances the existing title if you already possess it.*

Congratulations! You have gained the title Creator! This title is gained or enhanced any time you create a new ability, spell, or skill. This grants the following bonuses:

As the creator of the ability, spell, or skill you gain double the efficiency and power.

Any battle with another being where you both are using the ability, spell or skill, in a test of wills you will always win and be able to shut down their use of said ability, spell, or skill.

The efficiency and power increase exponentially for all abilities, spells, and skills you create.

"WOW! That's a potential game changer if I can come up with more unique abilities."

My excitement further soared when I read what '**PURITY!!!**' did.

Ability: PURITY!!!
<u>Description</u>: Purity magic goes beyond healing and removal of corruption from the mind, body, and spirit caused by magic, curses, toxins, and poisons. Purity has the power to transform one thing into another. It is at the heart and foundation of your transformed Omni-core.
<u>Passive effect</u>: Naturally purify and cleanse your mind, body, and soul/spirit. This grants you immunity to diseases, poisons, curses, and corruption. Protects and strengthens your channels increasing growth and purification of all existing toxins within you. You no longer must wait for magic to enter your core to purify and transform it. In addition, allows you to naturally resist negative effects from Eldritch magic.
<u>Active effects</u>: Absorb external power and transform it prior to reaching your core. Tap into an external power source and purify it to what you desire. Can be triggered to cleanse a particular area of containments. If used while meditating to speed up cultivation progress and increase rates of reaching key thresholds.

Note: When using the active ability and contesting with outside sources you must succeed in a battle of wills. All bonuses apply during this conflict.

"Now this is even more useful! I can only imagine how bad a magical enhanced disease could be. Also, good to know curses are actually a thing, but even better to be immune to them!" I commented after reviewing all my hard work.

That was when I realized the sun was setting and I had been at this all day. As my external awareness came back to me, I realized my body felt stiff, you know the stiffness that comes from remaining in the same position for too long. Man I'm starving! Why does my body feel icky?

"Wait! What is that awful smell!!!" I exclaimed as I looked down and saw my body covered in some kind of black sludge that stunk something horrible.

The small rug I was on also was partially covered in the stuff. "Food can wait! I need a shower!" I complained as I rose to my feet and rushed to the shower!

After I rigorously scrubbed every inch of my body and removed every possible dead skin cell, I felt somewhat better. The shower-tub combination was filthy with parts of that black sludge flung everywhere as a result of my very aggressive scrubbing. The bathroom still stunk from the combination of my dirty clothes in a heap on the floor and specks of sludge everywhere.

"Man, another pair of pants ruined! Dammit!" I complained as I thought about how to clean up and throw away everything without having to touch any of it.

My new ability came to the forefront of my mind. "I wonder... the ability did say it could cleanse an area I focused on. Worth a shot." I said to myself as I focused my new ability on my clothes.

As the power of the ability heeded my call, I instinctively knew I had to create the image of what I wanted. So, I visualized my clothes being spotless and clean.

"**PURITY!!!**" I called out as I used the active part of the ability.

There was a flash and my clothes looked completely clean and practically brand new.

"Hey, it even removed that stain on my shirt I got from some soup splatter last week. That's freaking awesome!" I exclaimed.

After a few quick uses of my ability the entire bathroom was spotless.

"Man, where have you been my whole life?! I feel great!"

That was when I realized I felt better than I had in years. It always felt nice after a good shower, but this was on another level. I was still starving but felt like I had energy for days. Something was up.

Finally, I noticed the minimized notification in the corner of my view. Mentally willing it to expand, I read the new information.

*Congratulations! Your efforts have begun to purify the existing toxins and corruption within your mind, body, soul, and spirit. Your new ability focuses on the purification of all of these elements of yourself. As you expel these impurities you can further strengthen different aspects of your mind, body, soul, and spirit. You have grown your channels resulting in strengthening your body. Casting speed increased through channels. +13 **Constitution**, +13 **Intelligence**, + 3 **Dexterity**, + 2 **Strength**. You have reached the first minor threshold: **Passive Cultivation**.*

Passive Cultivation
Description: This threshold allows a caster or cultivator to passively draw in outside energy and cycle that Magic through their channels. This is the most basic and critical of thresholds that allow for slow yet automatic growth over time. Once this threshold is crossed, one must periodically remove blockages and impurities to reach future thresholds.

"Interesting. So now if I do nothing else my level or at least capacity should grow. Useful, yet it sounds like I should dedicate time to meditate each day."

GURGLE

Okay, okay. I hear you stomach, time to eat." I replied to my stomach's sounds letting me know it would no longer be ignored.

I cleaned the rug using my new favorite ability and got to work to cook up another four elk steaks...

GURGLE

... okay five elk steaks.

————

"Ahh. That hit the spot." I said while patting my stomach in satisfaction.

I ended up fixing and devouring six elk steaks. Man, my appetite has definitely grown, especially for meat. Luckily Paul had a fully stocked deep freezer with several slabs of elk. Man, I don't know where Paul is right now or if he was saved but my heart sent out a silent prayer in appreciation for meeting and befriending the man.

As I sat on the comfy homemade recliner I thought about my day. In some ways on the outside, I hadn't done much but in other ways I had accomplished a great deal. I still didn't have a defensive spell or many utility spells. Yet at the same time, the new ability I created if applied correctly could serve as a defensive spell against magical attacks, and it had the added benefits of being a very useful utility too.

KNOCK, KNOCK, KNOCK

'Man, that sounds so loud in this quiet cabin.' I thought, as a banging could be heard on the other side of large front door.

I heard rustling on the other side before more banging came.

KNOCK, KNOCK, KNOCK

I rose to my feet and approached the door "Who is it?" 'What, I couldn't help it.'

The only response I got was more banging and some growls.

Once again, Paul's design of this place proved useful. The door was re-enforced steel covered by oak. The thing was solid, and he had two bars you could place sideways to further lock the door in. He had also installed a peep hole, but it was on the side in the wall and worked similar to a periscope, allowing me to see outward from part of the roof. It was an ingenious design and he had a few of them all over the house to provide improved situational awareness, and boy was that a must right now.

In looking out the modified peep hole periscope my eyes widened. There was a large bear just periodically slamming into the door. Its movements seemed off, almost mechanical. That was when I noticed it looked wrong. It had patches of fur and skin missing exposing muscle and in some cases bone. It's eyes glowed and it looked like something out of a bad Thriller nightmare. That was when my System interface identified what I was looking at.

Undead Mutated Forest Bear

Description: Mutated forest bears tend to be more aggressive, and erratic compared to their forest bear kin. This mutation is usually caused by exposure to a concentration of magic. This corruption can increase the size and strength of the bear. This mutated forest bear was killed and resurrected by a necromancer strong enough to infuse enough death magic to animate the corpse and turn it into one of its puppets.

"Well... shit!"

Chapter 3- BOOM Baby!

If this undead bear is here, its necromancer can't be too far. I searched the area looking for some signs of other enemies. As I scanned the scene, I noticed some rustling in the bushes near the tree line.

THUMP, KNOCK, SCRATCH

The undead bear's attack was picking up intensity. I did my best to ignore it as I studied the brush. Three green skinned creatures about three feet tall stepped out of the bushes. The two held clubs and wore crude leather armor that looked more like scraps from an unknown animal. The third one held a wooden staff taller than he was and was wearing some kind of dark robe.

My System returned an identification for each of them.

Goblin
Level 5
Description: *Goblins are semi-sentient creatures with aggressive tendencies. As they level, goblins can evolve into different subspecies or gain classes. Their race has no qualms about eating other sentient beings which tends to lead to an attack first ask questions later approach to diplomacy. Typical alignment can be evil or chaotic. Powerful Dark aligned forces will use their race as general fodder to grind against their enemies.*

Goblin
Level 6...

Gr'ex
Goblin Apprentice Necromancer
Level 18
Description: *Goblins with some higher level of intelligence compared to their peers may sometimes gain a class in service of their master. This goblin has been granted access to the necromancer class and has gained access to Dark and Death magics.*

'Well, there's the necromancer. How powerful are these three that they took out that mutated forest bear?' I thought in resignation to how screwed I was right now.

"Go help my new minion you two fools! Our portal may have opened right in its path, but it was worth the almost complete loss of our entire war party of over twenty for me to gain such a powerful servant. Do not make me feed you to my new pet! Ugh, how the two of you were the last to survive I do not know! Now, go! I sense life within." Gr'ex commanded.

"Yes, great Gr'ex!" The remaining two goblins said in unison.

'Oh, well if it took them over twenty men to take down the bear these guys might not be as powerful as I thought. The bear is still a problem as I'm sure the apprentice necromancer is too.'

I started to formulate a plan. If I opened the door the bear would charge in, buuttt... if I removed the firing panel, I could shoot my assailants. Yes, that's right, Paul thought of everything. He set up metal panels that could be slid open to use to fire weapons and defend the cabin.

I had a few rifles and handguns that my System interface told me would still work as long as fire magic wasn't being used in the area. Such mana fluctuations with fire magic could accidentally make the gun powder explode. A possible tactic I could use later but for now I could at least use it on the goblins.

Grabbing my rifle, I slid open the panel closest to the door and took aim.

CRACK!

CRACK!

I fired both shots. One was a clean headshot and made the Level 6 goblin's head explode like a smashed watermelon. The second shot ricocheted off some kind of energy shield the necromancer had protecting himself.

I reloaded and the necromancer dived for the bushes while the level 5 goblin just stared in shock as his companion's body dropped to the floor.

"Move you fool! They are attacking us!" Gr'ex called as the goblin caster ducked behind a tree and bushes.

That yell seemed to spark the primitive part of their brains that told goblins to follow the orders of their superiors in battle. The level 5 goblin turned his head and began to move but there was nowhere he could easily use for cover. Sadly, for the little goblin my reload and aim was faster than his sprint to the front porch.

CRACK!

CRACK!

The first shot took it in the left leg, causing the level 5 goblin to lose his balance and face plant into the ground. The second was a clean head wound that ensured the goblin wasn't getting back up.

That left the giant undead bear which I doubt very much my rifle would do much damage to and the necromancer hiding behind a tree and some bushes.

I turned to look at my arsenal of weapons and as soon as my eyes fell on the elephant gun, yes, I owned an elephant gun, and you would too if you ever watched one of the Tremor movies!

I grabbed the weapon and took aim. Unlike any living enemy this undead creature would keep coming. I needed to reduce its mobility.

BOOM!

The first shot took out its right front leg and claw.

BOOM!

The second shot took out the right back leg causing the undead bear to flop to the ground with an earth-shaking thud.

For whatever reason the right side of the bear had more exposed bone than the other side. I did my best to hit those weak spots. Practically point-blank range helps at times.

I knew the thing could still attack one handed and its left side was far more intact, so I didn't trust the effectiveness of the elephant gun. Time to see how effective my one offense spell, Lightning Bolt, can be. I began charging the spell, I hoped the extra mana would give the spell more kick. Feeling like I couldn't hold on any more I released the spell again almost point-blank right at the undead bear's head.

ZZZAAAPPP!

The lightning bolt hit the bear right on the forehead and knocked the bear back and as I cleared the stars in my eyes from the bright flash, I noticed the head was gone and the remains of the undead bear's body were smoking.

"BOOM BABY! That was awesome!" I cheered.

I knew the fight wasn't over, I still had a necromancer to deal with.

"NOOOO!!! My minion! How dare you!" Gr'ex cried out.

The goblin had stepped out of his cover. He had rushed to his previous undead minion and had a look of utter loss on his face.

"Do you know how much mana I had to use to make this minion mine?!" Gr'ex said, as his focus was solely on his dead minion.

I decided to answer him with a Lightning Bolt. The necromancer must've dropped his magical shield or lost concentration, I wasn't sure how the defensive magic worked. What I do know is that the force of the blast lifted the goblin off the ground and flung him hard into the tree behind him. This had the added benefit of knocking the caster out.

I wasted no time and removed the bars from the door, flung it open and rushed towards the unconscious goblin with some lasso rope that was hanging on the wall. What? Again, if you ever watched a Tremor movie you would know that lassoing is a life skill.

The caster had dropped his staff by the bear's remains, but I quickly patted the goblin down and removed a necklace and his robe. That left him in a loin cloth and not much else. I tied the goblin caster up and took out a handkerchief from my pocket and used it to gag the guy. Yep, no way I want that back even with my ability to cleanse things.

I gathered up the enemy caster's things and brought them inside. I then took out my hunting knife, that reminded me of Crocodile Dundee's blade, and began to cut into the bear. I was looking for the bear's core and after some digging, I found it.

Mutated Forest Bear Core (Corrupted)
__Magic Types__: *High concentration of Death. Low concentration of Nature, Life, and Chaos magics.*
__Description__: *This core has been corrupted with death magic. Any of the creature's original abilities are lost. Warning: Corrupted cores can only be absorbed if you possess a strong enough affinity to the magic within.*

'Interesting. I wonder if I could purify the core?' I thought after reading the item notification.

I heard my captive starting to stir. Putting the usefulness of the core mentally to the side, I picked up my prisoner and threw him onto the porch. This had the benefit of helping the goblin to finish waking up.

"Wakey, Wakey, hands off snakie! Oh, that's right you can't move, oh so sad." I taunted Gr'ex.

Was it petty of me? Sure. Did I care at this moment? Not at all. I was more focused on killing him the moment he tried anything.

"Mmrrr, mmrrr." Was all I got back from Gr'ex as he was still gagged.

"I will remove the gag but if you try anything you'll regret it." I warned.

I slowly reached over and pulled down the gag.

"**Curse of Agony**!" Gr'ex yelled out.

SMACK!

THUD!

I backhanded the little jerk.

"I've kept my pimp hand strong so any time you test me I'm going to bitch slap you!"

'Good thing my immunity to curses works. Thank you, God! That made me realize I had understood what this goblin has been saying all along.'

I mentally asked my System, *"How am I able to understand these guys?"*

Query Accepted

Your System interface has a built-in automatic translation function.

"My System interface?"

Query Accepted

Yes, your System interface was upgraded to a higher version as a reward for selecting this option for how humanity will interact with the new world. Your version contains additional functions and greater information packets including language translation.

The term 'Enlighten Self Interest' came to mind. I wanted something that would help me, and others understand what was happening. This made the most logical sense. Nice I was getting a bonus for it.

Turning my attention back to the goblin. "So Gr'ex, shall we try this again?"

"Very well huemon. It is clear my gamble failed. How I do not know but Gr'ex has not survived this long being a fool. What is it you want to know?" Gr'ex replied.

"To start, how do you know what I am and how did you get here?" I asked.

"We were told of the dominant species of this world and our people have experience dealing with huemons before. We call you long pig as you can be tasty over an open fire." Gr'ex grinned evilly.

SMACK!

I backhanded the annoying jerk.

"Owe! What was that for?" Gr'ex groaned.

"For being a jerk and straying off topic. Back to my questions." I responded as I raised my hand again.

The system had told me that goblins respected strength and cunning above all else. That meant I had to be much harsher than I might be normally.

"Alright, alright, don't get your loin cloth twisted. You look like every other huemon we have encountered, but that crazed look in your eyes is scarier. As to how we got here... we entered through a portal."

"Um, System, want to tell me more about this portal."

Query Accepted

As the realms merge portals from different realities will open allowing monsters and other creatures to enter your world.

"Is there a way to close these portals?"

Query Accepted

Depending on the type of portal, yes. The portal the goblins entered from is called a contested portal, meaning it is not part of the realms merging and instead is allowed as a separate process to create challenges for humanity. If you can defeat the challenge the portal closes and those who participated can gain additional rewards and experience.

Contested portals can be closed primarily in two ways. The first is to defeat all the enemies that come through the portal. The second is to enter the *portal and destroy the focusing crystal or casters responsible for keeping the portal open. Once the source of the portal's power is destroyed you have a small window to return to the other side before being trapped in another realm or world. **Please Note**: There is technically a third way if you have access to spatial and reality or Planeswalking magic. You can use this magic to enter a contest of wills and force the portal to close.*

'Well, I'm going to have to try to figure out portals at some point. Add it to the list.'

"Is there a way to know how many enemies remain before the portal closes?"

Query Accepted

Yes. When you enter an area under an active challenge your quest log updates. This new quest will track the remaining enemies on this side of the portal.

"Great. Please display remaining enemies."

Quest: Defeat the Detachment of Goblin Invaders

Description: Goblins under the control of a powerful necromancer have opened a portal near you. If they are not stopped, they will bring devastation to the area. Defeat the detachment of 25 goblins to receive additional rewards and experience.

Remaining enemies: 1/25

Well, that was helpful. I now knew Gr'ex was the last remaining member of his unit. I wonder what constitutes defeat, do I have to kill him?

"Are you done staring off into space huemon? How someone such as you bested me I do not know." Gr'ex complained.

For some reason killing the little weasel sounded better and better as time went on.

"Yes. I was just checking my quest log. You are the last survivor of your group. Don't prove useful and you die. Got it?!" I said the last part giving him a wicked grin.

The goblin visibly gulped. "Understood."

"Now who do you serve?" I asked.

"My clan serves the great Kit'erak. He is a powerful necromancer and agreed to claim this area of your world as his future dominion. He is also working with others in the Dark to spread zombies and other undead across your world. As one of his lowly apprentices, Kit'erak would gloat about how easily some factions of the Dark agreed to his proposal of sending and seeding undead in your world."

"Seeding?"

"Yes. Portals are temporarily opened as rituals are cast to use death magic to create a miasma that can increase the chance of the dead rising from the grave to wreak havoc. Some undead minions are sent through, but the portal is always closed. The minions succeed or are destroyed, it matters not to my master." Gr'ex expressed glee as he thought about all the destruction.

"Then why is your portal contested?"

"Our clan is not undead. Though he may treat us as meat for the grinder, Kit'erak still needs us to establish multiple beachheads in this world. Opening portals can be costly, it takes time and resources. Our clan agreed so we could establish a new home here in a world about to be overrun with magic and conflict." Gr'ex explained.

"Well thanks for the info." I said as I withdrew my hunting knife. "Know that you are of no more use to me..."

Gr'ex interrupted me. "Wait! I can be of service! I know dark and death magic. I can teach you what I know."

"And how could I even trust you after you tried to kill me?"

"A magical contract and oath! I will pledge my power to teach you what I know and be a good necromancer. I know how to serve."

A prompt appeared in my vision.

Gr'ex is offering a magically binding contract and giving an oath balanced on his power. The agreement is as follows: Gr'ex will teach you his magic and be a good necromancer. Do you agree to the terms as stated? Yes, or No? Please note: You can modify the terms of the agreement.

Well, this is an interesting turn of events. I doubt very much what Gr'ex considers to be a good necromancer would be the same way I would consider a good necromancer. Either way, I knew his proposal had large enough holes in it to drive a semi-truck through it. I mentally selected the option to modify the agreement.

You have sent Gr'ex a modified agreement. Under his oath he will teach you magic, serve you, never strike or attack you himself, and has to be your ally in combat... **Gr'ex has accepted your agreement**.

A light flowed down and seemed to settle on Gr'ex. Shortly after I received a few more prompts.

Congratulations! You have defeated a contested portal! As the first person in your world to do so the rewards will be increased. For being the sole survivor, all rewards will be tailored to your needs.

Congratulations! You have gained the title **World's Champion** *for being the first to defeat a contested portal on your own. This title grants you* **+15 Strength, +15 Dexterity, +20 Constitution, +20 Intelligence, +25 Wisdom, and +30 Charisma**. *Other titles and perks will gain increased bonuses and rewards. In addition,* **when fighting in contested portals your stats are increased by 25% and rewards from successful completions are increased**.

You are granted a one-time opportunity to choose from a section of rewards. In addition to the experience you will receive, you may choose three from the following list below:
• *Magical weapon*   • *Combat skill to Adept rank*   • *Utility spell*   • *Offensive spell*   • *One random monster core*

"Umm, huemon can you untie me now? Huemon? Master?" Gr'ex kept trying different ways to get his new master's attention.

"Hold on a minute I'm choosing my rewards."

"It is letting you choose, that is most uncommon." Gr'ex commented.

"The notification said I am the first person to complete a contested portal on my world." I replied.

"Ah that is why. Get anything good?" Gr'ex inquired.

"I can choose from a magical weapon, combat skill to adept rank, utility spell, offensive spell, or a random monster core." I replied absently as I re-read the list of options.

"I was not expecting you to actually respond. I would recommend the combat skill to adept rank." Gr'ex advised.

"Why?" I asked.

"Do you know how long it can take to get a skill to adept rank? Some battle-hardened warriors do not even achieve such a thing in their lifetime. A combat skill does not exactly mean melee, it could be anything. That one reward is worth more than the others." Gr'ex explained.

"Well, I get to choose two more from the options." I said as I mentally selected that option for my first reward.

"Three of them?! How did you get so lucky huemon?!... Of course, the world's first. You are lucky the mutated bear took out almost my entire unit and I was low on mana from turning it into my minion."

I realized the goblin was correct. I'm not sure if I could've beaten 25 goblins all at once.

"If you want more advice, I suggest ignoring the magical weapon as an option." Gr'ex recommended.

"Why is that?" I asked.

"Simple. Whatever magical weapon you get now you will quickly outgrow." Gr'ex answered.

That threw me for a loop, so I inquired further. "How do you figure that?"

Gr'ex shook his head and started speaking like he was talking to an idiot child. "Simple. Contested Portal Quest rewards are determined at the point and level you are at completion, before you gain the experience from the start. You will gain a massive amount of experience from completing a contested portal quest by yourself. They are meant to be completed with a small to midsize force. The longer they are open the higher the difficulty will ramp up to close it. Our portal was one of the first opened to this new world, my previous master saw to that."

"So, the weapon I get would be for me at level 1 but as soon as I finish, I should be several levels past that meaning I would need a new weapon shortly after. Plus, the fact that the combat skill I get may not work with the magical weapon I get as a reward." I summarized.

"Exactly." Gr'ex said as he rolled his eyes.

"Okay, magic weapon is out. That leaves two spells and a random core."

"I would have suggested the core of it was not random. I would recommend taking the utility and offense spells." Gr'ex advised.

"Why the core if it wasn't random?" I inquired.

"It's simple. Magic cores that are the same magic type as your core are precious. They allow us to grow our own core. You can even gain additional experience and new spells, skills, or abilities. However, cores not of your alignment are of minimal use. It can be dangerous to try and absorb them, but they can come in handy for crafting." Gr'ex once again explained his reasoning.

His thought process made sense. What he didn't know was that I had all magic types so no matter the core it would benefit me. That left me to decide either a utility spell or offensive spell. As I couldn't take both I would have to choose.

I already had my Lightning Bolt spell, that had worked pretty well as an offensive spell. I did have my ability to cleanse things, but I figured the more utility I had the better in the apocalypse. My final choice was made; I confirmed my selections.

Flash of light and new prompts filled my vision.

*You have gained **+150 experience** for killing a level 5 goblin.*

*You have gained **+175 experience** for killing a level 6 goblin.*

*You have gained **+11,500 experience** for killing a level 20 undead mutated forest bear.*

*For completing the first contested portal quest on your world and doing it alone you have gained **+25,000 experience** plus an additional **+25,000 experience** for a **total of +50,000 experience**.*

*Level Up! Congratulations! You have reached **level 10**! +13 stats points per level. **Total stat points to distribute: +117!***

*Congratulations! You have learned the combat skill **Weapons Mastery** at Adept level... Your combat skill level has been upgraded to **Master rank** as part of your one-time bonus!*

The flood of knowledge brought me to my knees as I cried out in pain from the information overload. "AHHHH!"

"What is it, master?!" Gr'ex expressed confusion.

"The combat skill is **Weapons Mastery**... So much information..." I gritted my teeth try to get the words out as more and more weapons and fighting styles flooded my brain.

"You have got to be kidding me?! You get the one skill that is at the core of a weapons master class?! It takes grueling years of battle and practice to master multiple weapons skills. After that you must get them to merge into that one skill! Then you must level it up again to one day hope to reach adept!" Gr'ex explained in frustration with how lucky his new master was.

"Master..." I gritted out.

By now I was on my hands and knees struggling to breathe and stay upright as all the information kept hammering into my brain one weapon and form at a time. The constant movements were triggering a vertigo effect.

"Yes, you gained the **Weapons Mastery** skill at adept... or are you saying I forgot to address you as master. If that is the case..."

I cut him off and did my best to grind out the answer. "No... One... time... upgrade from adept... to master rank."

The last thing I remember was Gr'ex exclaiming, "You have got to be the luckiest son of a troll I have ever met!"

It took a while for me to come to and I only knew that because it was pitch black at night. I was laying on my back.

"Welcome back master. Can you please untie me or at the very least take me inside? Your world is being saturated with wild mana. Anything could be out hunting tonight. As I am currently tied up and I have limited ways to defend myself." Gr'ex complained.

"Sure." I said as I got to my feet on unsteady legs.

I picked up the goblin who felt much lighter than before. I brought him inside and shut the door. I plopped him on the floor and put the bars over the door for added protection.

That was when the next wave of information hit me and brought me right back to my knees.

*Congratulations! You have learned the spell **Create Water**! This spell grants you the ability to create up to 50 gallons of water in a single cast. This one-time reward has been upgraded to **Create or Destroy Water (Greater)**. This advanced spell allows you to create or destroy up to 100 gallons of water in a single cast. The less water created or destroyed the less mana used.*

I had the advanced spell shoved in my mind and once again I felt like I was trying to drink from a fire hydrant.

"New spell?" Gr'ex asked.

"Yea. Advanced version of **Create Water** spell."

Gr'ex shook his head.

"What?" I asked.

"The utility spell you received can provide enough water for a small community. That is no minor utility, it is a lifesaver!" Gr'ex replied incredulously.

"Well, I guess that is over." I commented.

Just as I said that a rather large spherical object appeared into existence next to me with an audible POP!

"You chose the random core? Of course, you did. With luck like yours, why not? That core is huge! It is literally bigger than I am! What did you get?!" Gr'ex commented as he shook his head.

Gr'ex was right, the magical core was huge. The core was probably about 4 and a half feet tall and wide, or to translate that into something the rest of the world will understand was roughly 1.33 meters tall. The core glowed with bright colors shifting from starry nights to golden hues of white, it was breathtaking.

A prompt brought me out of my revelry as my System identified the item.

*You have found a **Primordial Celestial Dragon Core**!*
*Description: Primordial Celestial Dragons are some of the rarest and oldest of all dragons, only second to Omni-Dragons. Celestial dragons will travel the cosmos as they seek to unravel the mysteries of the universe. Each celestial dragon will begin to embody the aspects of the fundamental forces it studies. When a celestial dragon reaches 'Ancient' status it radiates the very power it sought to understand. However, Primordial Celestial Dragons fully embodies and master the fundamental forces they seek to understand. This primordial core contains the very essence of **Time, Space**, and **Gravity**.*
Warning: Absorbing a Primordial Celestial Dragon core can overwhelm your own core and result in death!

"System, this thing can kill me?"

Query Accepted

*You **Divine Infinitum** will be able to absorb the core. However, it will take it time to fully assimilate the power within. Warning: the process will be potentially extremely painful and could have unforeseen side effects to your body.*

"Well, shit." I exhaled before I turned to my new companion. "Sorry Gr'ex, but you're going to have to remain that way for a while longer. If it makes you feel any better, what I'm about to do is going to hurt a whole lot."

"You know that does make me feel a bit better." Gr'ex answered.

I deserved that. I was going to keep him bound until after I was done. Sure, we had a binding agreement, but I didn't trust the creepy jerk as far as I could throw him... You know in this new reality I could probably throw him pretty far. I shook my head realizing I was just distracting myself from the inevitable.

I placed both my hands on the **Primordial Celestial Dragon core** and selected 'Yes' when asked if I wanted to integrate the core's power.

Power flooded into me. I could feel it going directly into my Divine Infinitum. At first, I thought everything would be fine. It felt like I was holding on to a storm or live ball of electricity, yet it was contained... until it wasn't. I screamed as the energy flooded my channels, only my **PURITY!!!** ability kept the power from ripping all my channels to shreds which would've crippled me in this new reality.

Even with my new ability the celestial power leaked from my channels and hit several of my organs. I felt the orb and I lifted off the ground hovering and the magic continued to flood my system. As it exited my body, for the first time I felt a tangible connection to my soul and spirit as the energy infused my soul and then it hit my brain and I blissfully blacked out.

Interlude - Gr'ex

Gr'ex grumbled. How did he get himself stuck in this situation? He thought back to how he got here on this hard wooden floor all tied up. Where did it all go wrong?

His master, Kit'erak, had given him 24 of his goblin clan to command and ordered him to establish a foothold on this newly integrated world filled with huemons. Most of the men under his command were battle hardened warriors with only a handful of lowly weaklings that were there to be his personal bootlickers and builders.

When they arrived through the portal there was nothing but forest. The portal was in a clearing surrounded by trees, it was a perfect location to begin building a base. No huemons around to interfere before they had time to build up a strong defensive position. Gr'ex was thrilled with his luck.

"Yes, Master will be pleased, and I will be rewarded with my choice of slaves from this new world." Gr'ex commented as he watched his men finish transporting the supplies and weapons they would need.

That was when it all went to troll shite. Gr'ex was chastising a couple of his bootlicking builders who were chopping down trees to make logs for their new base. They had nearly dropped a tree right on top of him. Just as he was about to unleash a few curses of agony on the two, one of his scouts rushed in.

The scout clearly ran all the way here and was completely out of breath as he tried to talk as he kept pointing back the way he came. "B-b-be-be-b-b-b-b..."

In frustration Gr'ex yelled at the scout. "Out with it you fool!"

"B-bear... b-big... bear... big bear, really big bear!" The scout stammered out as he kept pointing back the way he came.

That was all the warning they got before the massive Mutated Forest Bear charged into the clearing and roared.

ROARRR!!!

His men were shocked, and it took them a moment to move into action. The bear bowled over multiple goblins to get to the tasty morsel that ran from it. The poor scout tried to reach out to Gr'ex in the hope his boss would help him, but Gr'ex just pushed the scout in the bear's charging direction.

"I don't have to outrun that bear just you." Gr'ex sneered.

A few of the goblin warriors were able to get in good blows on the bear's right side as it initially ignored them so it could kill the prey that dared to run from it.

The scout had just enough time to look up into the bear's gapping maw before the monster clamped down and bit the goblin in two. Its initial hunter instincts satisfied; it turned its ire on the insects attacking it.

The bear's massive claw swung out and separated arms from their owners and split one goblin in two.

Gr'ex had to do something otherwise his unit would be gone, and he would be next. He started casting curse after curse all from the safety of a tree. Once he had enough damage over time (DOT) spells on the mutated forest bear, he started throwing dark bolts at the bear's weakened right side.

After a few dark bolts Gr'ex used a magic spell, his master had taught him. The spell was called **Eldritch Fire**. It was a tier 5 spell and would use up all his remaining mana. Focusing as hard as he could, Gr'ex cast the spell. Green fire shot out and hit his target on its right side. The spell seemed to splash on impact. Wherever the spell hit it seemed to melt the flesh away.

The mutated bear was on its hind legs swatting his men away like flies. However, even a swarm of flies can hurt a large beast. The bear cried out in agony as it swiped faster and faster. Until the combination of the **Eldritch Fire**, curses, and weapons attacks finally took their toll.

Sadly, for the remaining goblin warriors they were caught underneath the bear when it collapsed on top of them, killing all instantly.

"Idiots! I am surrounded by idiots!" Gr'ex complained as he got down from his perch on the tree, he was using to better attack the bear. 'Yes, that's it, it had nothing to do with getting away from the bear at all!' Gr'ex thought as he made his way to the dead bear.

There were only two bootlickers left, the rest of his force was dead or dying. Those wounded would cry out for help.

"You!" Gr'ex pointed to the two remaining goblins who had vacant looks on their faces.

"Yes, great Gr'ex?!" They both replied.

"Pick up a weapon and go around and put these wastes of goblin flesh out of my misery. I can't stand listening to their whining and complaining!" Gr'ex ordered.

"S-sir... they are dying." On one his remaining two men said.

"Yes, but clearly not fast enough. So, go! Besides the added death energy will help me as I recover my mana." Gr'ex pointed in the direction of his dying men.

Order given, Gr'ex no longer cared. His mind was focused on the other high-level spell his master taught him. **Animate Greater Undead Minion**. Perhaps Gr'ex's luck was improving. With this corpse he could finally have a powerful undead minion that would be far more powerful than his worthless warriors.

————-

Everything was great and all was right with the universe according to Gr'ex. He now had a powerful undead minion and could finally call himself a proper necromancer. Sure, his mana still had a long way to go to refill, but so what, Gr'ex did not care. Any creature that dared to cross him would die thanks to his new favorite minion.

The goblin caster knew they needed to find either slave labor to build a foothold or take over an existing base. Gr'ex figured either option would not be very difficult. He just needed to find some huemons. That was why he was using his **Life Sense necklace**.

It took some time to sort out all the life signs in the forest. It was rather annoying. "Too much life in this place. We will have to change that once we take it over."

"Yes, great Gr'ex!" Both goblins said in response. They had learned the hard way how cruel their commander was, and they had zero intention to end up as snacks for his new pet.

The magical necklace led them to a structure built out of tree logs.

"This will serve as a base for now. I sense life within. Time for my new minion to show me how amazing it is." Gr'ex said as he mentally commanded the Undead Mutated Forest Bear to take down the door so they could introduce themselves to the inhabitant.

———-

Gr'ex just looked over at the unconscious form of his new master. "How was I supposed to know he had impressive, ranged weapons or that powerful lighting spell. If I had not been so low on mana my shield might've held out longer, but no, he smacked me around like I was nothing. Me, the great Gr'ex taken out by a level 1 huemon. All because I had no mana. My mana is still not fully recharged."

Gr'ex tried to better position himself to be as comfortable as was possible, but it was difficult to say the least. "How did a level 1 have such powerful magic or weapons at his disposal? His luck must be off the charts."

Moving as best he could, Gr'ex surveyed the room. Only a few feet away from the goblin he could see some well-built furniture with what looked like very comfortable padding on it. "Why couldn't he have dropped me off on one of those."

Still grumbling at his lot in life Gr'ex continued to move and look around as best he could. The place was clearly a home for a king. "Perhaps that is why I was defeated. If this level 1 huemon, well level 10 now, was royalty that would explain how he beat me. True royal huemons were granted authority by their God, it was not something anyone of us that serve the Dark can ignore."

The possibly royal huemon, no, Gr'ex would not accept anything less. The one who bested him had to be a true royal huemon. Gr'ex watched his new master as his body glowed and periodically twitched or morphed then would shift back. "Creepy. I wonder what magic core he absorbed. I didn't get a chance to inspect it before the light blinded me and it was gone."

After the giant magical core was gone his new master looked like he morphed and changed but the light was too bright to make out into what. Then out of nowhere the huemon dropped from his place floating in the air. "What kind of power makes you float in the air like that? Maybe aeromancy? Nah it was too bright. Maybe Storm magic with lightning. Nah, that would not explain the golden glow. Whatever it was, it is clear he was compatible and will survive."

Just then Gr'ex got a cramp in his neck from trying to remain twisted for so long to watch the huemon. "Owwww! Hells' bells! I hope this guy wakes up soon! Pins and needles!!!"

Chapter 4- If I Pass Out One More Time

I woke up to the sound of complaining. "Are you awake yet master? My limbs have somehow both fallen asleep and feel like I'm being stabbed with thousands of pins and needles!"

"Ugh." I said as I sat up. "Give me a few to sort myself out."

"Look huemon, let's be real here, it is going to take you longer than a few to sort yourself out. The least you can do is let me out of these bindings."

"Enough!" I exclaimed as I mentally reached out on instinct to shut him up.

Gr'ex lifted off the ground and flew into the nearby wall.

SLAM!

"Ugh... I'm good... forget I said anything." Gr'ex said in a daze and a bit of fear.

"How did I just do that?" I asked out loud.

Query Accepted

You have finished the first stage of absorbing the Primordial Celestial Dragon core. You used the new ability you have gained: Gravity Momentum Manipulation. The second stage of absorption will complete in 5 more hours.

You have gained the following benefits:

Mana Capacity and Mana Regeneration have increased.

*Total stat point increases: +13 **Strength**, +9 **Dexterity**, + 5 **Constitution**, +10 **Intelligence**, +16 **Wisdom**, +10 **Charisma**.*

New Ability Gained: Gravity Momentum Manipulation

Gravity Momentum Manipulation
Description: *Primordial Celestial Dragons understand gravity and momentum at a fundamental atomic level. Once mastered, they use this ability to traverse the stars and change the momentum of celestial bodies.*
Passive Effect: *Learn to move your body's momentum and position in space.*
Active Effects: *Use Mana and Stamina to adjust the gravity and momentum of objects within your soul's aura. Warning: This ability drains mana and*

stamina quickly. Please Note: Finer control of this ability will reduce mana and stamina consumption.

Well, that explains that one. I stood up, withdrew my hunting knife, and walked over to Gr'ex.

"Seriously master, leave me here as long as you want! I'll shut up, you won't hear a peep from me, I swear!" Gr'ex exclaimed as his eyes were focused on my blade.

I waited until I was right up next to him and bending down to cut his bindings before I spoke. Sure, I could've alleviated his fears sooner, but the little jerk annoyed me, and I still hadn't forgotten he tried to kill me.

"Oh relax. I'm just cutting you free." I said as I cut the little goblin free.

The goblin rubbed his wrists and cracked his back. "Oh yea, that's the stuff. Thank you, master. Is it possible I could get my clothes back? I mean I know I have a very attractive figure, but I think I might've messed up my loin cloth after being stuck there for so long. I would like to wash it and don't want to make you jealous of my goblin endowments." Gr'ex yammered on.

"Do you ever shut up? Hold on one second." I replied as I cast **PURITY!!!** on his loin cloth and the puddle he had left.

Gr'ex's eyes went wide. "What-What did you just do? My loin cloth is completely clean!"

"It's one of my abilities. Here is your robe." I said as I hit him right in the face with his robe.

THUD!

I used my **Gravity Momentum Manipulation** ability to fling the robe right into him and knock the goblin on his butt.

The goblin glared at me with a 'was that really necessary' look.

I shrugged my shoulders. "I'm still learning how to use that ability."

That was technically true, but I did intentionally ramp up the speed. And yes, it was totally necessary. You would be practicing every chance you got if you could fling things about with your mind.

The ability was interesting. If I tried to push too hard when I first made it move it took way more mana and stamina, but if I lightened the gravity first then rev up the momentum after it was already in motion and then return gravity to normal to give it that extra impact when it hits. Something to practice and play with.

For now, it was time to finally sort out my new companion. Man, his face makes me want to hit him. I shook my head. As much as I didn't want to play nice, I knew I would be a fool to waste the resource. The caster could teach me more about magic than I knew currently, which I could sum up as point and shoot.

GRUMBLE

My stomach let me know I was once again starving. Well time to break bread. "Are you hungry Gr'ex?"

"Starving. Last time I ate was taking a few bites out of one of my dead warriors before we started scouting." Gr'ex answered.

"You ate your dead?" I asked incredulously.

"Waste not, want not. They were dead and just flesh. I needed to recharge after casting such a powerful necromancy spell and they were just lying there."

"Well, I'm not going to unpack all that right now." I said as I made my way to the kitchen.

"Unpack what? You already know I have nothing on me. Where do you think I have hidden something to unpack?" Gr'ex asked in confusion as he followed me.

"No, it's a saying from my world. Don't worry about it. Hopefully you like elk cause that's what I'm fixing."

"I have no idea what elk is but if it's meat I'll eat it. Worst case I can go make use of what is left of my two bootlickers." Gr'ex commented.

I paused for a moment, looked at Gr'ex, and decided it just wasn't worth the conversation. My body felt like it was put through the ringer, and I ached in places I didn't know it was possible to ache in. My stomach growled again as I took out 10 elk steaks this time.

As I was preparing the steaks I decided to chat with my new companion. "Tell me Gr'ex, how much does a goblin usually eat?"

Gr'ex watched what I was preparing and answered. "Two of those cuts of meat should be sufficient. I could survive on one but with all the magic I flung around today my body needs the extra."

"Explain. I thought Mana Capacity, Mana Regeneration, and the related stats were the primary factors in using magic." I said as I tried to wrap my mind around the need for more food. 'Maybe that's why I've been so hungry lately.'

"For the most part you are correct. However, casting can still take a toll on your body and mana channels. Eating more when you tax your system helps it grow stronger, faster."

"Makes sense." I commented.

"Today I cast two higher tiered level spells that I normally cannot cast. The trip through the portal gives us a bit of a boost to our mana and magic. That and I had two single use items that helped me as an arcane focus."

"Arcane focus?" I asked as I began to grill the elk steaks.

"Certain castings, usually more common with rituals or higher tiered spells required materials to act as a conduit for the magic. To do otherwise risks you burning out your mana channels or causing you permanent harm. Most creatures aren't built to handle that much magic running through their bodies. That becomes truer the higher the tier you attempt. Some like my staff serve as an arcane focus for my magic to use, other materials are spent or consumed in the magical conversion process." Gr'ex explained.

"Magical conversion process?" I inquired.

"Think of it as a catalyst that gets consumed to fuel or finish the spell. My master gave me a few mana crystals to use in case I needed to cast the more powerful magic he taught me."

"Interesting. And you're going to teach me all this magic and what you know?" I said as I held up a steak but waited to put it on his plate until he gave me an affirmative.

"Yes! I already agreed so stop teasing a poor starving goblin." Gr'ex said in exasperation.

I chuckled as I put the two steaks on his plate before I started to dig into mine.

Gr'ex grabbed one of the steaks with his hands and took a big bite out of it.

"No, use the utensils." I admonished.

"The what-now?" Gr'ex asked in confusion.

I waved the fork and knife I had in my hands and then pointed to the ones by his plate. Then I glared at him before he finally put his steak down and picked up the fork and knife.

"Fine! Waste of time. Using your hands is so much quicker." Gr'ex complained.

"Perhaps, but it's definitely messier, and if you ever end up around other humans, things like this matter to them." I advised.

"Huemons are dumb."

I stared at him.

"Present company excluded for now, but I reserve the right to change my mind." Gr'ex replied.

"Fair enough. Speaking about other humans, I don't think they will take very kindly to a goblin in their midst. They may shoot first and ask questions second."

"That's easy." Gr'ex said as he revealed a ring on his finger. He rubbed it and a shimmering wave washed over the goblin. In the goblin's place sat a short ugly man that looked like Gr'ex only if he was human. Somehow this made him look both uglier and ornerier.

"Minor Illusion Ring." Gr'ex pulled out another one and set it on the counter. "I received two of them for later infiltration and spying on huemons up close. They are preprogrammed."

Gr'ex wiggled his finger with the ring on it. "This one is specifically keyed to my mana signature and makes me look like the most handsome huemon possible."

I tried not to say anything. 'Hold it in. Ask him about the other ring to distract you.' I told myself before speaking up. "What about the other one?"

"It is unbound, meaning someone has to attune to the ring so it can sync up with their mana signature like this one is to mine." Gr'ex replied as he waved his ring around again.

"How does one attune to an item?" I asked.

"It is different for each person and each item. The easiest way to explain it would be to flow a trickle of your mana into the item and get a feel for the item's magic type and functions. The process usually takes several hours of meditation. You can start and stop the process; you lose some momentum, but it gives you the flexibility of taking your time." Gr'ex explained the process.

"Mind if I try it out with that one?" I pointed at the ring on the counter.

"That depends." Gr'ex said cautiously.

"On what?" I asked.

"The magic core you absorbed, are you still 'digesting' it?" Gr'ex asked.

"It says phase two is still another few hours. Is that what you're referring to?"

"Phase 2, interesting. My guess based on its size and brilliance there will be at least three phases, possibly more, for your body to fully absorb and integrate the power you consumed."

"Good to know, but what does that have to do with the Minor Illusion Ring?"

"It's simple. Your own core and body are in flux. You should not attempt an attunement while that is occurring. Take the time for you to assimilate what you have within you, then I will help you with the ring." Gr'ex answered.

"Sounds good." I answered.

"By the way, would you be willing to tell me what kind of core it was. It might help me understand what you're going through and what to expect." Gr'ex stated.

My hackles rose as did the hairs on the back of my neck. "No, I think I will keep that to myself for now."

"Fair enough. By the way... this 'Lkkk' is rather delicious." Gr'ex replied.

"Yes, it's my favorite meat." I said as I put the last piece of steak in my mouth.

"I can tell, you ate all eight of those steaks. Hopefully there is more food." Gr'ex commented.

"Oh, there is plenty of meat in the freezer. If you're finished, I can show you around and get you settled in one of the bedrooms." I picked up the dishes and did a quick once over with my ability.

I was not a fan of doing the dishes, but this changes everything. Of all the abilities to get in the apocalypse, being able to stay clean is got to be one of the most useful.

"You seem rather prepared for the end of your world as you know it. Why is that? Were you granted some kind of vision?" Gr'ex asked.

"Ha, ha, ha. No nothing exactly like that. Some of us like to be prepared for worst case scenarios. A friend of mine built this place to withstand various catastrophes. I just so happened to be staying out here when the energy hit, and we all received the notification." I chuckled in response.

"Your Luck stat must be through the roof." Gr'ex commented.

"Hey System, is Luck stat a thing?"

Query Accepted

The simple answer is yes, and no. Luck is a stat you can display in your attributes, but it is not pure chance as most believe it to be.

"Please explain."

The Luck stat is more accurately based on a combination of any blessings you may be receiving, your power signature, spiritual impact, and presence. Your other stats also can factor into the overall stat. Some systems grant the user the ability to increase this stat, but it does not always directly translate into tangible results. Please Note: Your system does not allow Luck stat modification. That functionality was locked out for all remaining humans on the planet as part of the consequences of their actions and spiritual decisions.

"In other words, humanity screwed up and you won't let us un-do it artificially. It will take hard work to survive. I will say Gr'ex does seem to have a point that my luck seems to be good as of late."

Query Accepted

One primary reason is broken down into two. First, you chose to sacrifice yourself in the hope to save others who turned away from salvation. Second, your spiritual impact, strength of will, and high imagination will naturally influence the universe around you. Please Note: This is also the beginning of the apocalypse, and many calamities await your world.

"So, in summary, I made good choices in life and those choices are helping to pay off now. Oh, and these minor benefits in the grand scheme of things pale in comparison to what humanity is left will have to face."

Correct. No more can be shared at this time related to this subject.

'Interesting. Again, I feel like I am beginning to scratch the surface of some greater understanding. The fact that my system seems to speak to me directly is significant in and of itself. More to sort out later. Time to focus on finishing Gr'ex's tour of the cabin.' I thought as I was showing the little goblin around.

The tour did not take long. Gr'ex gave me many confused looks as I showed him around. I'd say the conversation about the importance of using the toilet and flushing was the most eye opening. At first the goblin did not understand why I was so adamant. His attitude quickly changed as he saw the water change into clean water.

"And you say this is not magic? You're joking right? Do you know how strong goblin urine is? I used to send my men into the woods and make sure I wasn't downwind. This removes that problem. Goblins do not care much about hygiene and until this day I did not think that was too important either. I just avoided the stinker of my kind." Gr'ex commented.

"Well let's make a point for me to never find out. Just make sure to flush and we are good. Now let me introduce you to the shower."

"Rain on command! This 'show-er' is amazing as well. You huemons may have some merit. Huemons will make great slaves to build such wonders..." Gr'ex commented.

I interrupted Gr'ex as I lifted him off the ground with my **Gravity Momentum Manipulation** ability. "You were saying?"

"I was just saying how other huemons would make excellent slaves, of course not you, master. Ahh!" Gr'ex cried out as I elevated him higher off the ground. "Okay, okay, no huemon slaves."

I began to lower the little goblin to the ground. "What about the dumb ones? Maybe they can be slaves?"

I just shook my head and chuckled a bit. "Ha, I make no promises. Though I doubt the dumb ones will last very long to begin with."

Gr'ex thought about my words before speaking up. "You would be surprised master. We have many dumb goblins that grow in strength or some skill but still are more trouble than they are worth. There is a reason Gr'ex is the last one alive, use the dumb ones as fodder first."

"Hmmm, perhaps that rings true with humans too at times. Still not agreeing to give you any slaves. Let me show you upstairs." I said as I led Gr'ex to the next floor.

The most hilarious part of the tour was showing the little goblin the bedroom. Paul did not skimp on mattresses, they were the kind that supported your body yet were extremely comfortable, almost guaranteeing a good night's sleep. Gr'ex jumped up onto the bed.

"This is for me? So huge. Only goblin kings can hope to have a bed so large. I forgive you for your prior poor treatment of me, for the most part. Keep it up huemon. Now to try this out... Wait... soooo comfortable. Ahhhh!" The goblin sighed in contentment as he partially sunk into the bed.

It was at this point in the tour where it was like I didn't even exist anymore. His attention fully focused on the comfort he was experiencing. I was lucky to get a hand wave and an "Uh-huh" before I heard snoring.

Leaving the bedroom, I shut the door. "Crazy little goblin."

As I started to walk to my bedroom down the hall, I said to myself out loud, "Well at least I should be able to get some decent sleep in my comfy bed."

Phase 2 Integration Commencing...

I barely got out the words, "You couldn't wait until I got to my bed?!" before I fell face first into the hallway floor and passed out.

Chapter 5- Oliver

Oliver woke up on the floor. "Ugh. What happened. That raid was crazy last night. Huh? I can't remember how the raid ended. Oh well."

Oliver sat down on his bed after doing a quick stretch. Sleeping on the floor rarely results in great rest. "Man, I have got to stop doing late night Taco Bell runs. Well, guess I should start my day."

Just as Oliver stood up to grab a quick shower, words appeared in his vision.

Greetings! Your world has forever been changed, what was separated shall now begin to return. Magic is real as are the beings you called monsters. Many of you have left your world and reached salvation. Now it is time for you to determine what you will do with the rest of your life on this planet.

This system has been chosen to help you interpret the changes to yourself and the world around you. Think or say "status" should you want to view your character sheet or information regarding your skills and abilities. You can concentrate on an ability or area to gain additional information. If you desire to adjust your notifications or display think "system settings" and your options will appear. These options are limited by person due to a multitude of factors.

"Is this a joke? Am I still dreaming?"

Query Accepted

This is not a joke. You are awake. What your people understand as the apocalypse has begun. Prepare yourself.

"Okay..." Oliver said as he slumped back onto his bed.

"So, I have a system and if I believe the words appearing before me, the apocalypse has started."

Correct

"And the system listens and interacts with me..."

Correct

"That's not creepy at all."

Good

"Okay, seriously system, are you just messing with me right now?!"

Query Not Accepted

"Yea, you're totally screwing with me. Of course, the apocalypse starts, and I get a snide system."

Query Accepted

"That wasn't a question!" Oliver quickly cried out.

As stated in the initial release, each system will have subtle differences, settings, and permissions based on a multitude of factors. Your mind is filled with sarcasm and random fantasies. Based on your memories, your preferred form of communication is snide sarcastic behavior. The system settings have been adjusted to compensate.

"Okay, that's fair. Let's see, system do you know the one about..."

Query Accepted

Yes! Again, in your mind. Initiating scan to determine if brain was damaged during integration.

"Hey! Come on now! Why you gotta be like that?!"

Scan complete. Results inconclusive. Additional observation required.

"Geez. Okay, got it. You're probably right, a completely helpful system without snide comments would probably be more of a shock to me than the apocalypse. Well, if we are stuck with each other let's get started. What was it again?... right show me my Status."

Name: Oliver	**Race**: In Transition	**Level**: 1
Strength: 6	**Dexterity**: 6	**Constitution**: 8
Intelligence: 17	**Wisdom**: 14	**Charisma**: 9
Spiritual Attunement: Unaligned	**Core Stage**: Not Formed	**Spiral Stage**: Not Formed
Health, Mana, Stamina Values & Regen Rates per hour (pH)		

HP: 20	HP/pH: 5	MP: 43	MP/pH: 42	SP: 70	SP/pH: 24

"Well, no surprise that my physical stats aren't the greatest. A life of video games and good books has rarely driven me to be very active. Though I would go with James and others on trips and such. What was one of the rules of surviving the apocalypse..." Oliver snapped his fingers as he remembered. "Oh yea, cardio! Well, I'll work on it. My intelligence looks pretty good, and my Wisdom isn't too bad either, must be from all that reading. I'm surprised that my Charisma looks decent. I mean maybe it comes from being part Italian, who knows, but I'll take it."

A new notification popped up.

You have been granted one perk and based on your stats one basic spell. Please choose from the following...

"Alright! You are making a better impression now system, keep it up."

DO NOT PUSH IT

"Okay, okay. Got it, you can mess with me, but I can't really mess with you, is that it?"

EXACTLY

NOW CHOOSE!

"Got it. Please display the available perks."

— — — — —

A few hours later...

"Alright system I will go with the Favored Magic Type perk."

Favored Magic Type
Description: *Choose a magic type or 'school'. All spells of this magic type have double the potency and are a quarter of the mana cost. In addition, spells of this type do not require magical components or an arcane focus. This grants you access to one tier higher spell.* **Magic Type Chosen:** *Fire.*

You must now choose your first Tier 1 spell. Due to your chosen perk, you may also choose one Tier 2 Fire spell.

"Sweet! Two spells to choose from!" Oliver exclaimed.

First spell selected: **Weak Fire Arrow**

Weak Fire Arrow
Description: Summon and shape a Fire arrow that shoots a target causing fire damage. Please note: The fire damage from this spell is increased due to related perk.

Tier 2 Fire spell chosen: **Minor Fireball**.

Minor Fireball
Description: Form and shoot a minor fireball causing force and fire damage. Please note: The fire damage from this spell is increased due to related perk.

As he was now working with fire Oliver had to say the classic Beavis & Butthead line. "Fire! He, he, he, he, he. Cool, he, he, he, he, he!"

Smiling Oliver summoned a fire arrow before dismissing it.

"Ye be a wizard, Oliver!" Oliver exclaimed in excitement.

Query Accepted

You cannot choose a class until you reach level 13.

"That is not what I meant, and you know it!"

Correct

"You son of a... woosah, woosah. It's not like you can do anything to the damn system to begin with."

Correct

"Errrrrr... Okay you know what, no. I am going to be the bigger man here."

Debatable

"Son of a... wait you know what? I walked right into that one, didn't I?" Oliver exclaimed.

Query Accepted

Correct

"Alright. I'll give you that one. Now what can I expect out there? Man, I wish I had gone on that birthday trip with my buddy. One, I feel kind of bad he was alone on his birthday. Second, that cabin is stocked and a great place to hole up and survive this apocalypse."

QUEST RECEIVED

Find Old Friends
Description: You have realized that you will need resources and a place to use as a base of operations in the hopes of surviving this apocalypse. You also realize the most precious resource is someone you can trust to watch your back. Lucky for you, you know exactly where to find these very things. Unluckily for you, the location is not exactly close.

Objective: Reach Shadow's Cabin before you or your friend are overrun. HINT: It will take time for the realms to merge. The faster you get there, the easier it will be. WARNING: Do not take too long to decide. The clock is ticking... like seriously, why aren't you moving already?

Please note: This quest has been auto accepted on your behalf as it is the best course for survival. This is mandatory and cannot be rejected.

"Okay system we are going to have a serious talk." Olive complained as he finished getting dressed, started to figure out what he needed to take, and began to load up his backpack.

Once Oliver finished his packing, he loaded everything into the old pickup his buddies had spent time fixing up. Oliver and his friends were preppers, not on the extreme side, but they all had emergency rations and had some level of additional resources should the end of the world occur.

"You're not paranoid if you're right!" Oliver repeated the popular prepper saying to himself.

As part of his final preparations before heading out, Oliver did a quick 'circle of safety', which consisted of doing a 360 degree walk around the truck and checking the tires and popping the hood to do a quick check to see if anything wrong stood out. He wasn't a mechanical wiz like one of his buddies, but he watched his buddy and his buddy's friend Kevin rebuild the engine, so Oliver knew just enough to know everything looked right. As this truck had zero computer chips in it, he figured it had a far better chance of starting up than his car, plus extra fuel was already loaded into the back of the truck.

'The quest said make it to Shadow's cabin. If that was the case Paul was no longer with us.' Oliver thought as he remembered the crazy old genius.

Paul adored Oliver's best friend and made it clear if anything happened to old man, his buddy inherited the cabin along with everything Paul owned. Oliver remembered the conversation as they were all sitting there on the cabin porch enjoying the quiet.

"If I ever die or am raptured, and you didn't join me, then I want you to have the place. I never had any kids, wife cheated on me while I was at war, so I kicked his ass and booted her to the curb. I consider you like the son I never had... Shadow. Why you youngins like to use your gamer tags makes no sense to me. Though I guess when I think about it, when I was in the war, my buddies and I gave each other nicknames too." Paul said as he shook his head and stood up, "Now, let's go inside and you can try some of the moonshine I made."

That was how Paul was, he would get right to the point, maybe reminisce for a moment, then act.

"If the cabin doesn't reference my best friend's name, then it looks like my buddy took on one of his gamer monikers. Shadowalker, or Shadow for short, was one of a few handles his best friend went by when they gamed. Oliver had a few go-to names himself. One of his favorites was from a sci-fi series he loved, Farscape. It wasn't what he used when they raided every week, but it still was one of his go-to handles. "Eh, why not. If everything is changing, maybe I should too. System can you update my name to Laraaq?"

Query Accepted

System settings update complete. Name has been changed from Oliver to Laraaq. If someone inspects you, they will now see Laraaq.

Displaying Status changes:

Name: Laraaq
Perks: Favored Magic Type (Fire)
Known Spells: Weak Fire Arrow (Tier 1), **Minor Fireball** (Tier 2)

"Thanks System." Laraaq said out loud.

You are welcome... sci-fi nerd, I mean Laraaq.

"You just couldn't pass up the dig, could you?" Laraaq stated.

Correct

Cannot having you die of shock from your system being nice to you.

Shaking his head at his system's antics, Laraaq got into the truck and started up the engine. His mind shifted to the journey he was about to undertake. That made him think of his buddy. "Funny enough I bet Shadow would appreciate the fact that I'm bringing the truck to him. I doubt his electrical car is going anywhere, ha, ha, ha. Time to do this."

"Alright System, time for a Road Trip!" Laraaq said as he pulled out of the driveway after shutting the garage and locking up.

As Laraaq drove off down the street, he did not know if he would ever come back to the place, he called home. Laraaq thought to himself, 'I sure hope so.'

Driving down the street Laraaq immediately noticed how no one was on the road. It had been at least half a day since the initial notification. "It looks like after the notification everyone found the nearest place to bunker down in." Laraaq commented to himself as he slowly drove by several abandoned cars. Some had rolled to a stop somewhere; most had crashed into something.

Query Accepted

Millions of humans chose to be saved and were immediately taken when this event started.

"Wait, what? Why wasn't I given that option?"

Query Accepted

You have no faith. There was only one path to initial salvation, that option required strong faith or innocence.

"Innocence? Explain please."

Query Accepted

Those that did not have enough mental development or had limited capacity were automatically saved unless they had committed great acts of cruelty.

"I am not sure I understand that answer. Could you please elaborate."

Query Accepted

Most human children under the age of 16, most pets, and mentally disabled were automatically taken and spared what is to come.

"I guess kids make sense as their cognitive brains are still developing. Why stop at 16? The brain still develops way past that age."

Query Accepted

That was the average age. Cognitive development was considered, some children older than 16 were taken and some younger were left. It was decided that by that age they should have enough cognitive development to begin to understand faith and the difference between right and wrong.

"Have you met the younger generation? I would not make that assumption, especially with some of the crappy non-existent parents out there." Laraaq commented.

Do I need to run another mental health scan? Think about it.

After a long pause...

Query Accepted

It falls to the parents to develop the cognitive skills of their children. Many cultures have different ages of adulthood. The decision was made to take the average of 16 and factor parental responsibilities for any children from 16 to 18 years of age. Some were saved, some were not. Cruel acts were considered for those children without faith.

"So, what I am understanding is anyone from 16 to 18 if they are here, it was because the parents didn't raise them right. Also, any kid younger than 16, if the kid wasn't a little shit chances are they were taken. That means, any kids I see under 16 I might want to be wary of." Laraaq summarized.

Correct

"Well at least that means I don't have to feel bad about throwing a fireball at some little jerk off if they are still here."

That's the spirit!

Laraaq pondered what he just learned. He mentally resolved himself to be very cautious around younger kids still around and decided to take a 'shoot first, ask questions later' policy in that regard.

Keep that mindset and you just might survive this apocalypse.

An hour into his drive Laraaq encountered his first monster. At first, he just thought it was someone who was in shock or maybe drunk as they just meandered around listlessly. As he got closer to the individual, Laraaq realized they were missing half the skin on their face.

"Of course, the apocalypse had to have zombies. Just great." Laraaq lamented before steeling his resolve. "Well let's find out of this is a fast moving or slow-moving zombie."

Laraaq maneuvered the truck closer to the zombie. Whether it was the sound or proximity of the truck, Laraaq didn't know, but the zombie began to move in his direction. "Slow moving, that's perfect."

Laraaq took his foot off the gas and rolled down his window. Sticking his arm out the window, he cast **Weak Flame Arrow** and shot it right at the zombie. The first shot went wide and missed the zombie entirely. Not wanting to give the zombie further opportunity to get closer, Laraaq cast a second Weak Flame Arrow. This one flew true and smacked the zombie right in the chest and ignited the zombie's clothes.

"Uhh, uhh." The zombie moaned as the fire spread from the clothes to the zombie's torso and face.

Shortly after the whole zombie caught on fire and then collapsed in the middle of the road.

Notifications appeared in Laraaq's vision.

*Congratulations! You are the first human to kill a former human turned into a monster within 1,000 kilometers. You have gained the achievement: **Kill Them All & Let God Sort It Out**! This achievement grants you the Titles of **Ruthless Hunter** and **Early Adopter**.*

*Congratulations! You have gained the title **Ruthless Hunter**! This title is gained when you kill a former human who was transformed into a monster or dark aligned creature. This grants the following bonuses:*

Stats and damage increased by 25% when battling with former humans that have turned into monsters or dark aligned creatures.

*Congratulations! You have gained the title **Early Adopter**! This title is gained when you are the first to kill a former human turned monster or dark aligned creature This grants the following bonuses:*
Experience gained on first kill tripled. When you level up, humans will gain 5 attribute points, which are commonly referred to as 'stat points', to distribute into any area you choose. This title grants you an additional 5 'stat points' per level. This is not a retroactive title and only applies to levels gained after receiving this title.

*Congratulations! You have gained **+125 experience** for killing a level 4 undead zombie. This experience is tripled due to achievement title. Total **+375 experience**.*

Level Up!** Congratulations! You have reached **level 2**! +10 stats points per level. **Total stat points to distribute: +10!

"Sweet! Now that I am a hunter, I should get a 1967 Chevy Impala. System can you notify me should we encounter a 1967 Chevey Impala, preferable in black?"

Query Accepted

Should one come within your sensory range, and you miss it a warning notification will go off in your brain.

"Thank you, System."

You are welcome, Dean, I mean Laraaq.

"Okay, so that confirms you can read my thoughts and or past memories."

DUH. I thought we already established this. You sure are slow on the uptake.

"Hey! I just didn't know you could go back into memories of past shows I used to watch."

Do you really want to get into a conversation on things you have watched in the past?

"Uh... no, we are good. And for the record... never mind, let's stay focused on the present System, yes that's it, better to focus on the present right now for my safety." Laraaq replied as he put the pickup truck in gear and continued along his journey.

Chapter 6 – Suzie

Suzie ran as hard as she could. Her legs were tired, and her body ached. She felt like she had been running all day, and in fact, that was not too far from the truth.

The twenty-six-year-old woman was visiting her family in the small town in the middle of nowhere. To say Suzie's relationship with her parents was estranged was an understatement. When Suzie turned 18, she moved to California in the hope of getting her big break in the movie business. That choice was not something her very religious parents had approved of.

In truth, Suzie, like so many of her peers, really didn't have a plan or idea of what they wanted to be or do with their life. She just knew she had to get out of the small town if she wanted to figure it out. Shortly after arriving in Los Angeles Suzie learned how expensive everything was. Even though she had a few successful commercials ads, and some 'extra' work, it was hard to get by. Her original awe at the industry quickly faded after multiple 'auditions' that just turned out to be attempts at getting her to do porn. She had nothing against the industry, but it wasn't what she wanted.

It took a few years and several failed relationships, but Suzie had finally met someone, and they decided to move in together six months ago. Both worked one or more jobs and still they struggled to survive and make ends meet in the city. She would call her parents every so often, but they just didn't understand her, so the calls home became fewer and fewer. When they would call her, she would say she was busy or working and let them go quickly.

She did love her parents; they just didn't understand how things were now. They were strong in their faith, and it was clear they loved each other very much. Suzie just could not get them to understand how dating was and how the world worked now.

"No, my little Suzie-cue! The world only works that way if we allow it!" Suzie's father would tell her all the time.

To which her typical response would be to roll her eyes and say, "Okay dad."

Both of her parents were loved in their small-town community as well. Her father was a doctor, and her mom was a part-time schoolteacher. Her mom kept the household and finances, with it she had invested well, and they were able to both retire early. Retirement for them only meant they could be more active in their church and community, both giving back as much as they could.

They did not approve of her moving in with her boyfriend. Her parents never admonished her, but rather just expressed concerns about settling for less than she deserved. Suzie did not tell them why she had come home to visit. They could tell something was wrong, but they did not push. Instead, they did what they could and welcomed her home with open arms and her mom did her typical country mom response. "Sweetie, you look like skin and bones. Sit down and let mamma fix you somethin' to eat."

Suzie didn't have the heart to tell her parents they were right. She had come home early, only to catch her boyfriend in bed with her best friend in LA. A part of her had wanted to resort to violence, as her father and older brother both had served in the military and made a point to teach her survival skills. Heck her own mother taught her how to use a bow so she could go hunting with the family when she was young. Suzie knew how to handle herself as a true country girl. In this instance, however, her heart hurt too much to even bother beating the crap out of them. She just grabbed her keys, hopped into her car, and drove straight to her parents' house, only stopping to use the restroom, fill up the tank, and grab snacks along the way.

That was how she ended up in her small hometown when the apocalypse came. She was sitting down at the table for an early morning breakfast her mom was making. Her older brother, his wife, and their twins Matt and Micah had just arrived for a visit. The reason, according to her brother, was so the two eight-year-olds could get quality time with their auntie while she was in town. In truth, her brother wanted to know what happened and whose face and rear-end he needed to rearrange.

They had all just started digging into the amazing food her mom had just made, when her whole family disappeared in flashes of bright light. Then the words appeared in front of her vision and a voice echoed in her mind. The apocalypse had come. Her family had been saved, but she was now left alone to figure out how to survive.

The system gifted to everyone left reminded Suzie of the role-playing games, or RPGs, several of her boyfriends had played. She was no stranger to them either but found it best not to make them look bad. To say her exes were not the sharpest tool in the shed was an understatement. Suzie's problem was her like of pretty boys. Other than the lack of good conversation and the fact that it was darn near impossible to build a life with a moron, her biggest dating issue was that most of her exes ended up being one narcissist after the other.

One thing she learned about narcissists, you can't be better than they are at anything, otherwise they make you suffer for it. So, she played dumb as best she could, but now that it was the apocalypse, she could not risk falling for another evil person. Even though her heart was recently stomped on, she focused on the problems at hand. Suzie decided she would lean into her RPG skills and learn as quickly as she could what this system could do.

Suzie reviewed her Status page.

Name: Suzie	Race: In Transition	Level: 1
Strength: 8	Dexterity: 18	Constitution: 16
Intelligence: 13	Wisdom: 6	Charisma:17
Spiritual Attunement: Unaligned	Core Stage: Not Formed	Spiral Stage: Not Formed
Health, Mana, Stamina Values & Regen Rates per hour (pH)					
HP: 40	HP/pH: 5	MP: 33	MP/pH: 18	SP: 145	SP/pH: 48

Congratulations! You have earned one perk and based on your stats one spell or stamina-based skill.

"Well, my agility and reflexes are pretty good since I have such a high Dexterity. Guess that comes from stretching and running every day. My Constitution is high as well. Must be from all the yoga, exercise, and healthy eating. Intelligence not bad, Wisdom is kind of low, maybe that explains my poor choice in men. Lastly, my Charisma is good, that should help with interacting with other survivors." Suzie summarized as she thought about what kind of 'build' would play to her current strengths.

Suzie decided to choose the Weak Point Detection skill first. She was already skilled at hand axe and knife throwing thanks to her father and brother's training. It only made sense for her to lean into that skill set.

Weak Point Detection

Description: Sharpen your eye to find and exploit weakness in an enemy.
Passive effect: Naturally gain insight into an enemy's weak spots, increasing your chances of inflicting a critical strike.
Active effect: Expend stamina to have weak point areas on an enemy highlight or glow to make it easier to hit.

It took Suzie some time to decide on her perk. In the end, she decided to embrace this new RPG like world and chose a perk that allowed her to change her race to Wood Elf. This gave her a racial perk called Elven Precision.

Elven Precision

Description: Elves are known for their quick reflexes and graceful movements. This racial characteristic grants them increased accuracy in both ranged and melee attacks. Minor decrease in costs on Stamina based skills and actions.

Susie screamed as her whole body contorted and began heating up. She could feel muscles tearing and bones breaking, only to be reformed a new. What felt like agonizing hours passed, but it was only a few minutes. She came to lying on the floor, blood and other bodily fluids lay in a puddle everywhere around her.

The scream had apparently drawn attention to her. As she stood there on shaky legs, a banging was being made on the door. Suzie grabbed a few nearby kitchen knives just as the door burst open. A short green skinned figure with an axe charged straight at her.

Without even thinking, Suzie threw one of the blades she had in her hands. The blade flew true and in a blink was buried handle deep into what her System identified as a level 4 goblin. The moment the goblin dropped dead on the floor another goblin charged in club raised.

Seeing a steak knife on the table she stood next to, Suzie grabbed it with her free-hand and chucked right at the oncoming goblin. The blade flew true as well, once again burying itself up to the hilt into the goblin's skull. That was two dead.

Suzie did not get a breather or even a chance to take a moment. A third goblin appeared in the doorway and charged at her. Again, with lightning quick reflexes she grabbed another steak knife and took out the third and final goblin.

Rushing to the kitchen door, Suzie did a quick look outside. Further down the street she saw more goblins checking houses and doors. She ducked her head back in and then proceeded to drag the two goblin corpses by the doorway further inside her house. Once the bodies were clear of the door, she shut it.

The latch was broken on the door, so Suzie ran to the kitchen table and pushed as hard as she could. The solid oak table slowly moved towards the back door. Once the table was firmly blocking the door from being opened again, Suzie slumped to the floor. She wasn't safe yet, but she had a moment to review her notifications and get cleaned up.

"Ugh! I smell awful! I'm so taking a shower, goblins, or no goblins." Suzie said as she tried to multitask, reading her notifications while taking a quick shower.

*Congratulations! You have killed a level 4 goblin. You gained **+125 experience**.*

*Congratulations! You have killed a level 4 goblin. You have gained **+125 experience**.*

*Congratulations! You have killed a level 5 goblin. You have gained **+150 experience**.*

Congratulations! For killing multiple enemies of dark alignment in quick succession and leveling up within the first few hours of the apocalypse you have gained the achievement and title Skillful Hunter.

Title: Skillful Hunter
<u>Description</u>: *Within the first few hours of the apocalypse, be one of the first in your area to kill enough dark aligned creatures to level up using your natural talents and skills. Those who adapt quickly to this new world reap the benefits. +4 stat point per level gained after obtaining this title.*

Level up! *Congratulations! You are now **level 2**! As a wood elf you gain +6 stat points per level. With your **Skillful Hunter** title, you have a total of **+10 stat points** to distribute.*

Suzie was sure glad she had selected the **Weak Point Detection** skill. Without thinking about it her new wood elf mind used the skill in tandem with her racial perk to easily pinpoint and strike critical killing blows on her attackers.

Her quick shower over she was dressed in some form fitting yet comfortable gear that gave her good range of motion. She grabbed her father's weapons belt and leg straps. This allowed her to equip and carry multiple hand axes, small blades, and a few handguns to her waist and legs. She threw on a hoodie to help keep her warm and cover her now pointy ears. That done she snagged her dad's rifle, all the ammo she could find, and grabbed her compound bow, quiver along with holster and a backpack.

"These goblins are about to meet a true country girl!" Suzie declared.

She wanted to pay back these goblin invaders from daring to come into her hometown. "Wait when did I get so possessive of this place?" Suzie asked before she answered herself. "The moment I had to defend it."

Even with that drive to fight, Suzie used the upstairs windows to do some scouting. Her parents had regularly commented on how each room upstairs faced a different direction, giving you a 360-degree view of the town, they so loved. Careful poking her head up and doing what she could to remain unseen, she checked each cardinal direction.

The goblins seemed to be coming from both the southwest and southeast direction into town. A handful could be seen slowly making their way deeper into town, but her scouting confirmed the northern direction was completely clear. This left Suzie with a choice, to make her way out of the town and into the forest north before the goblins closed in around her or bunker in and take a stand.

Doing one more headcount on the number of goblins she could see, Suzie realized one simple fact. She might've killed three of the bastards easily enough, but she doubted she could take on the over thirty goblins attacking her from all sides. She had to flee. Perhaps she could find a well-built cabin to hunker down in and figure out a plan.

Just as Suzie was about to head downstairs, she heard gunshots. She turned and saw Old Man Jones shooting at the nearby goblins with his assault rifle.

"Come get some you green skinned demons! I'm gonna send you back to the hell you came from!" Old Man Jones declared.

"Crap. I can't just let him die. My parents loved that old coot." Suzie cursed as she booked it downstairs and headed for the door.

Several goblins were running towards the old man. Several shots could be heard, and more goblins dropped dead. "Yea that's right, come get some ya little ugly bastards!" Old Man Jones roared.

Suzie noticed a few goblin archers taking up positions. One was almost at an angle to flank the crazy old man. She drew her bow, activated her Weak Point Detection skill, knocked an arrow, and fired. The arrow flew true and took the goblin archer right in the throat.

The goblin archer fell from his perch catching both Old Man Jones and a few nearby goblins' attention.

"Nice shot Darling! I remember when you won the Archery State Championship. Your parents were so proud." Old Man Jones yell out to her as he took a step further from his spot on his porch.

In his distraction a goblin archer hit Old Man Jones in the shoulder causing him to drop his assault rifle. "Son of a..." Old man Jones cursed as he fell back trying to take cover.

Suzie paid the archer back for his transgression with an arrow to the back of the head.

More goblins were making their way up the town's streets, coming from the south. Suzie bolted towards Old Man Jones's house. One of the downed goblins apparently wasn't dead yet and lunged for Suzie as she was passing by. Completely caught off guard she could only watch as the goblin's dagger was heading straight for her stomach.

BANG! BANG!

Two bullets hit the goblin twisting the body and giving Suzie the precious space to dodge the attack. The goblin dropped to the ground dead. Suzie looked towards the sound of the gunshots and saw Old Man Jones holding his 9MM. "Little bastard was playing dead."

Old Man Jones leaned against his door showing clear signs of fatigue and injury. Suzie helped him maintain his balance when she reached him.

"Good to see ya darling."

"You too Mr. Jones. Let me take a look at that wound." Suzie greeted, as she began to inspect the injury.

"It's nothing darling. Just give me a couple shots of whiskey and I'll be right as rain."

"Nonsense. Let me patch you up. Then we gotta get out of here. All that noise is attracting more goblins." Suzie said as she withdrew some gauze from one of her first aid kits in her backpack.

In mere minutes she had his shoulder bandaged and gained a skill for her efforts.

Skill Obtained: Healing (Mundane)

Healing (Mundane)
Description: Rare is the healer that can save someone's life without the use of magic. +25% increased chance to treat injury and illness to save a patient's life.

"I remember when you would work at your father's practice and go with him on house calls. You always had a gift with healing darlin." Old Man Jones commented as he moved his injured shoulder.

"What was that Sir?" Suzie asked.

She was a bit distracted by the notification and then the rush of memories as she recalled all the time, she worked alongside her father to be his personal nurse. 'Why hadn't I pursued a life in medicine? I used to love helping people feel better.'

"I said, you got a gift for healin. Now help me with my things so we can get out of here." Old Man Jones said as he gestured to the duffel bag near the door.

Suzie helped the man who had to be in his 70s put the strap over his other uninjured shoulder so he could carry the bag.

She put Old Man Jones's arm over her shoulder to help him lean on her as she headed north out of town.

That had all happened hours ago. They both were exhausted, and it was getting dark.

"I'm sorry Sir but I can't keep going. We have been running for hours. My body is about to collapse, and you don't look much better." Suzie exhaled as she leaned up against a tree.

"Call me Jebediah, or Jeb for short. Ya earned it for helping me get outta town. Plus, I can't forget you helped fix up my injured shoulder. There are a few hunting cabins up ahead. We can wait out the evening and get some sleep in one of the ones close by. Then in the morning we should head to my old war buddy's compound several miles deep into the forest." Jebediah stated.

"Compound? What are you talking about Mr Jones... I mean Jeb." Suzie said the last part after Jeb raised an eyebrow at her formality.

"You haven't been back for years Suzie. Seven years ago, my war buddy Paul, you might remember him..."

"Kind of." Suzie answered unsure.

"Well anyway, Paul bought a bunch of land for cheap from the town up north deep in the forest. He then proceeded to build a bunker compound. The man was a genius. Paul said he built the place to survive the apocalypse." Jebediah continued.

"That sounds like a good destination. How are we going to get in if he built it so well?" Suzie asked.

"That's the easy part. Paul left it to a hunting friend of ours, a young gentleman who was like a son to him. Good man who was always respectful to us old timers. He would listen for hours to use droll on about past experiences. He stopped by several days ago to say hi and let me know he would be up there for a week or more. Goes by the name of Shadow, he was some kind of gamer, we called him that cause he was always our shadow everywhere we went. If he's still alive we can hole up there." Jebediah explained.

"Sounds like a good plan to me. My memory of this forest is starting to come back to me. One of my ex-boyfriend's had a place nearby. His cabin should be up this road. I know where he used to hide the spare key." Suzie stated as she realized how close they were to Duncan's place.

"Lead the way darling."

A few minutes later they were walking up the driveway to her ex-boyfriend Duncan's place.

"Who goes there?! I got my guns! Don't think ye got a chance trying to loot me!" A nervous voice called out of one of the cabin windows.

"Duncan?! Is that you? It's Suzie!"

"Suzie?! Yea right! Suzie moved away years ago! Now get off my property!" Duncan called out.

"I came back home a few days ago! Now quit being an ass Duncan Donuts and come help a lady and Old Man Jones!" Suzie got another side eye from Jeb. "I mean Jebediah!"

"Suzie-cue?! It is you! Hold on a sec, I'll be right out!" Duncan called out, clear recognition in his voice.

Suzie and Jeb heard a latch, and several bolts were unlocked before the front door swung open revealing Duncan. The man was easily two meters tall and had the look of a linebacker. Which made sense, as that was what he was in high school, they were state champions thanks to his skills on the field. The boy was built like a tank, but his friends called him Duncan Donuts because he would never pass up a donut, he loved them. He wasn't the smartest and probably took one too many blows to the head, but he was notorious for being able to take a hit and shrug it off like it was nothing.

Duncan's eyes lit up seeing his old friend and past girlfriend. He ran out of his house, closed the distance in an instant, and picked up Suzie in a big ole bear hug. "It's good to see ya again Suzie-cue! I missed ya!"

Trying hard to breathe, Suzie wheezed out, "Let... me down ya big oof!"

Duncan put his friend down and rubbed the back of his neck in embarrassment. "Sorry about that Suzie-cue. I just got excited to see ya. It's been years and everything has gone all crazy. Poor Pookie vanished in a flash this mornin and then all these words showed up in my vision."

"Pookie?" Jebediah asked.

"His dog." Suzie answered.

"Ah, yea my Duke vanished in a flash too." Jebediah put his hand on Duncan's shoulder. "It's for the best my boy, you wouldn't want them living through this nightmare."

Duncan sniffled. He always got sad thinking about his dog being gone. The big man just nodded and led them inside. "Come on in. It'll be a bit tight, but I'll make room. You two eaten anything?"

"Not since this morning." Suzie answered as her stomach growled at the reminder of food.

"Same. Been a bit distracted since." Jebediah commented.

Chapter 7- Road Trip

Laraaq was about 200 kilometers into his journey to reunite with his best friend. He was cautious as he drove but did take some time leaving their suburban city. The quest text implied a timer and that one or both would become overrun at some unspecified point in time.

Knowing he was on the move and his buddy was most likely holed up at the cabin turned compound, dollars to donuts Laraaq was convinced his buddy would need his help. With that said, his drive to level up was not something he could ignore. He had taken his time leaving the suburban city because he made a point to roll down his window and set each undead zombie a blaze. It was like shooting fish in a barrel.

Now that Laraaq was finally out of town he looked at his gains. Working with his System settings he was able to get his kill notifications to aggregate into one summary prompt after combat.

*Congratulations! You have killed 78 Undead Zombies ranging from level 4 to level 6. You have gained **+11,700 experience**.*

Level Up! *Congratulations! You are now **level 5**! You have **+40 stat points** to distribute.*

"Not too bad, if I do say so myself."

Eh

"Of course, you would say that System. I could've stayed much longer but I didn't trust that more were going to show up. Let's consider the fact that I never had to get out of the truck and not even one made it to me before they succumbed to the fire damage." Laraaq defended his current progress.

For Laraaq's perspective he was level 5, well on his way to level 6 and every single one was accomplished from the comfort of the driver's seat. He even got to try out his **Minor Fireball** spell which had a good amount of knock back effect from the combination of force and fire damage creating a mini explosion. That got him thinking.

"Hey System. Are all Tier 2 spells that much more powerful than Tier 1's? What are the other tiers like? What can you tell me?"

Calm down young grasshopper!

Query Accepted

Each Tier is exponentially more powerful than the prior tier. The difference between Tier 1 and Tier 2 is minimal in comparison to the other tiers. As you go up in tier rank the spell form becomes more and more complex, typically requiring greater understanding of the concepts and nature of the magic you are working with.

"Okay, so when can I learn a Tier 3 spell?"

Impatient, aren't we?

You must first gain a class before you can gain any higher Tiered spells beyond Tier 2. There are rare cases due to high affinity and other factors but those are so minimal, you should not concern yourself.

"How many Tiers are there? Could you at least give me some kind of summary of of the different spell Tiers?"

Say 'please'

"Screw you!"

*Only after several drinks. Scratch that, with your mug, it will take a whole case. In fact, I advise you to put more points into **Charisma** to help your future prospects.*

"Ha, ha, very funny. That was a good one. Now can we get back to my questions?"

Sometimes you are no fun.

"System!"

Alright, alright. Very well

Query Accepted

Spell Tier Summary:

——Spell Tiers———
Level 0 - Simple Magic/Copper
Tier 1 - Weak/Iron
Tier 2 - Minor/Silver

Tier 3 - Gifted/Gold
Tier 4 - Enhanced/Platinum
Tier 5 - Potent/Mithril
Tier 6 - Superior/Orichalcum
Tier 7 - Powerful/Epic/Adamantite
Tier 8 - Mythical
Tier 9 - Legendary
Tier 10 - Grand Scale Magic
Tier 11 - Pinnacle Grade Magic
Tier 12 - Supreme God Tier
Tier 13 - Ultimate God Tier

*Most do not consider Tier 0 an actual tier and acquaint it to simple parlor tricks, hence the zero value. True magic starts at Tier 1 and goes all the way to Tier 13. Tier 1 through Tier 7 is considered the **Material realm**, which is why some use metals to depict the level of power contained within that range. Tier 8 and Tier 9 are considered the **Transcendent realm**, some spells within Tier 7 could also be considered in this realm. Tier 10 and Tier 11 are considered the **Ascension or Theosis realm**. It is here that the magic itself is likely divine or deific levels of power. Those that possess such ability to cast such spells are those that are gods or who could fight them. Tier 12 and Tier 13 are typically called the **God realm** or tier but that is an underrepresentation of the power levels such tiers can unleash.*

"Thank you for the summary and explanation System." Laraaq had learned early on to show appreciation to his system, or it seemed to get testier and for lack of a better term it would mess with him far more. At some point he was going to have to start dishing it back but not until he felt more comfortable in his abilities.

Laraaq was glad he got out of town before it got dark, but he also knew he was going to have to find a place to hunker down, distribute his stat points and get some sleep. With that in mind, he found a small airport after a few hours of driving.

The airport looked to be a private one. It had two runways, two hangers, and what looked like an office building. One hanger was a good size and by Laraaq's estimation could probably fit three or four small planes or helicopters. The second hanger was much smaller, maybe big enough for two small planes max. Pulling up to the smaller hanger, he parked the pickup with the headlights facing the hanger door. The door was held in place by a heavy-duty deadbolt lock that was threaded through a hole between two sides of metal, one connected to the door, the other to the frame of the hanger.

With a quick mental command Laraaq summoned a fire arrow but he condensed the fire, bringing it close to his hands as he increased the intensity of the heat. He was rewarded twice. The first reward was the lock melting away. The second was a notification.

*Congratulations! You have discovered an existing Tier 2 spell: **Heat Metal**.*

Heat Metal (Tier 2)
Description: Focus your fire to bring about intense heat. Then pour that heat into a metal causing it to burn white hot and melt. Anyone in contact with the Metal will take severe fire damage and be burned. Time required to cast the spell varies based on type and size of Metal object and amount of mana expended.

"Sweet!" Laraaq said as he pushed the hanger door open enough to let the glow from the headlights illuminate the hanger.

What Laraaq saw was a small biplane, some shelving, equipment, a backroom, and a desk. More importantly, there was enough space to easily fit the pickup inside and close the hanger back up, which is exactly why he had come here in the first place. Opening the hanger more, he decided to back up the truck into the hanger.

Not wanting to waste time, Laraaq began inspecting the hanger and the backroom. Much to his relief he didn't find anything but plane parts, grease, and dust. Inspection complete, Laraaq went to close the hanger door and that is when he heard the growling.

Four deformed coyotes stepped into the area illuminated by the headlights which were now facing outward towards the road. A quick inspection of the wolves told Laraaq what he needed to know.

Mutated Desert Coyote
Level 7
Description: Desert coyotes are scavengers and pack hunters. These desert coyotes have been mutated from exposure to intense mana fluctuations in the area. Mutated monsters tend to be more aggressive and bloodthirsty.

These mutated desert coyotes have gained enhanced strength, speed, and constitution. In addition, their sense of smell has been increased so that once they have the scent of their prey, they can track them for hundreds of kilometers.

Mutated Desert Coyote
Level 8...

Mutated Desert Coyote
Level 7...

Mutated Desert Coyote
Level 8...

"Well, that means I can't leave a single one of you alive."

Two of the mutated desert coyotes rushed forward, only to be thrown back by two consecutive explosions from Laraaq double casting Minor Fireball. Though he was successful, the accomplishment gave him one hell of a headache.

The other two darted to the sides. It was clear to Laraaq they planned to hit him from two directions. Meanwhile the other two coyotes were slowly getting to their feet.

Not wanting to contend with more enemies than he had to, Laraaq double cast two Weak Flame Arrows, each one hitting one of the injured monsters. His headache intensified.

Laraaq gritted his teeth in frustration and anger. "Errrr! You bastards are really beginning to piss me off!"

Both uninjured monsters leapt at him, one on his right side, the other on his left. Once again Laraaq tried to double cast Minor Fireball. The pain was getting so bad he dropped to one knee and almost lost his concentration on the spell forms. He doubled down on his will, working through the pain and refusing to fail.

"I'm not getting taken out by some overgrown puppies!" Laraaq roared just as both spells completed, and each fireball hit one of the coyotes right in their open maws, both throwing them back away from him. One hit with such force that it ripped the head right off the body. The other had a busted jaw and the entire body was on fire.

Laraaq quickly turned to the first two coyotes to assess their threat levels. One was clearly dead as the fur was on fire and the final coyote tried to run. Unluckily for the beast, its front paw was burned so bad it couldn't put weight on it, dramatically reducing its speed.

A couple Weak Fire Arrows later and that coyote too was a smoldering flame. The area smelt like cooked meat.

Perfect time to roast some marshmallows.

"Better yet, s'mores." Laraaq said as he grabbed the ingredients from one of his backpacks and proceeded to make s'mores as the coyotes slowly burned to ashes.

"You know System, it's the little things that make life worth living."

Correct

"Hey System, are these coyotes' edible?" Laraaq asked.

Query Accepted

Yes, your body should be able to ingest the cooked meat. You should always first check if the creature has a core before worrying about any other parts. These coyotes were very low leveled but as they are mutated by errant mana it is possible for them to possess a core, even if it is a small one.

"Core? Please explain."

Query Accepted

Cores are a key component in growth. If you consume magic cores, it can help you in the formation or evolution of your own core. Think of it as your main battery in powering your magic.

"But I'm casting magic now. Does that mean I have a core already?"

No

"Please elaborate."

Fine

Query Accepted

Cores are required if you want to cast any magic higher than Tier 3. It is recommended you already have a core when attempting to use Tier 3 but it is technically not required. A core helps you gather and strengthen your magic. If you combine that with a Gathering Spiral...

"Gathering Spiral?"

Getting there. Do not be so impatient.

A gathering spiral is a mental and metaphysical construct used to help gather and funnel mana into your core so it can grow stronger and denser.

As you move on to more complex spell forms you will find the need for greater mental control and visualization.

If those monsters have cores, they should be made up mostly of unaligned mana or small amounts of certain magic types. Normally you never want to attempt to absorb magic cores that contain magic types you do not have within your own core or have no affinity for. As you do not have a core of your own you can attempt to absorb the small amounts of mana within.

"Alright. Where do I find the monster's core?"

Query Accepted

Most cores are found in their chest near the heart. The other common locations are in the head somewhere near the brain. As each creature has a unique physiology it can vary greatly, but those areas seem to be the most common locations.

"Well let me see if they have any."

After about 30 minutes of cutting open the burnt remains of the four corpses he found three tiny cores, all smaller than a marble. Both level 8's and one level 7 held a tiny magic core.

"Now that is done, what about the meat?"

You should be able to eat it. The trace mana you will find in their meat will help you recover quicker and recharge your mana faster. Please Note: This is only possible because they are low level and you have not formed a core.

Inspect one of the magic cores.

Laraaq took the System's advice and inspected one of the tiny cores he had.

Mutated Desert Coyote Magic Core

Description: Tiny magical core formed from a mutated desert coyote. This core contains small amounts of earth magic and unaligned magic.

The other two cores said the exact same thing.

Laraaq decided to ask his question. "Each says it has small amounts of earth magic. If I absorb the core, will I be able to learn earth magic."

Query Accepted

You have some existing affinity to earth magic so you can absorb the magic. As you do not have a core of your own you cannot gain any spells, skills, or abilities from those coyote cores. Please Note: As tiny as those cores are the chance is minuscule, they contain any spell, skills, or abilities.

"How do I absorb a core?"

Query Accepted

It is recommended you eat some of the coyotes cooked meat to help with the process. Due to their size and power level, swallow the core after you have consumed some of the coyote flesh. It is recommended you meditate on try to feel the magic flowing through you.

Laraaq took out his butcher's knife and began to cut strips of meat from the coyotes. Once that was completed, he salted and stored the meat in one of his portable coolers. After closing the hanger door, Laraaq ate some coyote meat and swallowed one of the magic cores.

Tonight, he would attempt to meditate until he fell asleep. In the morning, he would spend his stat points and plan out a few things. Tomorrow, he decided to make a run to Lowe's and Home Depot down the way. If he was lucky enough, he would find a good trailer he could use to load up as many supplies as would fit. If they decided to stay put at the compound, they were going to need everything he could gather.

Interlude- Tek'tar & Jek'jon

Tek'tar stood at the center of this huemon place of gathering, something they call Town Hall. His master had sent three of his necromancers to conquer this area. Other than finding slaves, Tek'tar could not understand why this place had such value.

Each necromancer was given command of their own battle force. The number of men given to command was based on their rank and standing.

Tek'tar was a level 39 journeyman necromancer, he held the highest rank and therefore he was given command of 200 goblins. Jek'jon was a level 28 apprentice necromancer on the cusp of journeyman rank, he was given 75 goblins to command. Lastly, there was Gr'ex, a level 18 apprentice necromancer, he was only given 24 goblins to command.

Jek'jon and Gr'ex were not told about the other portals, only Tek'tar was given such knowledge. As the senior necromancer, it was his job to take command of the other two forces and lead the entire goblin army. Jek'jon fell in line easily enough, but Gr'ex still had not shown up and Tek'tar was unsure on how to proceed.

Tek'tar despised the fact his master seemed to favor the piece of troll dung for some reason. Though Gr'ex was only given 24 goblins to command, his master had given Gr'ex something very precious, high-level spells and artifacts to be able to cast them. Master called it balancing the scales.

Each portal took great power to open and could only send so many people through. If multiple portals were being opened near each other further limitations were put on who could go through. Each clan invested what they could to opening and maintaining their portal. If the portal could be anchored, then it would become a permanent gateway between worlds.

A total of 9 clans participated in this endeavor. Three clans were dedicated to this area alone. The other 6 clans were focused on other locations.

Tek'tar did not care about those other locations, he only cared about this one. If his master had invested so many resources to claim it, then this place would be more important than the others. He did not know why but that was not required to accomplish his master's goal.

"What are we going to do about Gr'ex?" Jek'jon asked.

"Stupid Gr'ex, what a piece of troll dung!" Tek'tar spat on the ground. "He is most likely dead, taken out by some locals. It matters not. This huemon town is ours and we did not need his help to do it."

"But should we not investigate? If the local huemons took Gr'ex's unit out they could pose a future threat." Jek'jon advised.

Tek'tar slammed his fist on the makeshift throne he had them make for him out of human bones. "No! And do not question my orders again! Master put me in charge! You may barely be a journeyman necromancer, but I am the senior leader here and my clan has the numbers to control this place without yours. If Gr'ex is dead than I say good riddance!"

Jek'jon bowed his head. "As you command great and terrible Tek'tar."

Tek'tar smiled evilly. 'It is about time this worm showed me some respect!' "Better Jek'jon, much better. I will take your advice under advisement. For now, we consolidate our control of the southern area of this land. So far there are more huemon structures south. Let us finish raiding them and collect more slaves before we bother with the north."

Jek'jon bowed as he backed away and walked out of the room. "As you command oh great and terrible Tek'tar."

'Little does that idiot know I call him terrible because he is the worst commander, I have ever had the displeasure serving. If I had known the master was sending his clan I would not have volunteered. But such is the life of Jek'jon, one moment of suffering to the next. I did not even want to be a necromancer. Oh well such is my lot in life.' Jek'jon thought as he carried out his orders.

"What are your orders Jek'jon?" One of his men asked as Jek'jon exited the Town Hall building.

"Consolidate our control over the south. Collect as many slaves as possible. Our clan is not like the Bone Marrow clan. Use our sleep poisons to subdue them. Finish our base in the Southeast and store most of the huemons we find there. Bring the rest here."

"Yes, wise Jek'jon" The goblin warrior replied.

It was clear to Jek'jon that his warrior had more to say. "Out with it! It is clear you have something you wish to know."

"Yes, wise Jek'jon. Are we sure this town is what the master wants?"

"No, I am not. The master said to take control over a structure in the area. He did not say a town. But it does not matter, Tek'tar is convinced we are to conquer this town. I am not strong enough to take over. He is now 9 levels above me since I reached level 30 through this conflict."

"What of Gr'ex? If his men were alive, could we not work together?"

"Tek'tar thinks he died along with his men. If Gr'ex perished in the north, then we shall stay to the south. We will act like good followers and remain while the Bone Marrow clan can no longer ignore the north and must take it. If we are lucky enough perhaps what killed Gr'ex will kill them." Jek'jon answered.

"That is why we call you the wise Jek'jon" The goblin warrior said as he bowed and carried out his orders.

Jek'jon walked towards the slave pens. So far, they have 50 people in these cages. In truth, Jek'jon's men had recovered over 200 people but most of them were back at their war camp. Most of these people were captured by the Bone Marrow clan and anyone who could not work ended up as food. There was a reason Tek'tar's clan had the name it did.

"Please let us go."

"We never did anything to you."

"Let me go, I don't care what you do to the rest of them."

On and on they pleaded. There was nothing Jek'jon could do, even if there was, he was not inclined to help. Each clan was given a certain number of slave bracelets. Those devices ensured compliance, but they were not foolproof.

Once Jek'jon neared his war camp he looked out longingly at the farms and their fields. That was what Jek'jon wanted to be a farmer and herbalist. His clan specialized in herbs and poisons. They had a pouch or vial when thrown it would release a noxious gas that could easily subdue a target. This was how his clan captured so man more huemons alive than Tek'tar's clan did.

As Jek'jon looked longingly at the southeastern farms he made up his mind. "I am going to use my skeletons to work the fields. It is not like Tek'tar will care and our people will need food eventually. It may be my lot in life to be miserable, but I will enjoy this one thing."

Chapter 8- Growing Pains

I knew intense suffering. If this was a dream, it was, by far, more real than any other I had before. My skin felt on fire. One moment my organs felt like they were being ripped apart and completely shredded, then the next moment everything was put back together as if nothing had happened.

Organ after organ I would be wracked with unimaginable pain and then heat and burning, then it would be fine, and another organ went through the same process. The entire time my skin felt like it was both on fire and being poked by millions of pin pricks. No matter how badly I wanted to wake up I couldn't.

I did everything I could to shift my thinking and I tried to remember happier times. Then I tried to focus on what I wanted, to be whole and healthy. I refused to give up even as my body and soul felt like it was being crushed by intense weight.

Then as I felt darkness was all around me, I was blinded by intense light.

I woke up gasping for air! "Ah-ha, got... to... breathe... holy... what... was... that?!"

Words both appeared in my vision and echoed in my head.

Temporal Encoding Complete

Congratulations! You have finished the second stage of absorbing the Primordial Celestial Dragon core. You have gained the following benefits:

Mana Capacity and Mana Regeneration have increased.

*Total stat point increases: +15 **Strength**, +10 **Dexterity**, + 25 **Constitution**, +15 **Intelligence**, +25 **Wisdom**, +13 **Charisma**.*

"What the hell does that mean?"

Query Accepted

The Primordial Celestial Dragon core you absorbed came from a very old dragon.

"I figured that much by the word 'Ancient' but..." I started to say but was cut off by my System.

NO. You do not understand. Old as in the beginning of this universe and others.

"Oh. Wow, but how does that explain what just happened?"

Query Accepted

You have completed phase 2 of the assimilation process. During this stage more of the energy flows through your soul and body. If there are remnants of the creature's soul within it has a chance to resist or in this case judge the worthiness of the recipient.

"But what do the words 'Temporal Encoding Complete' mean?!" It was not like my system to withhold information and it was causing my frustrations to rise.

Query Not Accepted

"WHAT?!"

I couldn't believe it. It may have only been over a day, but my system has always been more than willing to help me understand things. I wasn't sure what to do about this. That was when a new notification appeared in my vision.

You have completed phase 2 of the Primordial Celestial Dragon core. You have an opportunity to immediately combine and finish phase 3 and phase 4. Do you wish to proceed, Yes or No?

"I wanted this over. If I'm going to die then so be it system, but if I die because of lack of information I'm going to be seriously pissed off!" I said as I mentally selected the 'yes' option.

I immediately screamed in agony as everything I had just experienced hit me again but times thirteen!

My vision was blinded by light, and I think I passed out. I'm not sure as when I opened them, I was floating in a golden bubble in space.

A deep voice spoke, and every fiber of my being thrummed to every word. "Do not blame your system for not being able to answer your question. It was not meant to know."

"Who are you?" I asked.

"That is one of my questions to you." The voice replied.

A few moments passed before it asked two questions in a commanding voice. "Who Are You?! What Do You Want?!"

"Hey, I know those lines. They are from one of my favorite sci-fi series of all time." I replied.

"Yes, I know. I have been inside your Mind, Body, and Soul. Those questions have power and meaning behind them. Yet I do not think you fully understand what that means, not yet anyway."

"Will you help me understand?"

The voice boomed with laughter. "Ha, ha, ha, ha! Now that is the right question!"

A moment passed and it continued. "I am the remnants of the Primordial Celestial Dragon core you are absorbing."

"Nice to meet you. Do you have a name?"

The voice replied. "You are being rather cavalier about possibly being destroyed."

"My parents taught me to be respectful and my Nanuz and Uncles taught me to be honorable even in the face of danger." I answered.

"Wise people and their wisdom show in your very soul. Very well, to answer your question I have had many names, as names have power, I will gift you with that knowledge should you survive what is to come."

"I'm all ears." I replied.

The voice boomed in laughter once again. "Ha, ha, ha, ha! That would be a very uncomfortable state of being if you were all ears."

"No, it is just an expression..."

The booming voice cut me off. "Ha, ha, ha. I know that but the visual it inspires is quite hilarious."

"You know you're right." I replied as I thought about how weird that would look to be covered in ears.

"Of course, I am right I tend to be. As do you do you not?" The voice replied.

That caught me off guard. "Well, I tend to use both my mind and heart, yet when I truly listen, I tend to be pointed to the solution. It tends to be so clear to me, but others have a hard time, yet I tend to be proven correctly. It's hardest when I'm blinded by emotions. I never really thought about it before."

"Yes, there are reasons for what you do. Your mind, your very soul are touched by time, as is mine. You see we are fractured in time and space, in being one thing and it's the opposite. That duality is your greatest burden as it was mine. Do you understand?"

"No but perhaps I am beginning to."

"And that was the right answer. Knowing you understand very little but seeking out the truth is the true measure of wisdom. Of all the magics and powers in existence Time is not understood by Intelligence alone, no it is your Will and your Wisdom that helps you understand." The voice stated.

A long pause went by before the voice continued. It was clear to me the voice wanted their words to sink in. "If you had not a Divine Infinitum you would be dead already. I embodied time and space. I embraced my charge and traveled through time and journeyed across the stars and realms. Along the way I gained both Light and Dark traits, your system calls them abilities."

"How did you die?" I asked. This being sounded very powerful, and it made my mind wonder what could kill it.

"Some would call it hubris, but I call it self-sacrifice. I helped both the Light and the Dark lock away several ancient Eldritch beings that were the antithesis to the Light and the Dark. It was one of the rare times they banded together to stop a greater threat. The apocalypse your world is suffering is only the beginning. It is a chance for Light to give a final chance for redemption. It is Dark's chance to further claim as many as they can for their side. In the end it matters not. Perhaps there is a third choice. What I do know is the greater enemies are those who exist outside."

"Outside? You mean the Eldritch?" I asked.

"Yes and no. Those that serve the Eldritch are not always like their masters, they are those who are lost and beyond madness. I cannot speak more about this, and that is not the purpose of our conversation. The apocalypse is THE event, but it was not the catalyst. I was wounded in the greatest of battles. That wound left me with a choice. Sacrifice much of my power to heal and live or instead sacrifice myself to entrust my power to another. I chose the latter."

"My respects to you for such an honorable act." I commented. I was not sure I could do such a thing.

The voice continued. "There were five options to bequeath my legacy. One of the Light, and one of the Dark, three caught in the middle and possibly falling to one side of the other. In the end I chose you."

"What?! I thought I received your magic core as a quest reward for closing the portal. My understanding is that reward is random. Also, why me?" I asked in confusion.

The voice laughed. "Ha, ha, ha, ha! To most things are 'random' but that does not mean without the ability to predict probabilities to one such as I. To answer your question, why you. It is simple, you did the same selfless act as I had done."

"Huh? No, I didn't. I did not kill myself. I'm pretty sure at least up until this moment I was very much alive." I answered perplexed.

The voice chuckled. "Ha, ha, ha. Perhaps you do not realize what you have done. You sacrificed your guaranteed salvation to save those you both knew and did not know. You chose to return just for the chance to save others. That is the same thing I do now. Your Divine Infinitum will give you the chance to absorb my power, but you must change and adapt just as your core and spiral have."

"What do you mean?"

"Simple. A human body has infinite possibilities but as you are now you cannot contain my powers. So, you must adapt."

"I feel like you are leading to something."

"Yes, I am. It is why I prevented your system from showing you the results of phase 2 and why I forced it to initiate phase 3 and 4 together. Temporal Encoding Complete." The last sentence the voice spoke thrummed and I felt it in every fiber of my being.

"What does that mean?" I asked the disembodied voice.

The voice boomed in response. "It means you are now both a part of time and beyond it. Yes, I have picked up several abilities over the eons, but my greatest attunement was to time itself. To be both a part of it and separate. Even the god of time could not find me, for I was everywhere and nowhere simultaneously. That is what Temporal Encoding Complete means you now can never be hindered by any negative time or slowing effects. Only time magic you wish to experience and wield will occur. Your system is as much a part of time as the universe itself so it cannot comprehend what this fully means. I will allow it to understand some but only you will understand it's full meaning."

I was speechless. Not even a time god could touch me. Good to know there was a time god. Lower case g which means lesser and not the big guy.

"Sadly, this also means from this point forward you will no longer age. Though your cells can die this will give you a natural resistance to necrotic damage. Most death magic spells tend to have elements of speeding up cell death, that part of the magic will have no effect on you, but that does not mean you are immune to that type of magic in totality." The voice explained.

"Good to know. Let me first say thank you for this and what you are doing. If I already received the Temporal Encoding as part of phase 2, what is phase 3 and 4?"

"As I said earlier your very spirit is fractured. Such a profound choice you made has consequences. Who you were, what you are, and who and what you will become has been broken. This affects your very mind, body, and soul. I cannot fix this completely, but I can put in motion the eventual healing needed for you to be made whole again. That shall be set in motion but also means you cannot remain solely human. Your body must adapt, and you must become as I was, a Primordial Celestial Dragon."

"Hold up. Wait a minute! You mean to tell me I'm going to become a dragon?! I mean an actual dragon?!" I said in disbelief.

"Yes, it is the only way to both begin to heal you and it will be needed for phase 4."

"So, I get to be a dragon?! One of my rules in life: be yourself, cause everyone else is taken... unless you can be a dragon then be a DRAGON! My friends would say be Batman but that pales in comparison to being a real dragon! Let's do this!" I said in giddy excitement.

"Do you not wish to understand phase 4?" The voice asked.

"Oh, yea right. Sorry just excited. Why does me becoming a dragon help the next phase? Also, what happens in phase 4?" I replied.

The voice explained. "By becoming a primordial celestial dragon your body, including all your organs will be able to handle the influx of my power. Your Divine Infinitum would have survived and grown regardless, but you might remember the intense pain you felt everywhere, your body, as it is, cannot handle what I give you. One of my kind is built to survive the extremely harsh environments of space, the stars, and other realms. Some of my power will be used in this transformation. For the power contained within my core this is easy as it is like genetic memory and cell replication. It will still be excruciatingly painful; of that I am sorry."

"It's okay. I get to be a dragon. Sorry believe it or not, lifelong dream coming true here. If pain is what it's going to take so be it." I replied, not deterred in the slightest.

The voice continued. "Very well. Phase 4 is when my magic core fully infuses with you as the last vestiges of who I was becomes a part of you. As part of my sacrifice, I ensured that many of my abilities, spells, and skills would transfer over. Several will be made available to you when you awaken. However, there will be some that will remain dormant until you reach an appropriate level, or the right circumstances are met. Much of my magic is related to time, it will take you a great deal of reflection and hard work to use that power to the fullest possible. Lastly, I will tell you this, do not tell others about me or of what you have become. My kind were forces of nature that could be seen as being both Light and Dark. If others discover you to be a dragon, do not reveal your type. Yet of all these warnings the most important is never reveal what Temporal Encoding truly means. You will begin to understand my unique power soon enough."

"Thank you for everything." It was all I could think of to say. This being was giving its life for the chance to help save others. It would always have my respect and appreciation.

"AND SO, IT BEGINS!!!" The voice boomed.

Then every part of me exploded. I was a scattering of feelings, thoughts, and emotions. As I felt like I was starting to be stitched back together the pain came in roiling waves of intensity. Once I felt like I had organs again, they only brought with them pain and agony.

Each organ morphed and changed, while they filled up with liquid fire. That fire poured out of each organ and burned through every vein and artery. I screamed and screamed until I felt that same liquid fire scorch my throat as it continued to spread. Then it hit my brain and I recalled every painful memory I had ever experienced in exacting detail and magnified exponentially.

Then ever so slightly a memory of hope or love with show itself. I felt the joy of knowing my best friend would always be there for me. It redoubled my commitment and love for him as my brother. Then I remembered other family members, many who I knew were now gone, saved from such brutality and horror this apocalypse would bring.

Then I saw flashes or images that felt like memories but different. I saw the local town overrun by goblins. People were in cages or used as slaves or worse, food. I saw my best friend traveling across the country, fighting zombies and then coyotes. A flash of three people armed approaching the compound. An image of magic pulsing and flowing. Then in an instant a flash and everything was gone.

I gasped awake. I bolted upright and then jumped to my feet.

"Holy cow! What was that?!" I exclaimed as I immediately checked my vitals.

"Eyes, ears, nose, mouth, arms, legs, family jewels. All check! Whew! Wait I thought I was turned into a dragon? Was that just some weird extremely painful dream? Why am I still human?"

Welcome Back!

Query Accepted

Congratulations! You have completely absorbed the Primordial Celestial Dragon core! As a result, you have gained the following changes:
***Race change** to **Primordial Celestial Dragon**...*

"Wait if it says it right there that I am a dragon, why am I human?"

Query Accepted

You are using a shapeshift ability that has you completely in human form. Even if someone inspects you, they will only see the race you take the form as. Please Note: Finish reviewing the summary of changes.

"Sorry System. Please continue displaying the changes."

> Congratulations! You have completely absorbed the Primordial Celestial Dragon core! As a result, you have gained the following changes:
>
> - **Race change** to **Primordial Celestial Dragon**
> - Your **Divine Infinitum** has grown in power. **Mana Capacity** and **Mana Regeneration increased.**
> - You have greater control over your ability **Gravity Momentum Manipulation**
> - You have gained the ability **True Shapeshift**
> - You have gained the ability **Partitioned Mind**
> - You have gained the ability **Dark Mantle**
> - You have gained the ability **Flight.**
> - You have gained the ability **Draconic Regeneration**
> - You have gained the ability **Seer's Gift**
> - You have gained the ability **Claws of Time**
> - You have gained the spell **Magic Missiles (Time Variant) (Tier 1)**
> - You have gained the spell **Plasma Bolt (Tier 3)**
> - You have gained the spell **Black Hole Arrow (Tier 7)**
> - You have gained the spell **Time Boost (Tier 4)**
> - You have gained the spell **Rift (Tier 8)**
> - You have gained the skill **Quick Step**
> - You have gained the skill **Probability Calculations**
> - You have gained the following stat increases: +10 **Strength**, +10 **Dexterity**, +25 **Constitution**, +25 **Intelligence**, +25 **Wisdom**, +13 **Charisma**

"Damn that's a lot of stuff from one core!"

Correct

Query Accepted

Such a high number of benefits is so improbable that the only conclusion was the core came from a being who imbued as much of its power in its core. Such an act would result in its death.

"Good to know System. Let's learn what all the new abilities do. I'll wait to read up on the spells and skills after I get a better handle on all the changes."

Query Accepted

Ability: True Shapeshift
Description: Many dragons possess the ability to turn into any race they desire. The ancient dragon can not only look like the race, but their mana signature and physiology are indistinguishable from true beings of that race. This form cannot be forcefully changed, granting immunity to polymorphic magical effects.

"Nice so that explains why I feel as human as ever. Good to know it can't be forcefully removed. Also, nice to know I can't be turned into a sheep or something like that." I said as I continued reading.

Ability: Partitioned Mind
Description: Your mind is now your own. This ability provides two primary functions. First, it allows you to completely compartmentalize parts of your mind preventing all others including the system access. Second, it grants you the ability to split your thought processes to perform true multitasking. You can now perform multiple computations and thought calculations in parallel.

'So finally, my mind is my own again. Isn't that right system?' I mentally thought inside what I visualize as a separate bunker in my mind.

I waited to see if the system would respond. Several minutes later and nothing. 'Sweet! Okay time to move on.'

Outside my mental bunker I mentally thought, "That will be very useful. Let's move to the next one System."

Ability: Dark Mantle

Description: The vast void of nothingness can strike fear to even the most devoted. Warning: This can cause some to become fanatics to your cause and others to wet themselves in your presence.

Passive effect: Those that oppose you will second guess their choices reducing their battle effectiveness. Dark aligned creatures will naturally see you as someone worthy. For several Dark aligned beings, those with this ability deserve to be served and obeyed. Others may be stricken with fear. Warning: This part of the ability cannot be turned off.

Active effect: Can inspire both fear and awe in those around you. This ability weakens Outsiders and Eldritch beings within your vicinity. Please Note: This ability could draw Dark aligned creatures to your side.

"This complicates matters a bit. I don't really want people to piss themselves when I walk by. I should probably invest heavily in Charisma to help compensate. Alright next one System."

Ability: Flight (Gravity Variant)
Description: This form of flight allows you to create opposing gravitational forces between you and the ground or air molecules to enable flight. This can still be used in space even if objects are separated by vast distances.

"Well, that is going to be one of the very first abilities I'll be testing out! Okay these keep getting better. Bring it on, System."

Ability: Draconic Regeneration
Description: The healing powers of some types of dragons are legendary. This ability will automatically heal any wound. This ability uses 'True' healing meaning it cannot be blocked by any magical means. Mana and stamina can be expended to increase the rate of regeneration.

"Alright now we are talking! Just what I need to help me survive the apocalypse! Man being a dragon is so freaking cool! What's next, System?"

Ability: Seer's Gift
Description: Some might consider this a curse. This ability taps into latent bloodline powers granting you periodic clarity and insights. Sometimes granting visions or moments of just knowing. Without proper control these flashes are completely random. Please Note: This ability is one of the most difficult gifts to master.

"Hmmm. A bit vague but sounds promising. Let's just hope it doesn't trigger during a battle. Wait did I just cause a death flag?! Cancel, cancel, cancel!

Nothing to see here death flags! Moving right along! Okay, System, show me the last new ability."

Ability: Claws of Time
Description: Shift your hands into wicked claws. These claws can pierce through time. Attacks inflicted use time magic to bypass any resistances in the current moment. Can be used with devastating effect. Warning: Pushing too hard and you can create a tear or rip in time that you must close.

"Wowzah! Bypassing resistances by piercing time, that's wicked! My offensive capabilities just increased dramatically! Though the warning is a bit ominous so I might want to error on the side of caution. Either way, it was a weapon I plan to use."

That was when the smell hit me. I was completely naked; my clothes were shredded... again! And I was covered and standing in blood and filth! "Yuck! Man, I need a shower! Times to use PURITY!!!" Saying the last part as a used the ability multiple times to make both myself and the hallway clean, and I do mean multiple! There was black sludge on the walls and the ceiling! "How the heck did it get on the ceiling!" I said after losing count of the number of times I used my favorite ability.

"You know it has got to be almost lunch time and I've been making all sorts of rackets. Is Gr'ex really still asleep?"

My curiosity got the better of me as I walked back to Gr'ex's room and opened the door.

SNOOREEE!

I found Gr'ex completely knocked out, snoring, with two pillows stuffed over his ears. "That little shit heard me screaming in pain and what does he do?! Stuff his ears and go back to sleep! Why I outta... no, no... woosah, woosah. I'll get him back for this somehow!" I said as I closed the bedroom door and headed downstairs to plot my revenge!

"How'd ya sleep darling?" Jeb asked Suzie when she joined him in the kitchen.

Jeb was cooking some eggs, bacon, and some other dishes. It all smelled heavenly. "Mmmm! That smells amazing!"

"Thank ye kindly. Duncan said I could help myself as long as I left some for him. I figured it would make sense to use up all eggs and bacon before they went bad." Jeb explained.

"Good idea. Where is Duncan?" Suzie asked.

"He said he wanted to do some scouting back the way we came to make sure nothing was heading this way from town. He left several hours ago, should be back soon. Ah I think I hear him approaching now."

Jeb put some eggs and bacon along with something else on a plate just as Duncan stepped through the front door.

"It's just me guys." Duncan stated as he walked into the kitchen and took a seat at the table.

"We figured that based on your whistling on the way in. Did you find anything?" Suzie asked.

"Nah, not really. The town is overrun with what my identify says are goblins. They don't look like much but there are a lot of them, plus some looked pretty well equipped." Duncan stated.

"Any coming this way or doing any scouting?" Jeb asked as he put a plate full of food in front of both Suzie and Duncan before grabbing a plate of his own and sitting down.

Suzie didn't realize how hungry she was, but the moment food was in her presence she instantly dug in with abandon.

"Easy darlin, there is plenty more where that came from." Jeb said as she started to inhale her food.

Suzie wiped her face. "Sorry. Ever since the apocalypse I find my appetite has increased."

"That's what running for your life and not being sure when your next meal will be does to a person. I felt the same way when I was in the war. Now slow it down." Jeb stated.

Duncan just ate. It was clear he was enjoying his meal.

"This is really good, what is it?" Suzie asked pointing to the dish that looked like some kind of meat slop mixed with gravy and potatoes.

Duncan spoke up for the first time since he started eating. "Shit on a Shingle or SOS for short. My dad used to make it. Said he learned how to make it in the army."

"That's right! Who do you think taught him how to make it?" Jeb answered.

Duncan just smiled, nodded, and went back to eating.

"Why is it called that?... wait don't tell me; I don't want to know. All I can say is this food is amazing Jeb, if you were thirty-five years younger, no thirty years younger, I'd marry you in a heartbeat with cooking like this."

"Hey I can cook. What about me, you had my cooking before." Duncan admonished.

"Yes, I did have your cooking and it was good but it ain't nothing like this." Suzie replied while pointing her fork at her empty plate.

Jeb got up and grabbed Suzie's plate. "Want some more darlin?"

"Absolutely! Yep, if you were 20 years younger, no fifteen." Suzie replied with a smile.

Jeb just chuckled as he piled up her plate and gave it back to her. Seeing Duncan's plate was empty, Jeb just took it, filled it back up, and set it back in front of the big man without even saying anything.

"Thank ye kindly Sir." Duncan said in gratitude.

"Jebediah or Jeb, none of this sir stuff. We are going to be fighting side by side for our lives, first names or nicknames are best in such a situation." Jeb replied.

"Understood Sir, I-I mean Jebediah." Duncan stammered out.

Jeb put his hand on the big guy's shoulder. "And I'll call ye Donut or Donuts, haven't decided yet but I'll let ye know, he, he, he."

Duncan just shrugged and went back to eating.

After everyone was done eating, they decided to talk more about their next course of action.

"Why not just stay here? I know it's kind of crowded but I know the place." Duncan suggested.

"Not that I don't mind the hospitality but Paul's Compound, well I guess it's Shadow's Compound now. Anyway, it has multiple bedrooms and plenty of facilities to help us survive. Heck there's several whole facilities underground that Paul told me about." Jebediah explained.

"What kind of name is Shadow? Sounds kind of shady to me." Duncan asked.

Jebediah looked at Suzie. She just sighed, "he didn't do that on purpose. It takes a while for his brain to catch up."

"Huh? What are you talking about Suzie-cue?" Duncan asked in confusion.

"You just said the name Shadow sounds shady. Those words can mean the same thing. I thought you were intentionally making a bad joke until I saw that clueless look on yer face." Jebediah answered.

"Oh." Duncan said then it clicked for him, and he let out a big ole belly laugh. "Ha, ha, ha, ha! That's a good one. I am funny even when I don't mean to be, ha, ha, ha, ha."

"Yea, a genuine comedian you are Donuts. Now to answer your question... the guy is a gamer. He had different gaming handles he would use, one of em was Shadowalker. Paul and I used to tease him and instead call him our Shadow because he would follow us around everywhere. He was kind and respectful enough not to correct his elders so the name kinda stuck." Jebediah explained.

"That doesn't sound very nice." Duncan commented.

"No, I guess it wasn't, but we meant no harm by it. Paul loved the guy like a son, so he left the place to him. Shadow swung by to see me about a week ago, just before you got into town in fact Suzie."

"Oh." Suzie replied. 'Like what does that have to do with anything.' Suzie thought.

Jebediah continued his explanation. "Yea, he stopped by and let me know he would be at the cabin and to let him know if I wanted to go hunting with him. Shadow said he would be there for a couple weeks, give or take. If he wasn't saved and is still alive, that would be our best bet to make a stand. And let's not kid ourselves, we will have to make a stand against those ugly, green-skinned goblin bastards."

"Still sounds like the best plan." Suzie stated before she turned her attention to Duncan. "You still got that open dolly trailer? What about ATV? Could we load up supplies on the trailer and use the ATV to haul everything there?"

"Nah I sold the ATV years ago. I got plenty of points in strength and the dolly trailer has got wheels. I could probably set up a chain harness and pull the thing behind me." Duncan suggested.

"Right weird new world. I keep forgetting. My system says we can share our stats and form a 'party' which lets us share experience and let our systems relay simple messages to each other. How about it?" Suzie said as she sent both men a party invite.

A few seconds later she got the confirmation notifications.

Jebediah, Human, level 8 has joined your party.

Duncan, Human, level 6 has joined your party.

"Oh cool. I can see little health bars next to a picture of your faces in the lower righthand corner of my view. This will come in handy." Suzie said in excitement as the familiarity of some of her past gamer experiences helped bring a sense of confidence to her mind.

They all took a moment to share their status pages with each other.

Name: Suzie	Race: Wood Elf	Level: 7
Strength: 16	Dexterity: 40	Constitution: 20
Intelligence: 20	Wisdom: 18	Charisma:24

Spiritual Attunement: Unaligned	Core Stage: Not Formed	Spiral Stage: Not Formed

Health, Mana, Stamina Values & Regen Rates per hour (pH)						
HP: 110	HP/pH: 6	MP: 112	MP/pH: 64.8	SP: 370	SP/pH: 75.6

Titles: Skillful Hunter

Name: Jebediah	Race: Human	Level: 8
Strength: 20	Dexterity: 30	Constitution: 24
Intelligence: 23	Wisdom: 20	Charisma:20
Spiritual Attunement: Unaligned	Core Stage: Not Formed	Spiral Stage: Not Formed

Health, Mana, Stamina Values & Regen Rates per hour (pH)						
HP: 132	HP/pH: 5	MP: 129	MP/pH: 60	SP: 367	SP/pH: 75

Title: Murderhobo

Name: Duncan	Race: Human	Level: 6
Strength: 30	Dexterity: 23	Constitution: 30
Intelligence: 16	Wisdom: 13	Charisma:18
Spiritual Attunement: Unaligned	Core Stage: Not Formed	Spiral Stage: Not Formed

Health, Mana, Stamina Values & Regen Rates per hour (pH)						
HP: 330	HP/pH: 10	MP: 90	MP/pH: 39	SP: 435	SP/pH: 93

Title: Stalwart Defender

Suzie wasn't surprised by Jebediah's stats and his Murderhobo title. He was killing goblins with wild abandon and clearly loving every minute of it. Duncan, however, was another story.

"Wow Duncan that Title is impressive as is your Strength and Constitution. How did you reach level 6 already?" Suzie asked after reviewing his stats and title.

"Oh, that. Yea I saw a little deer when I went outside to check on my chicken coop. Several forest wolves tried to come after the deer and my chickens. I fought the wolves and defended the poor deer and chickens. I had a metal shovel I used to bash their heads in. When the fight was over, I had killed eight level 10 wolves and earned that title. It gave me a boost for the first battle, so the experience gain was temporarily boosted. Brought me all the way to level 6." Duncan explained.

"Yea you're definitely going to be our tank." Suzie said after hearing that story.

"Tank?" Jebediah asked.

"It's a gaming term, it means the one out front soaking up all the damage so us more fragile folk can bring the pain. You better get used to em Jeb." Suzie replied.

"We'll see, we'll see. I noticed you aren't human. Wood elf?" Jebediah said.

"It came from the perk I took. Resulted in a race change." Suzie explained.

"I still have to pick my perk. I will look at options while we walk." Jebediah said as he turned his attention to Duncan. "I would say looking at Donuts' high Strength score I don't think he will have a problem pulling the dolly, especially if we keep it light. We can always make a second trip if we have to."

Both Suzie and Duncan nodded in agreement. With that, they got to work loading up the little open trailer.

It took them about an hour to load everything they wanted. Then roughly another hour to set up a chain harness with some leather straps over Duncan so the chains wouldn't dig into his skin too much. One final check and they locked up Duncan's place.

"Ready Donuts? Let us know if you need to take any breaks or the load gets to be too much." Jebediah said sincerely as he looked the man in the eyes.

Duncan nodded and started pulling. "Let's get moving."

As he started to get a grove going, he pulled out a donut from his pocket and started eating it as he was walking.

Jebediah just leaned over to Suzie and whispered. "Where did he get that from?"

Suzie smiled at her friend. "Don't ask. Ever since he was a kid, he always kept a stash somewhere for emergencies. I'd say the apocalypse would be a good example of emergency."

"Fair enough." Jebediah said as he picked up his pace to keep up with the hulk of a man.

——————————

I started cooking a late lunch. After what I just went through, I was absolutely ravenous. I decided today would be the perfect time to make honey glazed bacon-wrapped scallops.

I made a point to leave Gr'ex's bedroom door open. Once the bacon was good and cooking, I took a kitchen towel and fanned the delicious smell towards the bedrooms. Then I went back to preparing the rest of the food.

In oh I'd say a minute or two tops I heard Gr'ex practically fly out of bed and run down the stairs, making a beeline for the kitchen.

"What is that amazing smell?!" Gr'ex commented as his big nose was raised in the air and inhaling deep.

"Good afternoon to you too Gr'ex. That is bacon, my little goblin. One of the greatest gifts from God put on this earth. See take a good long whiff." I said as I picked up the skillet and waved the cooking bacon right under his nose.

Gr'ex literally licked and smacked his lips as his mouth started to salivate. "Mmmm. I cannot wait to taste something that smells so divine."

"Oh yes they do taste even better than they smell." I claimed, as I wrapped them in scallops with a dash of honey.

"How is that possible?! The bacon has to be the best thing I have ever smelled in my life." Gr'ex said in surprise.

Then I looked at Gr'ex a wicked grin across my face. "Sadly, you won't get to find out as I don't reward a lazy good-for-nothing jerk!"

Gr'ex's mouth fell open in shock. "Wh-What do you mean I don't get to have any?!"

I popped one in my mouth and chewed, exaggerating my sounds. "Mmmm, so good!" I even licked my fingers after I popped in another bacon-wrapped scallop.

The whole time I just smiled and stared at the goblin. After I swallowed, I spoke up. "You do remember last night, don't you?"

L-last night?" Gr'ex said hesitantly.

"Yea, you remember. I was screaming in utter agony and suffering the whole night!" I said the last sentence in clear fury.

Gr'ex was about to lie or deny he knew what I was talking about, but he could not hide the horror on his face.

"You covered your ears and went back to sleep you little bastard! I could've died! What were you thinking?!" I yelled at the jerk.

Gr'ex slowly stammered out a reply. "We-well. The bed was so comfortable... and I figured you would call me if it was urgent."

"What do you think screaming is a call for?!"

Gr'ex visibly gulped. "I figured if you didn't call for my help and you died, I'd be free to do whatever I wanted. If you were screaming because you were purifying your body as part of absorbing that core, then I would most likely be the one left to clean it up. No offense but that kind of gunk lingers and stays with you." Gr'ex said the last part in a quick rush.

I wanted to throttle the man but then I remembered why I staged this little display and put a cold smile on my face and ate another bacon wrapped scallop. "Mmmm, these really are amazing."

Gr'ex dropped to his knees in front of me his hands up in supplication. "Please! I'll never do it again! I swear!"

"I know you're a self-serving bastard, but I don't care. I consider such an act a form of betrayal!" I said the last part as I turned on the active effects of my **Dark Mantle** ability.

Gr'ex literally fell backwards onto his butt, had a complete look of terror on his face, and... proceeded to wet himself. A puddle formed around him, and an awful stench wafted up.

'I don't think that's just piss. Whoops. I might have overdone it there. I just wanted to get him back not scare the actual crap out of him.'

I immediately deactivated my **Dark Mantle**'s active effects. Then used several instances of PURITY!!! to clean up Gr'ex, his clothes, and my floor.

I bent down, grabbed the goblin by the shoulders, and lifted him to his feet. "Sorry about that buddy. Guess I overdid it a bit."

"Ya-ya-ya think?! What was that?! I have never been both so scared and in awe in my whole life! And I used to talk with my former master, and he was scary." Gr'ex replied.

"It's called **Dark Mantle** and..." I started to explain but was cut off by Gr'ex.

"No need. There is a legend about that ability among my people."

"There is?" I started to ask then refocused. "Never mind. Tell me about it later. We good? You ever going to not come to my aid again?"

"Never. I swear. My apologies. I never slept in such a comfortable bed, and it got the better of me. I am not a laborer and admit I can be a bit lazy. I'll try harder." Gr'ex apologized.

The little goblin still seemed a bit shook up, so I let it go and opted to move forward. "Fair enough. Come let's eat."

I put a plate full of bacon-wrapped scallops in front of Gr'ex and he proceeded to inhale them.

The goblin necromancer patted his extended stomach. "You were right master! They tasted better than they smelled. You are too good to Gr'ex. I re-pledge myself to you and your cause. Especially if we can have bacon again."

"Done! You can start by teaching me the spells you know." I said as we clasped our wrists.

————————-

"Some of my most effective spells are my curses. They each cause an effect and damage over time to the target. To use them you must envision great suffering on your target. I was seen as somewhat of a savant when it came to such magic. I think this above anything else is why my previous master favored me with higher tiered spells." Gr'ex explained as we were in the study discussing magic.

"Sounds effective but I can also see how using curses could twist you up inside." I commented.

"To use such power, you must grow hard inside, or the curse will rebound and affect you too. I may be cruel, but I do not take pleasure in the act as some do. No, I remain focused on the goal, beat or stop my target or enemy. This is where my previous master was wise. His gift was death magic, necromancy, but that is not the only magic he wields." Gr'ex clarified.

"What kinds of magic does he wield?" I asked curiously. Something told me I would have to face this guy someday, best to get as much intel as I could.

"I am getting there. In this you must let me be the teacher. Back to curses. As you seem to be immune to curses it will be difficult for me to teach you that magic." Gr'ex answered.

"So then what do you recommend we start with?"

Gr'ex continued. "Master taught me more than curses. As you already are aware I know **Death** magic but what you have not yet seen is my **Dark, Air, Water, Hellfire,** and **Eldritch** magic. My core is more aligned to the darker elements. Beyond curses, death magic is my highest affinity then water and ice, then air."

"You didn't mention your affinity to **Hellfire** or **Eldritch** magic. Why is that?"

Gr'ex nodded. "Yes, that is because those two magics use higher energies and work differently. I would recommend we cover those later. Let us start with the basic elements. Most of my curses come from **Dark** magic but they are not all the spells I know of this type."

Gr'ex conjured a bolt of energy that seemed to suck in the light around it and was pitch black. "This is called **Dark Bolt**. It is a simple Tier 1 spell but still quite effective. It uses very little damage and when hit it can cause dark magic damage. If you hit them in the face with it, you have a chance to cause temporary blindness. In battle, I am sure you realize how much of a boom it can be to blind your enemy. Let me show you the spell form."

And so, he did. The form was rather easy to pick up. Especially after he hit me with the spell so I could better understand the effects. According to him it helps speed up the visualization step. I think he just wanted to use the loophole that allowed him to attack me. As long as the attack wasn't lethal, and it was part of magic training the oath did not trigger. He was far too happy about this fact.

I felt the use of my exceptional imagination would be a far better way to learn the spells, but Gr'ex had gleefully insisted, the jerk!

So, for several hours I was hit with the Tier 1 **Dark Bolt** spell. After that Gr'ex moved on to **Death Bolt**, which dealt had similar forms to the **Dark Bolt**, but was a Tier 2 spell and caused decay damage. From there he used **Ice Lance**, another Tier 2 spell, which caused cold and limited force damage. Finally, to round out the torture was **Miasma Blast**, this was a Tier 3 spell and created a forceful blast and then spread miasma in the surrounding area of effect. Miasma is the antithesis to life. The undead thrive off of it but needless to say it messed you up if you weren't a walking corpse.

My ability **PURITY!!!** saved the day as it could completely purify the area of any of the miasma and helped me heal from the many, many, and I do mean many injuries from my sadistic magic trainer.

At one point I reactivated the **Dark Mantle's** active effects just to get him back a bit, and to keep him on his toes, but mostly just to get him back.

When we called it a day several hours later, I had to admit Gr'ex was a good teacher. Though I won't be telling him that... ever. I was able to learn **Dark Bolt, Ice Lance, Death Bolt**, and even **Miasma Blast**.

My **Partitioned Mind** ability helped me mentally practice each spell form hundreds of times, which added to the rate I was able to ingrain the spells and add them to my repertoire. However, this also added to my fatigue and exhaustion. My mind had a headache, and my body ached all over. Yep, this was definitely the apocalypse.

We were sitting down drinking some herbal tea I made, enjoying the quiet. My headache was rapidly disappearing. One giant benefit of having really high Wisdom is how fast my mana fills back up when I'm not constantly chain casting.

"Ah, this is nice." I commented as my headache was now completely gone.

"Shhh, don't ruin it." Gr'ex replied.

'That little shit. I'm going to...' I was mentally interrupted when I looked over and Gr'ex had a big smile on his face. 'He was messing with me.' I mentally sighed. 'I've got to remember his nature and just dish it back.'

I smiled right back at him. "Ah, for a moment I forgot you were even here. Shame you ruined it."

His smile never wavered. Gr'ex nodded. "Good one."

We both went back to sitting in the study which had a great view. We just watched the sun begin to set.

After another few moments of silence Gr'ex spoke up. "You did remarkable today. You learned each of the spells in hours. I have never heard of anyone learning so quickly. I'll admit I was hoping to torture... I mean teach you further."

"I'm sure we can pick up the torture tomorrow." I replied.

I was starting to get used to Gr'ex's personality and despite my better judgements the little goblin was growing on me.

"What happens after I have taught you everything I know?" Gr'ex said, clear uncertainty in his voice.

"Then we figure out our next move together. Perhaps scout out the town, see what supplies we can scavenge, or see if we find any survivors. This place could probably be converted to a decent base at some point." I answered as my mind began to think about what was next. 'I won't rush in, but I also don't plan to remain hidden away.'

"You-you mean you aren't planning on killing me after you have learned everything?" Gr'ex asked.

The question threw me for a loop. "No why would I. There is more you can help me understand and navigate. Why would you think that was my plan?"

"That is what I would have done. I know many that would do such a thing." Gr'ex answered.

"No wonder you're such a jerk. You think I was planning on killing you. No, you big dork. Don't cross me or betray me and we will get along just fine." I extended my free hand, and we clasped our wrists once again.

We both caught movement out of the corner of our eyes that made us turn to see what it was. Three people were coming up the dirt road. They were all armed and the biggest one that looked like a tank, looked like he was pulling an open trailer behind him.

A memory triggered in my mind. I had seen these three in a flash, I'm guessing from when I first gained my Seer's Gift ability.

"Best go grab your staff and activate your ring Gr'ex. We have company. Let's see if they are friendly or hostile."

We both moved to the other room to take action. Once I had my elephant gun in hand, figured I'd need it for the one pulling the trailer, I inspected all three of them.

Duncan, Human, Level 6.

Jebediah, Human, Level 8.

Suzie, Wood Elf, Level 7.

"Wood elf huh? That's interesting. I didn't expect to encounter an elf out here." I relayed back to Gr'ex.

"How are you able to identify them already? There are still so far away." Gr'ex replied.

"Don't know. Good eyes I guess."

Query Accepted

Yes, your eyesight has greatly improved but the inspection range of your system is also much farther than standard.

"What? Why is that System?" I mentally asked.

Query Accepted

As you chose this form of interaction with your new world it was deemed appropriate additional interface options and settings be available.

"Sweet, thanks System!"

You are welcome.

I turned my attention back to the three people approaching.

"Hold it right there!" I yelled out.

"Shadow, is that you?" A familiar voice yelled back.

"Jebediah?!"

"Yea it's me son. I have a couple of friends I made along the way. Mind if we have this conversation inside? It's getting dark and I don't feel like tangling with the wildlife in the dark!" Jebediah yelled back.

"Sure! I'll open the garage so you can pull your trailer in!" I called back before shutting the murder hole and heading to the garage.

"Better come with Gr'ex. I know Jebediah but I don't know the other two." I said over my shoulder as I made my way to the garage.

Gr'ex followed me into the garage.

The garage was huge. It could easily hold 6 to 8 vehicles plus a boat and a motorhome if I wanted. Currently, it has a couple ATVs, a van, some tools, and several Powerwall batteries to store solar power. The garage was a faraday cage, so it made sense to store the power backup in here.

I opened the massive door just enough to let the three in with their trailer.

Once everyone was inside, I closed the garage door while they helped their friend out of his chain harness. The three newcomers were all heavily armed, but no one had any of their weapons drawn, except Gr'ex with his staff.

"It's good to see ya alive my boy. I feared the worse." Jebediah said as he embraced me in a big hug.

"Good to see you too, Sir." I greeted him while returning the hug.

After we separated, I noticed Jebediah had tears in his eyes. "Are you crying, Sir?"

"No, just got something in my eyes. And stop with all this sir stuff. Jeb or Jebediah, we are in your home, I should be the one addressing you as Sir. Paul left this place to you."

"Here I was worried you might try to take this place from me. The apocalypse does weird things to people." I was honest and expressed my concerns.

Jeb looked shocked. "I may be a bastard that likes killin what needs killin, but I haven't lost my humanity yet. Let me introduce you to my traveling companions and party members."

"Party members?" I asked.

Gr'ex was the first to answer. "Yes, the system lets you group up, share experience, and gain limited communication functions."

I looked back at my companion. "That is pretty cool. Thanks, Gr'ex." Then I turned to the newcomers. "Let me introduce my buddy Gr'ex. He is a magic caster and very knowledgeable about the system."

Jeb nodded in acknowledgement. "Nice to meet ya Gr'ex. My name is Jebediah." Then he waved to the woman beside him, and then the mountain of a man. "This here is Suzie, and he is Donuts... I mean Duncan but I call him Donuts. You two this is Shadow."

"It's Shadowwalker. I let you and Paul call me that out of respect but..." I started to say but Jeb gave me the most intentional innocent look. "Ah screw it, I don't care. It's nice to meet you both."

"Thank you for letting us in. Things are pretty crazy out there." Suzie said while shaking my hand in greeting.

"Yea I can imagine. Come on in and let's talk over some tea."

"Nice to meet you, Sir." Duncan said as he shook my hand as he passed.

Gr'ex led them to the living room while I went to the kitchen to get the currently lukewarm tea back up to hot. It did not take long and by the time they undid their gear and set it aside so they could sit comfortably, I had returned with the tea. I handed each of them a cup or mug of tea before grabbing my own mug and taking a seat.

Duncan surprised me and spoke up first. "How are you level 10 already? And how is your friend level 18?!"

"Wait what?!" Suzie said before she took on a far-off look that I learned was a tale tell sign someone was interacting with their system.

"Duncan Donuts is right! And here I thought we were high level." Suzie replied.

Jebediah just smiled. "Good for you, my boy. Must've killed a whole bunch of those green-skinned pukes."

That seemed to get Gr'ex's attention, and he looked at me.

I answered Duncan's question. "Killed some goblins yes. Also killed an undead mutated forest bear. What earned me the most was being first on the planet to close the portal that brought them here. According to the prompt, all the goblins had been defeated, but it sounds like you all had a run in with goblins too."

Realization dawned on Gr'ex, and he spoke up. "There must be more than one portal!"

"I don't know about any portal-thingies, but I do know that goblins invaded the town."

"Which way did they come from?" Gr'ex asked.

Suzie was the one to answer. "From what I saw, there were two separate groups. One came in from the southwest, and the other came in from the southeast. Each group seemed to dress differently and sport some kind of common colors."

"Three portals. Why three? To create a three-pronged attack?" I asked as I looked at my companion.

Gr'ex looked thoughtful. "Three portals would be the maximum number of conflict portals that could be opened in such a close proximity."

"How do you know that?" Suzie asked.

I chimed in. "Very knowledgeable about how this new world works, remember."

She didn't seem thrilled with that answer, but she accepted it.

Gr'ex was oblivious as it was clear his mind was working in overdrive. "What colors or symbols did you observe?"

"I just saw a lot of red but that was probably from all the bloodshed. I did notice one group wore more armor and heavy leather. The other seemed to wear light leather and cloth." Jebediah stated.

Duncan chimed in. "I saw a willow tree on some of them."

Suzie finally gave her observations. "One wore lots of browns and reds. They had bone symbols on some of their gear and came from the southwest. The other force that came from the southeast wore lots of muted greens and browns. They were the ones who had what could pass as a willow tree symbol on their gear."

"Well done, Darlin. That is some great intel gathering." Jebediah commented as everyone else nodded in agreement.

"Ah troll dung! Damnit!" Gr'ex swore.

"What's wrong Gr'ex?" I asked.

"The two clans Suzie described are the Bone Marrow clan and the Sleeping Willow clan."

"I take it they are bad news." Jebediah stated.

"The Sleeping Willow clan is known for its very effective sleeping potions and other poisons. Their common tactic is dropping a vial or pouch into a group to knock out an enemy and come in to mop up after they are incapacitated. Bone Marrow stays true to their clan's namesake, they love to feast on the bone marrow of their victims. They are one of the more bloodthirsty of the goblin clans and usually have the most equipped warriors." Gr'ex explained.

"There were definitely double the number of brown and red clothed goblins than the others." Suzie conveyed.

Duncan chimed in again. "When I went scouting, it was clear the town was overrun. I would say there were hundreds of goblins from what I saw."

"That is way more goblins than the group I faced!" I stared in shock at what I just heard.

I then looked at Gr'ex and asked the questions on my mind. "Why were so few sent with one group and so many more with the other groups? Also, that is a lot of forces for a small town, what do they want?"

"How do you know so much about these goblins, Gr'ex? And don't give me the excuse you just know a lot about this new world!" Suzie said in frustration.

"Darlin, careful. We are guests here." Jebediah said quietly.

Suzie rose to her feet. "No! I want answers! You almost died Jeb!"

"I know Darlin, I was there, but our host hasn't even agreed to let us stay." Jebediah cautioned.

Suzie was having none of it. "The town I grew up in has been overrun by monsters! I have been fighting and running for my life practically nonstop! If this little man has answers and if your 'friend' is keeping stuff that could get us killed I will kill them before they get a chance!"

Gr'ex chuckled. "Ha. You wouldn't get two steps."

That was apparently not the thing to say.

What happened next was a quick series of crazy in my opinion.

Suzie pulled one of her blades and lunged at Gr'ex! Unfortunately for Suzie, Gr'ex had been prepared and hit her with a Curse of Agony that immediately dropped her to the floor screaming in pain.

Seeing his lifelong friend hurting, Duncan rose to his feet and attempted to charge. "Hey! Leave my friend alone!"

Duncan too only took one step before he dropped to his knees: pain written clearly on his face.

However, Jebediah just sat there sipping his tea. "Huh?"

Gr'ex looked at the old man. "What?"

Jebediah shrugged his shoulders. "You said they wouldn't get two steps and you were right."

Gr'ex just smirked and then turned to me. "I like this one."

I replied with a smile. "I do too. Release them."

Gr'ex did as I commanded and visible relief showed on Suzie and Duncan's faces.

After they took some time to collect themselves, Suzie and Duncan both resumed taking their seats.

With a frown Suzie turned to Jebediah and spoke with clear continued frustration in her voice. "Some help you were! Is that how you help your party members?!"

Jebediah just shook his head. "Ah the impatience and impetuousness of youth. You aren't the only one to learn what they can from the system. While you were busy staring daggers I was reading."

"Reading what?!" Suzie said as she crossed her arms over her chest as she considered how to still attack Gr'ex and I.

"Guest Rights. Also known as hospitality rights. You and Duncan are too young to be familiar but back in the day there were clear expectations between guest and host. My pappy always told me they were sacred and old traditions passed down. I asked my system about them. And you know what I found out?" Jebediah replied.

"What?!" Suzie said through clenched teeth.

"That in this new world if you commit an act of violence or attack a guest while under guest rights the host has the right and obligation to act. The guest you attacked has a right to kill you if the host doesn't do it themselves." Gr'ex answered.

Jebediah just nodded. "That's right."

Both Suzie and Duncan had looks of horror on their faces.

"That is barbaric!" Suzie admonished.

"This coming from the person who attacked someone under my protection after I opened my home and hearth to you. The world you knew is gone. Like

Jebediah my family raised me right. Guest rights are not barbaric but the exact opposite."

Jebediah chimed in. "If we are to build a society from the ashes, we will need such things to prevent us from becoming the monsters we are fighting."

"He's got a point Suzie-cue." Duncan said softly.

Suzie sighed loudly and dropped her shoulders in defeat. "You're all right. I'm sorry I attacked you Gr'ex. I have been on edge since I lost my family, and it has just been a lot."

"That is something we can understand, right Gr'ex?" I chimed in.

"Not really." Gr'ex deadpanned.

I quickly spoke up. "Gr'ex is just screwing with you. He likes to use humor to reduce the tension in the room. Rather than decide anything tonight, why don't I fix us something to eat, and we can discuss everything tomorrow. I'm sure you all could benefit from a shower and some much-needed rest."

"A shower sounds nice." Suzie sighed.

"Jebediah, you know where everything is. Why don't you show your friends to the facilities while I cook us up some food." I instructed.

"Aye son, that sounds like a great idea. Suzie-cue, Donuts, follow me." Jebediah said as he stood and guided them upstairs.

After they were out of earshot, Gr'ex spoke up. "They are struggling to adapt, but they are not as bad as they could be."

"We will sort it out in the morning. I'm concerned about these other two clans. Why don't you tell me what you didn't want to say in front of them." I replied as I prepped the food for dinner.

Gr'ex spoke quietly. "My master told me that I was limited on the number of warriors I could take as the portal was encountering interference. My master felt that meant my portal was most likely close to the target."

"In other words, the town may not be what your master wanted to claim." I hypothesized.

"I believe you may be right. If their portals were farther away, then they would've been allowed to send more men." Gr'ex explained.

"If I recall, this compound is north and slightly east of the town. The Sleeping Willow Clan was half the size of the Bone Marrow clan. If this compound is the real target, it would explain why Sleeping Willow, who came from the southeast, could not send more men. What were..." I cut off what I was going to ask as I heard my guests coming downstairs.

"Smells divine my boy!" Jebediah said as he took a seat at the table.

Duncan took a seat as he finished the donut in his hand.

Suzie was drying her hair with a towel. "That shower was amazing. Much better than what my parents had. Theirs would have already run out of hot water by now."

"Paul built this place to also tap into some geothermal energy as both a backup to solar power and to heat the water." I explained as I put plates down in front of everyone.

Gr'ex immediately dug in. He had zero interest in waiting for anyone or talking while he was eating. No one really wanted to talk as they all seemed focused on the food.

"You always were an amazing cook, son. That was delicious." Jebediah said after finishing his meal.

"Yes, it was very good." Duncan chimed in.

"Man, where have you men who can cook been all my life. I think that was better than what Jeb fixed for breakfast, and I thought that was the best meal I've ever eaten until now." Suzie commented.

"It's the elk. The richest flavor of meat I have ever eaten came from elk." I explained.

"Nah, it is definitely more than that. I've had elk before." Suzie replied.

"Side effect of the apocalypse." Gr'ex finally spoke up after he finished his food.

"Huh? What was that?" Suzie asked.

"Mana and ambient energy are in the air. You also have gained physical stats that are enhancing your body. These things increase your appetite and make your taste buds more sensitive. It also increases your food consumption until you can develop and grow a strong enough core to help subside the massive energy requirements your empowered body needs to thrive." Gr'ex explained.

"Well, now I know why I'm hungry all the time." Duncan commented.

"Shadowalker doesn't realize he's doing it, but he's infusing some of his mana into the food when he prepares and cooks it. In doing so, it makes it far more nutritious for all of us. Eventually you will be able to eat monster meat and that will already have mana infused into its flesh." Gr'ex continued.

"Hmmm. I didn't realize I was doing that. Wouldn't that weaken me instead of filling me up more?" I asked.

"No. Two reasons. First, you are only using the smallest amount. Second, your mana regeneration rate is so high you recover faster." Gr'ex once again proved a wealth of knowledge.

"Who votes Shadowalker prepares all the meals?" Jebediah asked.

"Hey!" I protested.

They all raised their hands. Gr'ex raised both his hands.

"Fine, we will discuss it in the morning. I recommend you take some time to meditate and channel your energy. It really does help." I offered as I was picking up the plates.

We all said our good nights and adjourned for the evening. It took me several hours of active cultivation, gathering and moving the mana around my channels before I was tired enough to be able to sleep. While I lay there, my thoughts kept drifting to the realization that they may have been sent for his compound and he didn't know why.

Chapter 10 – Gathering Resources

Laraaq slept surprisingly well last night. After eating the coyote meat, he used his **Heat Metal** spell to seal himself in and provide an extra layer of security. The old pickup had one long comfortable seat that let him lay flat and stretch out.

Killing those coyotes had boosted Laraaq's level to 7, which meant he had +60 stat points to distribute. Not wanting to waste any time or get distracted, Laraaq allocated his points.

He had learned from his system that a point score of 10 was a normal average healthy human. Sadly, Laraaq was lower than 10 in several stats. It really was his mental stats that set him up for success with his casting, but he couldn't ignore his health or movement speed. Cardio was important to survival in the apocalypse.

Getting a stat to 20 was like that of a peak athlete or scholar. For survival Laraaq focused on reducing his deficiencies and playing to his strengths.

Stats distribution finished, Laraaq felt a surge of power that was beyond euphoric. His muscle mass increased, his body slimmed down and firmed up. The mental fog that would be there at times vanished. He felt good! Better than good! Laraaq felt healthier than he had his entire life.

Now starving, Laraaq cooked and ate more of the coyote monster meat. After several twenty-ounce steaks devoured, he was starting to feel normal.

"System, why was I so hungry all of a sudden?"

Cause you are an idiot.

Query Accepted

The energy you collect when you level up is used up to improve different aspects and processes of yourself. However, if you wait too long some energy degradation naturally occurs, especially without a core or gathering spiral. This also can happen when you distribute too many stat points at once. You have lost small amounts of energy; your mind and body translate that as needing food. Though that is important, what you want most is mana enriched food like what is in the coyote meat you ingested.

"So, until I have a sufficient core and gathering spiral, don't wait so long to level?"

Is this thing on?!

Query Accepted

Yes. It is also highly encouraged to meditate and work on your magical pathways or channels while practicing your cultivation.

"Good reminder, I'll make a point to set time aside each day. Time to review my status." Laraaq stated as his Status page appeared in his vision.

Name: Laraaq	Race: In Transition	Level: 7
Strength: 12	Dexterity: 20	Constitution: 20
Intelligence: 30	Wisdom: 26	Charisma:12
Spiritual Attunement: None	Core Stage: Not Formed	Spiral Stage: Not Formed

Health, Mana, Stamina Values & Regen Rates per hour (pH)					
HP: 100	HP/pH: 5	MP: 150	MP/pH: 78	SP: 280	SP/pH: 60
Titles: Ruthless Hunter, Early Adopter					

Laraaq was pleased with his progress. He was now at peak of what a pre-apocalypse human would be capable of for Dexterity and Constitution. Strength and Charisma were now above the average standard human. Finally, his Intelligence and Wisdom are now beyond genius levels which means a bigger mana pool and faster mana regeneration. His system reminded him that without a gathering spiral he was only benefiting from a fraction of what his Wisdom should be capable of. He figured the higher mental stats would help in his cultivation visualization.

All that done, Laraaq did some morning stretches to limber up and get a better feel for his improved body.

"No way! I have a six-pack! Freaking awesome! I have never had a six-pack in my life!" Laraaq exclaimed to himself.

Stop feeling yourself up. Get back to leveling.

"You're right System." Laraaq replied.

Of course, I am right. We established this already. Do I need to do another brain scan?

Shaking his head Laraaq spoke out loud to his system. "I got carried away there for a moment. Time to focus on some scouting and resource gathering."

It was clear to Laraaq as much as his system messed with him it did a good job of helping him control his emotions, stay focused, and on task. He did not feel alone in this place with his sarcastic testy system, and he appreciated that fact.

"Okay. First things first, check out the rest of this private airport. If this can work for a temporary base, I could scavenge whatever I can find from around the area before heading out."

Good idea

The inspection of the private airport was uneventful. The second hangar had a few biplanes and some fuel, so Laraaq earmarked it to take when the time came. The combination office building and control tower had some interesting and possibly useful radio and radar equipment but that was about it. Some technicians had left some schematics, manuals, and books regarding radar and radio operations. Figuring it would make a good read and it would help him figure out how to extract and transport the equipment.

Temporary base sorted out, Laraaq hopped in the pickup and headed to the Home Depot he had seen back down the road several kilometers back. It took him about thirty minutes to get there. The building was in a shopping center that was clearly set up for the residents in the area to do all their shopping in one convenient location.

The shopping center had a large chain grocery store, the Home Depot, an electronic store, and a few random home and clothing stores. Laraaq headed straight for the Home Depot to find a trailer or something he could use to transport all the stuff he wants to haul off.

Entering the store was surprisingly easy. Laraaq found the place was unlocked and completely untouched. He kept his guard up and did a quick sweep of the store, checking every isle, office, and back room. The place was completely empty.

Situational awareness seen to, Laraaq checked out the trailer options. The toe hitch trailers were small and not worth it. However, he did find a trailer for towing a vehicle and this Home Depot was one that rented those giant moving trucks.

"Well, I might as well load up the giant moving truck, drive that, and just tow the pickup behind." Laraaq said to himself out loud as he got to work.

After Laraaq had the old pickup truck on the trailer, he started his shopping spree. The hardest part of this was deciding what to take. He had a finite amount of space. Granted the giant moving truck was a major increase in available space, Laraaq still had to be selective.

Top of his list were tools, from shovels to a welding torch and soldering kit, Laraaq grabbed multiples of each as you never knew what could come in handy. After tools came key building components like different size nails, sandpaper, bolts, and screws. These tend to be things people forget about that couldn't hurt to have on hand. A few more passes and a couple hours later and Laraaq was done with Home Depot.

"Time to check out the electronic store. Not sure how long that stuff will last but worth a look. That makes me wonder, hey system, how long will electronics work? Will we have to worry about stuff going out?"

The short answer is it depends.

"Sys, come on!"

Do not push it!

"Sorry, system, I'm asking for your vast knowledge and insight."

That's better.

Query Accepted

The more different kinds of mana saturate an area the sooner it will cause your very sensitive electronics to go on the fritz. There are skills and classes that focus on mana-infused equipment and technology that one can eventually learn. Use of such technology is not as common as you might think as for the most part magic and other energy cultivation solutions tend to be far easier.

Laraaq had already noticed in his travels how few places had power. With so many people gone, there were limited people to run the power plants and water pumps so it was only a matter of time for water and heat would be critical scarce commodities.

Even with the thought of dwindling power plants Laraaq was still intrigued with the prospect of learning magic-tech. "Hey system, it would be cool to learn more about magical technology. Can you keep an eye out for that kind of stuff? I'd like to explore it if such techniques become available." Laraaq noted.

It has been added to the list.

Laraaq didn't spend much time in the electronics store. He grabbed a few items, but after his system's explanation of what was to come, Laraaq thought it best to use that precious space for other things, he still wanted to snag the radar and radio back at the airport.

The final planned stop was the grocery store chain. Laraaq figured he might as well stock up on food, especially meat if it hadn't spoiled already.

Entering the grocery chain store, Laraaq instantly noticed the place had been ransacked. It was clear people had been through here. Slowly, quietly, and with a metal bat equipped he searched the store isle by isle.

As Laraaq got further into the store he heard movement. With the bat in one hand, he used the other to prepare and do his best to hold a Weak Fire Arrow spell at the ready. If it was undead, he would end them quickly. 'Now if it is survivors, that will be interesting, as I haven't seen many that aren't zombies.' Laraaq thought as he walked further into the store.

Silently creeping closer, Laraaq heard people talking before he saw them. There was an end-aisle display that gave him a view deeper into the store but blocked his shape from being seen. About twenty to thirty feet away were clearly two sets of people.

The first set of people consisted of a girl in her mid to early twenties standing protectively in front of a younger girl who could be between 13 to 16. Next to the girl were two guys, one in his mid to early twenties, and the other was clearly mid-forties to early fifties. The older man had a pistol. The younger man held a metal bat similar to what Laraaq was carrying. Both girls held blades. The older girl held what could be classified as shortsword or just a long dagger and a butcher's knife. The little girl held two daggers.

The second set of people were two guys, both in their late twenties to early thirties. They both wore camo-gear. One had a rifle, the other had a shotgun. Both weapons were pointed down but still drawn.

The guy in camo holding the shot gun spoke up. "Look, the world has gone to crap. Survivors need to stick together. If you come back with us, you have a better chance of survival. We have a well-fortified camp, weapons, and armor.

The younger guy from the other group couldn't hold back his words. "Yea right! I see the way your buddy has been looking at my girl! No way we are going with you jerk-offs!"

"This kid is a hot-head, Carl. They have no clue what they are in for." The camo guy holding the rifle commented.

The guy in camo holding the shotgun, Carl, replied. "Boss's orders are to bring back any survivors. These people are just scared. Let's not escalate the issue, Tom."

"Look, we don't want any trouble. We just came here looking for supplies. If you have got a problem with that, we will leave. The kid is not wrong, we don't know you and aren't going to just go with you." The older gentleman said.

Now that Laraaq was looking, he could see a subtle familial similarity between the two girls and the older man holding the pistol. 'Must be their father. If I had to guess by the way he called the younger guy kid, they probably aren't related.' Laraaq thought as he watched this byplay.

Everyone heard a crash and turned to see several zombies coming out of the back room. 'These idiots! All the yelling back and forth must have drawn the zombies' attention. Laraaq thought as he did his best to assess the situation and figure out what he was going to do.

Tom cried out as he lifted his rifle. "Carl let's bail man; these people are idiots. I'm not going to die for some idiots, I don't care how fine that girl looks!"

"Tom, we need people!" Carl replied.

There were eight zombies in sight, possibly more coming behind them. Laraaq had to make a choice. He either would quietly extricate himself and leave these people to their fate or help the survivors. A big part of Laraaq wanted to kill Carl and Tom, then track down this boss and kill him. The problem was the zombies. 'I'll take them out later, worst case they can be distractions and I can take them out after.'

Carl raised his shotgun. "Get down you four!"

The group of four were frozen in shock when they saw the zombies. Carl's words knocked them out of their stupor as they all ducked.

Carl ended up being a pretty good shot and made one of the zombie's heads explode as the shotgun blast hit it. The second shot took one right in the chest and knocked down the two zombies behind it from the force of the hit.

Mind made up, Laraaq stepped out of his hiding spot and fired his overcharged Weak Flame Arrow taking one zombie in the eye and lighting the whole head in a blaze of flame. Then he cast his Minor Fireball spell and sent it to the remaining charging zombies. The impact knocked them all back and off their feet.

"Who the hell is this guy?!" Tom asked as he raised his rifle and took a moment to line up a headshot to take out another zombie.

The dad did not stand idle and turned out to be a good shot with his pistol. Every shot he took a zombie was hit in the head for an instant kill.

The younger kid stood side by side with the older girl as they both stood in front of the youngest girl.

Laraaq cast another Minor Fireball spell and set the remaining zombies clustered up in flames. The force damage did not disappoint either as several zombies lost burning legs, arms, or split in two burning halves.

"Whoever he is, he is a badass!" Carl stated as he watched the astounding damage this recent arrival just did. 'I'm not sure we could've handled all those zombies. Yet this guy just wiped them out like they were nothing! Maybe he could help us.' Carl thought.

Before he approached the stranger, Carl decided to send Tom to do a quick sweep of the area. "Tom, go do a quick sweep. You know the drill, run away if you see something, don't be a hero."

Tom did not look pleased, but he agreed. "Yea, yea, heroes get dead. I know, I know." The surly man walked out of sight to check the direction the zombies came from.

Carl walked up to Laraaq and put out his hand. "That was some very impressive work, stranger. I'm Carl. What's your name?"

"Laraaq." Was the only reply Laraaq gave before shaking the man's hand.

What surprised Laraaq was Carl's handshake. It was firm yet not overbearing. He was expecting the man to have a 'fishy' or loose handshake.

Laraaq turned to the group of four to check on them. "You four all okay?"

The dad replied as he held his hand out. "Yes, thank you Laraaq. I am not sure we would've survived that. I'm Mack."

Laraaq was expecting this man to have a firm handshake based on the way the man carried himself yet was beyond bone crushing. If Laraaq hadn't put the points in strength he had the man might've broken his hand.

The younger kid stepped up and was clearly excited to meet Laraaq with how fast he started talking. "Man, Mr. Laraaq, what you did was super impressive! Where did you learn magic? I'm Colin by the way."

"This is a whole new world. I am just doing what I must to adapt to it." Laraaq said as he spined on the balls of his feet and clocked Carl with his bat knocking him out cold.

Colin had a shocked look on his face. Mack just looked at Laraaq with apprehension.

Laraaq explained himself. "I had a chance to catch the tail-end of your conversation with those two. It kind of sounded like they were trying to force you guys to go with them. Is that what it felt like to you?"

"It totally seemed that way!" Colin chimed in.

Mack raised his hand. "Now Colin. I'm not so sure either way. I didn't like that Tom character as he seemed to spend too much time glancing at my girls."

"My father is correct. I'm Christy and that's my sister Sarah. I do agree with my dad that Tom concerned me, but Carl seemed okay. I kind of felt like he kept his friend in check."

Laraaq handed Colin some zip-ties he grabbed from Home Depot; he had stored them in his pack just in case. "Use these to tie him up. Mack, why don't you come with me to go retrieve Tom."

Mack gave a nod and followed alongside Laraaq as they moved as quietly as they could in the direction Tom went off in.

Tom wasn't exactly being quiet himself. He had his rifle ready to shoot the moment he caught movement, but rather than silently move and check each room, he talked to himself and whistled a tune as he lazily looked around. 'Eh nobody is around, time for a drink.' Tom thought as he withdrew a flask from one of his camo-jacket pockets.

"Ahhh, that's the stuff. I should pick up more alcohol while I'm here." Tom said to himself, clearly not worried about being quiet or stealthy.

Laraaq and Mack on the other hand crept up quietly. They were careful not to make a sound. Rather than magic, Laraaq opted to us his bat to hit Tom across the head. Tom went down like a sack of potatoes.

Mack then proceeded to kick Tom so hard in the side Tom was flung into the side wall. Then proceeded to kick him a couple more times. "That's for staring at my daughter!" Mack said with barely kept in check rage.

Laraaq commented as he picked up Tom's rifle. "I don't really care if you kill him as I get it, but how about you carry the unconscious guy while I take his rifle. Let's get some answers first. Sound good?"

Mack just nodded and picked up Tom's flask before picking the man up like he weighed nothing. "Fine by me. I might as well take this as he won't need this anymore. I can wait to kill him."

"Strength build?" Laraaq asked when he saw how easy it was for Mack to pick up the unconscious man.

"What are you talking about?" Mack asked in confusion.

"I take it you have a good number of points in Strength, am I right?" Laraaq replied.

"Oh. Yea. I started with a higher strength as I used to go to the gym all the time. I was a professional body builder for a time. Even over a decade after competing I can still bring the pain." Mack explained.

The two men quickly returned to the group. Colin used more zip-ties to constrain Tom.

"Colin, while you're down there, check his pockets for any weapons and useful items." Laraaq instructed.

"What now?" The older sister asked.

"That's up to all of you. I can't ignore this 'boss' of theirs. I plan to go have a little chat with them and get a feel for the place. If I find people are being forced or treated poorly, I will deal with them. Your party can go on your way, or you can join up with me." Laraaq stated.

"Mack and Christy, I think we should go with Mr. Laraaq. I'll go where you guys decide but I think this has a better outcome." Colin commented.

The older sister turned to her dad. "What do you think Mack?"

Laraaq noticed her use of her father's first name and thought it was odd but figured some parents tried to be 'friends' with their kids instead of being parents. 'Though Mack doesn't seem like the type to be that way. Oh well, their family dynamic is their own.'

"We've been scavenging what we can and avoiding the cities and zombies. Where you headed?" Mack asked.

"Overall, I'm heading farther East. My buddy has a secure and self-sustaining compound near a local town out there. You are welcome to come with me if interested and make a new life for yourselves at the town or compound. Totally up to you." Laraaq answered.

"It's as good a destination as any other." Mack said after a moment of thought.

"What do you want from us?" Christy asked.

"Follow my orders. Beyond that it depends. Can any of you drive a big moving truck?" Laraaq said.

"I was a truck driver after my professional body building career ended. It won't be a problem for me or Christy." Mack replied.

"That's how I learned to drive was on his big wheeler." Christy commented.

Colin spoke up. "My dad was a trucker too. That's how I met Christy, her dad and mine were friends. Dad taught me to drive one too. Why are you asking?"

"I packed up a bunch of stuff in a big moving truck from Home Depot. I noticed another three of those around the back of the building. Plus, I noticed a large semitrailer around back of this store. If it is one of those refrigeration trucks, we could transport a bunch of food along with more supplies. I doubt this will be the only shopping center we will come along." Laraaq relayed the plan that was forming in his head.

"We are in, but I drive the refrigeration truck." Mack stated.

"I got no problem with that." Laraaq answered.

"That is going to be a lot of gas to get wherever we are going. How are we going to deal with that issue?" Colin asked."

"I found a private airport nearby that seemed to be a mix of commercial transport and small private flights. I found a stockpile of fuel. We could load it up in one of the trucks and use that when we don't find a working gas station." Laraaq revealed a bit more of his plan.

"That should work." Christy replied.

During this conversation, Colin had removed a few knives and another two flasks of alcohol from Tom. Decisions made. Laraaq turned to Mack. "If your minds are made up, no reason not to start checking out that semi and starting to load up the food. We don't know if they have any friends nearby. I can interrogate them while you guys are loading up the trucks."

Mack picked up on the unspoken message, Laraaq wanted to spare the girls watching the interrogation. "Yea that's probably for the best. We can get that done while you handle that. Just keep Tom alive if you can. He's mine at some point."

Laraaq nodded in agreement. "I'll do my best, but I make no promises."

"Come on let's go check these trucks out and start loading up what we think we should take." Mack said as he guided them to the loading bay in the back.

After they were out of earshot, Laraaq bent down, and slapped Carl awake. "Hey time to wake up!"

Carl jerked awake from the blow, dazed, and confused. "Huh? Wha... where?... why can't I move?"

Then Carl's eyes seemed to focus as he looked at Laraaq. "You hit me with a cheap shot! I didn't do anything to you, and you attacked me!"

"Oh, quit your whining. I didn't kill you. Besides from my vantage point it looked like you and your buddy there..." Laraaq pointed to Tom's still unconscious & bound form before he continued. "Were trying to force that family to come with you even though it was clear they didn't want to go."

"They're just scared. It's the damned apocalypse! I wouldn't have hurt them. It was clear they were just going from place-to-place scavenging. You know that's not sustainable. We have to put down roots, grow a community if we hope to survive!" Carl became more passionate the longer he spoke.

Laraaq didn't necessarily disagree with the man. The rub was really all about who was in charge. Heck Laraaq didn't want to be in charge or responsible for people. He knew his buddy was better suited for that role, even if his friend was reluctant, he had the experience leading thousands of people. Laraaq knew next to nothing about these people and that was about to change.

"Calm down Carl. Let's say for a moment, I believe you. What about your buddy Tom over there? He doesn't seem to share your ideals. He was willing to abandon that family to their fate and according to that same family he seemed to be far too interested in the girls of the group."

Carl winced. "Look, Tom can be a bit of a hot head and volatile but he's a good fighter and right now we need that to survive."

Laraaq chuckled. "Ha. Not much of a fighter if he runs away. Besides, tolerating that kind of behavior only leaves you dead when it really counts. He's weak willed."

Carl sighed. "I'm kind of stuck with the man. He's the nephew of our boss and was assigned to me to keep him in check."

"Nepotism even in the apocalypse. Tell me about this boss of yours and the current state of your base." Laraaq inquired.

"The boss is strong; he is already level 6. He has some chi attacks he used to fight some undead and earn his levels. He's also an expert marksman. He saved my life and many others." Carl started to explain.

"Interesting. What about the others at the base?" Laraaq asked.

"Before I left, we had about fifty people. Half of that are non-combatants. Everyone contributes even the non-combatants." Carl explained.

"No such thing as a free lunch." Laraaq commented.

"According to what my boss said, he discovered there were many people in the cities but lots of those were overrun and converted into mindless zombies. Which for some probably wasn't much different from their previous life. He rescued who he could but people outside the city had a higher chance of success in survival." Carl stated.

"Where are you all holed up in?" Laraaq asked.

"It's an old warehouse. Well-built, plenty of space and easily defendable. I can show you the way." Carl answered.

Laraaq slapped Tom. "Alright time to wake up!"

"What the hell?!... You! Release me! I'm gonna kill you when I get free!" Tom said as he saw who was in front of him.

"That's not much of an incentive. I mean what kind of idiot tells their captor they are going to kill them if they get released." Laraaq replied.

Tom looked dumbfounded as he was unsure how to react to Laraaq's deadpanned response.

"You were bound because I don't trust you and you made the girls feel super uncomfortable with your ogling." Laraaq stated.

"Ha, those girls should be grateful my uncle and I would take them in and protect them! And if they aren't grateful, I'll make em grateful! I've done it before, and I'll do it again until they all learn!" Tom spat out.

Upon hearing those words Laraaq immediately summoned a Minor Fireball. Laraaq took some deep breaths and dismissed his spell. "No, killing you now would be a waste. Better to make an example of you."

"What does that mean?!" Tom said in fear.

Laraaq picked up each bound man one at a time and hauled them outside. 'Man, I would not have been able to do this before I improved my strength. Maybe I put a few more points in the stat. It would've been nice to carry each of them one handed. Would've saved me some time too.' Laraaq thought as he brought the men outside.

Christy came lightly jogging up to Laraaq. "You guys almost ready to go Christy?"

Christy nodded. "Yes. We could probably take more food but it's a good start. Mack wanted to know if you wanted backup in dealing with these men and their friends."

"As much as I want to say yes, Carl here assures me the group isn't all bad. I'm going to make an example of Tom over there. If they try to get dumb, I'll have a few surprises for them. You guys keep loading things up. Remember the three of you are driving a truck. We will want supplies where we are going. If I'm not back before nightfall, find somewhere safe and secure to hold up in." Laraaq stated before going to his truck.

Pulling out a walkie-talkie he handed it and some batteries to Christy. "Take these. I already have it programmed to a set frequency. When I get back within range, I will click the button a few times to get attention. If I don't hear back from you, I will find my own place to stay secure overnight and return here in the morning."

"Understood. Good luck and thank you again earlier for your help." Christy said before giving Laraaq a big hug and kiss on the check before heading back to her family.

Laraaq threw Carl in the front seat and there was enough room to throw Tom on the floor of the passenger seat. It made the space for the two men a bit cramped, but he didn't care. With Carl's help, Laraaq was able to navigate to the warehouse turned makeshift base.

As he drew closer, he noticed the warehouse was surrounded by a large fence that went around the entire property. Several guards were on duty stationed outside. Laraaq got out of the truck. "Let me talk to your leader!" Laraaq yelled out.

Noticing several wood moving crates, Laraaq went to the passenger side and pulled out Carl and set him down in a way that made him clearly visible to those outside on guard duty. The Laraaq pulled Tom out of the truck and unceremoniously threw him to the ground. He dragged the scum to the back and grabbed a small can of gasoline.

Laraaq noticed one of the guards ran inside the building. Deciding to wait a few for more people to come out of the warehouse to see the commotion, Laraaq dragged the bound Tom, now covered in gasoline, up onto the wooden moving crates.

About twenty to thirty people came out of the building to check on the commotion. A lean yet muscular man looking to be in his early fifties was leading the crowd. "What is the meaning of this?! What have you done to my nephew?!"

Laraaq cleared his throat loudly before speaking so everyone could hear him. He tied the man to the wooden moving plats making it so the man could not move or run away. "This scum tried to have his way with a few girls under my protection! He has admitted openly that he has forced himself on others and has every intention of doing it again! Some of you here are probably some of his victims! This may be the apocalypse but that is just more reason not to tolerate such trash! This man admitted his guilt and for his crimes I sentence him to DEATH!"

On Laraaq's final word he summoned a Weak Flame Arrow and shot it at Tom. The flame ignited the gasoline that was liberally poured all over the man. Tom and the wooden moving crates he happened to be attached to burst in a bonfire of flames. Tom screamed bloody murder!

"MY NEPHEW!" The well-built man said.

Two of the men beside him held the boss back. A few ladies started speaking up. "Good riddance!

"He rapped me in front of my daughter!"

"Justice!"

The fight seemed to leave the boss as he heard the words of the very same people he had sworn to protect. The man dropped to his knees and wept. "I'm sorry sis, I couldn't protect your boy from himself."

Tom's screams of pain did not last long, and the body continued to burn long after Tom had died. Many of the onlookers stayed and watched. Something in his gut told Laraaq many of those people were either bullied or taken advantage of.

The 'boss' had been escorted back inside by two of his men, so he could grieve and not have to continue to watch the gruesome sight.

Laraaq went to Carl and cut his bindings. "You're free to go."

Carl rubbed his wrists to help get the feeling back into them. "Thank you for keeping your word and releasing me."

Standing up, Carl spoke up again. "You should meet the group. Some I imagine will even want to say thank you for what you did."

"And some will probably want to kill me." Laraaq answered.

"Look. I know you did what had to be done. I had my suspicions that Tom wasn't all there or alright, but I had no proof and kept my focus on finding more resources and doing what I could to keep the man in line." Carl replied.

"Sounds like you failed miserably based on how many people yelled out. Besides I don't think your boss would be that interested in talking." Laraaq stated.

Carl winced. "Fair enough. Yes, it's clear the boss is grieving but he's also a practical and pragmatic man. He will listen if you have something to say."

Laraaq thought for a moment. 'I did come here to possibly recruit these people. I also don't want to leave an enemy at my back. Time to push and see who tries to push back.'

Mind made up, Laraaq replied, "I'll make my pitch and then go."

Carl nodded and guided Laraaq to the gate and spoke to one of the guards nearby. "Caleb, let us in. Mr. Laraaq here wants to talk to everyone."

Caleb's attention, like so many others, was transfixed on the burning body. It took him a moment to turn to Carl. "You sure that's wise Carl?"

"Yea. He means us no harm unless we cross him and his. It's starting to get dark. Open the gates and let us in. You know it's not safe to be out at night." Carl replied.

Caleb did as Carl asked and opened the gate. After letting them both in, Caleb secured the gate and escorted both men inside. The setting sun seemed to grab the remaining onlookers' attention and they too returned to the safety of the warehouse.

Carl talked with Caleb as he escorted them inside. "I see we found more people."

"Yea. We found about another twenty people. Most are in their mid to late twenties. Only a handful are beyond level 1. There's over 70 of us now."

Laraaq kept quiet but inside he was shaking his head. If most were level 1 that means they haven't done much to survive but hide. As he walked, he noticed most of the people he saw were people in their twenties and early thirties. There were a few in their forties or fifties and most of them seemed armed and more battle-hardened. 'My generation probably more equipped to shift to this game like world of survival. The younger generation were too young to remember what the country was like when everyone came together with some common principles. Now we are too divided and too entitled. Let's see how many of these people can adapt.'

Other observations Laraaq picked up on were the makeshift privacy screens to give some semblance of shared but private living quarters. He also noticed they had sections for weapons and crafting or repairing of clothes and armor. There seemed to be a station for communications, with what looked like radio equipment. There was even a section for food storage and cooking. That last section seemed the most guarded, which made sense to Laraaq. It was easy for people to get desperate and do something irrational when they were hungry.

Caleb led them to a raised platform towards the end of the big open space. It had a microphone and megaphone. Carl instructed Caleb to start gathering people up.

Laraaq noticed how Caleb showed deference to Carl, so he decided to ask him about it. "He seems to follow your orders without question. How'd you earn that level of respect?"

"I led the team that saved his life and rescued him from some zombies. Plus, I'm second in command next to the boss." Carl answered.

"Ah. Well, it is impressive what you've been able to build in a few days." Laraaq commented.

"It hasn't been easy, but I'm ex-military, as are a few others. Several of us gained some good survival skills based on our past experiences. Those perks have come in handy." Carl answered.

Twenty minutes later there were probably close to fifty people gathered by the podium. Carl quietly spoke to Laraaq. "This is probably it. The rest would be either on guard duty or returning from patrol."

Laraaq nodded and took up the mic. He hated public speaking but clamped down on his emotions and pushed through it. "My name is Laraaq. I came here for two reasons. The first was to dish out justice to those of you here who were suffering in silence from what that scumbag did to hurt or take advantage of you! I don't care if it's the apocalypse, such behaviors won't be tolerated! So let that be a lesson out there for anyone else involved or considering such things..."

Laraaq conjured a **Minor Fireball** to emphasize his point and held it there before dismissing it. The act had the desired effect as many gasps and whispers could be heard. "Magic is real and anyone I find or come across attempting such abuse I will burn to ash!"

After the rumblings died down Laraaq continued. "The second reason I came was to offer you a chance at a fresh start. You have the right idea to work together, and it is impressive what you have done in the time you've had... but it is not sustainable."

"What do you mean?" Some random woman called out from the crowd.

"To survive we will need to grow crops, hunt food, not just scavenge what is left out there. And lastly and more importantly, we all must grow stronger." Laraaq answered.

"I am not a fighter! I don't want to die!" One of the younger guys yelled.

Laraaq had asked his system if there were other ways besides killing to earn experience in the hopes of being prepared for questions like these. He was pleasantly surprised at what he learned.

"Look there are many ways to grow stronger. You can earn experience if you use your skills and perks to help yourself and others grow. Sure, the fastest way is to become a hunter, but it is not the only way to earn and contribute. Dedication to your craft can also yield experience and offer you a profession related class when you hit level 13. This is the apocalypse; we are the ones left behind. We won't survive forever if we don't think differently than what led us here. If you want that chance come with me."

Carl was the one that asked the question in everyone else's mind first. "Where?"

Laraaq wasted no time responding. "East. My best friend and I were preppers. He owns a self-sustaining compound outside a remote town. The land there should be good for growing crops and the nearby forest a good source for animals to hunt. The town can be resettled, and a new community can be formed."

Whispers were heard across the crowd as they began to discuss the offer. One voice was louder than the others, she asked the question others were discussing. "How will we get there?"

"Simple, moving trucks and buses. We use the giant moving trucks at some of the moving companies around the area. Also, I saw a school not too far from here. A school district has buses."

An older man spoke up. "I was a bus driver before I retired. I know where the district yard is!"

Laraaq pointed to the man. "Good job. Throwing out solutions instead of just problems. We load up what resources we can in the moving trucks and use the buses to move the people. If we run out of bus space, some people will have to use the back of a moving truck or scrounge up a few extra vehicles. I also recommend we grab some reliable motorcycles to act as scouts."

The mood in the warehouse seemed to shift as people started to realize this plan was a viable one.

Laraaq decided now was the time to make a few things clear. "My buddy runs the show. I follow him and have his back. Cross him and you are crossing me."

Laraaq resummoned his **Minor Fireball**. "I am not the nice one. If you cause problems and I was the one who brought you... I will take that as a personal offense!"

Some people gasped at the open promise of violence.

The Laraaq dismissed his Minor Fireball and pointed outside in the direction of where the smoldering embers still burned Tom's corpse. "With that said, know my buddy shares the same sentiment as I when it comes to the strong taking advantage of women and children, they have no place in the new society we will build!"

The crowd was silent and unsure to take the next step. Carl came to the rescue. "I for one am going! Sure, we should all be proud of what we accomplished but deep down we know this..." Carl waved his hands around. "... is not sustainable. Plenty of mistakes were made. I had my suspicions of Tom, but I did not act on those suspicions, for that I am sorry."

A voice spoke up as the crowd parted for Carl's boss. "No Carl. You should not be apologizing for my failures."

The man continued to walk until he came to stand beside Carl and Laraaq before he spoke again with clear sadness and defeat in his voice. "I made a promise to my sister to always keep an eye out and look after my nephew. I knew Tom wasn't right in the head... but a man shouldn't be asked to harm someone from their own family. I did what I could by partnering him up with Carl as We all know he is a good man. Based on how many of you cursed his name while he burned, my nephew still found his ways."

Carl's boss turned to Laraaq and held out his hand. "I hold no ill will towards what you did, as you did for me something I could not do. My name is Jacob."

Laraaq shook Jacob's hand. That one handshake told Laraaq everything he needed to know. He wasn't a limp fish or attempting to crush his hand like Mack tried. Jacob's handshake was like Carl's; firm, solid, yet not overbearing. It conveyed the message of being a reliable and reasonable man.

After the handshake Jacob turned back to the crowd. "In good conscience I can no longer lead you good people..."

Several murmurs and outcries of dissent came from the crowd.

"We only got this far because of you and Carl!"

"We need your leadership!"

"Tom's crimes are not yours!"

That last one seemed to strike a chord with Jacob. "No! What my nephew did, he did on my watch! I was blinded by my own emotions and old sentiments. We all need more from a leader. If Carl says he is going, I am too! I will follow this friend of Mr. Laraaq's! If he can convey such loyalty from an honorable man such as himself then he is worth at least giving a chance to."

Jacob turned to Laraaq. "I will help in any way I can to get our people organized. Based on what I heard of your plan, we could probably be ready to go by midday tomorrow. You should stay the night. It is already dark, and more monsters seem to come out at night."

Carl chimed in. "Absolutely. You should not be going out at night. Plus, it would be good for our people to see you among us. Let me show you to the makeshift mess hall and then get you a cot or some blankets."

Laraaq reluctantly agreed. He knew he might have to stay the night, but among all these strangers, he knew he would not get much sleep.

Chapter 11- Paul Planned Ahead

I woke up early and was surprisingly full of energy. Rather than wait in bed, I went downstairs to do some light stretching before fixing breakfast. Not sure if I was nervous about my guests or I just had more energy period.

I wasn't exactly looking forward to the conversation later with my guests, but I knew it had to happen. Clear ground rules had to be set if they were planning on staying. The fact that there were more portals and goblins had my mind thinking of solutions to deal with that problem as well. Rather than continue to feel pulled in multiple directions, I used my Partitioned Mind ability to split my focus on multiple things at once. Somehow the ability brought a sense of calm and order to my thoughts and feelings in a way I hadn't experienced before. It was like I just knew I could handle multiple issues at once and solve them just as easily. That sense helped me further focus on my Gravity Momentum Manipulation ability or GMM for short.

As I went through my series of stretches and light exercises, I would lift and move small objects with my ability. Development of these new abilities was key. If I could establish default thought patterns and triggers for my abilities to execute specific commands or things, I wanted them to do, it would become a game changer in combat.

Knowing that specific incantations, hand movements, and material components were all just cruxes, I was determined to not allow those to be my downfall. If my hands were ever tied or I was captured and gagged, or any other of a thousand possible situations that could prevent me from casting the traditional way. I knew my Partitioned Mind ability was key in overcoming these traditional constraints and in the development of these mental triggers. So, I practiced even after my morning warm up.

It was almost like child's play to split part of my mind to work on understanding my magic as I started cooking breakfast. "This is easy as…" I began to say while cooking until I was hit with the most massive headache that brought me to my knees and stopped all other thoughts.

"Breathe in, breathe out." I repeated it over and over until I felt like I had control of my faculties again.

"System what the heck was that?!"

Query Accepted

Your Partitioned Mind ability overloaded when you attempted to understand the Time Magic part of your core while also focusing on other magic and spell comprehension.

"What?! Please explain."

Query Accepted

You overloaded your ability by not allocating enough partitions to understand Time magic. Your Partitioned Mind ability is still growing and will continue to do so as you master the ability but in the interim, you must be careful not to take on too complex a calculation without enough attention.

"So, I found my limit with the ability, but that is a temporary limit as I keep pushing the use of my Partitioned Mind ability."

Correct

Please Note: Time Magic is one of the most complex Celestial magics to comprehend. That is why it is one of the rarest to be embraced and studied.

"Good to know. Sounds like the more I study Time Magic the more I can expect those mental overloads. Yet if I do put more focus and attention on that magic type both my magic and my Partitioned Mind ability will advance. Did I get that right?"

Correct

If you apply your hypothesis, your Time magic and Partitioned Mind ability will synergize. This could also result in the creation of new abilities, spells, and skills.

"Please make a reminder each day for me to dedicate a minimum of two hours to the combination mastery of these two aspects of myself."

System Setting Applied - Reminder Set

"You rock system! Thank you!"

I started to smell the bacon sizzling, so I quickly refocused on saving breakfast. My attempt worked and only a few pieces of bacon ended up extra crispy. "Where is my buddy, he loves crispy bacon that melts in your mouth."

One negative side effect I discovered was how my headache seemed to make it hard to multitask and how sluggish my mind was for several minutes before I could reactivate my ability. "That's a dangerous risk in combat. Note to self: don't do too many separate calculations in the middle of combat until I have developed my ability further." I said out loud to myself, but my system responded.

System Setting Applied - Warning Message Set to Trigger Upon Conditions Specified

"Wow! You really do rock System. Can you also tell me when I've mastered the ability."

Additional System Setting Applied

"Thank you!"

That done, I refocused on finishing breakfast for everyone. My cooking skill had evolved from '**Cooking**' to '**Gourmet Cooking**'. With that evolution a wealth of knowledge flooded into my mind, and I had to endure the pain from using my Partitioned Mind ability to process and understand the information provided. Using this newfound knowledge, I adjusted the spices slightly for breakfast. As I was my own personal taster, this time when I tasted the food it was like I had a thousand more individual tastebud. I also learned more about the skill.

Skill: Gourmet Cooking
Description: The base cooking skill grants the wielder the ability to infuse energy into the food they prepare. This enhances the flavor and provides greater sustenance to both magic casters and body enhancers. This skill also imparts inherent knowledge of what can be made edible from monster meat to mutated crops. The Gourmet version of this skill enhances the user's taste and smell. Additional universal knowledge is provided on ways to prepare food in this new reality. Energy infusion into food is drastically increased as you learn how to draw out the natural energy contained within all food. Meals you prepare can also provide temporary buffs to those who consume it.

That was a whole lot of words to say: I learned all sorts of new ways to prepare food and make it more nutritious. The temporary buffs would be fun to explore. Heck, I'll take it. Guess this is what comes from being the primary food preparer and making a point to experiment with the food.

Savory smells roused everyone from their slumber.

Gr'ex was the first one to the breakfast table and did not even bother waiting for anyone. "This is the best thing I have ever eaten. How is the food so good?!"

"Mmmm, that smells divine!" Suzie said as she took her seat at the table.

Suzie could not believe how much better she felt this morning. She slept deeply and peacefully. For some reason she felt safe and secure here. 'The idea of crossing Shadow instantly fills me with dread but if I at all consider staying here or following him, I am filled with a sense of rightness. Maybe it's the food or the fact that I can sense he is strong?' Suzie thought as she dug into her food.

Jebediah was already scarfing down his food. The most we got out of him were grunts of approval. "Good eats... more..."

Duncan was eating a donut while he was sitting down for breakfast.

'This man always has a donut. I have to ask.' I thought before asking my question. "Duncan how is it you seem to always have a donut on you?"

"It was the perk I chose." Duncan replied as he started to dig into breakfast.

His response brought everyone short and the whole table looked at him. Jebediah spoke up first. "Son, explain that one."

Duncan swallowed a mouthful of eggs before answering. "Man, this meal is amazing. Sorry, what was that Jeb?"

Sighing, Jeb repeated his question. "What did you choose as your perk?"

"Oh that. Everyone knows I love donuts, well guess my system recognized how much I loved em too. I had a special perk I could choose called Endless Delicacy. It will summon the food you love the most several times a day. The food provides the nutrients I require for a meal. I can sometimes think really hard on the type or brand of donut, and it will come out that way. All I have to do is activate the ability while reaching into a pocket or bag and out comes a delicious donut."

"Of course, that's what you would go with as your perk." Suzie commented.

"It's smart when you think about it. Endless supply of food. Well, it sounds endless, within limits. Are you able to share?" Gr'ex chimed in.

"I can only share one per person, per day. Not sure if there is a limit of number of people, but I'd be down to test it. Everyone should have the chance to enjoy the yumminess of the donut. Though your food this morning is even better than last night!" Duncan replied.

"Well, that is probably because my Cooking skill evolved into Gourmet Cooking." I shared.

Gr'ex dropped his fork. "You already have evolved your Cooking skill?!"

"Yea, why?" I asked.

"Yea why he asks. To gain one of the cooking skills, you must either have a good amount of past experience cooking or a high aptitude for the skill. To gain a skill evolution your affinity would have to be exceptionally high. When you reach level 13, one of your class options will be some variation of Chef or cook." Gr'ex explained.

"Is such a class any good?" Suzie asked.

"Yes and no. For combat not so much. However, a cook can be invaluable as a profession." Gr'ex stated.

"So, our skills will influence what classes we can get when we reach level 13?" Suzie asked.

"Of course. I encourage all of you to spend time asking your system some of these questions. Choosing your class is an important step on your path to strength." Gr'ex explained.

"Speaking about classes, is it possible to gain more than one class?" I asked.

"Good question. In rare cases it is possible to get more than one class. Some can gain a profession class and a combat class. Much will depend on your potential and energy capacity. And before you ask about those two things, I cannot tell you about the specifics for multiple reasons. What I can tell you is that all of you should focus on the development of your core, gathering spiral, and channels. These things will have the greater impact on future growth and available class slots." Gr'ex stated.

"Can you at least tell us what class slots are?" Suzie asked.

Gr'ex sighed and then further explained. "Most people will only ever have a base class slot and one evolution or as some call it an advancement slot. When you choose your class, your core keys itself to that class. The effectiveness of that synergy is dependent on many things like advancement of your core, affinity to both your class and magic type, etc. As the three main components of your cultivation, core, spiral, and channels grow, you can possibly gain more capacity for additional classes. Think of classes like a part of your foundation. As you level and grow stronger that foundation increases giving you an advancement slot. Simply put, this allows you to evolve your class to either a higher rarity or more powerful version of the class you have. Unless you have horrible affinity or poor cultivation everyone will be able to advance their class at least once."

"That's a lot to unpack there. All I really took from that was work on forming your core and when it comes time to pick a class, choose one you have a high affinity with." Jebediah summarized.

Gr'ex gave the universal 'so-so' hand gesture. "For the most part that is accurate and a good initially focus."

"What is your core like?" Suzie asked.

Gr'ex looked horrified and shook his head. "It is considered extremely rude to ask someone about their cultivation levels or anything about their core."

"Oh, sorry I did not know. This is all new to me." Suzie apologized.

'She's much more understanding today than yesterday. Amazing what food and a good night's sleep can do for one's disposition.' I thought.

"I will tell you this much. My core primarily uses Death, Dark, and Air magics. That means I am limited to only learning spells and cultivation techniques related to those magic types." Gr'ex explained.

Duncan finally spoke up. "Those sound very ominous. You are sure you're not a bad guy?"

"We all do what we must to survive. My magic was hereditary and part of my, let's just call it, learning. I have pledged myself to Shadowalker's cause, so do not cross him and I see little need for concern."

Jebediah turned to me. "Well, that brings us to a more important topic. Stay or go."

"Yes, now that breakfast is over, I guess it is time to have that conversation." I commented.

Suzie spoke up first. "I am sorry for how I acted yesterday. I was out of line. The last few days I've been on edge just trying to survive and I took that out on you and Gr'ex. You both have a right to your secrets."

"I appreciate the apology. I understand what life and death stress can do to fray the nerves." I replied.

Jebediah sighed. "If we are giving apologies, I should give one too."

"Huh? What do you have to apologize for Jeb?" I asked in confusion.

"When we arrived, I should've told you, heck when you stopped by earlier in the week, I should've told you then."

Giving him a confused look. "Told me what?"

Jebediah continued. "You see Paul was my good friend and I was a bit bitter that he left this place to me..." he raised his hand to forestall me from speaking up. "Let me get this out. I can be stuck in my ways, but I also know when I'm being a fool, especially how you took us in, fed us, and gave us warm beds. Paul was right to leave this place to you. I think he always held out hope I would be saved, but I guess I still hadn't let go of the pain inside me."

Jebediah gave a sad chuckle. "Ha. How sad is it to hold on to my pain and bitterness for the ones I lost that I prevented my own salvation. We think we have all the time in the world but that's just a lie we tell ourselves. I just wasn't ready to let it go. My friend had faith in me and in you. So, I should too. Do you know why Paul and I called this place the compound and not just the hunting lodge or something like that?"

"I just figured because of how huge it was and the giant greenhouse garden and garage or the fact that this place is built like a fortress." I answered.

Jebediah chuckled, this time with a feeling of fondness. "Sure, that is part of it but nowhere near the main reason. Most of this place is completely underground."

"What do you mean most of the place?" I asked.

Jebediah replied with a question of his own. "Do you know how many acres your property covers?"

"100 acres I thought Paul said." I replied with suspicion.

"The forest is easily over 1,000 acres. You technically own all of it." Jebediah replied.

"What?!" I immediately asked.

Just as I asked my question, Suzie rose to her feet and asked a question of her own. "How is that possible?!"

"Does that mean he own my family's plot too?" Duncan asked a moment later.

Jebediah waved to Suzie to sit down. "My buddy Paul was a genius, that's how Suzie. Several years back the town was in a bit of financial trouble. Paul had made so much money from all the patents and things he made. He offered to bail out the town on a few conditions.

"First, he was allowed to build this compound in secret. Second, he was allowed to buy the land the forest covered so we and others could always go hunting whenever we wanted. Lastly, Paul was a prepper so of course he had a clause added related to the apocalypse. It stated, should an apocalyptic event or major crisis occur ownership of the town and surrounding borders belonged to Paul or his heir. The town council all agreed as Paul offered to pay every landowner a fair price ahead of time. We all got nice payouts and were able to stay in our homes, knowing we only lost them should a catastrophic event happen. Everyone was happy to take Paul's money, even your parents Suzie. No one believed the end would come. They also had no idea why Paul wanted the whole area so bad."

Duncan realized something. "Wait is that why I got that nice lump sum check?"

Jebediah looked at Duncan incredulously. "What did you think it was for?"

"I don't know. I just figured I won some sweepstakes or something. Paid off the mortgage. Used the rest of the money to buy a boat for the lake." Duncan replied.

"What was Paul up to?" I asked.

"His ultimate purpose he didn't even share with me. What I can tell you is that most of this compound is underground." Jebediah stated.

"What does that mean?" I asked.

"There are several interconnected buildings and tunnels that span acres and go several kilometers down. I can show you if you want." Jebediah offered.

"Absolutely! Lead the way." I replied.

What I knew of the man continued to evolve. The mystery of why Paul did what he had still made me wonder.

Jebediah led us to a hidden panel in the walk-in pantry. He touched it and one of the walls in the pantry fell away like a hidden door revealing an elevator. "There is this lift elevator, another special elevator and a set of stairs in the master bedroom, elevator and stairs in the garage, and some emergency exits." Jebediah explained.

"Why so many ways just inside this cabin?" Suzie asked.

"Just in case there was a breach, and you couldn't get to another one. Paul thought ahead. Each of these panels will prevent anyone without access from getting down into the subterranean levels. Your bio signature should already be stored. Give it a try in the elevator." Jebediah said as he walked into the elevator.

I was concerned. I was no longer human; would that interfere with the bio scanner? I put my hand on the panel inside the elevator, thinking about what excuse I could come up with to explain why it wasn't working.

To my surprise it responded in the affirmative and we all descended underground.

Mentally I asked my system what was going on. *"Uh System, any clues as to why that worked?"*

Query Accepted

Your form of transformation is closer to a dragon's. When dragons turn into a specific race, they become that race not just look like them. Your energy and power are still that of a dragon, but your bio signature shifted back to what your mind was most familiar, your human form. Even in your human form you have access to your enhanced stats.

"Good to know for the future. Thank you again System." I mentally replied.

You Are Welcome

It did not take too long for the elevator doors to open again. When we all stepped out what greeted us was something out of a science fiction movie. There were several large chambers with hallways that reminded me of the underground halls of Cheyenne Mountain from one of my favorite sci-fi series.

Walking to look at one of the chambers we found various crops, then we saw different animals from cows, deer, elk, to chicken. They were separated into their own grazing section that had to be several acres each.

"Each of these herds have several acres of grassland to graze with different fruit trees scattered throughout. With a good farmer or several farm hands you could easily feed thousands with what is under here." Jebediah explained.

"What about sunlight?" Suzie asked.

"Each section has their own set of UV lights. For all intents and purposes, the light those animals and plants are getting is sunlight. The land has deep soil and collectors to periodically collect the animal waste and turn it into fertilizer. The septic system upstairs is also connected to that to help turn our waste into fertilizer too."

"Very impressive. Paul was a genius." I commented.

"This is just the beginning." Jebediah replied.

"What do you mean?" Duncan asked before I could.

"The elevator we took takes you to this level because it is coming from the kitchen. If you were coming from the kitchen, you most likely need food..." Jebediah waved his arms out. "Hence why it brings you to the food production section of the compound. We can take the connecting elevator or stairs up ahead."

We took another elevator deeper down. Once the doors opened, we saw a series of tunnels and what looked like heavily insulated rooms. As we walked, I noticed an actual forge in one of the larger rooms.

"Is that a forge?!" I asked.

"Yes, this room is the smithing room. It connects directly to one of the storage rooms where you will find many different metal bars and different tools for use. Paul called this level the production and communication level or as he jokingly would call it the PC level." Jebediah explained.

"Yea Paul did have a weird sense of humor." I commented.

Jebediah continued his tour. "You will find several crafting rooms with various stations. There are sleeping quarters down here to help non-combatants feel secure and be close to their craft."

The living quarters seemed spacious and as homey as Paul could make them. They even had fake panels to look like windows to help those who might be down here awhile. A good hundred people could probably live down here comfortably.

"Follow me." Jebediah said as he led us to a section filled with various weapons and what looked like radio equipment. "This is the Command and Communication section of this level. This will also branch off further to additional sleeping quarters and rooms to practice different art forms of war. There is an archery range, shooting range, rings for melee combat, and an obstacle course to work on your coordination." Jebediah explained as we checked out each room.

Leading us back into the communications room Jebediah spoke up. "This room was a hold out hope room. Meaning it is large enough to be used as a war room and if the different radio equipment works, we might be able to reach out to find other survivors outside the town."

"This is very impressive stuff." Duncan commented as he looked over the radio equipment. "My dad worked in radio and would teach me how to tinker with it. Mind if I see if we can get the radio working?" Duncan asked.

"I don't see why not." I replied.

"Give me a hand Suzie-cue." Duncan said as he took his seat.

Gr'ex watched in fascination as Duncan and Suzie worked on the radio.

"That works out great. The next section is for you alone son." Jebediah said as he led me away from the others.

Jebediah led me to a dead-end corridor. It turned out this was not a dead end but led to a secret room with another elevator and some stairs. "This is one of the stops the elevator in your bedroom will take you. That elevator aka this elevator..." Jebediah put his hand on the panel. "This one can make three stops. Here, the food production level, and a special third level Paul called the hub. I don't even have access to that level. Paul said it was meant for you and was pretty tight lipped about it. Go on, I'll wait here until you come back."

I hesitantly stepped into the elevator and took it down to the third level. The elevator seemed to take some time which told me the next level was deep down. I got out of the elevator into a rather large and spacious room that seemed to have tunnels that went off in different directions. Closer to the elevator was a corridor leading to another two rooms. One looked like a private work out or meditation chamber and the other looked like a giant office with a desk.

The office had a nice mahogany desk that was huge, something you would expect to see in some CEO's office. I took a seat in the comfortable leather chair. Sitting on the desk was a thick envelope with my name on it.

"Well let's see what this is all about." I said to myself as I picked up the thick envelope and took out its contents.

On top was a letter in Paul's handwriting addressed to me.

"Hello Old Friend..." I read that line, and it reminded me of the old tv show Babylon 5, we both had enjoyed watching the show together. We would address letters to each other if we ever needed to. People forget the impact of a handwritten letter. Shaking off the nostalgia I got back to reading.

... I am writing this letter to you for a few reasons. First, I wanted to explain a few things. Second, I wanted to give some advice. Lastly, to say goodbye.

First, you know for the longest time I have been a prepper. What you don't know is why. You know I am strong in my faith. The story I haven't told anyone until today is what happened to me on the day of my baptism. I was a teenager and everyone that walked up would be asked a simple yet important question, get dunked, and then go get changed.

When I was out under the water I was hit with such intense force and a blinding light came over me. I saw a vision of the end of the world. I had read scripture. At first, I just thought it was my imagination running away with me until I didn't come up and somehow knew I was still under water with my eyes closed yet I could see just fine. I started to see battles taking place, but they weren't for land but for people and for something within the earth. I saw demons, monsters, and other sentient races. Then I saw some dark shadow reach into the earth and grab hold of these lines of light and the lines twisted and turned wrong somehow. Then I saw a massive dragon glowing golden white and hope immediately filled my being. The dragon reached out and took hold of these lights and both the dragon and the lights grew bigger and brighter. People across the globe, survivors I realized flocked to the glowing dragon. They helped him make more lines of light grow brighter.

Then I heard the words. "The battle had already begun. The die is cast. Time is my ally and so shall it be yours. A willing sacrifice shall be made. Do this not for you but for what will come."

I went home after that and just sat in my room for the whole day. From that moment on my life was changed forever. I would read everything I could about how things worked. I would pray every day and each decision I would ask for guidance. And you know what, the more I did that the more I got. It was a profound realization and helped me achieve strong discernment to make the right decisions in life. With that I survived two wars, invented all sorts of things, and built this place you are in now.

It took a great deal of research and I found there were concerted efforts to distract or conceal actual history and real science instead of what was pushed. Those fragmented truths helped me find this place. As I started this project, I began to have doubts, then I met you and your cousin at a gun show and the moment I shook your hand I knew. A man can tell a lot about a person from a handshake, but you know that already. I built this place for you, my friend. I knew you would sacrifice your guarantee to help save others. This place is designed to help you achieve that goal. That and one more thing which sadly I cannot say because I don't quite understand it myself, but I think you will soon enough.

Now, for my advice. You aren't quite whole, but you will be in this journey. Do what you feel is right not what is easy. You have a hard road ahead of you, but it was the road you chose so embrace it. Something is only ever impossible until someone does it. Ever since I've known you, you have made the impossible possible. Never forget that.

Be a monster not a tyrant. You and I talked in great length about the true definition of 'Meek' and how that definition was intentionally twisted to turn people passive and weak. Unleash your sheathed power to protect others and to do the right thing. Some will see you as a monster due to all their past programming that tells them right is wrong and wrong is right. Do what you must, this is where you must be made whole to fully temper the rage inside.

Last bit of advice, as you are saving lives make sure to live yours, servant leaders can sometimes forget that. You are in the marathons of marathons; changes may happen overnight but for you to truly succeed you must use Time wisely and consider yourself most of all in those choices! You are the one granted THE <u>authority</u>, not someone else, YOU. I can say no more about that.

Finally, I wanted to say goodbye and good journey my friend. Be the man and the <u>Dragon</u>, I know you are! I have faith and I know you do too, that faith is your greatest weapon and defense. Lead them well!

Your ever faithful friend and ally,
Paul

Interlude- Alice

"AAAHHHAAA!" The man screamed as his arm was shattered.

"That is what happens when you dare to touch me." Alice said as she did a little curtsy in her cute little dress as she held onto her doll.

A hulking brute two meters tall in a top hat and trench coat stepped back out of the shadows. It had a gaunt almost skeletal face and wicked grin.

"See, my imaginary friend doesn't like it when you try to put your filthy hands on me. Only my daddy is allowed to touch me." Alice said as the brute crushed the man's other arm.

"AHHHAAA! Please... please let me go. I-I'm sorry... I didn't mean it... please..." The man sniveled and pleaded as tears ran down his face.

She had cut the man's Achilles tendons when he tried to run. Then he tried to grab her and her imaginary friend took immediate action.

Alice looked to be 10 to 12 years old and was the picture of innocence if she wasn't covered in the man's blood.

She met the man along the road. He had stopped as it seemed she was traveling alone. But Alice was never truly alone. She always had her friends with her.

Shortly after he took her back to his place "to protect" her, he did what every man seemed to do. Men and some women seemed like they couldn't resist her cuteness and always wanted to touch her.

Every time one of them did touch her it always resulted in what was before her now.

With a thought her imaginary friend flipped the man over onto his back.

Cheerfully she materialized her blade and gleefully stabbed into the man's gut and cut him open. "Shhh. Hush now. Isn't that what you boys say before you try to do something naughty." Alice said as she sliced open his abdomen.

"AHHHAAA! Please... please... stop... I'll be good... I swear! AHHHAAA" the man pleaded and then screamed again as she began to pull out his intestines.

Her imaginary friend put his hand over the man's mouth.

"Daddy sent me here to make new friends. I like to make boys like you play with me and my other friends but my way." Alice said and she pulled out more of the man's intestines.

"Let's play jump rope, it's one of my favorite games." Alice said cheerfully as she began to use his intestines as her jump rope.

"See isn't this fun!" Alice said as she continued to jump rope for a few more minutes.

The man was barely holding on to life.

"Oh, don't worry, you'll be joining my friends soon enough, and then we can play forever." Alice giggled.

Alice re-summoned her blade and began to cut into his skin. The man died screaming and begged for his life.

"Now for even more fun." Alice said as she cast one of her favorite spells.

Spell: Create Soul-Forged Minion
Description: Seize the soul of the departed and use that soul as fuel to transform the body into a completely obedient minion. Any damage these minions incur can be healed with your mana.

Soul and death magic merged to surround the corpse and lifted it off the ground. The body morphed and stretched into a slenderer form. Armor and a mask formed over the body. Glyphs began to etch themselves all over with glowing lines of green and black. Then settled back to the ground. The lines and glyphs periodically would glow and thrum with power.

The creature rose to its feet then kneeled before its new master.

Alice clapped her hands and giggled. "Goodie! More friends who will never leave. Time to use Daddy's gift.

Ability: Soul-Space Realm

Description: _Using soul and spatial magic to create and store an unlimited number of minions tied to your soul and any soulbound weapons and items._

She opened a portal in her shadow. Pointing her finger, Alice ordered her new minion into her Soul-Space Realm. "Go join the others."

"Uhhhh." Was all her new minion said before walking through the portal.

Alice waved her hands and the blood vanished from her hands and dress. "There, all better."

"Come let's go see if we can find some new friends." Alice told her imaginary friend.

———

Alice had been traveling with her little doll for a while now. She had been following road markers to head to the next town. Not a care in the world Alice skipped along on the road.

She finally saw the outskirts of town when she was surrounded by a bunch of green creatures in muted brown and green leathers. Alice identified as goblins. "Hello." she said cheerfully.

The goblins surrounded her pointing their spears and other weapons at her. One of the goblins spoke up. "Girl comes with us goblins. We take you to other humans."

"Okay. Sounds fun. Maybe I'll find more people to play with." Alice said cheerfully.

The goblins took her to the slave pens filled with other survivors the Sleeping Willow clan found on their scouting missions. One of the goblins opened the gate and pointed for her to enter. Alice did as she was asked.

Inside the cage were five women, three were older in their fifties and the other two were mid-twenties. Alice realized she would have to pretend and possibly even put on the waterworks. She put on a mask of worry.

The three older women came over to check on her.

"Are you okay?"

"Did those nasty goblins hurt you?"

"Don't worry we will look out for you."

"You remind me of my granddaughter."

"What's your name dearie?"

Alice squeaked out. "Alice."

"Nice to meet you, Alice. I'm Melody. You know you remind me so much of my granddaughter. Is that your doll?" Melody asked.

"Yes. He's my imaginary friend. My daddy gave him to me to protect me and play with me." Alice said innocently.

Melody wrapped Alice up in a hug while the other two ladies patted Alice's back to soothe her.

Alice just let them comfort her as she inwardly cringed at their touch.

Melody spoke up as she held Alice. "Don't worry Dearie, we won't let those mean goblins touch you."

'I liked the goblins; they didn't eye me like some others.' Alice thought to herself as she looked at one of the other cages.

Inside the cage was a woman that hadn't taken her eyes off since Alice entered the adjacent cage. Alice saw the woman lick her lips. 'Maybe she will play with me later?'

Chapter 12 — Reach Out and Touch Someone

I put Paul's letter down. One of the additional documents included with the letter was instructions on how to add or remove people from the approved access list. There was an old school computer terminal and receptacle to deposit the DNA sample. It was a closed system so there was a limited chance for interference.

After I figured out the access terminal, I picked up one of the other documents. It was a mineral and soil sample report. The old mine had been shut down for decades. To learn it wasn't as dry as people believed was a pleasant set of news. The report showed large veins of iron, copper, silver, and some gold deep underground.

"That will come in handy later if we need materials for building and trading." I commented as I set the report down and picked up the rest of the documents.

One piece of paper was a simple note that said the filing cabinet behind me held many of Paul's notes and sketches on his inventions and ideas. It would be a treasure trove of ideas to further help us grow a community if we could solve the goblin problem.

The last set of documents consisted of the purchase of the compound lot, the forest, town, and surrounding area. This also included official copies of his will and Living Trust that left everything to me.

"So, Jebediah was right, according to this I own this territory. Wait what is this?" I asked as another piece of paper with Paul's handwriting on it fell out of the stack of documents.

PS: Something I have researched is how ownership authority seems to work. If there is meaning and intent tied to it and an exchange of value, there is more significance tied to it. Note: If you're reading this my friend, I think this will matter in the apocalypse, but I can't say why. Hope this helps you.

"How weird. It's like Paul had some glimmers of insight into how things might work in the apocalypse. Maybe Gr'ex or the system can yield some answers." I told myself as I stood and left the office.

Returning to the second subterranean level, I found Jebediah right where he said he would be.

"How did it go, son? Get some answers?" Jebediah asked.

"Some answers and more questions." I replied.

"That is usually the way it works." Jebediah commented.

"Come on. Let's go see how the others are doing." I gestured for Jebediah to follow me.

We found Duncan and Suzie excitedly working on the radio equipment and Gr'ex eating a donut. When the little goblin saw me, he pointed to the donut he was eating. "Duncan's donuts are pretty good. He gave me one to shut me up while they worked."

That comment made me laugh. "Ha, ha, ha, ha. I'm not surprised Duncan's donuts are good."

Gr'ex clearly didn't get the joke, but Jebediah and Suzie laughed.

Suzie spoke up after she stopped laughing. "He, he. As you can see Duncan has been at it the entire time. What's exciting is we think we got in contact with someone out there. Duncan is trying to get them back!"

"That's good news. Any idea who it was?" Jebediah asked before I could.

"It sounded like Mrs. Burns." Suzie said.

"Carol? If I recall she worked at a radio station back in the day. Her son Carl was ex-military. I think he ended up in Southern California. Hmmm. I thought she moved to Nevada a few years ago when we all got our payouts from Paul. I think she wanted to be closer to her son. What did the old bat have to say?" Jebediah asked.

"I'm pretty sure she's younger than you Jeb. And we didn't get much, she was trying to talk about some survivors before we lost the signal." Suzie replied.

I took the opportunity to grab Gr'ex's attention. "Hey, Gr'ex, you got a few moments to chat?"

Gr'ex just nodded. He ate the last of his donut as he followed me out of the room.

"What's up?" Gr'ex asked.

"What do you know about territory ownership? Does significance in the process mean anything to you?" I inquired.

"You referring to Jeb's statement that you own the area?" Gr'ex asked.

"Yes. Looks like it's true. I found an official copy of the transactions. Paul seemed to think such exchanges were important in gaining ownership. Does that mean anything to you?"

"Of course. Energy exchange or trading something each party sees value in creates the impact of the exchange, which adds the meaning needed for the system to act. Soon that will matter for those who make deals and agreements and then try to break them." Gr'ex answered.

"Matter how?" I asked.

"Your world is not yet fully integrated. Mana has only yet begun to flow and change your world. The other realms have not yet fully connected to this one." Gr'ex explained.

"What does that mean?" I impatiently asked.

"I am getting there huemon. It means that this apocalypse is happening in waves or phases. Once there is enough energy or mana more functions will become available. The reason why my oath worked was the fact there is already a high amount of energy in the local environment. Why I don't know. This will allow territories to be officially recognized by the system. For that to occur there must be significant impact for the system to acknowledge this place as yours."

"So, you're saying the system could take this place from me?"

"In a way that could be possible, but very unlikely. Possession is a big factor in assigning initial ownership, but it is not the only thing considered. If Paul really went through all that trouble and everyone recognized his right of ownership, the system would weigh that heavily in your favor." Gr'ex further explained.

Just as Gr'ex finished his explanation a new notification popped up in my view.

New Quest: Right of Ownership

Description: _As you have just learned possession is a factor in determining initial ownership. Two factions of goblins occupy a portion of what should rightfully be your territory. Eliminate the invaders to gain ownership of this new territory. Ownership will unlock the **Territory Management** function of the system. Resolve these two threats before phase one of the apocalypse is completed. Each threat resolved prior will grant additional quest rewards. Time remaining before phase 1 completion in area: 5 days, 13 hours, 18 minutes..._

Gr'ex noticed the distant, glassy-eyed look of someone reading a notification. "What did you get?"

I answered Gr'ex's question as I finished re-reading the notification. "A new quest. I must resolve the goblin invasion in roughly five days. The challenge to my right of ownership of this territory must be resolved before then."

"That does not leave us much time. To deal with the Bone Marrow and Sleeping Willow clans." Gr'ex stated as he pulled out a ring and handed it to me. "Here. If you have finished absorbing the core you can start to attune to this ring. We will need to scout, and you and I should be able to do that better as goblins."

"The extra **Ring of Minor Illusion**?" I asked in surprise. When we first discussed the item Gr'ex seemed very hesitant to part with it. 'Perhaps he's beginning to trust me.' I thought as I just nodded in thanks.

Suzie poked her head out of the doorway. "Come quick! We got her back!" She didn't even bother waiting for us before she went back to the radio.

We entered the room and heard an excited conversation.

"It's good to hear from you too, Mrs. Burns!" Duncan said.

"Is that my donut? How have you been sweetie?" Mrs. Burns said on the radio.

"Surviving ma'am. I've got Suzie-cue and Mr. Jones with me." Duncan replied.

"Suzie-cue? Did you finally go home for a visit?" Mrs. Burns asked.

That one question made Suzie begin to lose the wall she had erected around her emotions. "Y-yes ma'am. I got a chance to spend time with them... before they vanished."

"Sounds like they were the lucky ones, sweetie. Don't fret. Don't fret. I'm glad to hear you and Duncan have each other right now." Mrs. Burns comforted.

Duncan squeezed Suzie's hand to let her know he was there for her. She just nodded and wiped away some tears that started to form.

Jebediah decided to chime in to change the subject. "How are you holding up you, crazy old bat?"

"Is that Jebediah? You're like twenty years older than me. I'm doing just fine you old coot! It's just me but I'm well stocked on food, and I don't eat a lot. My place is secure enough, and I've got no reason to leave."

"That's good to hear. What can you tell us about your area? Have you talked to other survivors?" Jebediah asked.

"I've seen some weird monsters and some undead, but they seem to be looking for other prey. As for survivors, I've talked to a few people, they are scattered all over in small pockets. My son's group is probably the largest I've heard of so far." Mrs. Burns shared.

"You talked to Carl?" Duncan asked.

"Yes, my sweet donut. Carl was able to get out of the city. Luckily, he was smart and lived in one of the suburban cities in California and was still armed. He helped form a group of survivors of over sixty people." Mrs. Burns beamed with pride about her son.

"Wow. Good for him. Glad to hear he's doing okay. Did they find a good place to defend?" Jebediah asked.

"They found an old secure warehouse but yesterday he told me they are packing up."

"Packing up? Is it not safe?" Suzie asked with concern.

"Oh no sweetie, my son just said it's not sustainable. Carl said they met someone who is leading a convoy northeast. My son said they should be stopping by and picking me and other survivors up along the way." Mrs. Burns explained.

"Do you know where they are going? And do we know anything about the person leading the convoy?" Jebediah questioned.

Mrs. Burns shared what she had learned. "The new leader of the group seems to be tight lipped about the destination. My guess is he doesn't quite trust everyone yet. Carl made mention of some awful business with a man named Tom who was the nephew of their old leader. Tom took advantage of their people. Mr. Laraaq killed him for hurting people. Said he wouldn't tolerate such behavior."

That name caught my attention. Gr'ex was the only one looking at me, so he picked up on my change in posture. "What is it?"

I raised my hand to forestall my goblin companion. I wanted to hear what they were saying.

"This Mr. Laraaq seems like he doesn't mess around. Sure, you didn't trade one tyrant for another?" Jebediah asked.

"No, I don't think so. I got a chance to talk to him on the radio last night. He assured me he would keep an eye on my son and watch his back."

I spoke up for the first time. "Is it possible to get a message to him?"

"Who is that? I don't recognize your voice." Mrs. Burns inquired.

"He's a friend of mine. Goes by the name Shadowalker. We are staying at his place currently." Jebediah explained.

"What's with all these weird names." Mrs. Burns commented.

"It's a gaming thing ma'am. Do you think you can get a message to Laraaq?" I asked.

"Most assuredly. Carl is supposed to call me soon before they pack up their equipment and head out. What is it you want me to tell him?"

"That Shadowalker is happy to know he is alive and to be safe. We are dealing with a goblin problem, but I don't want him risking his life to get here. The more survivors he can pick up along the way the better, but again take only calculated risks." I stated.

Mrs. Burns said in concern, "Goblins? That doesn't sound good."

"It's not ma'am but I'd rather my friend get here safely than rush." I replied.

"Well, I'm going to sign off now. I don't want to miss my son's radio message. You all stay safe yourselves."

"You too Mrs. Burns." Duncan and Suzie said.

Jebediah said in farewell, "Try to stay out of trouble Carol."

Everyone turned to me. Jebediah asked, "So... want to tell us more about Laraaq?"

"Laraaq is Oliver." I replied.

"No way. Ha, ha, ha, ha. Good for him dealing with that scumbag. I knew he had it in him." Jebediah chuckled.

"Laraaq was one of his gaming handles, like Shadowalker is one of mine. If he's leading a convoy then that means we can expect reinforcements at some point. It would behoove us to start working on recon and gathering information on our enemies." I explained.

"That is a good idea but also very risky business leaving this compound." Jebediah replied.

"That's why Gr'ex and I are going to go scouting." I answered.

"What? We are? Why would we do that?" Gr'ex asked incredulously.

"Because we can blend in with your illusion rings. We can make ourselves look like goblins." I stated as I gave my companion a pointed look.

"Wow you can do that?" Suzie asked.

"Yes. Gr'ex show them your goblin form." I ordered hoping my ally would pick up on my message.

"Ah yes, my goblin form. Here let me show all of you." Gr'ex replied as his features slowly changed until the goblin was in his true form.

"Wow that looks so real. Let's see yours Shadowalker." Duncan said in awe.

Gr'ex chimed in. "He still has to attune to the ring, but it will work the same as mine does."

"Man, you look just like them. It's kind of creepy." Suzie commented.

"Creepy, I can show you creepy!" Gr'ex offendedly replied.

I quickly stepped in. "Gr'ex why don't you help me learn how to attune to the ring. Maybe we can go upstairs so we can get started. Jebediah you are the only other person who can access the subterranean levels. Mind staying here and helping Suzie and Duncan?"

"Sure, not a problem, son." Jebediah nodded.

It was clear now that we had contacted someone they knew in the outside world, Duncan had zero interest in leaving the communications room.

Suzie chimed in. "Jeb, if you're staying can we go take a more detailed look at our supply cache? If we are expecting over sixty guests in a few days, it would be good to have a handle on everything while Shadowalker and Gr'ex are out scouting."

"Good idea Suzie. Duncan, you good to stay here?" Jebediah asked.

Duncan just waved his hand as he ate a donut and fiddled with the radio equipment.

Jebediah chuckled. "He, he, he. I'll take that as a yes. Alright Suzie-cue let's take an inventory of what we've got."

As Gr'ex and I returned to the surface level I gave him a quick warning. "You have to be careful. They only know goblins as invaders and killers. Give them time."

Gr'ex shrugged. "They are not wrong. Goblins aren't as driven for battle like Orcs are, but we can be a bit bloodthirsty when riled up. I will do better."

"That is all I ask my friend." I responded as I exited the elevator.

Gr'ex stood there for a minute before stammering out, "Do you mean it?"

I stopped and turned to face my companion. "Do I mean what?" Then it clicked, did I consider him a friend. "I believe we are well on our way to being friends. So, yes, I would say we are new friends. Come and explain this attunement process."

Gr'ex smiled at my response. 'Who would have ever thought I would be friends with a huemon.' He thought before saying, "As I mentioned before, reach out with your magic and attempt to connect it to the ring. Usually, one has to do that for several hours or days, but something tells me you won't have much difficulty."

True to Gr'ex's words, the moment I put the ring on and fed it a trickle of my mana I immediately received a prompt.

*Congratulations! You have attuned to a magical item that uses a magic type within your core. Item Attuned: **Ring of Minor Illusion**.*

Ring of Minor Illusion
Description: *Think of the image you wish to convey as you visualize pushing that image into the ring. This illusion is strong enough to provide false data on common identification magic.*

I immediately took the form of a goblin caster, wearing similar robes to Gr'ex. I looked at myself in the mirror. "So, this is what I would look like as a goblin."

"Not the ugliest goblin I've seen. Then again, not everyone can be as good looking as Gr'ex." My goblin companion commented.

I chuckled. "Ha, sure, sure. Let's get going. I want to get an idea of what we are up against."

We walked out the front door and I locked it behind us.

Chapter 13 – Convoy

Laraaq woke up early and was checking in on his truck before heading out to meet up with Mack, Christy, Colin, and Sarah. After doing his circle of safety to see if any damage or looting occurred last night, he opened the truck door.

Caleb came running out and calling out to Laraaq. "Mr. Laraaq! Mr. Laraaq! Wait!"

Laraaq groaned as he shut the moving truck door. "Now what?"

Caleb caught his breath. "Carl needs you at comms. There is a message for you."

Laraaq gave him a puzzled look. "A message for me?"

"Yes sir. Please come with me." Caleb said as he guided the man back inside.

'This better not be a trap. I don't have time for such nonsense.' Laraaq thought as he recalled his experiences the prior evening. Last night he had talked to Carl's mother. She was a nice enough lady but what interested him was the fact that she had already was in contact with multiple small groups of survivors. The woman lived a few hundred miles from their location, and he had promised Carl, they could retrieve her on the way to their destination.

Lost in his thoughts Laraaq finally noticed he had entered the communications area of the warehouse. Carl was speaking to his mom over the radio.

"Here he is mom. One sec." Carl said as he gave up his seat for Laraaq.

Taking his seat, Laraaq asked his question. "What can I do for you Mrs. Burns? I hear you have a message for me."

"Indeed, I do sweetie. I was told by a Mr. Shadowalker to tell you he is happy to know you are alive. Stay safe. Oh, and that they are dealing with a goblin problem, but he doesn't want you risking your life to get to him quicker. He said the more survivors you can pick up along the way the better, but only do so with the right amount of risk. I hope that all means something to you sweetie."

Laraaq just sat there in stunned silence. He had convinced himself that the quest he had meant his friend was still alive. Now though he knew it to be true. In this whole big wide world, Mrs. Burns somehow was able to contact him. 'Small world after all.' Laraaq thought before finally speaking up. "T-Thank you Mrs. Burns. We will hopefully make it to your place today and hunker down for the night. Do you think it might be possible to talk to my friend at that time?"

"I don't see why not. Donut is manning the radio." Mrs. Burns replied.

"Donut? Who the heck is donut?" Laraaq asked.

"Duncan Donut. My son knew him growing up." Mrs. Burns answered.

"You must be joking. His name is Duncan Donut?" Laraaq looked at Carl for confirmation.

"It was a nickname. The man loved donuts so that became his moniker. He's a good guy and handy when it comes to working a radio. Mom is right, if Duncan is there, we should be able to reconnect once we reach my mom's place." Carl explained.

"Fine, but we are burning daylight. I want to retrieve some additional resources. I should be back in about an hour or two. I want everyone out of here by then. We shall rendezvous at the private airport nearby. Got it?" Laraaq made it clear he wasn't really asking.

"Understood, Sir. We will be ready and meet you at the airport in just over two hours. Drive safe." Carl said as snapped to attention.

"Thank you, Mrs. Burns. I look forward to meeting you in person later today." Laraaq stated before he left to go find the family he found yesterday.

It took Laraaq about 45 minutes to get back to the shopping center. As he promised, when he was back within range, he used his walkie talkie. Christy's voice was heard a few minutes later. "That you Mr. Laraaq? Over."

"Yea, it's me Christy. How did you guys do last night? Over." Laraaq replied.

Christy quickly answered. "Nothing to worry about on our end. We had a few zombies, but they were the slow dumb ones. We took them out easy enough. Heard some howling but no contact. All and all one of the easier nights. Over."

"I should be there in a few minutes. Everyone ready to roll out? Over." Laraaq informed.

Christy's voice had a hint of joy in her voice as she replied. "Music to my ears. We should be ready to go by then. Mack and Colin are doing a quick sweep to make sure we have a clear shot of the trucks. See you outside. Over."

True to her word, when Laraaq pulled up all three drivers were in their trucks and the engines were running. Laraaq jumped out to hand Mack and Colin each a walkie talkie already set to their frequency. Getting back into the moving truck, Laraaq used the two-way radio to talk to everyone at once. "Good job everyone being ready to go this morning. That is appreciated. We are heading to the nearby private airport to meet up with the rest of the convoy. The other group had over sixty people. Even though they had so many, they worked through the night to be ready on time to leave this morning. The group is well organized. Over."

Mack's voice was the first to come over the hand radio. "Any problems or backlash from dealing with Tom? I just need to know the kind of atmosphere we are walking into. Over."

"Good question. Went better than I could've hoped. I burned the man in front of everyone and most people seemed to cheer or at least be happy about it. Seemed like he was taking advantage and bullying a bunch of people. Carl and Jacob, their old boss, helped quite a bit with the transition. I don't anticipate much issue. We have a planned destination to get to by tonight. Over." Laraaq answered.

Some random chatter was heard over the radio but nothing of consequence to Laraaq, this led to him focusing on the road and keeping an eye out for threats.

It took their smaller group about an hour to get to the private airport. Laraaq pulled up to the control tower and got out to do a quick sweep for enemies. Using his radio, he let his team know what he was doing.

The quick sweep was non-eventful. "Nothing found on my sweep. One or two people keep an eye out for trouble and for the convoy. I need at least one other person to help haul out the radio and radar equipment I found.

There is also a bunch of fuel stored here so we should take as much as we can carry. That way all our vehicles will make it to our destination. Over."

Colin's voice came over the walkie talkie. "I can help. I'm not as strong as Mack but I played around with some radio equipment when I was a kid so I might be able to help there. Over."

"That works. Mack and Christy keep an eye out. We will be back. Over" Laraaq ordered.

As Laraaq and Colin were moving the equipment, Laraaq decided to talk to the kid. "How'd it go last night? Christy said you guys had to deal with some zombies and heard howling."

"Yea the zombies seemed to just be wandering around. Was easy to take them out if you know what you're doing and there are only a few of them." Colin replied.

"Never let your guard down and never assume it will be simple or easy. That's how you end up dead." Laraaq stated.

"I'll keep that in mind Sir." Colin acknowledged.

"What about the howling? Did you see what was making the noise?" Laraaq inquired.

"Not a clue. Whatever was making that noise never showed themselves. Christy and I both took night-watch and didn't see a thing. The zombies attacked shortly after you left yesterday. Other than the howling, nothing else happened." Colin reported.

They finished moving the radar and radio equipment. Laraaq showed Colin where the fuel was stored as he continued his conversation with the young man. "How are Christy and Sarah holding up?"

Colin thought about it for a minute before answering. "Christy has always been strong and very mature for her age, has been ever since I've known her. She's been a bit more agitated lately and I periodically catch her and Mack arguing but can't really catch on to what they are arguing about. Sarah on the other hand stays pretty quiet. Mack keeps her very close at all times unless he's out scouting. Sarah pretty much only talks to Christy or her father, so I'm not really sure how she is holding up."

As they brought out the final barrel of fuel Laraaq could see the large convoy approaching. Carl in the lead vehicle pulled up alongside Laraaq.

"Looks like you found more fuel. That's a relief. With this many vehicles it's going to require a lot of fuel to get there." Carl said, letting Laraaq subtly know he knew they were heading to his hometown.

"Load it all up. Where is Jacob?" Laraaq asked.

"He's in the back of the convoy watching our rear." Carl answered.

"Get him up here. I see you guys have some walkie talkies. I have more in the truck. Pass them out to who you feel should have one." Laraaq ordered.

Five minutes later Jacob was standing next to Carl, Laraaq, and Mack.

"Gentlemen, this is Mack. He and his family will be driving the food and supply trucks you see behind me. I'd prefer to keep them closer to my vehicle and I plan to be upfront leading the way." Laraaq instructed.

"Nice to meet you, Mack." Jacob said as he shook the man's hand. He did not even flinch as Mack tried to crush the man's hand only to get equal pressure applied from Jacob.

Jacob just smiled and turned to me. "It should be fairly easy to integrate them into the formation. The walkie talkies will come in handy as well. I have a feeling, however, that those reasons are not why you called this impromptu meeting."

Laraaq gave a smile of his own. "Good guess. I wanted to tell you now, so you have time before you answer me later tonight. Now that I know my friend Shadowalker is holding down the fort we can afford to take some additional time to help save more people."

Carl looked confused. "What do you mean?"

"Your mother has been talking to various groups of survivors." Laraaq stated.

"Yes, what about it?" Carl asked.

"That means she can help map out where these survivor groups are." Laraaq continued.

Jacob smiled. "I think I know where he's going Carl. You want to take time to rescue as many people nearby as possible."

"Exactly. If possible, we will wait one additional day to give Mrs. Burns time to make contact and get the information we require like location, number of people, current situation, and local threats." Laraaq explained.

"What do you need from us?" Carl asked.

"You two know your people better than anyone. I need to know who we can trust to send out on rescue missions. You two pick the teams and start sending them out. If we already know where some survivors are, then don't wait for tonight, go retrieve them. We meet up at Mrs. Burns' place. Then we plot out the locations and determine how many we can save."

"This will help a great many people. We should grab some additional vehicles as we can." Jacob commented.

"Let me be clear, we do this the smart way. I am onboard with saving people. I am not onboard with lost causes or finding out we just let a bunch of vipers into our midst. Understood?" Laraaq firmly stated.

Both men nodded, which was all Laraaq required. "Alright, let's move out!"

From there the day fell into a rhythm. Laraaq drove in silence and responded to various calls on his walkie talkie. Several vehicles would break away from the convoy as they hit certain forks in the road. Some would meet back up shortly after.

As Laraaq was alone in the moving truck he had an opportunity to talk with his system and get some more answers.

"Hey System, when I tried to cast two Minor Fireballs at the same time, I got an excruciating headache, and I almost lost my concentration on both spells. Why is that?

Query Accepted

You do not possess the Dual-Casting Skill or an equivalent ability or skill that lets you divide your mental focus to do complex calculations in parallel.

"Well, how do I get the Dual-Casting skill or something like it?

Keep attempting to cast more than one spell at the same time. DUH

"So, until I unlock this skill, I risk losing control of my magic spells if I try to cast two spells at the same time?"

Correct

"Seems risky to attempt during a fight."

That is why you practice outside a real fight. Do I need to run another brain scan?

"Okay, okay, I got it. What about modifying a spell on the fly? Is that possible?"

Of course, DUH!

"How would I go about doing that?" Laraaq grinded his teeth as he asked his question.

Query Accepted

Spell modification can be dangerous. First one must master the spell, know every aspect they can. This will allow you to know where or how you might adjust without blowing yourself up. Overcharging is the easiest way to modify your spell by continuously and slowly feeding it mana before you release it. This can cause headaches or spells to backfire if you are not careful but that is the most common modification.

"What about range or distance or adding a delay or another magic type?" Laraaq asked.

Query Accepted

You must first form your core before such modifications are possible. With a developed core, spiral, and channels you will naturally gain more control over your magic and therefore be able to modify it more easily.

"Thank you, System." Laraaq said before returning his focus to driving.

By the time they all pulled into the town Mrs. Burns lived in everyone was happy enough to stretch their legs.

Even though everyone was tired, they all were seasoned hunters. They would exit the vehicles armed. Some stayed to protect the convoy, the others would sweep the area. Some shots would be heard and then an 'all clear' or 'zombies put down' would come over the radio. It was a good hour before they felt comfortable letting people out for bathroom runs and to eat.

Mrs. Burns place was an old radio station building and parking lot she converted into her home. It was a bit away from the rest of town. This provided plenty of space for the convoy to set up temporary residence near her place.

When Mrs. Burns stepped outside to give her son Carl a big hug, Laraaq did not expect to see a tall slender woman who looked like a cross between a schoolteacher and a movie star. It was like her outfit couldn't make up its mind. Part of it was flashy with bright colors and frills while other parts looked to be homely yet professional.

"Mom, this is Mr. Laraaq. Laraaq this is my mom." Carl introduced the two of them after his mom released him from the long hug.

"Pleasure to meet you ma'am." Laraaq greeted.

"Oh, none of that ma'am stuff. Call me Carol. Come give me a hug! You kept my Carl safe. That makes you family now!" Mrs. Burns said before barreling into Laraaq and wrapping him up in her arms for another long hug.

After Laraaq, she gave Jacob a big hug.

"Alright, why don't you all come on inside. I'm sure we have a lot to talk about." Carol Burns said before practically dragging her son inside.

"Nice lady." Jacob said before following behind the mother-son duo.

Laraaq shrugged and closed the door behind himself after he entered the building.

Carol had converted one of the radio stations' meeting rooms into a map room where she had a few maps laid out or tapped on the walls. Each map had pins in them, some with several pins with flags or numbers on them. Some were in a cluster or section of the map. Noticing everyone looking at the various maps, Carol spoke up. "Each pin is a confirmed contact with a survivor. If I don't hear back after a day, I remove the pin. I wrote down what I could about each one."

Pulling out a thick notebook, Carol opened it up. "I did everything I could to get the information I figured you might need."

"This is impressive, mom!" Carl exclaimed.

"I agree, what a cunning and attractive lady." Jacob commented causing Carol to blush slightly.

"Most helpful. Though I did not expect to see so many marked locations. I think this is going to take us longer than an extra day to hit all these. Speaking about that, what were today's results?" Laraaq replied.

"We rescued another 21 people today. No injuries, but we did have a few close calls. Both Carl and I have talked to those teams and reinforced the importance of always maintaining situational awareness." Jacob answered.

"That's impressive. Seeing this list, how long do you think we will need to rescue all these people?"

Both Carl and Jacob looked over what Carol had put together. After about 30 minutes, the two men looked at each other before Carl was the one to speak up this time. "Realistically, we probably need a week. We could probably shave off time if we thin the teams a bit at the lower risk locations."

Laraaq turned to Mrs. Burns. "Can any of the groups make it here on their own or get to one of the nearby survivor locations?"

Carol Burns thought for a moment before speaking up. "Good question. I would say some are either in lower risk areas or could travel a short distance if they knew someone would be retrieving them shortly after. Some I flagged in red are running low on food or supplies. If those groups move, they would be going on good faith but probably also more inclined to meet you part of the way if they could get food and water."

"That is just the kind of assessment we needed. Thank you, Carol. Well, Jacob and Carl, with all that in mind how much time can you shave off?" Laraaq asked.

"Hmmm. I would say we could probably cut that time in half." Jacob answered.

Carl chimed in shortly after. "If we retrieve the ones East of us while we are on the move, that might shave off another day or more."

"As you already know where we are going Carl, I will ask you a follow up question. What would be your best estimate on when we would arrive at your hometown?" Laraaq asked the question he really wanted answered.

"I would say we would arrive at our hometown in roughly five days give or take." Carl relayed his best guess.

"That will have to do. Shadowalker did say not to rush. Speaking about my buddy can we give him a call?"

"Sure, sweetie. Let me see if I can get ahold of Donut." Carol answered as she guided them to her equipment.

Chapter 14- Goblins, Goblins, Goblins

It didn't take Gr'ex and I long before we spotted a goblin patrol. We slowly and quietly followed them from the shadows and bushes. The goblin patrol seemed to be either completely oblivious or we were being exceptional at sneaking around.

After about 30 minutes of this, I was rewarded with a new notification.

*Congratulations! Your ability to stalk your prey without their notice for an extended period of time has earned you the **Stealth** skill.*

Skill: Stealth
<u>Description</u>: *To go unseen or walk so softly you can sneak by an enemy or strike a foe without knowing what happened is only possible with a high enough Stealth skill.*
<u>Passive effect</u>: *Increased muscle and breathing control. Reduce the possibility of detection while moving by 10%.*
<u>Active effect</u>: *Use the shadows to help reduce detection. This effect can reduce the chance of detection by an additional 10% in normal lighted areas, with an additional on top of that for low-lit areas.*

Congratulations! Your Stealth skill has a natural alignment with Dark and Shadow affinities. As you possess these affinities, you can now influence Stealth with Dark or Shadow magic to increase skill efficiency by an additional percent per point of Dark mana used and two additional percent per point of Shadow mana used.

I immediately felt more in control of my movements. Without realizing it I had started to pull the light out of the area I was in as my mind had subconsciously extracted or converted the Omni mana into Shadow mana. If I can figure out how to consciously control this, I could figure out other benefits with my other spells, skills, and abilities.

Further blending into the shadows, Gr'ex and I moved past the patrol and headed further into enemy territory.

Our path southeast led us to the edge of a clearing. What we saw in the clearing brought us up short. A series of camps and simple wood huts and canopy tents dotted the clearing. In the center of the haphazard encampment were multiple pens or cages filled with people. Out in the distance I could see another portal shimmering in the light of the sun. Near the portal was the start of a walled fort in mid-construction. Past the partial fort multiple fields could be seen with humans and undead tilling the soil.

I crouched down low to whisper to Gr'ex. "Thoughts?"

Gr'ex looked at me. "Turn around and run far away."

"Be serious Gr'ex."

"I am being serious. The Sleeping Willow clan is dangerous with their poisons and sleeping draughts. Their skills with small blades are not to be underestimated either. I don't see a winning strategy here." Gr'ex replied.

"What else can you tell me about them?" I asked.

"They are smart and cunning. Like most goblins they respect strength and power. They hold no oaths to my master, rather they serve out of fear. Their leader is no fool and our clans have been allies for a few generations." Gr'ex explained.

"By my count, I'm seeing well over a hundred goblins. If there are this many Sleeping Willow clan members here, and our guests said there were more Bone Marrow clan members..." I let my question trail off as a party of three level 15 goblin scouts were mere meters from us.

'It doesn't look like they see us. Must be just heading out on patrol. Crap their path is going to cause them to pass right next to us!'

I thought about my Stealth skill. 'If I could funnel more Shadow mana into the skill... no, I need something to hide both Gr'ex and I. There seems to be a lot of Death magic in the area. Maybe I can draw that in and start to convert it. No time like the present!'

Concentrating on pulling in the Death mana in the area and converting it into Shadow to hide us. Focusing my visualization, I realized I didn't have time to convert all the Death mana into Shadow I wielded both types to push us from their vision. I felt the mana gathering and I felt Gr'ex grab my arm so tight I almost lost my concentration.

Gr'ex knew he couldn't say anything with the goblins so close but worry and confusion were clearly written on his face. Then I felt something shift and my **Dark Mantle** seemed to respond as the magic took hold. Notifications popped into my vision almost making me fall back startled.

*Congratulations! You have created the spell: **Death Shroud**!*

Death Shroud (Tier 5)

<u>Description</u>: *This tier 5 spell was created from the combination of primarily Death and Shadow magic with some Space magic. Death Shroud wraps targeted in a blanket of magic and shifts them into the veil between the Shadow realm, the reality you are in, and the Realm of the Dead. This thin veil prevents others from seeing or interacting with you. Caster's intent can move targets into either realm. Attacking will bring you out of the effects of this spell but increase the chance of a critical strike. Be warned both the Realm of the Dead and the Shadow Realm are antithetical to life, do not stray too far.*

*Congratulations! You have gained the achievement: **Spell Creator**! This achievement grants you the Title of **Creator** or enhances the existing title if you already possess it.*

*Congratulations! Your **Creator** title has increased from double to triple the applied bonuses to all abilities, spells, and skills you created.*

Congratulations! Your **Dark Mantle** ability has gained a new effect: **Shadow of Death**!

<u>**Shadow of Death effect**</u>: *Your **Dark Mantle** ability now resonates authority with those realms. You can now move those within your aura into either the Realm of the Dead or the Shadow Realm. The denizens of those realms will heed your call.*
<u>**Additional Passive effects**</u>: *Increased influence with Dark aligned and undead creatures. This effect is increased while in either realm.*
<u>**Additional Active effects**</u>: *Move you and others within your aura's range to and from shadows. This uses both mana and stamina. Call denizens of those realms to your aid and/or service. Please Note: If you use their motivations in your call this can increase success.*

The world around us grew darker and a cold chill ran down my spine. When the goblin squad walked right by us without any notice, it was clear we were not in their field of vision.

Gr'ex sounded a bit panicked. "What did you do?!"

"I created a tier 5 spell called **Death Shroud**. It brings us into the veil between our reality and the Realms of the Dead and Shadow. They can't see or interact with us." I replied distractedly as most of my attention was on the squad of goblin scouts.

"You just nonchalantly announce you created a tier 5th spell that brings right smack between the realms of Shadow and Death! Do you know how dangerous this is?! The creatures of either of those realms despise the living! As a Dark and Death Caster they are less inclined to kill me as I will 'smell' of their magic but you!!!" Gr'ex exclaimed, clear fear and worry in his tone.

"Oh, about that... apparently in the process of creating this spell I accidentally upgraded my **Dark Mantle** ability. I can now call on the denizens of those realms to aid us." Again, I replied partially paying attention to Gr'ex.

"Of course, you can, cause why not?! You are the luckiest person I have ever met in my life. You..." Gr'ex replied but I stopped paying attention to him all together.

"Hold on I'm going to try something." I replied before I willed myself to appear behind the trio, coming up through their shadows.

"What the?!" Gr'ex exclaimed as I disappeared from next to him only to then appear behind the squad.

I immediately struck out with two branches I picked up off the forest floor. Both flew true as I hit two of the three goblins on the back of the head, knocking them out and making them crumple to the floor. Dropping both makeshift clubs, I wrapped my arm around the third goblin's neck as he was turning around to see what happened to his squad mates.

"Ah-kkk!" The goblin choked out before my arm around his neck silenced him. He could no longer breathe as I lifted him off the ground. A few moments later, the third goblin was unconscious as well.

No longer surrounded by shadows, the world around me brightened back to daylight.

Gr'ex walked up to me, also no longer wrapped in darkness. "Now what? We cannot exactly just leave them here."

"Let's hide them in the bushes over there. We don't have much time and need to finish our recon." I replied as I started moving the unconscious goblin into the denser bush.

"Aren't you going to help me?" I asked Gr'ex as I noticed he wasn't moving.

"Your mess. You clean it up." Gr'ex said in frustration.

"Fine! Give me a minute and while I'm doing this, make yourself useful and come up with a plan." I replied as I continued to hide the scouts.

After I was done, I rejoined Gr'ex who had returned to the edge of the clearing to watch the goblin camp. "Come up with a plan yet?" I asked quietly as I crouched down to join him.

"Yes and no. Our biggest problem is the portal. Every day it is opened the invading force is allowed to send more forces through. That is why you are seeing so many from the Sleeping Willow clan here, they have had two days now to bring more forces through. Each day that number increases."

"Well, that sucks." I commented.

"Yes, it does. The problem is if you close it there is a possibility the Bone Marrow clan will be notified. There is also the chance they won't. It's a crap shoot really." Gr'ex complained.

"You said you had a plan." I encouraged.

"I said yes and no. I have an idea. My clan and the Sleeping Willow clan have been amicable over the years. I say we just walk right into the chief's hut and..."

"And what?" I asked.

"And that's about as far as I got okay!" Gr'ex said in frustration.

I thought about using Death Shroud again to hide us when I thought about the upgrade to my Dark Mantle ability. "Okay, let's do it."

"What?!" Gr'ex asked in confusion.

"You gave me an idea. Get me into the hut and make introductions and I'll handle the rest." I answered.

Gr'ex gave me a dubious look. "Alright... if you say so. But, let me go on record that I think this is a really bad idea."

"Noted. Let's go." I said as we rose from our hiding spot and walked into the clearing.

I whispered to Gr'ex as a followed behind him, still disguised as a goblin. "Walk like you're the badass goblin necromancer I know you are."

Gr'ex didn't reply but rather his unsteady movements became more sure-footed. He stopped slouching and seemed to have a surer gait to his walk.

Meanwhile I slowly released the hold on my **Dark Mantle** aura. The ability was a part of me. I could hold it back and contain its power, but it was always there. I only needed to release my hold to let its effects spread.

I only allowed the barest trickle, but it was enough for any of the goblins thinking about stopping us for questioning to reconsider. More and more heads turned our way. Even the humans in the slave pens seemed to turn our way. Most were in their twenties to early thirties, with a few older men and women.

Then my eye caught a little girl. She couldn't have been older than 10, maybe twelve. She wore a cute little dress and was absolutely adorable. My rage began to peak at the sight of a child being held as a prisoner, but I clamped down on that rage as I felt my Dark Mantle flare in response and more onlookers found a reason to suddenly look away. For some reason I could feel the little girl's stare. It felt like she couldn't take her eyes off of me.

'I will rescue that little girl and these other people, but for sure the poor helpless little girl. What sicko imprisons a child!' I thought as we entered the larger chief's hut.

"What is this intrusion. Can't you see your chief is busy!" Jek'jon jerked to his feet and moved what looked like a farmer's almanac under some papers.

"Is that anyway to greet and old friend?" Gr'ex asked.

Jek'jon's eyes widened as recognition dawned on his face. "Gr'ex! You are alive!"

Jek'jon ran up to Gr'ex and embraced him in a hug. "I thought you died!"

Gr'ex was a bit surprised by the sudden display of affection. They had been friends, but goblins didn't show weakness for fear it would be exploited.

Jek'jon realized he might've overstepped with Gr'ex not returning the hug. He then saw me and immediately let Gr'ex go. "My apologies old friend. I was just excited to see you alive. Who is your friend? Is he the only one left of your unit that survived?"

Gr'ex realized he might've inadvertently hurt his friend from his shock and gave Jek'jon a quick hug in return. "Sorry my friend, I was just caught off guard. We will get to him in a moment." Gr'ex said as he waved back to me before pointing at the partially covered farmer's almanac which had a picture of a farm on it. "I see you are still dreaming of farming."

Jek'jon gave Gr'ex a sour expression and whispered. "Why would you reveal that to a goblin I do not know?"

"Him?" Gr'ex waved at me again. "Oh, he's not a goblin."

I took that as my cue to drop my illusion.

"Hello. I am Shadowalker. Nice to meet you." I replied in a friendly tone.

"Huemon?!" Jek'jon exclaimed.

Gr'ex clamped his hand over his friend's mouth.

"Look away Gr'ex." I said as I released more of my Dark Mantle aura in Jek'jon's direction.

Gr'ex saw the horror on his friend's face. He imagined it was similar to his own terror. Even though Gr'ex wasn't facing Shadowalker he wanted to drop to his knees in supplication. The only thing holding him back was that he knew he was in service to the man. Gr'ex spoke softly to his friend and Jek'jon dropped to the floor. "You have nothing to fear if you do not challenge him. I have chosen to serve him."

Jek'jon whimpered and wet himself. Gr'ex took his hand off his friend's face and stepped away from the growing puddle. "Don't worry, I did the same thing." Gr'ex admitted.

"You-you... serve him?" The terrified goblin asked his friend before looking at me and asking, "what-what-what are... you?"

I withdrew my aura, and I could see the visible relief in Jek'jon's face, and I also noticed Gr'ex's shoulders seem to relax a bit too. 'Man, I've got to be really careful with the ability.'

I cast my **PURITY!!!** ability on the goblin to remove the stinky puddle that had formed before I reached down and offered my hand.

The goblin scooted away from my offered hand. It was very evident the goblin was still attempting to regain control over his emotions.

I took it in stride and walked over to the desk and pulled out the farmer's almanac book. "Good book. It has some great tips in there. So, you like to farm huh?"

That question seemed to get Jek'jon's mind to reboot, and the goblin stood on shaking legs. "I do not know what you are talking about. I am an apprentice necromancer like my friend Gr'ex here."

"You can trust him my friend. He does not see such things as a negative." Gr'ex advised his friend.

Jek'jon looked at Gr'ex for a moment before he spoke. "You serve this... being?" He then realized I might take offense to that and spoke quickly. "I-I meant no disrespect terrifying one. I just do not know what you are. You look huemon but no huemon could make me so horrified."

"For now, you can consider me a huemon with authority and I expect you to respect my authoritah!" I chuckled to which both goblins just stared at me in confusion.

I waved them off. "Forget it. Guess it's a human thing."

Gr'ex shook his head at me and picked up the conversation as I had turned back to thumb through the other papers on the desk.

"Yes, I have given Shadowalker an oath that I will serve him and teach him what magic I know. He has treated me well and is an exceptionally quick study when it comes to magic."

"You have taught him your magic?!" Jek'jon asked incredulously.

"Not all of it. We have been busy after all. He has potential System Authority over this territory. That is why we are here." Gr'ex explained.

Jek'jon's eyes widened once again. "System Authority is exceptionally rare. Usually most only hold provisional authority over an area."

"What's the difference?" I asked.

"Provisional authority is limited and only granted by some ruler or chief. However, **System Authority** is as it sounds, the universe itself recognizes your authority. Some say that power comes from God the Creator himself and as such holds more impact to what you can do with a territory." Gr'ex explained.

"Wait... can Dark aligned beings have authority? If God is the originator..." I asked as my thoughts wandered.

"Yes, of course. God has the System impart Dark authority over their domain. They can also subvert but that isn't the same thing as System granted Authority. It's different and would take too long to try and explain at the moment." Gr'ex answered.

"Fair enough." I said before turning to Jek'jon. "So, how about it?"

Jek'jon looked at me with confusion. "How about what?"

"Oh sorry, guess I jumped the gun there. I'm offering you and your clan the chance to join me. I plan to close the remaining two portals and that means either you join me or..." I said as I once again released some of my aura. "Or I would have to wipe you all out... starting with you." I said the last part with a wicked grin.

"Careful boss, your monster is showing." Gr'ex commented in the hopes I would reign in my aura.

I gladly did so, having made my point.

Jek'jon sighed. "Well, you are much more terrifying than my current master and if we can kill Tek'tar I am in. I cannot stand that pompous jerk!"

"Done." I replied.

Gr'ex chimed in. "Make the oath."

Jek'jon did as his old friend instructed. "I Jek'jon pledge myself fully in service to my new master Shadowalker! His enemies become mine. His allies shall be given aid. I bind myself and, as chief of the Sleeping Willow clan, bind my people in service to our new Master Shadowalker!"

A thrumming began in the tent.

I replied. "I accept your oath of service and fealty. I shall do what I can to give you sanctuary in my lands and protect our people!"

The thrumming of meaning washed out from the tent and every Sleeping Willow clan member received a similar notification.

*Congratulations! Hark and rejoice! Your chief has pledged an oath of service and fealty to **Shadowalker**. You have been bound to his authority and service. He has pledged to provide you with sanctuary as long as your people remain loyal and in service of your new liege.*

I received my own notifications.

*Congratulations! You have gained the fealty of the **Sleeping Willow clan**. The clan consists of 893 goblins. Only 180 goblins are on this side of the portal. Please Note: Goblins tend to be one of the most commonly enslaved and persecuted races. There is an increased chance your **Dark Mantle** ability will turn this goblin clan into fanatics doing everything they can for you, especially if you treat them fairly.*

Congratulations! You have resolved another contested portal. Due to the nature in which you resolved this conflict you are being given a choice. Rather than immediately closing the portal you can choose to allow your remaining goblin followers on the other side to join you on this side of the portal. Any number restrictions have been temporarily removed. They have up to four days to cross over. Any rewards will be delayed until the portal is closed. You can of course choose to close the portal now. Warning: Your goblin followers are not the only ones that can come through the portal during this time.

I spoke to my new follower. "Jek'jon. Interestingly enough, I am being given a choice to keep the portal open so the rest of the clan can cross over. Oh, and it says the number restriction on forces has been temporarily removed. How long do you think would be needed to bring the rest of the clan?"

"That is great news master! I would figure two days. My biggest concern would be keeping our numbers hidden from Tek'tar and his Bone Marrow clan. They already have double our numbers and in two more days I would expect them to have over 500 goblins here." Jek'jon explained.

"Well, that is a problem. How big is their clan?" I asked.

Gr'ex was the first to answer. "I would guess a couple thousand. They are one of the largest and most consolidated goblin clans I know of."

"Damn. We are going to have to come up with a way to start picking them off to reclaim the town. I doubt all of your remaining clan members are warriors." I stated.

Jek'jon shook his head. "Not many warriors left. What we do mostly have are herbalists, alchemists, healers, some hunters, rogues, with a few assassins mixed in. We have our women and children and elderly which will take most of the time to transport."

"Waiting two days before we start doing anything sounds like a great recipe for getting overwhelmed by numbers. We will need to come up with a few plans." I replied.

Jek'jon smiled. "Come it is time for the clan to meet you, master. Oh, and I recommend you not hide your ability. It will go a long way to gain their understanding on why we are changing sides in the conflict."

"I think he just wants to laugh as you make them soil themselves." Gr'ex commented.

"I have no idea what you are talking about my friend. This is about results." Jek'jon stated.

"Yea results on how many people wet themselves. I got twenty silvers on over 100." Gr'ex said with his own smile plastered on his face.

"I will take that bet." Jek'jon answered before pulling me along to exit the tent.

I heard Gr'ex whisper, "Don't hold back and I'll split the money with you."

Chapter 15- Alice Finds a New Father

"We need to get her out of here Melody. She is just a child." Nina said.

"I'm aware of that but I don't see how that's possible Nina." Melody commented.

"We should get one of these useless men to do something or cause a distraction." Nina complained.

"Hush Nina. We are already well aware of your dislike of men. Now is not the time to sacrifice people, we must stick together." Melody commented.

"What-what is that?!" One of the younger men spoke up in fear.

"I sense it too." Nina trembled.

"I feel like someone just walked over my grave." Melody commented.

"Look at those two goblins. They look like bad news." Another man said.

Alice didn't bother getting his name. She felt it too. A feeling that sent pleasure through her in anticipation. The adults were once again talking nonsense. She did not see two goblins. One looked human and had a shimmer around him.

'What was it father called it? Glamour? Yes, that was it. The trick was fooling the adults but not me. Silly adults.' Alice thought.

The adults seemed to start to calm down once the duo went into the big tent.

Melody pulled Alice into a hug. "Don't worry sweetie. Those two bad goblins are gone now. Nothing to worry about."

'This lady clearly does not understand how much I want to play.' Alice thought as she said. "I'm not scared."

"Of course, you're not. There is nothing to be scared of." Melody said as she held Alice closer.

'She sounds more like she is trying to convince herself. Why are these adults so weak.' Alice thought.

Alice was giddy with excitement. She wanted to play.

Twenty or thirty minutes later, Alice wasn't quite sure the exact time, two goblins and a man stepped out of the large tent. The three of them seemed friendly but Alice was still learning those cues.

"Gather around my Sleeping Willow clan! Hurry up, we do not have all day! Your chief wants to introduce you to our new master!" Jek'jon's voice boomed across the clearing.

The various goblins began to head toward their chief. Alice did a quick count and found over a hundred goblins before she got bored, and all her attention shifted to the man behind the goblin chief.

"I AM SHADOWALKER, YOUR NEW LIEGE" A dark aura surrounded the man and washed over the clearing.

The goblins and the adults all dropped to their knees and wept. The feeling excited Alice like no other. She saw most of those around her weeping and soiling themselves.

'Ah yes, I so enjoy it when they are scared so fully, they cannot control their bodily functions. That raw dark power reminds me so much of father. Perhaps he will be my new daddy.' Alice thought in growing excitement.

"RELEASE THE HUMANS!" The man called Shadowalker commanded as he covered his nose and started casting some magic to make all the puddles disappear.

"Told you he would make over a hundred soil themselves. Pay up." Gr'ex said as he laughed.

Jek'jon pulled out twenty pieces of silver and passed to Gr'ex. "Fine. You win, here you are."

Gr'ex took and pocketed ten of the coins before handing the rest to Shadowalker.

"Hey! You cheated!" Jek'jon complained.

Shadowalker turned to Jek'jon. "No, you bet against me in doubting what I was capable of. Consider that a lesson."

Gr'ex just laughed. "Ha, ha, ha, ha, ha! You only felt a trickle of his Dark Mantle. Having been on the receiving end I knew what to expect."

"Dark Mantle?! That's what that is. No wonder I felt so compelled to serve." Jek'jon whispered.

Gr'ex clapped his friend on the shoulder. "Yep, I had that exact expression on my face when I found out. You were wise to pledge your clan to him."

Jek'jon just nodded in agreement.

Shadowalker withdrew his aura as the goblins scrambled to release their human prisoners. He walked over to the slave pens with Gr'ex and Jek'jon by his side.

The moment Alice's cage was opened she made a beeline for Shadowalker. She jumped up and slammed into him as she wrapped her arms around him. "Are you going to be my new daddy?"

"Uhhh..." Shadowalker stammered in shock as this little adorable girl had a Vice grip around him.

Melody approached cautiously. "Thank you, sir, for freeing us. Please forgive her. It is clear she has been through something terrible."

Nina came up and peeled Alice off Shadowalker. "Come now, stay with us women. I will take care of you. Men have no idea how to raise a child."

Anger flared in both Alice and Shadowalker. Alice spoke first, a pout on her face. "My daddy taught me everything I know!"

"I agree with the child! Fathers are critical in a child's development! I loved being a dad! That kind of bitterness only comes from one who is hurt so I will let it go for now." Shadowalker clamped down on his anger. Losing his family still hurts. To this day it was a wound that would not fully heal.

"I could kill her. I could use a new undead minion." Gr'ex commented as he stepped up closer as his hand started to glow.

Melody quickly intervened. "I'm Melody and that's Nina. She meant nothing by it. She's just not a big fan of men. Please forgive her. We have all been through so much and all of our nerves are beyond frayed."

"That much is to be expected. I can forgive for now, but what I say goes. Stand down Gr'ex." Shadowalker stated.

Alice liked how her new daddy carried himself. He shut that bad girl down and it is clear the goblins are smart enough to recognize his greatness.

"Sir..." Melody started but was interrupted by Shadowalker. "Call me Shadowalker."

"Mr... Shadowalker. It appears as if these goblins follow your orders..."

Nina spoke up. "Are you the one who had them round us up and take us as slaves?! Just like a man!"

Alice debated if she could slit this bad lady's throat and not get any of the blood spattered on her new daddy's outfit. 'Good for him to take you weak worthless adults in and feed you.' Alice thought. She was about to take action when Shadowalker let his voice carry across the clearing so all the humans could hear.

"I only recently have taken over this tribe..."

"Clan." Gr'ex interrupted.

Shadowalker turned to Gr'ex. "What's the difference Gr'ex?"

"Well to start..." Gr'ex began to say until Shadowalker cut him off. "Doesn't matter. Tell me later." Before he turned his attention back to the humans in the clearing.

"I only recently took command of the goblin clan..." Shadowalker glanced back to Gr'ex who gave him a thumbs up.

Shadowalker continued. "As I was saying, this goblin clan is called the Sleeping Willow clan. They are not the only goblin clan in the area. In fact, if you are familiar with the area a clan known as Bone Marrow has taken over the local town. I am going to work to free this area and lay claim to it."

"Of course, typical man." Nina mumbled.

Melody and a few other survivors gave her a dirty look.

"If you are willing to follow my lead and work together, I can bring you back to my compound north of here. We have food and can provide temporary shelter until we deal with the other goblin clan. There is no free lunch. Everyone chips in got it?!" Shadowalker explained.

Everyone nodded along. Some people were still in shock and seemed to just agree to any option that would get them away from the goblins.

"Melody. Can you organize the survivors? I would like to get you all escorted back before nightfall." Shadowalker asked.

Melody nodded. The older woman seemed reluctant to leave Alice but decided the man seemed to be protective of the little girl and did not want to anger their rescuer. "I'll make it happen."

"Thank you, Melody. Come see us in the chief's tent when you are ready."

Melody nodded once again before heading off to accomplish her task.

"Gr'ex, Jek'jon. Let's talk logistics. We will want an escort and we should also do what we can to not alert the Bone Marrow clan. We can discuss in the tent." Shadowalker said as he went to move only to realize Alice was still attached to him in a vice grip.

Seeing her opportunity to step in, Nina rushed forward. "I'll keep an eye on her."

"I don't know." Shadowalker said but Alice spoke up.

"It's okay new daddy, I'll go play with the lady while you are busy. I won't be a bother to my new daddy. I will be helpful."

Alice let go of Shadowalker but gave him a genuine smile. He ruffled her hair. "You are an adorable little one. Hmm, you kind of remind me of my daughter too. If you will be good and keep yourself entertained, then okay. I will see you later little one."

"My name is Alice, but you can call me whatever you want." Alice said.

Shadowalker ruffled her hair again. "Okay Alice. I will see you in a little bit when we are ready to leave."

Nina took Alice by the hand and led her away. Shadowalker heard her ask the woman. "Do you want to play with me?"

"Cute little girl." Shadowalker said before turning his attention to the goblins.

A few minutes later Nina was leading Alice further south. She moved quickly and practically dragged her along.

"Where are we going?" Alice asked.

Nina licked her lips. "I want to get us away from those people. I'll take good care of you, don't worry Alice. I'll show you things only another woman can teach you."

"Do you want to play with me?" Alice asked.

Nina turned to look at the little girl and could no longer hold back her urges to take the innocence of this little girl. Nina could no longer resist her hunger.

"Yes, I want to play with you Alice." Nina said as she put her hand on the little girl's stocking.

A blade flashed in Nina's vision.

"I guess we are far enough away now, but that doesn't give you the right to touch me." Alice said with a wicked grin on her face.

Nina looked down as the pain finally registered to see she was missing the hand she had put on Alice's leg.

"AHHHH!..." Nina began to scream but was silenced quickly as a giant hand big enough to grab her by the head and slammed Nina against a tree.

"Uhghhh..." Nina moaned.

"Yes. See I know they always want to moan with me but not like this I imagine. He, he, he. Meet my imaginary friend. Let's play a game. It's called fish. I cut your tendons while my friend collapses your voice box so you can't scream."

Alice sighed. "I do love when they scream but I don't want anyone to interrupt our play time."

Nina tried to get to her feet but wobbled. A giant hand wrapped around her throat and used its thumb to partially collapse her windpipe. Then in a flash Alice struck and Nina felt excruciating pain in her legs before she lost complete control of them, and they gave out from under her. Nina couldn't help but twitch.

Alice clapped her hands. "Oh goodie, goodie. You already know how to play this game."

Nina tried to scream to no avail, all that came out was a wheeze. She began to try to crawl away until she felt more pain in her right leg as Alice drove one of her blades right through the leg and into the ground, pinning her to the ground.

Alice sighed again as she looked at her imaginary friend. "Why do they always try to run just as we are having so much fun?"

Alice crouched down and used her other blade to lift Nina's head by her chin. "You see, you were mean to my new daddy! I can't allow that to go unpunished. I wouldn't be a good girl if I didn't take care of my new daddy. I'm going to use some extra runes that will add to extend the feelings of pain as I carve the symbols into your flesh."

Nina was crying and had a look of utter horror on her face.

"Ahhh. That's better. See, that's what happens when you are a bad girl. Do not worry I will turn you into one of my minions so you can play with me forever... but first..." Alice began to carve into Nina's flesh.

———-

Melody entered the chief's hut. She bowed her head in the trio's direction. She wasn't sure why she did that but felt it was right. "Sir Shadowalker, the group of fifty are ready to depart. Some are older so we will have to go slow."

Shadowalker nodded. "Very well. Let us depart. Jek'jon."

Jek'jon took that as his cue and began ordering several goblin squads to form up. "Protect our new master at all costs. Your lives are nothing compared to his..."

Shadowalker interrupted. "Okay, hold up. I appreciate the sentiment but come on."

Jek'jon just looked at him in confusion. The goblin chief turned to his friend for insight. Gr'ex spoke up. "He is pleased and wants you to continue."

Shadowalker looked at Gr'ex incredulously. Gr'ex smiled. "Just roll with it, trust me, it's our way."

Shadowalker shook his head but kept quiet.

Jek'jon took that as his cue to continue. "You see our new master is pleased! Protect him and if you must protect the huemons too, but only if you have to. Make sure no Bone Marrow goblin stumbles upon them."

"Wait where is Alice?" Melody asked.

"She was with that Nina lady. If she hurt her in any way, I'll..." Shadowalker began before his words were cut off when he saw Alice skipping into the clearing holding her doll.

Melody ran up to the little girl. "Where is Nina?"

Alice's smile dropped and was replaced with a frown. "That mean-lady tried to take me away from my new daddy. I told her I didn't want to go and then I came back here like a good little girl."

Melody hugged Alice. "I can't believe she tried to take you. You poor thing."

Shadowalker bent down. "Good riddance. She seemed like a problem anyway. Did she hurt you at all?"

"No, she pulled me really hard, but I got out of her grip." Alice answered.

"You want to come live with me and my friends? I'll do my best keep you safe." Shadowalker said.

Alice's face lit up and practical melted Shadowalker's heart. He ruffled her hair. "You are too cute."

Melody spoke up. "I can carry you Alice if you are ready to go."

Alice looked at Melody before opening her arms up towards Shadowalker.

Shadowalker chuckled and said, "Sure I'll carry you if that's what you want."

Alice's smile got bigger, and she nodded her head before wrapping her arms around his neck.

"Looks like she has chosen who she wants to carry her. I can relieve you if you get tired." Melody stated.

Shadowalker nodded. "I think I will be fine but thank you for the offer. Let's get going, we have a lot of ground to cover before dark."

With that they rejoined the group and started their trek back to the compound.

Chapter 16- Long Distance Call

"You know, you are really good with her." Melody said.

Alice had fallen asleep as I was carrying her and was now resting comfortably cradled in my arms.

"She reminds me of one of my daughters. I miss my family." I said quietly as we kept walking.

"We all do. I had a grandbaby about her age. I think all of us who are parents and grandparents miss the children. Though I am glad they have been spared this nightmare." Melody replied.

"Yes, I am glad mine were spared as well. How did the goblins treat you all?" I asked.

"I think we were the lucky ones." Melody said with sadness in her voice.

"How so?"

"I was with a friend of mine, Marsha, but we were separated. I saw her captured by the Bone goblins and I was captured shortly after by the Sleeping Willow. I overheard the goblins in the camp talking about how those bone guys like to eat their prisoners." Melody shuttered.

"Yea Gr'ex was telling me they are quite cruel, but we will be dealing with them soon enough. We will get justice for your friend." I replied.

"You are not what I expected when I first saw you coming out of that hut. I have never in my life felt something so terrifying and awe inspiring at the same time." Melody shuttered again.

"Sorry about that. It's a part of who I am now. I do my best to have it clamped down tight but sometimes I let up as it seems to have an interesting effect on Dark aligned creatures. I do apologize that you were caught up in that ma'am." I said sincerely.

"Please it's Melody, none of this ma'am stuff." Melody looked over at Alice sleeping so peacefully in my arms. "I'm serious though you are so good with her and patient with the rest of us. Nina was a pain so good riddance there. I can't tell you how many times I wanted to slap the woman for her comments."

"Being a dad was one of the greatest journeys of my life. Besides, at my core I believe in being the true definition of meek, sheathed sword you use only when you must. To the world you stand as an immovable barrier to protect others, but on the other side of that barrier, where your family is, you are patient and guiding. They get to see the softer side of you that you don't show to anyone else." I said as I recalled my Nanuz's words of wisdom that I tried to live by.

"Definitely not what I expected." Melody commented.

I changed the subject. "How long have you lived in the area?"

"I was a schoolteacher for many years in town. I loved this place and had zero interest in leaving it. The place has a small town feel yet had a decently sized population." Melody answered.

"Did you know Paul?" I asked.

"Of course. He was a crazy one. My husband and I took his money. Made our retirement all the sweeter. That is until my husband died of prostate cancer two years ago. Been angry at God ever since. I mean we just get that windfall of money so we can truly enjoy our retirement and my Daniel gets sick and leaves me." Melody said with a clear mix of sadness and anger in her voice.

'Man, this lady is a mess.' I thought before replying. "We don't know what time we have left. That is why it is best to make the best of the time you have while you have it. Those words may not help but you are here now, and it is best to make what you can of it. My understanding is as you level and put points into your **Constitution** stat it can extend your lifespan. Something to consider if we all get through this."

Melody seemed surprised. "Really? I haven't really messed with the blue boxes that have popped up from time to time. My grandsons were avid gamers. I tried to learn their lingo, but I only got so far."

"Yes. There is always some good even in the bad. My Nanuz, my grandfather, used to say that all the time and he was right." I quoted.

"Hmmm, I'll keep that in mind. Oh, back to Paul. Why did you ask about him?" Melody asked.

"He left me everything. I was staying at the compound when everything went down." I stated.

"Ha! That technically means you own this whole area. Who knew Paul would turn out to be right. Well, that means we are on your land, and I will help however I can." Melody seemed to have shifted to be in an upbeat mood.

"I appreciate that. We should almost be to the compound." As I spoke a goblin with a spear came running up. He dropped to his knees and practically slammed his head into the ground in supplication.

"Oh, great and terrifying one. Your humble servant brings you news."

I groaned. "Ughh. Get up. Get up. I'm not going to yell. Don't make me wake the child."

The goblin hesitantly rose to his feet, but he still had his head down. Gr'ex just smirked. He had been quietly listening to my conversation with Melody. Most of the goblins would come to him out of fear of bothering me. For this one to come to me directly meant something was up.

"Speak before you displease our master." Gr'ex chided the goblin.

"My apologies great Gr'ex. We have arrived at a structure but there are huemons inside that seem very upset. They took what we believe was a warning shot at us. We were unsure what to do. Some of us wanted to storm the place and unleash vengeance for daring to hinder your orders. Others wanted to get orders. We decided it was best to tell you directly so as to not anger you. I drew the short stick."

Gr'ex spoke up. "You made the right choice. What's your name soldier?"

The goblin winced. "My name is Goob'reks, but everyone calls me Goob."

"You've got to be kidding me. Lead the way Goober. He, he, he." I chuckled.

Melody and some of the other humans around giggled.

When I saw his confused look, I changed tactics. "Lead the way. Gr'ex, tell our people to not advance and that I will handle this."

I could tell the little goblin loved being able to boss people around and the grin on his face after I gave him the order only further proved it.

As I approached the cabin turned compound, I heard shouting.

"You green-skinned bastards take one more step and I'll fill ya full of holes! You are lucky Suzie-cue was on duty and gave you a warning shot. I wouldn't have!" Jebediah yelled.

"Calm down Jeb, they are with me!" I yelled out.

Surprisingly with all this commotion, Alice still slept peacefully in my arms.

"Shadow? Is that you? What are you doing with a bunch of green skins?" Jebediah asked when he saw my figure come out of the bushes and into the clearing.

"Gr'ex and I were able to convince the Sleeping Willow clan to join us against the Bone Marrow clan. Now open the door. We have other people that we rescued. They have been walking for the last several hours." I replied as I kept walking forward.

I heard Suzie speak up. "Is that a little girl in your arms?!"

"Yes. Her name is Alice, and she is one of the people we rescued. Now can you please open up. I'd use my keys, but my arms are a bit full."

"Fine! But I don't like it!" Jebediah grumbled out.

"Hold on." Suzie said as I heard her move and a few seconds later undid the latch and opened the front door.

First words out of Suzie's mouth, "How cute you two look. Awe she's holding a little dolly! Can I hold her?"

"Sure, take her up to my room. She can sleep there, and I can take the couch until we can figure out arrangements for her." I replied as I slowly moved her into Suzie's arms.

All the shouting and noise she didn't wake up at all. The moment I put her into Suzie's arms Alice started to stir. "Huh?"

"Go back to sleep little one. Suzie is going to take you to my room so you can finish your nap, okay." I said softly.

"Okay daddy." Alice said sleepily.

"Daddy?" Suzie teased.

I did my own grumbling. "Don't start. She wants me to be her new father. Whatever trauma she has been through, and I think with everything that is going on, I can keep an eye out for her."

I wasn't going to deny a child a feeling of security. If that is what she needed from me then I'd look out for her. She seemed like a sweet girl and for some reason I really liked her. 'Maybe it's the fact she reminds me of my daughter. Doesn't really matter either way. A man protects children, period.' I thought before turning my attention to Jebediah as Suzie headed upstairs.

"Let's get people set up downstairs in the bunks. There is enough food for them, and the first level is relatively secure." I instructed.

"Sounds like a plan." Jebediah answered.

"Where is Donut?" I asked as I did not see him anywhere.

"He's still at it with the radio. He has refused to leave since we made contact. I was just about to go down to check on him when I heard Suzie fire her rifle..." Jebediah explained.

Gr'ex walked up with a few goblins not far behind him. This stopped Jebediah mid-explanation. "Gr'ex? That you? Man, that disguise looks so real. I almost didn't recognize you."

"It's not a disguise, you old crazy fool. You are finally seeing how good looking I am." Gr'ex stated.

Jebediah looked at the goblin then back to me as a few things clicked and now made more sense.

I spoke up just to make sure the old hothead didn't do something stupid. "How else do you think he knew so much about the goblins and the system."

"You knew!" Jebediah said it more as a statement than a question.

"Of course. I defeated him and bound him to my service as I needed answers, and he has been a great source of info. Not to mention he knows the Sleeping Willow clan's chief Jek'jon."

"But he's a green skin?!" Jebediah said in confusion.

"Most goblins don't have much of a choice. We tend to be fodder for some tyrant or dark ruler." Gr'ex explained.

I spoke up. "It's not like you guys are all that innocent."

"Never said we were. I enjoy a good pillaging just like the next guy. The point is our culture has evolved around us being someone's minions. Some of us are a bit more blood thirsty than the rest of us, like the Bone Marrow clan." Gr'ex stated.

Turning my attention back to Jebediah. "As you can see these goblins aren't exactly fans of the other clan of goblins. Plus, they all have given me their oath of fealty and that can't exactly be broken that easily."

"What about whomever they were working for before? Didn't they have an oath of fealty with them?" Jebediah asked, clearly not completely convinced.

Gr'ex answered. "No Kit'erak would never bother with gaining our fealty. He just scared and threatened us into action. Fealty requires acknowledgement on both sides. It's an oath of service and loyalty. In a way that is true for both sides as our liege must do what they can to protect us too. Most would never bother to consider goblins as worthy of such an oath."

"Hmmm. Alright. I'll accept that... for now. Let's get these people settled down below and we can talk further." Jebediah answered before heading outside.

"Come on everyone! We have cots to sleep on and food down below. Wait is that, Melody?"

"Of course, it's me you old coot! Now help a lady up the porch, my legs are killing me from all that walking." Melody chided.

"Yes ma'am!" Jebediah replied as I saw him offer his arm to the old schoolteacher.

"We should talk." Gr'ex said as I watched the two elders chitchat amongst themselves as they walked to the elevator.

"What's up? Are you not having enough fun being my intermediary and bossing the goblins around?" I replied.

"No, that's lots of fun. Thank you for letting me do that." Gr'ex said.

"Oh, please you stepped right into that role without me even asking." I commented.

"True. Being the goblin with you the longest and how you treat me, they naturally came to me first. It's a goblin thing. You try not talk to the big scary boss unless you absolutely have to. They tend to be a bit unpredictable." Gr'ex explained.

"I can imagine. So, what was it that you wanted to talk to me about?" I asked.

"Many may see us as cowards, but I like to say we have a strong survival instinct." Gr'ex commented.

"Uh huh, sure. So, what's up?" I replied.

"Even though they are scared of you, several have asked to remain by your side, to be at your beckon call." Gr'ex stated.

"I would expect you to like that idea. More goblins to boss around." I teased.

"Of course, that is a given. No, my concern is the other huemons. They are still struggling to embrace this new reality as you have." Gr'ex answered.

"I'll do what I can with them. You do what you love and keep the other goblins in line." I stated.

A wicked grin spread over Gr'ex's face. "Within reason my crazy power-hungry goblin. We are changing things and will eventually be building a community. Be mindful of that when others are around."

"Fine." Gr'ex replied before heading off to find someone to give orders to.

I had to admit to myself that Gr'ex did a great job directing the goblins and in turn guiding the humans inside. The goblins that would pass by me would bow low and some would bow multiple times before they passed. I just internally groaned as I saw Gr'ex smirking.

Then I recognized one of the goblins. "Goober! Come here a moment."

The poor goblin practically jumped as he rushed forward. "M-me?" Goob'reks stuttered out.

"Yes you. Gr'ex is busy and I know you." I replied.

Goob'reks whispered to himself, "why did I have to draw the short stick?"

"Short stick indeed." I replied, letting him know I had heard him.

The look on Goob'reks' face was priceless. He didn't know whether to run or beg for his life. I let him sweat it out only for a moment. "Relax Goob. I may expect you to follow my orders, but I do not punish or harm my people without cause or good reason. You will find I am not like the leaders you are used to."

Goob'reks gave me a nod. "Thank you oh great and scary master."

"Are you any good at observation while not being seen?" I asked.

Goob'reks nodded his head again. "Oh yes Goob'reks is very used to not being seen or observed. Sometimes people just walk over Goob'reks as they do not seem to see me. It is a very sad life, but I make the best of it."

"Okay Zathras. You wouldn't happen to have any brothers with the same name?" I randomly teased as I noticed the similarities.

Goob'reks nodded along once again. "Oh yes. Goob'reks has several brothers and sisters. All named Goob'reks. My parents were not very smart. We had to fend for ourselves very early on. Again, very sad life."

My mouth fell open in shock. 'This guy has got to be messing with me.'

Then I heard Gr'ex on the floor holding his sides laughing. "Ha, ha, ha, ha! You should see the look on your face! I told Goob to tell you that story. After you told me all about that show you loved how could I not?! Ha, ha, ha, ha!"

I looked between the two goblins. Goob'reks was ringing his hands worried. I then used Gravity Momentum Manipulation to lift Gr'ex up and fling him into the bushes. I heard him laughing the entire time. Looking down at Goob'reks, "Is what he said true? Did you just make up that entire story?"

Goob'reks dropped to his knees. "N-not all of it."

I gave the goblin a hard stare. "Explain."

"A-All of it true except the part about my brothers and sisters. I have no brothers and all my sisters are dead. They were all eaten by Orcs. Gr'ex said I should say that part to make you laugh." Goob'reks stuttered out.

I couldn't help it. I wasn't truly angry. It was a good prank. I started laughing. "Ha, ha, ha, ha. It was a similar story I can see why Gr'ex put you up to it."

Gr'ex came walking out of the bushes still chuckling. "He, he, he, he. See Gr'ex is hilarious!"

I force laughed loud. "Ha... ha... ha!" At the end I used my ability to slam Gr'ex up against a tree. "That's what you get for messing with me you crazy bastard."

Turning to glare at Goob'reks who was still on his knees scared. I clapped the little goblin on the shoulder. "Don't worry I won't punish you for Gr'ex's little prank. It's not your fault you have a very sad life."

Goob'reks agreed. "Very sad."

I chuckled again. "He, he, he. I can see how Gr'ex came up with the idea just by talking to you. Anyway, I have a job for you."

"Job? Goob'reks serves. What can Goob'reks do for great and scary one?"

"Keep an eye on the other humans. Be discreet. It is clear they are struggling. That may be all it is and in time they will adapt just fine. Just in case it isn't I want to know." I explained.

Goob'reks bowed. "Goob'reks hears. Goob'reks obeys. My **Stealth** skill is very high. Master won't be disappointed."

After he finished the little goblin took off.

Gr'ex came up brushing leaves and dirt off his robes. "That was a good choice. Jek'jon told me the goblin has the makings of a good Shadow."

That sounded like a title or class, so I asked my question. "Shadow?"

"It is a class. Goblin Shadow. It is an advanced option off the rogue class which is what he is now." Gr'ex explained.

Interest peaked I followed up. "What is so special about a Shadow class?"

Gr'ex explained further. "Goblin Shadows as the name implies can use Shadow magic. They make the perfect spies and assassins if needed. They can partially do what your Death Shroud spell allows which is move into the Shadow Realm. The boy doesn't have the demeanor to be an assassin but he does have an affinity to Shadow magic so there is a chance. We goblins make good scouts and spies, since so many dismiss our race as insignificant."

"Speaking about spying. We should ask Jek'jon to have some of his men keep an eye on the town. It would be good to get actual counts and know how many humans they still have imprisoned." I stated.

"Easy enough. Most of that was already planned, minus the tally of how many huemons are left. I'll get it done." Gr'ex answered.

"I was going to go check on how things are going down below and check in with Donut. You should probably come with as I'm not sure Suzie noticed you in your true form." I commented.

"Fine. Give me a few minutes before you head down there." Gr'ex before walking towards a group of goblins.

As I was waiting for Gr'ex I noticed Suzie coming back downstairs. "How is she?" I asked.

"She went back to sleep easily enough. It was clear she was tired. I'm guessing she didn't sleep much." Suzie replied.

"Sad a child has to go through so much." I commented.

"Very much so. What are you doing just standing here?" Suzie asked.

I pointed to my friend. "Waiting for Gr'ex over there."

Suzie looked over then did a double take. "Wait is he really a goblin?"

"Yes. Sorry for not telling you but we weren't sure how you would take all of this." I replied.

"It was probably for the best. When we first got here, I'm pretty sure I would've shot him. Now, however, he's kind of grown on me. Plus, seeing all these goblins taking orders and helping people get to safety... it's clear some goblins are good guys." Suzie stated.

"Well said. Let's hope Donut agrees." I commented.

"The big guy is the first to give others a chance. He's going to love Alice by the way. He had a younger sister about Alice's age that had drowned. Duncan was the one to find her." Suzie shared.

"Oh geez. My son almost drowned. In fact, he did drown, but his mother knew CPR and brought him back. One of the most traumatic moments of my life getting that call at work." I replied.

Suzie looked at me for a moment with clear sympathy in her eyes. "You know in some ways it's easy to forget we all had lives before this. Heck, I ran home because I found my boyfriend in bed with my friend from Los Angeles."

"People can really suck." I commented then a thought struck me. "You know... if you had been in LA at the time of the event you might never have made it out alive. You might be all 'uhhhh' right now." As I made the zombie sounds, I imitated a zombie stumbling around with a lopsided grin on my face.

Suzie started to laugh. "Ha, ha, ha, ha, ha! You look completely ridiculous, ha, ha, ha! Ahhh... thank you for that. I forgot the last time I laughed so hard. He, he, he."

"Not a problem. We all need a good laugh every now and then. Gr'ex might be a selfish jerk at times, but he makes me laugh, and I am grateful for that, but don't tell him that. We wouldn't want to encourage him. He, he, he, he." I chuckled.

"Speaking of him, here he comes..." Suzie said as the little goblin approached us. She then greeted him with acceptance. "Hello Gr'ex. You know I think you look better as a goblin."

Gr'ex beamed before looking at me. "Told you! Best looking goblin here."

I just rolled my eyes. "Insufferable. Alright Adonis, let's see how everything is doing downstairs."

———-

As we rounded the corner into the Communications room, we heard Duncan excitedly say, "hold on a sec! Let me go get them!" Duncan practically bowled us over.

"Oh! Sorry guys! I heard you were back Shadowalker, and your friend is on the radio!" Duncan exclaimed.

"Lead the way big guy." I replied with a smile.

"I'm back Mrs. Burns. I have Shadowalker with me. Go ahead." Duncan said to the mic before getting out of the seat for me. "It's already set to on, you just got to talk, and they will hear you."

I could hear an older woman reply as I sat down. "Okay give me a minute dearie. Mr. Laraaq is right here."

A few moments later I could hear my best friend's voice over the radio. "Uh, hello? This is Laraaq. Am I doing this right Carol?"

"Yes, they can hear you just fine dearie." I heard Carol reply.

I spoke up, a smile on my face. "It's good to hear your voice brother. You went with Laraaq huh?"

I could hear the joy on the other end too. "It made sense. I almost went with another handle but figured you would know this one well enough. Shadowalker huh? I figured you would go with one of your other gamer handles."

I chuckled. "Ha! I almost did. I figured the apocalypse warranted walking through shadows so why not. How are you holding up?"

Laraaq chuckled. "Ha, as good as can be expected. It's been a crazy ride. Learned Fire magic so of course I had to learn at the very least a minor version of 'Fireball'. Been using it to kill a bunch of undead and a few mutated coyotes."

"That's freaking awesome that you know 'Fireball' you so will have to teach me." I replied happy for my best friend.

"Of course. How are you holding up?" Laraaq asked.

"Eh, doing good. We just turned one of the two goblin tribes to our side." I replied before I heard Gr'ex in the background chime in, "Clan!"

My buddy proved one of the many reasons why he was my friend. "What's the difference?"

"That's what I said. That was Gr'ex. He's a pain in the butt but he's been a great help navigating this new reality. Anyway, we have rescued over a hundred people so far. How are you doing on your end?" I asked.

"With the different squads we've sent out... so far, I'd say about 130 people. We were going to stick around a few days to help save several more. It sounded like you would be okay with holding out that long. I read that right brother?" Laraaq replied.

"Yea, you read that right. Especially with gaining the Sleeping Willow clan, we should be good. Save as many people as you can. We will need them if we plan to rebuild a community here. Oh related side note... apparently I own the whole town and all the surrounding forest and territory curtesy of Paul." I explained.

"Sweet! That will make things easier. Orders received my friend. I'll save as many as I can. By our calculations we should be there in about five days." Laraaq stated.

I shared my high-level plan. "Cutting it close but still should work out. We are going to start giving the remaining goblin tribe some trouble. Won't go all out for a few days. I want to give our allies time to move their clan here. If you guys can come in guns blazing from the southwest in five days, we can attack in a classic pincer move. That will leave Jek'jon and the other Sleeping Willow clan members to be our surprise to spring on the Bone Marrow clan when the time is right."

"That gives us a timeframe to work with. Hopefully we will find more fighters to join our ranks in the process. I have met some capable people who will be more than happy to help fight for a new home. It was good to hear from you and know you are okay brother." Laraaq replied.

"You too brother. It helps reduce my levels of concern. See you in five days." I answered.

I was excited with a strong sense of relief. I finally talked with my best friend and knew he was okay, I felt I could now focus on getting ready for our uninvited guests. I turned to my makeshift party. "Alright everyone. It's time we started leveling. We also need to work on shoring up everyone's cultivation foundation."

Chapter 17 – A Hunting, We Will Go

Laraaq woke up feeling well rested and excited for the day. Last night he was able to talk to Shadowalker and make sure he was okay. Sure, it wasn't as long a conversation as he would've liked but it checked the boxes as far as he was concerned. His friend was good. They had a high-level plan. Finally, he felt like he could get more involved in the rescue operations.

"Good morning, Carol." Laraaq said as he walked over to the coffee maker.

"Mmmm. That's good coffee!" Laraaq had to admit Carol made one hell of a cup of coffee.

Carol smiled. "Someone is in a good mood this morning."

"That I am. I am planning on helping the rescue ops over the next couple days." Laraaq replied.

"Yes, my son mentioned something about that. He said you were going with him." Carol shared.

"Yep. Excited to see how many people we can save and how many monsters we can slay. Let me know if you get wind of anything interesting. I'll have my two-way radio just in case." Laraaq explained before heading outside.

He knew from experience the last few days that Carl was an early riser. Sure, enough Laraaq found Carl with a squad of men near a bus. "Morning Carl."

"Morning Sir." Carl replied.

"Laraaq. Please drop the sir. I'm no fancy knight."

"Just a sign of respect Mr. Laraaq." Carl stated.

"Well as long as you follow orders, I don't care what you call me as long as it's not Shirley." Laraaq deadpanned.

The two of the three men just stared at Laraaq confused. Carl chuckled. "He, he, he! Nice Airplane movie reference. Let me introduce you to the squad."

Carl pointed to the tall gangly man who couldn't be more than 20. "This here is Jerome. Ex-army. Decent shooter."

Laraaq shook the man's hand. It was firm but not overly so. "Nice to meet you, Jerome."

"You too Mr. Laraaq. You tell us where to shoot and We will get it done." Jerome said it as a way of greeting.

Then Carl pointed to a shorter stalker man with tattoos on his arms. He looked like he had a hard life but was maybe mid-twenties by Laraaq's guess. "This is Mario. He used to be in the marines. Also, a decent shot. Good small blades skills."

Laraaq shook Mario's hand. It too was firm, but more strength applied but not over the top like Mack. "Nice to meet you, Mario."

"You too Laraaq. I wanted to say thank you for taking care of Tom. He was a menace." Mario replied in a thick accent.

Laraaq nodded. "Not a problem. I don't like people who take advantage of women and children or abuse their position. Where are we headed today?"

"A few locations. We are going to head to the farthest and work our way back. First up sounds like a family who have been trapped inside." Carl explained.

Laraaq decided to sit in the back of the bus and meditate while they drove. He knew he had to work on forming his core. As the group journeyed onward, Laraaq dived inward. Self-reflection meditation wasn't exactly his strong suit.

Since the apocalypse Laraaq was more of a man of action. To him, the apocalypse was a second chance at truly living rather than going through the motions like so many of us every day. Now he was asking his mind to shift, to slow down.

"This is infuriating! System any advice?"

You are lucky enough to have me.

Query Accepted

I can induce you into a meditative state and help your imagination but there is a cost. You must remain in that state for a minimum of three hours.

Laraaq opened his eyes. "Hey guys, how much longer?"

Carl called back to him. "I didn't expect you to be the 'are we there yet' type of guy."

Laraaq made a forced laugh. "Ha, ha! Cut the nonsense. I'm about to go into a deep meditative state that I won't be able to come out of for a few hours... so kinda need to know ETA."

Carl replied. "Got it. You should be fine. Our current ETA is just shy of four hours."

"Sounds good. Carl, watch my back. I'm trusting you." Laraaq stated.

"You got it, boss." Carl answered.

Laraaq's system brought up an image in his mind. It was a silhouette of a human body, of his body. He could see what looked like veins and arteries flowing through him. They would reach what looked like clusters and then continue on. Some clusters were larger than others, regardless of size, they all seemed to dim when he would look at them.

Mentally he asked. *"System what are those dim clusters?"*

Query Accepted

Those are your meridians; some call them your mana gates. They are key connection points that exist both in your spiritual and physical body. You must first form a core and gathering spiral before any attempts can be made to open your meridians.

'Interesting. It's similar to some of the cultivation fantasy stories I've read in the past. So, how do I form a core?' Laraaq thought to himself, yet his system answered him.

Query Accepted

You must gather the loose mana that flows through your system and condense it into a single place central to your body. Many gather it close to their heart to make it easier to open that meridian when the time comes.

"Wait, so I can technically form my core anywhere in my body?"

Of course, not all beings are bipedal or have a body shape as humans. They form their core where it most suits them. DUH! Do we need to do another brain scan?

"Well, that makes sense." Laraaq commented in his head as he studied the diagram of his body.

Of course, it does, I am explaining it to you.

Laraaq mentally sighed as he tried to ignore the system and focus. That was when he saw tiny motes of light randomly located in his body. They were haphazardly moving about, with some parts of his body more concentrated with the notes than other parts.

The other thing he noticed if he really focused was that the motes of light weren't uniform in color. Most seemed to be a mix of a neutral color and reddish orange, with a few deeper reds, browns, blacks, and blues thrown in.

Laraaq mentally talked out his observations. *"I can assume as I have been primarily using fire those are the reddish-orange motes. The neutral color must be the **Unaligned** mana. Hmmm, if that is the case perhaps the brown one is for **Earth** mana?"*

His system once again answered his question.

Query Accepted

*Correct. As you have been able to deduce on your own, the colors of the mote signify the type of mana. Neutral is **Unaligned** mana, typically the mana of the world itself. Some parts are saturated in a specific mana type. Your body can convert some but not all mana. Too much mana of a type you have no affinity can poison you to the point of death.*

"What about the other colors I see?" Laraaq asked.

I am getting there! Do not be so impatient!

Query Accepted

*Reddish-orange motes are **Fire** mana. Brown motes are **Earth** mana. Blue motes are **Water** and **Ice** mana depending on shade of blue. Black motes can either me **Dark** mana or **Death** mana depending on the shade. Finally, the deep red motes represent **Blood** Magic.*

"Blood magic? I have an affinity for Blood magic?" Laraaq asked in surprise.

Query Accepted

Correct. It is not a high affinity, but it is present.

"And what about the others?" Laraaq inquired.

Query Accepted

The dark motes are from the environment. There is much Death and Dark mana in the surrounding atmosphere. Lucky that you have affinities in these two magic types as well. You also have some minor affinity for Water, Ice, and Earth magics.

"What happens if I gather different mana types into my core? Will that change the core I have?"

Let's not get ahead of ourselves.

"System!"

Fine!

Query Accepted

The answer is yes and no. You do not possess a high enough concentration of any one type to affect your core. In time that will change as you begin refining the mana in your system. That is when your affinities will matter, and choices will need to be made.

"Long story short. It doesn't matter right now, but eventually it will."

Correct

"So, how do I gather them into one spot? They all just seem to be floating around." Laraaq inquired.

Query Accepted

You mentally will them to move and collect into one area. Once that is accomplished, you must visualize you mentally compressing them together and holding them there until the core takes shape.

"Do I have to gather all the motes inside me?" Laraaq asked in concern. He knew he would have a hard enough time doing what the system described. If he had to collect all the mana, he's not sure he could finish in time for the rescue mission.

Query Accepted

No. It is not required to collect all the motes of mana, just enough to apply enough mass and pressure to create your core.

"Got it. Well, no time like the present." Laraaq mentally commented before he put all him Mind towards his new task.

First thing Laraaq spent time on was mentally grabbing hold of one of the motes. He visualized a spectral hand grabbing the mote and attempting to move the tiny ball of energy. It was one of the Fire motes and it felt warm, almost hot, to the mental touch.

Laraaq doubled down as the heat seemed to rise and the warmth was becoming unbearable. Then he felt his spectral hand become more solid and the Fire mote began to move. He tried to move it directly to the center near his heart but found the mote would move very slow until he moved it near one of those arteries or veins he saw. Once it touched what he realized was a mana channel, the mote seemed to glide much quicker along to the center of his body. Progress would slow down again any time he tried to pass it through one of his dormant meridians.

Slowly but surely, Laraaq began to gather a mix of motes near the center of his torso by his heart. It was a loose collection of mostly neutral, some Fire and Earth motes as they seemed the most abundant and the most pliable.

Laraaq paused his efforts to ask the system a question. "System can you notify me when I have enough gathered to start my compression?"

Query Accepted

You have already reached that number.

"What?! Why didn't you tell me earlier?!"

Simple... You did not ask.

Rather than lose his concentration he just ignored the system and tried to visualize two spectral hands forming cups to scoop the motes together. Laraaq then willed both hands to begin to squeeze together. He pushed and pushed and almost felt like the motes were tiny magnets that would be repelled as they drew closer. Yet Laraaq refused to give up.

Sweat and pain from the strain was beginning to echo across his mental landscape. Laraaq was about to stop when suddenly, the resistance vanished, and his mental hands slammed shut into a cupped dome. When he dropped the spectral hands visual, he saw a small bright ball glowing where the hands met in the middle.

New notifications flooded his mental vision.

Congratulations! You have formed a magical core! Core is currently **Stage 1** *and* **Unaligned***.*

Congratulations! For creating a **magic core** *before level 13 you are granted an additional spell based on the types of mana motes used to form your core!*

Congratulations! For using a high concentration of Fire motes in forming your magic core you are granted the tier 2 Fire spell: **Flame Spear***!*

Spell: Flame Spear (Tier 2)
Description: *Manipulate Fire into any size spear of flames. Size and heat intensity dictate mana usage. Collateral splash and force damage is possible depending on mental control of flame spear and intensity of the heat.*

"Wow that is an awesome spell. Flexible too. For sure something to test out soon. I wonder if I could make it work like a flamethrower?" Laraaq mentally exclaimed before going back to his remaining notifications.

Congratulations! For using a moderate concentration of Earth motes in forming your magic core you are granted the tier 1 Earth spell: **Stone Skin***!*

Spell: Stone Skin (Tier 1)
Description: *Harden a part of the outside of your body to be as hard as stone. This greatly increases your defense rating in that part of your body. Adds resistance to damage from non-magical attacks and reduces the chance poisons and diseases take hold on that part of your body. This spell uses both mana and stamina. The amount of mana used dictates the area of the body covered and the amount of stamina used dictates Stone density.*

Congratulations! For forming a magic core prior to level 13 you are granted one additional level!

Level Up! *Congratulations! You have reached* **level 8***! +10 stats points per level.* **Total stat points to distribute: +10!**

Laraaq came out of his meditation mentally, physically, and somehow spiritually exhausted. He was sweating and every part of his body was sore, even the hairs on his head. "How does my hair hurt?! How is that even a thing?!"

"Oh, hey boss, you're awake. Meet Simon and Sharon." Carl introduced the two new people sitting on the bus. The guy looked to be in his mid-thirties and the girl was in her mid-forties.

Confused Laraaq asked, "How long was I out?"

"Five hours. We just finished rescuing the two and headed towards our next location when you woke up." Carl explained.

Sharon hotly spoke up. Disdain clearly in her voice. "You call that a rescue?! You killed my son! He was only seven!"

"What?!" Laraaq asked in shock.

Carl sighed. "Look lady. Your 'son' stabbed Simon and was coming after Jerome with a butcher's knife!"

"He only attacked Simon because he told him no. Simon is not his father and has no right to tell my sweet baby anything. His job is to provide and protect us, which clearly, he is failing at!" Sharon replied while looking down at Simon.

Laraaq noticed the large badge wrap on Simon's arm.

"New rule Carl, Jerome and Mario!" Laraaq spoke loudly to catch everyone's attention. When they all turned to him, he continued. "Any kid you find under the age of 15 you shoot to kill!"

Carl looked shocked. "S-sir?"

"You heard me. Ask your system what the age cut off is. Only kids with significant trauma or are completely void of strong morals will be left in the apocalypse! You did the right thing; it is clear Sharon is a horrible parent that didn't instill morals and boundaries or teach the kid anything of substance!"

Sharon looked offended and angry at the same time. Laraaq immediately summoned his new Flame Spear and pointed it right at Sharon. "You got a problem with that lady I can take you out right here and now and not bother wasting our food resources on you!"

Simon moved to put himself in between Sharon and Laraaq. "Please sir, she meant nothing by it. She is just in shock from the loss of her son."

Sharon's look of rage turned into a smirk, one Laraaq recognized. He canceled his spell and looked Simon right in the eyes. "She's playing you for a fool. Her kid was an evil narcissist, and that behavior is learned typically from the parents. This is the apocalypse, ditch her before she gets you killed!"

"Thank you, baby, for coming to my defense. I take back what I said. I'll reward you later." Sharon whispered to Simon.

Laraaq just turned away in disgust. He lost a man that was like a brother to a narcissist like this. A part of him wanted to kill the lady right here and now and throw the body out of the bus, but he knew he had to be better than that.

Turning back to his squad. "Strike that last order. Instead, we will sequester anyone under 15 until we can investigate which side, they are on, psycho or abused."

The three men seemed to relax, and all nodded in agreement. While Laraaq had been confronting the narcissistic woman all three men had confirmed with their system the truth of his words. They didn't like it, but it was another ugly truth about their new reality, and they knew one thing for sure, ignoring the truth gets you dead.

Laraaq took a moment to allocate his available stat points. This interaction showed him that as much as he hated the idea, increasing Charisma was going to be needed to deal with idiots like Sharon. Laraaq dumped 8 points into Charisma bring it up to 20 which should be peak levels for a normal human. The final 2 points he put into Strength as that was beginning to fall behind and he really was looking forward to hitting some people. 'Man, narcissists really piss me off!' Laraaq thought before he confirmed his choice and looked at his updated Character Sheet.

Name: Laraaq	Race: In Transition	Level: 8
Strength: 14	Dexterity: 20	Constitution: 20
Intelligence: 30	Wisdom: 26	Charisma:20
Spiritual Attunement: Unaligned	Core Stage: Stage 1 (Unaligned)	Spiral Stage: Not Formed

Health, Mana, Stamina Values & Regen Rates per hour (pH)					
HP: 110	HP/pH: 5	MP: 165	MP/pH: 78	SP: 280	SP/pH: 60
Titles: Ruthless Hunter, Early Adopter					

Chapter 18 — Rescue Rangers

Laraaq was pleased with his progress.

Laraaq was pleased with his progress so far. Today he took a giant step forward by forming his core before he gained a class. He had gained a level for the achievement, so he was happy about that. Even better, it had netted him some additional spells.

The Earth spell was the one Laraaq was most excited with. This would allow him a chance to grow his proficiency with Earth mana. Even better, the spell would finally provide some defensive options which were sorely lacking in his current build. If he hadn't distributed his stats more evenly, Laraaq would be a 'glass cannon'. Survivability rule for the Apocalypse, if you can't take a hit, you're dead. Firepower is great and all but is meaningless if you get one shot.

Shifting his focus externally, Laraaq asked, "What do we know about our next destination?"

Carl took his eyes off of scouting and looked back. His eyes seemed puzzled. "Did you get more handsome? The angles of your face seem more defined."

"I just leveled so put most of my stats into Charisma. Figured I'd need it if we have to talk to more people." Laraaq explained.

Carl just shrugged. "Makes sense. I'll keep that in mind. To answer your question, we are rescuing a family. The parents are in their late forties with a daughter in their mid-twenties. Mom said they seemed like a sweet couple with their heads on straight."

"I'd say that's high praise coming from Carol." Laraaq commented.

Carl relayed the intel he received. "You have no idea. Guess the dad is a mechanical engineer. The mom is an inventor and electrician. Their daughter is a civil engineer and artist. Guess the two of them came up with some cool gadgets that work with the mana in the atmosphere."

"Wow! Those three sound amazing. They sound like the perfect people to bring us magi-tech!" Laraaq said excitedly.

Sharon chimed in. "What is that?"

Simon answered seemingly as equally excited as Laraaq. "It is the combination of magic and technology. In theory to be able to do more with both than you could do with only one. I have listened to a lot of books about it..."

Sharon cut him off. "Okay no one wants to hear about your immature gaming and fantasy nonsense. Geez why couldn't I have found a real man."

Simon went from excited to sullen and withdrawn. "Sorry."

Carl and Laraaq both wanted to throttle the woman for how toxic she was being. Mario walked back to where Simon was sitting and quietly asked, "Can you tell me more about what you heard about magi-tech. I'd really like to know."

Simon seemed down and just replied, "No it was dumb, just childhood fantasies."

Mario put his hand on Simon's shoulder. "Man in case you haven't noticed we are kinda living in a fantasy now. Granted it's a bit on the darker side but still magic is clearly real. I bet all those people that were teased for their wild ideas and fantasies are going to be invaluable in this new world."

Simon seemed to consider Mario's words but one look at Sharon changed his mind. "No sorry. I got to man up and stop thinking about such things."

Mario shook his head. "Hombre, a woman can't tell a man how to be a man, just like a man can't tell a woman how to be a woman. Sure, we can have an opinion but don't let her limited mind stunt your growth."

Simon got defensive. "She has helped me grow a lot and encouraged me to step up and take more responsibility."

Mario glared at him. "Don't be a fool. That is classic narcissistic behavior. They do that so you will be of more use to them not because they know what's best or even really care about you."

"Don't listen to him baby. I know what's best. I haven't steered you wrong yet!" Sharon said as she gave dirty looks towards Mario.

Standing up, Mario walked back towards the front of the bus. He whispered to Carl, "She is going to get that man killed."

Carl just nodded before resuming his scouting out the windows.

Laraaq decided he would rather be upfront with the rest of his squad. The more he had to listen to their toxic dynamic the higher the chance someone, Sharon, was going to get a Fire Arrow to the face.

"So, any other intel on this situation?" Laraaq asked to get his mind focused.

Carl finished debriefing Laraaq. "Yes. They are dealing with a mix of Mutated Coyotes, Undead Zombies, and something they call the beast. The whole family claim to be good shots but the beast they mentioned wrecked their transportation. The thing seems to have a thick hide, as regular bullets just bounce off it."

"Sounds fun, not." Laraaq commented as they pulled into the suburb.

The squad spotted twenty undead as they turned into the cul-de-sac. "Well, that's not a small number of undead." Jerome commented.

"They came here to party but so did we." Mario said as he pumped his shotgun.

Carl grabbed the CB radio. "Let me call and let them know we are here for pick up."

After a few clicks they heard a girl's voice come over the radio. "This is Jennifer. I take it you're our ride. Over."

"That's right Jennifer. This is Carl. You spoke to my mom Carol. Are you guys ready to go? Over."

"Yes and no. Over." Jennifer replied.

Laraaq held his hand out for the radio. Carl nodded and handed it to him.

"Jennifer, this is Laraaq. I'm in charge of the rescue squad. We are going to need more than just a vague yes and no, the zombies seem to like your little cul-de-sac. Over."

"... Hold on I'm telling them..." It was clear she was talking to someone other than their squad. A few moments later she continued speaking to Laraaq. "Sorry about that. Mom wanted me to let you know we can't leave just yet. They are almost done with one of their prototypes. We have some equipment too that dad wanted to make sure we bring along too. Over."

"This isn't a…" Laraaq started to argue then he thought better of it. 'Man, that **Charisma** just might be helping after all.' He thought before replying. "Scratch that. We will start taking out the undead. We have to do that either way. That should give you some time to do what you gotta do so we can get out of here. Over."

"Roger that. Over." Jennifer replied.

Laraaq summoned a **Weak Flame Arrow**. "Alright guys. Let's light em up!"

"Allow me." Mario said as he opened the door and stepped out as he shot two zombies in quick succession.

"Hey, don't hog all the fun brother!" Jerome said as he too exited the bus and started taking out zombies with his rifle.

Carl turned to Laraaq and said, "We can't let them have all the fun." He joined the fray quickly after.

Laraaq looked at Simon. "Stay here. Keep your heads down and try not to make any noise. The zombies seem to be attracted to the vibrations.

As Laraaq stepped out of the bus he flanked Carl, covering his back.

"Looks like the initial twenty zombies were down to about ten…" Carl started to say before he saw Laraaq cast a **Minor Fireball**.

BOOM!

"Make that, six remaining zombies." Carl commented.

"Five." Jerome said as he blew the head off another zombie.

"Three!" Mario called out as he blew away two zombies close to each other.

Carl shot another zombie in the head. "Two."

Laraaq double cast his **Weak Flame Arrow**. This time it was easier, and he was rewarded with a notification.

Congratulations! Your core contains Fire mana. This has helped you connect with your fire spells and increase your mastery. You have gained the skill: Dual-Casting.

Skill: Dual-Casting

Description: Why cast one spell when you can cast two instead. Reduces the mental strain from maintaining two spell constructs at the same time. As this skill improves the increased mana cost required to dual cast will decrease over time.

"Finally!" Laraaq exclaimed as he used his two Weak Flame Arrow to take out the remaining two zombies.

Misunderstanding his words, Carl spoke up. "It didn't take us that long to take them out."

Laraaq shook his head. "No, I finally got the Dual-Casting skill. I have been trying to unlock that..."

Getting a sense of unease, Laraaq acted on instinct and tackled Carl to the ground.

Two giant shapes flew over them. One shape turned towards them. It was a **Mutated Desert Coyote**. The other coyote darted off toward Jerome.

"What the...!!!" Jerome said as he barely dodged out of the way. He didn't quite fully dodge the left paw and caught a gash to his shoulder.

"Son of a...!" Jerome began to curse but was cut short as he had to roll out of the way from a follow up attack from the coyote.

BAAM!

The head exploded spraying brain matter all over Jerome as Mario shot the coyote while its attention was on his squad mate.

Mario was out of ammo, so he drew a short sword that looked like a machete, waving it at two other coyotes that showed up.

Laraaq got a chance to see all of this before him and Carl had to focus on their targets. Another coyote joined the one that tried to pounce on them from behind.

So close to the coyotes Laraaq didn't dare use **Minor Fireball** so instead he cast his new spell **Flame Spear** and had the spear grow wide like a flamethrower.

The coyotes did what most animals instinctively know, 'fire bad' and you get as far away from it if you don't want to get burned, they tried to back up and run.

Sadly, for them the two coyotes were not fast enough and Laraaq released his **Flame Spear** in a rush of flames that caught both coyotes on fire.

YIP!

YIP!

The coyotes yipped and cried as they ran around not knowing what to do. This caught the attention of their packmates as they turned to see what happened. This too turned out to be a fatal mistake as Mario used the distraction to swing his machete to cut into the coyote's neck as Jerome killed the other one with his 9MM.

Carl used his rifle to put the two burning coyotes out of their misery.

"Hey I leveled!" Carl said excitedly.

"So did I!" Jerome exclaimed.

"Same here!" Mario chimed in.

The three men looked out at Laraaq expecting him to say something similar. He just looked back at them. "What?! I didn't level Okay." He said in irritation.

Carl headed towards the bus. "Well let me ring Jennifer and see if they are any closer to being ready to leave. Mario, why don't you look to Jerome's shoulders."

Jerome was holding his shoulder and wincing in pain, but he was still alert, demonstrating his resolve. "I can manage."

"Don't be an idiot brother. I can patch you up back in the bus with the first aid supplies." Mario chided the man as he cleaned off his machete and sheathed it before picking up his empty shotgun.

Laraaq did a quick circle of safety around the bus just to make sure there weren't any remaining enemies. By the time he was at the front door of the bus Mario had already dragged Jerome in and had the first aid kit out. Carl was in mid-conversation with Jennifer.

"Yea we heard all the commotion, sure hope that doesn't attract the big guy... Oh, Mom said she's almost done. Over."

"Sounds good..." Carl was interrupted when everyone heard a roar.

RRROOARRRR!!!

A giant honey badger plowed through someone's garage. Laraaq instinctually identified it.

Giant Mutated Honey Badger
Level 12
Description: Someone thought it would be a good idea to have a wild honey badger as a pet. When the apocalypse hit the concentration of mana mutated and corrupted him, increasing his size and ferocity.

Laraaq stared at the three meters tall, deformed honey badger. He turned to Carl who just said. "Good luck with that."

"What do you mean good luck with that?!" Laraaq asked in shock.

"Guns don't work on that thing. That kind of makes us not so useful." Mario said on behalf of Carl.

"I mean we are willing to try and distract it, but I wouldn't count on it doing much." Carl commented.

"You guys suck! Distract it if you see I need help." Laraaq said before turning his full attention on the honey badger.

The honey badger was sniffing in his direction. Laraaq, not trusting the bus to survive a direct hit from that thing, stepped away from his squad mates. That motion seemed to be all the monstrous honey badger needed as it started to charge.

Laraaq cast as quickly as he could two Minor Fireball spells, two **Flame Spears**, and he was about to cast more when the first set of spells detonated on the giant honey badger.

After the flames cleared the honey badger looked a little singed but no real damage, worst yet it was still charging straight at Laraaq not hindered in any way.

"Well, I'm screwed!" Laraaq commented as he was about to turn and run when the two **Flame Spears** hit.

The resulting blows left minor gashes on the honey badger's left front paw and right shoulder. Laraaq didn't have time to charge those spells, knowing the spells wounded the beast, he had one attack that could hurt the thing.

Seeing it get closer Laraaq cast Stone Skin as he dodged out of the way. As the honey badger barreled past him, the monster used its giant tail to smack Laraaq across the chest sending him rolling across the ground.

The honey badger's skin seemed to flow and shift directions. It somehow used that movement to transfer its momentum and change directions heading right where Laraaq lay on the ground.

"I COULD USE SOME HELP HERE!!!" Laraaq called out as he tried to regain his feet.

Rather than casting two **Flame Spears**, Laraaq channeled one and increased the heat before he had to release it and attempt to dodge once again.

His squad mates stepped off the bus and began firing. Carl and Mario were using rifles and Jerome was using a 9MM as his other arm was in a makeshift sling. They fired at the honey badger with impeccable accuracy and speed.

The gunfire did nothing to the monster and the beast completely ignored them. It had eyes only for the one that dared to challenge it, Laraaq.

The single **Flame Spear** hit the right paw as it was in mid-swipe at Laraaq. The blast saved Laraaq from being shredded as it blew the attack wide and severed a tendon.

"Ha! Take that you overgrown rodent!" Laraaq yelled as his spell put the limb out of commission.

The giant honey badger shifted its skin again changing its momentum allowing it to lunge towards Laraaq and clamp down with its jaws across his left shoulder and torso.

Once again Laraaq's magic saved his life. Laraaq had covered a good portion of his body using **Stone Skin**. The problem was, with all the running and fleeing, Laraaq's stamina was low so he could not make the Stone Skin as dense as he wanted, especially as the denser it was seemed to slow him down too much. This allowed the giant honey badger's teeth to pierce the stone. The spell still saved his life, but he was trapped in the jaws of the giant beast.

He could smell the stench of rotten flesh coming from its hot breath. "UGH! Eat a breath mint! You ugly..." was all the words Laraaq could get out before the badger shook its head further tearing gashes into his flesh.

Laraaq tried multiple times to form a Flame Spear but kept losing his concentration as he was shaken like a rag doll.

"Hey ugly! Try these on for size!" An unknown male's voice could be heard as the badger continued to shake him.

Then Laraaq heard explosions and the honey badger was knocked back.

BOOM!!!

BOOM!!!

The blows caused the honey badger to release Laraaq and he went flying into someone's yard.

"Ha, ha, ha, ha, ha! Looks like he didn't like that!" The male voice said.

An unknown female voice replied back. "Let's take this guy out together!"

BOOM!

"You got it honey. Let's give em the ole one-two punch!" The unknown male voice said.

As Laraaq lifted his head to see what was happening he saw a man and woman in a mechanical suit that looked like something out of a steampunk novel. It had giant arms and fists. It had some kind of arm cannons and the fists themselves seemed to crackle with energy. The two-man Magi-tech suit was being expertly piloted by the couple he assumed he was here to rescue. They were jumping around and practically boxing the giant honey badger then shooting something out of those arm cannons that were blowing literal holes into the giant monster.

His vision was soon blocked by a beautiful blond woman who ran to his side. "Don't move. You're badly injured. Let me heal you!" Laraaq recognized the voice as Jennifer.

A feeling of soothing warmth spread across his body. Laraaq's wounds began to close. He canceled his Stone Skin as the healing took effect.

"Ah. I see. You had some kind of defensive ability or spell. No wonder you aren't dead." Jennifer braced herself as she felt a wave of exhaustion hit her.

"Are you okay?" Laraaq asked in concern as he sat up.

"I'm fine. Just a bit tired. That much healing takes a lot out of me."

"Still pretty cool ability to be able to heal people." Laraaq commented.

They both turned to watch the couple in the magi-tech power suit finish off the honey badger.

Jennifer spoke up while she watched her parents. "I used my perk to gain a healing ability. It only made sense with my parents and their experiments. I lost count of the number of wounds I had to heal from one explosion or another. It was just prudent."

"Is that why there were so many enemies in this area? All the explosions attract them?" Laraaq asked.

Jennifer nodded. "Yea. The downside to their experiments, lots of noise. Before we knew it the neighborhood was overrun with monsters. Lucky for us, our house and their workshops were reinforced."

A notification popped up in Laraaq's vision when the monster died.

*Congratulations! You helped kill a Level 12 **Elite Giant Mutated Honey Badger**! Your help might have consisted of running away and being a chew toy, but hey, it counts! **+3,000 experience**.*

***Level Up!** Congratulations! You are now Level 9. You gain +10 stat points per level. You have **+10 total stat points** to distribute.*

*Congratulations! For rescuing three critical team members that will be crucial to the survival of your new community you gain the title: **Rescue Ranger**.*

Title: Rescue Ranger
Description: *Survivors are more likely to go with you or come to your aid. +25% success in favorable negotiations with survivors you helped rescue.*

+15% stats when conducting a rescue mission. One-time bonus of +1 level increase.

Level Up! *Congratulations! You are now Level 10! You gain +10 stat points per level. You have **+20 total stat points** to distribute.*

Standing up and dusting himself off. "I don't suppose you have some kind of mending option for damaged clothes?" Laraaq asked hopefully.

"Sorry I don't. Let me introduce you to my parents." Jennifer replied.

"Hey, I just met you. Don't you think you're going a little fast." Laraaq teased.

"Cute, but no. Good one though." Jennifer said before calling out to her parents.

They were using their power-suit to loot the corpse.

"Hey mom and dad, this is Laraaq, he is the leader of the rescue squad."

"Not sure who was rescuing who. Your power suit is awesome." Laraaq commented.

"We built it to deal with big guys like him." They said as the power suit pointed to the dead honey badger. "I'm Mike. That's my wife Marcia. You already met our daughter Jennifer."

"Nice to meet you all. I got to ask; how did you build the power-suit?" Laraaq asked excitedly.

"Facts we live by." Mike answered.

Jennifer smiled.

Laraaq looked confused. "Facts you live by?"

Marcia spoke up. "Fact 1: Realize you are on the same team. Fact 2: Tearing down your partner tears you down. Fact 3: Build and create together. Whatever you both help create will be far better than solo. We live our lives by those facts of life and relationships. Fact 4: If you both always put the other person first you both are always taken care of. Fact 5: Don't do something for someone expecting something in return. Do it cause you care and it's the right thing to do. That's real love. With all that in mind, it only made sense to combine our talents to create this baby."

Laraaq commented. "I got a guy in the bus named Simon who could really stand to get some facts and truth sent his way."

Mike laughed. "Ha! More than willing. We been happily married for twenty-six years!"

"That's my parents. God knows I love em, all their quirks and all." Jennifer stated as she smiled.

Mike chimed in. "We will grab our equipment and load it up. We have a giant moving truck we bought forever ago. The engine was torn up by the honey badger but now, we can pull it along using the suit."

Marcia spoke up. "That is if you don't mind us remaining in the suit and following you along."

"No problem I see. You want to ride with us on the bus Jennifer?"

"Sure. Sounds good to me. Let me grab my stuff."

Interlude- Tek'tar

"Terrible one. The ritual has been completed and the orb is powered." The apprentice necromancer reported.

Tek'tar looked down on the groveling apprentice. 'I am the only true necromancer sent to this backwater place. Why must I suffer these fools? At least they have some use.'

"Leave me. I must contact our master and I will not have trash like yourself bother him." Tek'tar stated.

"Shall I send for Jek'jon, terrible one?" The apprentice asked.

Tek'tar backhanded the goblin knocking him to the ground. "Do not presume to think! Your mind cannot handle the pressure! No, I alone will speak to our master. If Jek'jon is not here that is his problem. Now leave me!"

The apprentice scurried out of the town hall as fast as his legs would carry him. His mother had warned him to not dabble in necromancy, but he had thought he knew better. Now the apprentice wished he had listened.

Once Tek'tar was alone, he activated the communications orb. He assumed a position of supplication as his master's face appeared in the orb. "Greetings master. It is your most loyal servant Tek'tar."

"Where is Gr'ex and Jek'jon?" Kit'erak inquired.

"Jek'jon is too busy with patrols and fortifications, master."

Kit'erak's voice echoed in the hall. "TOO BUSY?! You dare presume..."

"No, no master. I would never presume. I merely relay his disrespectful words." Tek'tar quickly corrected.

"I will expect him next time you report, and I will deal with the insolence then. Now where is Gr'ex?!" Kit'erak replied.

"He and his squad are presumed dead, master. There has been no sign of him or his forces." Tek'tar reported.

"DEAD?! Did you investigate? Whatever killed them is a threat and must be destroyed!" Kit'erak ordered.

"We have secured the town as you have requested and then we were starting to scout..." Tek'tar began to explain before he was cut off by his master.

"YOU FOOL! What makes you think I care about some pathetic town?! I sent you there to secure the Master Leyline Nexus!"

Tek'tar was confused. "M-master? We have sensed no such power nearby."

"You are a fool! Do you not know anything?! The world you are on is reintegrating with the other realms. You haven't sensed it as the mana density is not high enough and the first phase of the integration is not complete!" Kit'erak explained.

"I have never been to an unintegrated world master. What do you mean?" Tek'tar asked.

"I'm surrounded by idiots!" Kit'erak exclaimed before sighing and continuing. "Ugh. I'll speak slowly so you can understand. When the first phase completes the hidden and dormant leylines will run all through this world. You at least know that when two leylines cross that is called a leyline node, correct?"

"Yes master." Tek'tar quickly replied.

"Places of power can be built or naturally form in such locations. You know this as well, right?!" Kit'erak asked.

"Yes master. I have seen your place of power. It must be the most wondrous of all." Tek'tar stated.

"Don't be a fool. My place of power is formidable, but it pales in comparison to what is there." Kit'erak replied.

"Master?" Tek'tar asked in confusion.

Kit'erak sighed again. "Ugh. That world will be contested with many forces. The more it reintegrates, the more forces we must contend with. Claiming nodes that have the chance to become a place of power are critical to gain a foothold in that world."

"I understand, master." Tek'tar said as he held his head high in pride.

Kit'erak fumed at his luck. Why did he send goblins there. His death knight will have to solve this matter once he is done laying waste to some place called Lost Angels. He had to negotiate with the Demon faction who already had a strong presence in some woods called Holly. He thought he recalled holly being poisonous so it would be fitting the demons were there.

Kit'erak shook his head. The Dark was not united, and it infuriated him having to placate factions he'd rather destroy, but that was his lot in life too. Even Kit'erak had a master.

Refocusing back on his idiot servant, he knew he had to tell him what was at stake. "No, you do not understand you moron! There are certain nodes that are considered a nexus and will be far more powerful than others. The continent you are on has over 10. Most of those had already been pledged to the Dark by those in power. One, however, was hidden more than the rest. That was until I discovered ancient texts from the time when the realms were connected."

"What was so special about this one, master?" Tek'tar asked.

"That planet is ripe with untapped potential. It has such high potential that it has more than one leyline nexus with the chance to connect to the Infinite Nexus. Do you understand what that means?!"

Tek'tar had only heard of the Infinite Nexus as a legend or story. A realm that sat between all other realms. A place that is connected to everywhere else. He voiced his thoughts. "Master, isn't the Infinite Nexus a fantasy story?"

Kit'erak's eyes glowed with rage. "NO, YOU UNEDUCATED MORON!... The Infinite Nexus is the greatest prize! With it you can break connections, shatter the veils between realms, and gain power to rival the old gods! If one can find a connected leyline nexus they can use it to follow the power to that sacred realm. Then you just have to crack the door just enough to slip in. The nexus you are near, I believe is one of those rarest of connections. That is why it was hidden and that is why you are there, not some crappy human town!"

"Oh... forgive my ignorance master. Had I been told..." Tek'tar began to say but was cut off once again by his master.

"Enough! Of course, you were not told. If the other factions of the Dark learn what I suspect you would all be dead already. I only tell you now because your bumbling and ignorance has jeopardized the mission! Gr'ex's portal was the one closest to the vicinity of where I believe the nexus will emerge. If he is dead, then whatever is there is a threat. One that you must destroy!"

"It shall be done, master." Tek'tar promised.

"It better. Now tell me, how many undead have you raised?" Kit'erak replied.

This time Tek'tar knew he could report good news. "We have raised over 500 undead. I have a ritual in progress that should finish within another day or two at the maximum. Once completed I will create a few Undead Abominations. I will use them to lay waste to whatever threatens your plans in the north!"

Kit'erak pondered for a moment before speaking. "Hmmm. That is surprisingly acceptable. How many human slaves do you have left?"

"We have captured over 600 huemons from the surrounding area. Of that, only a little under a 100 are left. Most turned undead or used to feed my men."

Kit'erak nodded. "Also, surprisingly acceptable. Keep the rest alive for now. See if you can find more. We will need as many as possible for blood sacrifices to open the way for me to enter that realm. Now focus on securing that nexus."

Tek'tar bowed. "Yes, master. It shall be done."

"I hope for your sake you are right. You do not want to find out what will happen to you should you fail me." Kit'erak said before the orb went dark and the connection was severed.

"So, a nexus is nearby. And by the sounds of it, one that shall be more powerful than most. If I could claim it and not just securing it for master... I might have enough power to rival my master. Then no one will ever dare to cross Tek'tar or think to disrespect me again! Ha, ha, ha, ha, ha!" Tek'tar laughed evilly as he thought of all the slights, he would pay back to Kit'erak and anyone else he wanted.

Chapter 19 – A Scouting, We Will Go

I woke up early as I did every morning. Last night after checking in on Alice to make sure she was okay; I came down to the third sub-level. There was a cot in the corner of the office. I imagine Paul put it down here in case the surface wasn't safe for some reason. As my bed upstairs was occupied with Alice, I didn't want to disturb her, so I came here.

The office was cozy for how big it was. The fact that no one else was allowed down here helped me get some much-needed rest last night. It wasn't that I was physically tired but rather mentally and emotionally drained. I had people depending on me and I would not shirk my duties. It was just nice to get some time to myself, even if it was for a few moments.

Deciding it was time to start my morning exercises I headed to the giant chamber that took up much of this floor. I first did some light stretches before running through some forms and katas I knew. Some were from past studies and others I had found in some older documents Paul had stored in the office. That guy sure collected a lot of random stuff.

After going through several forms, I shifted to my magic spells and abilities. Every fiber in my being called for me to master these wonders. I mean I could literally do magic. I have been dreaming about this practically all my life.

The power to directly influence the world around me and use my power to make it better for more than just me. This allowed me to further my goal of being meek. This required mastery of my gifts so when I needed them to help people I could.

I was focused on the nature of my magic when a wave hit me. The whole world shifted and when I finally focused, I was somewhere else.

"This is the town. How did I get here?" I said to myself.

There were hundreds of goblins and undead. They were milling about doing one job after the other. It was clear they couldn't see me. "So, am I having a vision? I must be." I told myself hoping my system would answer me back, but no response ever came.

I saw people in jail and other makeshift cages. There had to be about a hundred of them. They were all in various states of health. None were void of at least one mark or bruise. The goblins hadn't been kind.

That was when I came upon what I presume were their cooks. They had pots and various cooking pits. I could see animals and body parts that were clearly human on roasting pikes cooking over a fire. If I didn't have control over my stomach, I might've just lost its contents.

Then I felt drawn to these circles filled with dead bodies and a few undead inside. I could see the death magic swirling in the massive circles. Goblins were chanting and moving in complex patterns as the magic continued to move. One goblin stood out above the rest, literally. He was the tallest goblin I'd ever seen, at least head and shoulders taller than the rest. He wore loose-fitting black robes, but I could see the muscles underneath. This goblin was strong and powerful. He had a large scar across his face. He somehow had control of the magic flowing through and around the other goblins.

My focus changed from the brute of a goblin back to the magic circles. The undead began to merge with the flesh of the dead bodies contained within the circles. The new masses undulated and shifted about in the magic circles. They began to morph and take shape into a new form.

Standing in each of the magic circles stood a massive undead abomination. Each easily stood 4 meters tall. Some had two heads or an extra arm or leg sticking out of it. Some had other faces in their skin stretched in permanent horror. These were true monsters and they let out blood-curdling roars.

RAWRRWRRR!

"Yes! My new minions rise and bring utter destruction to my enemies!" The large goblin caster proclaimed.

Then I felt myself shifting again. Abruptly, I was back in my body on my hands and knees panting. I took a few moments to re-center myself and just breathe, concentrating hard not to throw up. I had dealt with episodes of vertigo for a good part of my adult life, which I believe now helped me regain control of my senses.

"Was that a vision of what is happening now or later?" I said to myself.

Query Accepted

You experienced a temporal anomalistic event. Not enough data to provide an answer. Time magic tends to operate on a different set of rules than most other magic types.

Well, that was good to know, but it still didn't answer my question. Deep down the only way I could get that answer was to go see the town with my own two eyes.

Stopping by the second floor to check in on the residents, I see Ann, one of the ladies in the cage with Alice.

"Good morning, Ann. You're up early."

"I was just about to say the same thing." Ann replied in greeting.

"How is everyone settling in?" I asked.

"Many are still shell shocked. Some stare at the walls. Others wake up screaming from nightmares. But all in all, most of us are doing much better now that we are out of those nasty cages." Ann explained.

"We help those we can, but there is no such thing as a free lunch. I expect everyone to contribute. If we can help those lost in despair we will, but in time I expect them to help too." I stated.

"That is a bit harsh don't you think?" Ann retorted.

"Not at all. Those of us left are a fraction of the population before. Many of those survivors are turned into undead or like yourself enslaved by others. If all of us do not contribute to fighting back the ever-creeping darkness, then we will all end up lost. I for one made a choice to help those that wanted help and would be letting them down if I ignore this issue." I gave in rebuttal.

Ann seems to ponder my words for a moment before signing. "Uh, I don't like it, but your point is well made. I'll keep you informed of those that seem lost and you can decide what to do, but that is the extent my conscience will allow. I was a nurse before the apocalypse, and gained a healing perk, I'll offer to help in that way. That suit you?"

"Most definitely. We will need healers. Please coordinate with Jebediah. He can be a bit crass and hot headed, but he means well." I replied as I patted the older woman on the shoulder before walking away.

I peeked in on the different living quarters. 'Man, all of this must've cost Paul a fortune.' I thought before my eyes picked up on one of the people Ann mentioned.

The young man just sat on a cot, staring at the wall. From what I could see on his face, it appeared to have a mix between a vacant stare and the look of being utterly lost. I'd seen something similar in my ex's face when our son had drowned. It's like your brain gets stuck, trapped between the trauma of the event and having any clue about how to proceed from that point forward.

My heart did go out to the young man, as it did with the other dozen or so I saw in a similar state. 'I'll give them some time. Right now, everything is so fresh and new. Hard to deal with the cold hard facts of how things really work when the infrastructure you depend on collapses.' I thought before heading up to the ground floor.

"It'd be great if we had someone who could heal the mind." I commented to Gr'ex as I saw him up already, sitting at the table in a pose that screamed 'feed me'.

"What was that? My stomach was growling too much to hear you." Gr'ex replied.

Shaking my head, I started to prepare some breakfast. "I said it would be nice to find someone with a gift for healing the mind. We have over a dozen people down below that seem lost in their trauma."

"Oh, that." Gr'ex just waved my explanation off with his hand.

"What do you mean 'oh that'?" Suzie asked as she overheard the conversation while walking into the kitchen.

Gr'ex turned back to her. "It happens on newly integrated worlds or large countries where many people live a different life in the city far away from the front lines. They don't understand how everything they were taught about entitlement or the rules on being a good person growing up don't work when the Dark comes for them."

"I could see that. Competence and working together are going to matter far more to our continued survival." Suzie commented.

"I agree there. I was just talking with Ann, one of the ladies we rescued yesterday. She is going to keep an eye on the people that seemed lost. I hate the idea of just tossing them out, but we can't afford to waste limited resources on dead weight. Man, I wish we had someone who could heal the mind." I said again, frustrated that I currently did not possess such an ability.

'Note to self: get a mind healing ability, spell, or skill.' I thought.

My system once again answered me.

Query Accepted

Notes have been added to your reminders and to do lists.

I mentally thanked my system.

Gr'ex chimed in after a moment. "You know, I could turn them into my undead minions. At least that way their dead weight would make a nice meat shield against me and any danger."

"Absolutely not!" Suzie quickly snapped back.

I raised an eyebrow at her and just stared as I cooked.

Gr'ex smiled at the display. "Though you are very capable for a Wood Elf... you are not the one in charge."

Suzie deflated. "You can't be seriously considering his proposal?!"

"Not at the moment no... buuutt, I will not outright dismiss anything. I appreciate the teamwork and you are very capable Suzie, but Gr'ex is right, you are not the one in charge here. Now in the future, I will most certainly delegate responsibilities, but in war, we must always have a clear chain of command. Make no mistake, we are at war for our survival."

"I do agree there. I will do my best to back your plays Shadowalker, but don't expect me to be silent if I disagree." Suzie sighed.

"I wouldn't have it any other way. Though I have final say, I required and welcome feedback and input. We are all stronger working together, but it is okay to talk through the issues and make counter proposals. That is how we end up with the highest chance of the best outcome." I replied.

That seemed to perk Suzie right up. "Sounds good. And that smells good. Is it almost ready? I'm starving."

"Oh, thank God you're cooking. Fix me a plate would you son." Jebediah said as his nose led him to the kitchen.

"That's an odd reaction." Suzie commented.

"Do you remember my friend Chuck?" Jebediah asked.

"You mean Mr. Cast-iron?" Suzie replied.

"That's not his actual last name. He used to be a cook in the army. The man could turn anything into a meal, with one caveat." Jebediah answered.

I was curious so I spoke up first. "What?"

"You rolled the dice on whether it'd clear out your digestive track. He always had a cast iron skillet and we stopped asking what was in it. We started calling him Cast-iron." Jebediah explained.

"Oh yea, he was the cook at the high school for a bit. I remember all the cheerleaders lost a lot of weight that year." Suzie chimed in.

Gr'ex looked at the two in horror before turning to me. "Please promise me I'll never have to eat his cooking!"

"Well now I know what to threaten you with." I teased.

"You wouldn't?!" Gr'ex said with concern.

"Be a good little goblin and you won't have to find out." I replied before asking Jebediah a question. "Why did you bring up Chuck?"

Jebediah answered between bites of eggs and bacon. "He is one of the ones you rescued and scared the literal crap out of him, his words."

"Oh yea, tell him sorry about that but Gr'ex and I had a bet to win." I replied has I high-fived Gr'ex.

Jebediah laughed. "Ha! Poetic justice to me. I can tell you how many times his cooking did that to me. Anyway, Chuck is cooking food for the survivors down below. He offered me breakfast, but I said I had to give you a status report. I noticed yesterday how you dumped the coordination of the survivors on me sunny-boy."

I looked at Gr'ex in confusion. "Weren't you coordinating them through the other goblins?"

Gr'ex kept eating. "That? I got bored so I just told Jebediah that you wanted him to do it."

"You little, green-skinned bastard! You're lucky it gave me an excuse to get out of eating Cast-Iron's food or we'd be having words." Jebediah said as he too cleaned his plate of any trace of food.

"Well, can we figure out an alternative cooking option than Chuck... one that doesn't involve me doing the job. I don't mind cooking for my party, but I have zero interest in that being my post-apocalypse career." I commented.

"Awe, but you do such a good job." Suzie teased.

"Don't make me cut you off with Gr'ex." I teased back.

"I've had Mr. Cast-Iron's cooking... the horror. I'll be good." Suzie smiled.

'I like that he dishes it back. You can't trust someone in a crisis if they can't handle some back-and-forth barbs.' Suzie thought as she considered Shadowalker.

"Now that you all have shoveled your food down. I wanted to talk about today. Gr'ex and I are going to do some scouting and investigate the town." I explained part of my plan for the day.

Jebediah spoke up first. "Seems risky my boy. You should take back up."

I waved his concern away. "Gr'ex and I can blend in, the rest of you can't. Besides I have some things I need you both to do."

"Like what?" Suzie asked.

Looking at Jebediah I say, "Jebediah, Gr'ex might've dumped the responsibility of organizing the survivors, but I ask that you keep it up." Turning to Suzie, "I'd like you to help him. Plus, I'm hoping you can work with Melody and Ann to keep an eye on Alice."

Jebediah grumbled. "Fine, but I might do some delegating of my own."

"I can do that. She's a little cutie. More than happy to help." Suzie replied.

"I'm fine if you two delegates. Just follow up and keep an eye out for issues. Try to get a gauge of what we have to work with. You know, things like skills, spells, abilities, and what they might be interested in doing."

"It'll take some time, but we can get the process started." Suzie answered.

"When we get back from scouting. I'd like our party to get together and go hunting." I explained the last part of my plan.

"Sounds fun. I've been itching to shoot something." Jebediah said as he pointed at Gr'ex. "Must be all these people I have to deal with."

Gr'ex smiles back at him, no shame in his voice at all. "Better you than me."

I decided to chime in on Gr'ex's lazy behalf. "Well, it is probably better a human work with them. I doubt they would like to take orders from a goblin after being in prisoned by them."

"Fair enough. Though I'm still going to figure a way of getting the little green skin back." Jebediah answered.

"Seems fair. Now let's get moving. As much as I want to check in on Alice. I'd rather get this scouting mission over with." I answered as I headed to grab a few guns.

———

I used the ring Gr'ex gave me to take on the visage of a goblin necromancer. We encountered few patrols north of town. It made no sense to me. "Gr'ex, why are there so few patrols north of town? You would think the Bone Marrow clan would leave the south to the Sleeping Willow and focus north."

"Ah. That's because you're not thinking like a goblin. Tek'tar won't trust Jek'jon. Their clans' dislike for each other is well known among goblins. Though my clan didn't care for the Bone Marrow meat heads either. Tek'tar will keep a contingent of his men south just in case Sleeping Willow betrays them."

"Well, that creates a problem for when the full assault comes." I said with concern.

Gr'ex shook his head. "Not really. Just because a goblin anticipates betrayal doesn't mean they are ready for it or that it still can't be used at the right time."

"Okay, I can see what you mean. But back to my point. I can see why there are less patrols, but this seems intentionally negligent on their part." I commented.

"You are not wrong. The only reason for it would be to guard something closer to town. Wait do you feel that?" Gr'ex spoke the last in concern.

A few seconds later I felt something. "It feels like when I use Death magic but off somehow."

"That's because you are also sensing Eldritch magic mixed in with the Death magic. I only know that because of the spell Kit'erak taught me twisted Dark and Death magic. Eldritch magic is from outside the inner realms. It can be very powerful but also tends to corrupt the wielder if one is not careful." Gr'ex explained quietly as we stalked towards the direction, we felt the large amount of mana coming from.

Crouching in the bushes, my mind reeled at the sight. My vision proved true. There were many goblins in the northern clearing in town. I counted five ritual circles straight out of some horror movie.

In each circle were dozens of corpses and undead zombies. Blood was everywhere and runic symbols were carved into the ground and wooden stakes positioned around each circle. The symbols looked wrong to my eyes for some reason. The barest of trickles of blood flowed from the goblins in armor as mana poured from the goblins in robes, both moving rhythmically through into the runes and then into both the zombies and dead bodies.

That is when I saw the goblin from my vision. He was rather large for a goblin, standing over one and a half meters tall. He wore a black robe without any sleeves, and it was clear the goblin was ripped with muscles all over.

I used my System to scan the goblin. I did not like what I saw.

Tek'tar (Goblin Chief)
Level 40
Class: Necromancer (Eldritch Corrupted)
Description: Chief of the Bone Marrow clan goblins. Reluctant servant to Kit'erak. Bone Marrow goblins territory borders Orc lands. This clan has adopted many of the Orc beliefs and tendencies to focus on physical attributes. Due to physical power being so prized among their clan, even magic casters will have several points in Strength. This goblin has dabbled both in demonic and Eldritch magics causing increased power but loss of all sense of morality. All previous beliefs have been corrupted beyond recognition.

"Why did I get so much info when I inspected Tek'tar?" I whispered to Gr'ex.

"Two reasons. You stared much longer, which gives your system more time to collect information. Second, he is considered the boss for your contested portal. The longer it remains open the more intel allowed for defenders" Gr'ex explained.

"What's with the corrupted status on his class?" I asked.

"It means everything he was as a necromancer has been corrupted. His spells etc. can be twisted or different. It also means he's going to be a pain to take down." Gr'ex further explained.

After a moment Gr'ex spoke up. "As scary as that guy is, those circles worry me more. That is a lot of power they are feeding them. They are using blood magic to slowly drain the life force while also supplying the ritual with large amounts of mana and materials. This is bad. My guess is they are making Undead Abominations."

"Giant deformed monstrosities, with extra limbs and body parts? About four meters tall? Super tough to kill?" I absentmindedly asked.

Gr'ex turned to me with a surprised look on his face. "Yes! How did you know that?"

"Educated guess." I replied.

Chapter 20 – Hard Choices

Laraaq just looked out the window and watched as a power suit about four meters tall was doing a light jog next to our bus as they towed a large moving van. The front of the van was shredded from an attack by the honey badger. According to Jennifer, the honey badger went after it when they had turned it on remotely. Luckily, it only shredded part of the motor, allowing them to easily put the moving van in neutral and drag it along like it didn't weigh several tons.

"How much can that thing pull?" Laraaq asked Jennifer.

She sat next to him. Jennifer and her parents wanted to beat the crap out of Sharon after meeting her and Simon for two seconds. After some choice words, Jennifer decided to sit next to Laraaq the rest of the trip back.

"From the tests, I'd say about 40 to 50 tons." Jennifer replied.

Laraaq whistled. "Damn! That's impressive. When can I get one?"

Jennifer laughed. "Nice try. You'd have to convince my parents and that's after they can re-establish their workshop and lab."

Laraaq had dreams of kicking monster butt with a power suit of his own. "I'm sure my buddy Shadowalker will be able to provide the right space, but he'll probably require a suit for the trouble. Just saying."

"Yea, I'm sure you're just saying. Well, I'm sure my parents will be willing if the lab is big enough." Jennifer replied.

"What will you need for your efforts?" Laraaq asked.

"Well, it depends. I can help with city planning. If I did that, I would need a drafting-desk and a big enough room for maps. If I help with the healing, we will need a clinic or hospital, which my parents and I can help design and build." Jennifer explained.

"Yea my buddy is going to be thrilled I found you guys." Laraaq chimed in.

Carl spoke up. "Hey guys. We are coming up on our next rescue location. Time to get locked and loaded."

Laraaq nodded to the man as he checked his 9MM sidearm. He left his rifle and shotgun with his truck. Carol promised she would keep an eye on everything, and Laraaq wanted to hone his spell casting.

Jennifer carried a rifle and a desert eagle as back up. Laraaq really liked her and her family's attitude. They were super easy to get along with, were willing to pitch in wherever, and as a bonus followed his instructions without any fuss.

The town they pulled into reminded Laraaq of a ghost town. They were in the desert so that combined with the lack of people might've had something to do with it.

"What do we know about the situation we are walking into?" Laraaq asked.

Carl gave the rundown. "Mom said it's a family of four. Two barely adult kids, one 16-year-old, and the mother. The boyfriend turned into a zombie and the two adult kids had to put him down."

Jerome picked up the CB radio. "This is Rescue Ranger squad. Anyone there? Over."

Static then a girl's voice could be heard. "Yea... this is Lisa... we are here..." Lisa was interrupted by another woman's voice. "Wh-what are you doing... you ungrateful child... hiccup."

The other woman's voice was slurred, and she was clearly intoxicated.

"I'm talking to the rescue team Natalie." Lisa's voice could be heard over the radio.

"I'm... your... your mother. Hiccup! You're lucky I let you stay... after you two killed my boyfriend." Natalie's drunk voice slurred her speech.

The chatter over the radio stopped.

"Sounds like she's drunk." Mario commented.

"My parents used to get that way. People do dumb stuff when drinking." Jerome chimed in."

"Agreed. We should be extra cautious until we get eyes on the situation ourselves." Carl instructed.

Laraaq nodded and turned to his squad including Jennifer. "Mario, you take point. Jerome, cover his back. Jennifer, you're with me. We may need healing if this goes bad. Carl, you take up the rear. Let's move out."

"Roger that." Jerome replied.

"You got it boss." Mario said in affirmation.

Jennifer nodded and checked her rifle. Carl did the same.

As they exited the bus. They signaled Jennifer's parents to remain and keep lookout just in case they required cover should they need to retreat. The power suit gave a thumbs up in acknowledgement and the squad moved in closer to their destination.

The run-down house was the only thing on the street for 500 meters. It wasn't hard to find. Though other houses were along the road. The one with the radio tower was probably the best bet as their destination.

Crouching low the squad moved together like they had done this countless times. Laraaq admired his team's efficiency and knew most of that was their previous military training. Carl also had a hand in their coordination, the man was an invaluable asset.

'So glad I didn't kill him. Between him and his mother, they have both been incredibly helpful.' Laraaq thought as the approached the back door.

They saw two zombies mewling about. Two quick shots from Jerome and Mario and both zombies were no more.

Mario checked the door. Jerome was on the opposite side of the doorway and gave his squad mate a nod. Finding the door locked, Mario kicked it open and moved to the side, he had zero interest in spooking those inside and accidentally getting shot.

Jerome did a quick scan of the room inside. Seeing no one Jerome and Mario took point and rushed into the house. Once in a better position they signaled an all clear and Laraaq and Jennifer entered with Carl watching everyone's flank.

Mario spotted movement. "What is all... hiccup... that racket! I swear I will beat you ungrateful kids again if you don't shut up!" A belligerent and clearly intoxicated woman stumbled into the room. She looked to be in her late forties, early fifties.

"Ma'am we are here to rescue you and your kids." Jerome said softly.

The woman swung the vodka bottle in her hand at Jerome's head. "Intruders! You won't get my alcohol! It's all mine!"

Mario used the butt of his shotgun to hit the woman in the back of the head.

THUD

CRASH

She dropped like a sack of potatoes. The bottle shattered as she fell.

"Sorry. I don't think I hit her too hard, but I had to do something. Drunk people do dumb stuff." Mario commented.

"You did the right thing." Laraaq agreed.

Just then a girl who looked to be in her mid-twenties walked in. The girl sported clear bruises on her face and arms. She immediately jumped back not expecting to see a room full of armed people. "AHHH!"

The squad patiently gave the girl a few seconds when they noticed she wasn't armed. She caught her breath after a moment. "Oh... man, you gave me an awful fright. You must be the people here to rescue us. I thought Natalie passed out again and broke another bottle."

The woman looked down at her unconscious mother. "She, okay? Oh, I'm sorry I'm Laura by the way."

Jennifer was kneeling next to Laura's mom using a skill that let her medically scan a person and her system would relay what was wrong. "She isn't dead."

Jennifer sighed and continued. "But your mom isn't doing good. She has severe alcohol poisoning. Her liver is in really bad shape, and she only has one functioning kidney. I'm not sure I can heal her. I don't exactly have a spell that purifies the body. I have a skill that lets me ensure a wound is clean but it's not the same thing as purifying the body to this extent."

One man who looked to be in his late teens, early twenties, walked into the room. "Hey sis, did mom pass out again?" The guy stopped dead in his tracks when he saw all the people. He too was sporting bruises over his face and body.

Seeming to take the scene all in stride, the guy spoke up. "I'm Bud. Nice shotgun."

"Thanks man. I'm Mario. That is Jerome, Laraaq, Jennifer our resident healer, and the one in the back is Carl." Mario replied.

Everyone nodded except Laraaq. He was pissed off and had half a mind to leave this woman. Laura's words brought Laraaq out of his musings.

"You're a healer?! Can you look at my younger brother?"

"Sure, show me the way." Jennifer said as she stood up and followed Laura into the other room.

Carl, ever the professional, dished out orders. "I'll stay here and keep an eye on this one. I'm going to bind her and turn her to her side. That way she can't hurt herself or choke on her own vomit. Mario and Jerome, why don't you two finish checking out the perimeter."

"You got it!" Mario and Jerome said as they checked the rest of the house.

"Go ahead and check on the kid. I know you want to. Bud will help me, won't you?" Carl commented.

"Sure, I can help. I have to carry her to her room all the time if she passes out somewhere in the house." Bud explained as he leaned down to help Carl.

Laraaq nodded before heading in the same direction as Laura and Jennifer. When the ladies entered the bedroom, Laraaq heard Jennifer gasp. "What happened to him?!"

Laraaq saw what shocked Jennifer a moment later. The older teenager was black and blue all over. He had a busted lip, and half his face was swollen so badly that there was no way the boy could open his eyes.

"My mom's boyfriend turned into a zombie. We don't know how. He just left to go score some meth from the bikers down the way. When he came back, he was different. He attacked my younger brother Jimmy."

Jennifer finished her medical scan. "So, that's how he ended up with multiple fractures, contusions, cracked ribs, swelling, two black eyes, a busted lip, and I lost count on the number of bruises."

"No. He only caused the one black eye, and my guess is the cracked ribs. My mom did most of that after we killed her boyfriend." Laura replied.

"What?!" Laraaq blurted out before Jennifer could.

"My mom did what she always does. She started drinking. She blamed my brother Jimmy for her boyfriend's death. She beat him. Bud and I had to break down the bedroom door. We got most of our bruises from her blind rage at, and I quote, 'killing the only person she ever truly loved'."

Laraaq was pissed but held it in as best he could.

Jennifer went to work healing Jimmy.

"Is my brother going to make it?" Laura asked.

"He... will live. I cannot heal all of this at once, but I healed the most severe issues." Jennifer exhaustedly replied.

Laura looked relieved. "Oh, thank God! I've tried to look after my brothers, but it hasn't been easy."

"Why didn't you take them and leave?" Laraaq asked.

"I almost did. Bud and I considered leaving with Jimmy once Natalie passed out. But then we heard from you guys and decided it would be safer staying put." Laura explained.

"That was probably the right call." Jennifer stated.

"I agree." Laraaq affirmed.

Jennifer then turned to Laraaq. "I'm not healing that evil woman. Even if I could heal her fully."

"I'm onboard with that too. I have half a mind to throw her to the zombies myself." Laraaq stated.

Mario and Jerome came into the bedroom at that time. "Ay, dios mío! What happened to the poor boy?!" Mario exclaimed.

"My mother happened." Laura replied.

"Permission to shoot the woman sir?" Jerome asked.

"Permission denied... for now. It's going to take Jennifer some time to heal Jimmy here to a point where we can move him. Go brief Carl on the situation." Laraaq ordered.

A few moments later Laraaq heard Carl exclaim, "She did what?!"

It took Jennifer over 5 hours to heal Jimmy to a point where he could be moved. She would use up all her mana to heal and then would have to wait for her mana to recharge before she repeated the process several more times.

Carl and Laraaq took the time to brief Jennifer's parents on the situation. No one was in the mood to talk to Sharon and Simon, so they were left in the dark on the bus.

Mario and Bud carefully carried out Jimmy. The boy hadn't woken up yet, but Jennifer said that was to be expected and advised he would most likely wake up on the return trip.

Everyone minus Natalie was outside the house discussing the next steps. They had a dilemma and Laraaq wanted Laura and Bud's input. "As you both know, Jennifer refuses to help your mom and I respect and back up her decision. The consensus of my team is to leave her here to her fate rather than just kill her outright. I know it's not an easy thing leaving family that is toxic, but we wanted to make the decision yours."

Bud didn't hesitate. "Leave her. Laura has been more our mom for years."

Laura hugged her brother. "Leave her."

"Alright. Do you have what you need?" Laraaq asked.

Laura and Bud both nodded.

"Good. You two go wait on the bus. Jerome and Mario keep them company. Carl and Jennifer with me." Laraaq ordered.

They entered the house. Natalie had woken up and was propped up on a couch sleeping. Jennifer slapped her awake, hard.

SLAP!

She turned to Laraaq and Carl who just looked back at her. "What?! We had to wake her up."

"We aren't complaining." Laraaq replied.

Natalie spoke up as she came to. "Owe! Why does my head hurt so much? Wait, why am I bound? Who are you people?! Don't hurt me!"

"It appears she's sobered up some." Jennifer observed.

"You may not remember us, but we came here to rescue you and your children." Laraaq began to explain.

"Where are those ungrateful little shits? How could they let you do this to me?"Natalie asked.

"As I was saying, that was the original plan. That is until we learned you are an alcoholic and beat your own kids." Laraaq continued.

"I don't know what you're talking about. My kids are prone to telling lies to get sympathy. They tell me stuff all the time, but there is no way any of it can be true. I'm a great mom. They are just ungrateful." Natalie said in rebuttal.

"You beat your own son to near death. Heck he would've died had we not arrived! You are a selfish person to wrapped up in yourself to realize you are a parent and have to care about more than just your own hurts and traumas!" Jennifer exclaimed.

"You know nothing about being a parent!" Natalie snapped back.

"I know enough to not beat my kids and put them through emotional head games because I'm too selfish to think about anyone but myself!" Jennifer retorted before turning to Laraaq and Carl. "I say we kill her!"

Carl raised his hands. "Now hold on. We talked about this."

"Carl, take Jennifer outside for some fresh air. I'll join you in a moment."

"Fine!" Jennifer said as she walked out of the house, Carl in tow.

"That woman is crazy!" Natalie commented once they left the room.

"Ha! You're one to talk lady. I happen to agree with her, but I'm not the one who was wronged by your actions, your children were. They are leaving with us. I'm going to remove your restraints." Laraaq stated as he summoned a Weak Flame Arrow.

Natalie's eyes widened and she froze stiff.

"Try anything and this goes right in your eye." Laraaq said as he leaned over and cut her bindings.

After her bindings were cut Laraaq backed up but kept his Weak Flame Arrow pointed in her direction. "You have a fighting chance at life now if you're willing to take it."

"Yea right! A fighting chance without my children. What kind of chance is that?" Natalie retorted.

"You aren't showing any real concern for your children. I bet you just want them to look after you. It's clear you care more about numbing your pain than living for more than just yourself. Don't bother trying to find us, not that you would try." Laraaq said the last part as he backed away from the woman, never taking his eyes off her until he left the room. He didn't deactivate his spell until he left the house.

"You kill her?" Jennifer asked.

Laraaq chuckled. "I like your thinking, Jennifer. I didn't kill her, but I came this close." Laraaq raised his index and forefinger showing hardly any space between the two digits.

After the intruders left her neighborhood, Natalie grabbed a bottle and a skillet. She made her way to her boyfriend's favorite hangout. His biker friends, who were also his dealers had all survived the apocalypse.

They were all hanging out at their compound. Everyone armed and laughing as they were drinking and making a ruckus. One rather large and buff man stepped out onto the porch. He had a shaved head, wore a sleeveless leather jacket but no shirt, so he could show off his muscles. He had guns and knives strapped to his sides. Everyone knew him as Titus, the leader of the Vipers.

"Is that Natalie? What are you doing here Natalie? Where's your beaux?"

"He's dead Titus. My kids killed him after he turned into a zombie."

"Damn! He must've been turned after he left our place the other night. Sorry to hear that, he was a good customer. Why are you here? You looking to score?" Titus asked.

"No, I came to ask for your help." Natalie replied.

"We don't run a charity! You know that!" Dom, Titus' right-hand man stated.

"I know that. This group of better-than-thou jerks came in and took my kids from me." Natalie said clearly upset.

"Damn! That ain't right taking a mother's kids from them. My mom was a good woman, dad bailed, but mom always bailed me out of jail. Not right for that to happen." Titus commented.

"I agree boss but what's that got to do with us?" Dom asked.

Natalie hadn't been as unconscious for as long as that group thought she was. She learned long ago to play like you're out and you can learn all sorts of things. Like one of them telling her son they were headed east towards some town they were going to build a community at. She knew exactly where they were heading.

"I looked out my windows when they left. They were towing a large moving truck and were meeting up with some others with resources at some town. I got to figure it would be a great score." Natalie knew how to appeal to men's selfish nature.

"That sounds promising boss." Dom chimed in.

"Sounds like a bonus. Maybe some new slaves. This place has been getting a bit stale anyway. The only problem is we are waiting to meet up with some of our boys up north. We can head out after they get here. I'm sure they'll want to join in the fun and mayhem too!" Titus explained.

"Looks like we are going to get to enjoy some mayhem boys!" Dom called back to the others.

Hooting and hollering was heard as were several gunshots into the air.

"Yay!"

BANG

"Oh yea!"

BANG

"Let's show those good for nothings what happens when you cross the Vipers!"

BANG

The loud noises attracted more zombies. Several could be seen shambling over in their direction.

"Oh goodie, more for the slaughter! Let's earn some more levels lads!" Titus cheered as he drew his weapons.

Chapter 21 – Magical Shenanigans

"Now what, buddy?" I asked Gr'ex.

"Now what? What do you mean, now what?" Gr'ex asked incredulously.

"Yea. You are the magic expert." I commented.

"Expert?! What part of 'apprentice' in my class title do you not understand?! I say we blow this place and find a new place to settle." Gr'ex replied.

"What about everyone we just saved and your fellow goblins?" I asked.

"Hey, I am not related to them, and even if I was, it would not matter. If I didn't have an oath with you, I would've already been running anywhere that wasn't here." Gr'ex exclaimed.

"Wait a minute. Why are we freaking out so much?" I asked for a minute.

"What do you mean? Do you see those things starting to form?!" Gr'ex replied.

My system once again answered my question.

Query Accepted

You are under a minor fear effect caused by the ritual being performed. As a side effect of the Eldritch magic being used, the ritual is generating a minor fear aura to make anyone not participating in the ritual want to run away rather than interfere.

Now that I knew what to look for, I mentally resisted by focusing on my intent to stop this from coming to pass. A moment later, my system let me know my efforts were a success.

You have resisted a minor fear aura. You are no longer frightened.

"Thanks System. Gr'ex, check your status. The ritual is giving off a minor fear aura. Focus on your will and you should be able to resist it." I explained.

Gr'ex had that far off look in his eyes like he was reading his status sheet. The panic on his face slowly fell away. "Ah, that is so much better. Thanks for the warning. Once I knew it was from the ritual, my mind was able to rationalize the effect was not completely real. Knowing what I do about

Undead Abominations, I still have a healthy fear of them, but they aren't made yet."

I patted the goblin on the shoulder. "Well now we have to figure out how to stop or at the very least delay those rituals."

"The fact that they are five ritual circles means they have to be drawing in more power from somewhere." Gr'ex commented.

"Um, you mean besides all these goblin warriors and casters?" I asked in surprise.

"Yes. Blood magic is strong, but Tek'tar isn't a blood mage and though he has Eldritch and probably demonic energy at his disposal, that is not the same as being a true blood mage. They have to be using some kind of magic item or artifact to act as a conduit. If we can find that and damage it, that would delay the ritual." Gr'ex further explained.

"Delay? Not stop?" I asked.

"That is the power of demonic and Eldritch magic, like Celestial, they can fill in the gaps or partially simulate a type of magic, some magic types better than others. If we find that magic item and damage it, their progress would dramatically slow down." Gr'ex stated.

"Slowed down by how much?"

"Right now, based on the rate of blood and mana being circulated, I would say these rituals should be done in a day at most. Take out the magic item and I would say the time to complete would slow to about three to four days." Gr'ex calculated.

"You sure about that?"

"Not exactly, maybe more, maybe less. Either way it would at least buy you two days minimum to come up with a plan to stop them and close the portal." Gr'ex replied.

"Fair enough. Okay, how do we go about finding this magic item?" I inquired.

Gr'ex offered some insight. "Most likely it should be close by. Because Tek'tar is attempting to do five rituals at the same time it has to be outside each of those circles. Knowing Tek'tar, he would also keep it out of sight for fear of some greedy goblin stealing it out from under him."

"So could he have it on him?" I asked.

"Not likely. This much power, it would be too big to haul around. No, it has to be something he could hide yet keep an eye on." Gr'ex stated.

"Could it be in town hall? It's not that far from here and I don't see the typical command tent like with Jek'jon." I hypothesized.

"Bone Marrow goblins are notorious for using what they conquer if they all plan to stick around, otherwise they just raise everything to the ground. As for the town hall. It would be a good place for it." Gr'ex replied.

I cast my spell and shadows wrapped around the both of us. I started to do short hops between the shadows we saw. I started to get glimpses out of the corner of my eyes. Little creatures grey or black as night in color and of various sizes could be seen in the distance if I looked fast enough. They easily blended into the shadows. Some looked like shadow bats, others like wolves, and a few humanoids in shape.

'These things must be what the spell description referenced. I'm going to have to experiment later when we aren't in the middle of an enemy camp.' I thought as we continued to jump from shadow to shadow.

There seemed to be more denizens of shadow that started to appear. First it was less than a handful, but as we reached the town hall there were dozens of them. I could feel Gr'ex trembling as we entered the city building.

I whispered to him when I noticed no one was around. "Are you alright Gr'ex?"

"D-Drop... y-your... s-spell." Were the only words Gr'ex stuttered out.

After double checking that no one was around I dropped my spell.

Gr'ex audibly gasped in relief. "Ah! So much better. Thank all that is holy for that being over!"

"Huh? I wouldn't have thought a goblin necromancer would thank the Light when he had served the Dark." I commented.

"Yea, well being around you makes one reevaluate things! Especially after that fiasco!" Gr'ex replied.

His words confused me, so I spoke up. "What fiasco? It was comfortable to me, like shade on a hot sunny day."

"Did you not see all those Shadow denizens getting closer and closer?! Those things are some of the more dangerous entities to any creature not of shadow. Their bite or scratch for some can inflict a shadow disease that weakens the body, mind, and spirit. Most health potions won't do anything to fix it. You need someone like a Life or Light master to cast the higher-level healing spells to cleanse you of such taint. The only beings I know immune to such things are those infused with Purity magic like archangels."

"Huh. Interesting. I have an ability that lets me purify things. It's what I use to clean clothes and the like. Remember I used it on you when you soiled yourself." I replied.

"First off, I will deny ever doing so. Second, I soiled myself because your Dark Mantle is one of the most terrifying things I've ever seen! Lastly and more importantly, you mean to tell me you've been using an ability with the power to purify anything to clean yourself and others?!" Gr'ex looked at me incredulously.

"Yea pretty much." I answered.

Gr'ex just stared at me for a moment before replying more to himself at first. "Of course, cause why not... luckiest son of a..."

I interrupted his little ty raid "What are you going on about now?"

Gr'ex took another moment to breathe. "True Purity magic is one of the rarest forms of magic in the universe. It is said to be a key component in the creation process. The lore I found stated that it is critical in harnessing the various magics to bring order to chaos or chaos to order. Not exactly sure what that means but I do remember hearing my old master share how much Eldritch beings are antithetical to the order of the universe. They are beyond chaos. Then there is the fact that any high-level healing spells that can cleanse or remove things like curses contain some aspect of Purity, but it is always mixed with something else. For you to possess a Purity ability, well, how do I put this? That has to be the most unique ability I have ever heard of."

"Well yea, I created it." I retorted.

Gr'ex's jaw dropped before he started mumbling to himself again. "He created it he says. Unbelievable! His Luck stat must be off the charts... no wonder he's not worried about the denizens of Shadow..."

"Okay, okay, can we get back on topic? Mind helping me look for this thing. I'm not exactly sure what I'm looking for." I called back to the flustered goblin as we scanned each room.

"With your Luck stat you'll probably stumble upon it anyway." Gr'ex grumbled.

"Not helping." I said back to him as I opened a door that led to a small office.

The room was pitch black and as I entered, I was looking back at my frustrated companion. This led me to not pay attention as I tripped over something, falling flat on my face.

THUD

"Owe!" I said as I rubbed my face.

"Ha! Now I feel better." Gr'ex chuckled at my misfortune.

As I stood up, I cast PURITY!!! to clean myself up and illuminate the room. The golden glow brought light into the room allowing me to see what I tripped over. Sitting in the middle of the floor was a grotesque effigy totem.

The thing had figures of demons and what I guessed some Eldritch beings might look like, all tentacles and mouths. In between those were runes that once again, like the runes I saw in the magic circles, looked wrong somehow. I couldn't place it. That's when it clicked for me.

"This is it, isn't it?"

Gr'ex realized what had just happened. "You literally stumbled upon it!"

I interrupted him before he could get started again. "Not another word... unless it's how we destroy this thing."

That was when I felt it. The totem seemed to be reacting to my PURITY!!! ability. It was like a wave of malice was radiating off the thing. The runes seemed to flare a sickly red and green. Red energy around the effigies of demons and green energy near the effigies of the Eldritch beings.

Gr'ex dropped to his knees clutching his chest in pain. "Uhhh! What is... happening? Can't..." My companion called out as he tried to breathe.

I could feel an intense weight trying to settle on top of me, the pressure slowly bringing me to my knees. The room was so thick with malice it felt tangible and seemed to make the air thick and difficult to move in. The force continued to bear down on me.

As the weight settled, I could feel emotions creeping into my psyche. First were feelings of fear, despair, and an overwhelming sentiment of not being enough, that I such an insignificant being would dare to be in the presence of greatness. It made me want to crawl away and hide.

My analytical mind reared its head. 'Wait a minute, those feelings are not my own!'

This realization made me angry that I would even entertain such a notion. 'I came back to save my friend, to save others. No! I will not be cowed by some alien entity. I CONTROL MY EMOTIONS NOT THE OTHER WAY AROUND!' Mentally, I cried in outrage.

Then the red runes seemed to react to my anger. Red flashed on the totem, and I was filled with pure rage. It was like the demonic red energy was fighting with the Eldritch sickly green energy.

The rage boiled inside of me. Rage at the stacked odds against me. Rage at the goblins who dared to invade my new home. Finally, a rage so primal that it burned away any fear or despair that had crept in.

One thought ran through my mind. 'How dare these Eldritch beings try to make me subservient!'

This thought prompted me to activate my Dark Mantle ability. The red runes instantly died out. The weight and pressure attempting to bring me to my knees felt like a feather compared to the weight of the Dark Mantle's authority. I rose to my feet and snarled at the totem.

"You want to dance, then let's dance you ugly..."

My taunt interrupted as tentacles made of a sickly green energy lashed out at me from the Eldritch effigies on the totem. They physically impacted my aura causing me to take a few steps back. It was an odd sensation to feel like you were hit both physically and spiritually.

My mind raced as to what to do as I took a few more slaps that sent me flying back into the side wall.

"Ugh." I moaned in pain.

I looked over at my goblin companion who was now unconscious yet had a horrified look on his face. That was when I remembered how effective my Dark Mantle's active effects were on others. I triggered those effects and fed power into them. The tentacles went from slapping me around to reeling back like they had been batted away.

This fact seemed to piss of the Eldritch entity as the tentacle swings increased in speed. Unfortunately for the tentacles every hit they made impacted solid walls as my aura tangibly solidified, the resulting impacts felt like a lite thud against my aura. I could not advance but neither could the tentacles reach me.

We were at a stalemate. I could no longer be harmed by the tentacles, but I was no closer to destroying this corruption. And that's when it hit me, "Corruption can be purified."

I could just cast my ability, but I would need to get closer.

'If I could only get within range, but those constant attacks on my aura make it hard to advance. Wait a minute? Isn't my aura just an extension of myself?' I thought, as an even crazier idea came to me.

A dear friend of mine had once told me, "You don't ask for permission, you just go and do it. That is what sets you apart from others, you don't even know or think you can't do something."

I focused on those words in my mind as I harnessed my will and intent, I attempted to try something new. I had no idea if abilities could be combined, but it didn't matter, I would make them combine.

Normally, I would cast my PURITY!!! ability through my hands. This time I willed it to activate in tandem with my Dark Mantle. In my mind, I grabbed both abilities and slammed them together. My friend's words echoing in my mind, I refused to not allow this to work.

The mental pressure was more intense than anything I felt before, even when going through the phases of absorbing the Primordial Celestial Dragon core.

"I HAVE BEEN GRANTED THE AUTHORITY! I AM THE MASTER HERE!" I cried out as I felt something click and my Dark Mantle swept out.

Little did I know at the time, but the active effects went far past the town hall building. Most of the town felt the pressure of my Dark Mantle. My words were like a cry echoing across the town. Goblins and humans alike fell to their knees. The rituals almost ended at that moment, but Tek'tar held it in place, if just barely.

'What is this pressure?!' Tek'tar thought as he too was on his knees.

Knowing none of this at the time, I did one last-ditch effort to deal with the totem. I poured all my remaining mana and stamina into both my abilities.

I roared. "**PURITY!!!**"

My **Dark Mantle** flared out with a new golden white glow so bright that I was blinded for a moment. The whole town lit up in golden light. I began to use the totem's own magic and transform it to my own needs. The pulsing light that now radiated across the entire town, this time it did make the rituals immediately fall apart and collapse. Those goblins involved cried out in agony both from the backlash of a failed ritual and the power of my aura.

Tek'tar screamed, "NOOOOO!!!!!" just before his eyes started to bleed as he took the brunt of the ritual backlash.

The human prisoners had their wounds healed, and for the first time since the apocalypse felt hope fill their hearts.

The building shook as the different energies warred with each other. Sadly, for the Eldritch being using the totem as a conduit, could not withstand the power that was its antithesis. My two abilities sucked the power out of the totem and used it to further fuel what I was doing. An otherworldly screech of pain echoed across the whole town.

ERRRRRR ARRRRR!!!!!

Then I heard it.

CRACK!!!

Like a soundproof door being physically slammed shut, the sounds of something shattering cut the screeches of pain off completely. Just before the sounds cut off it cried out vengeance for daring to take some of its power as my own.

"Screw you!" I taunted back in response.

As my vision cleared, I saw the totem both shatter and begin to melt at the same time. Then what was left started to violently vibrate in place before it imploded in on itself. The only thing left was a scorch mark on the floor where it had once sat.

That was the last thing I saw before I collapsed, fell flat on my face... again... and passed out.

Chapter 22 – Well, That Happened

I awoke to Gr'ex pulling on me as he attempted to drag me along. "I knew I should've put more points into strength. Freaking huemon has to weigh so damn much! I still don't know how he destroyed that thing."

"I'm awake you, grouchy gremlin. Stop pulling me." I called up to him.

Gr'ex immediately dropped my arm. "I am not a gremlin. Those little bastards are total chaos and mayhem for no reason. We goblins have reasons. Bout time you are awake."

Even though my mind felt a bit addled from the mana and stamina deprivation that caused me to pass out, I still couldn't ignore the chance to throw in a dig. "What reasons? Pillage and steal just so you can have it instead of them?"

"If you already knew the answer, why did you ask?" Gr'ex retorted.

"I forgot, no shame." I said as I sat up. "What happened?"

"I was going to ask you that. I felt unimaginable pain and must've passed out from it. When I came to, you were unconscious and there was a giant scorch mark where that Greater Totem used to be." Gr'ex replied.

"Greater totem?" I asked.

"I keep forgetting you don't know anything about magic. That magic item was a higher-level totem. Such things act as conduits for energy or entities. Greater totems can mix more than one energy together. I think the Eldritch being that used it as a conduit subverted the demonic energies and used it as door into our reality."

"So, the demonic energy may not have been a part of that willingly?" I inquired.

"Oh, I'm sure it was at first, until whatever Eldritch being took control. Demons rail against order and though they will serve other more powerful entities, they do not like Eldritch beings. It is one of the very few things that the Light and Dark agree upon." Gr'ex further explained.

"Good to know. I have a bad feeling that won't be the last time we hear from whatever that was." I commented.

Gr'ex talked out what he was thinking. "The question is how Tek'tar got his hands on it. I wouldn't put it past Tek'tar to make a pact with such a being but finding it is not some simple thing. Plus, he's not the sharpest knife in the kitchen. If Kit'erak gave it to him, then that implies Kit'erak may have betrayed the Dark pact. It would explain why he was trying to establish a foothold on some backwater planet. This is bad."

"Well yea, of course it's bad." I chimed in.

Gr'ex shook his head. "No. Kit'erak is a powerful lich necromancer with knowledge of opening portals to other worlds. If he has sided with any of the eldritch, not only your world is in danger. The Dark cannot be trusted but even more so that rings true for the eldritch."

"In other words, after we deal with the goblin invasion, we have to figure out a way to stop Kit'erak." I said in resignation.

Gr'ex nodded. "Exactly. Kit'erak is not likely to just give up if this invasion fails. Knowing my old master, he will not give up."

The conversation had allowed my initial grogginess to pass. "Where are we Gr'ex?"

"That's what I was originally gripping about. When I woke up, I found you unconscious. I may have smacked you a few times, but you were completely unresponsive..."

'No wonder my jaw was sore. I'm going to have to get back at him' I thought as I listened to him continue his synopsis.

"I figured it was only a matter of time until someone came to investigate. So, I started dragging you as best I could. I at least got you outside and into some grass and bushes near the town hall. It's not much cover but it's something." Gr'ex explained.

I stood and crouched down. I was just about to cast my spell to hide us in shadows when five goblins surrounded us.

"I'm not with him. I just found him here." Gr'ex quickly said.

A goblin with a good-sized belly and muscles spoke up. "Nice try, but you no fool Gr'onk. I am smarter than that. You are not from clan, nor do you wear colors of weak Sleeping Willow. Throw them in with other slaves. If huemons do not kill them then we wait for terrible Tek'tar to wake up. He will decide what to do with you."

The remaining goblins with spears approached. I was about to cast my spell when Gr'ex gave me a subtle shake of his head. Deciding to trust the self-preservation instincts of my companion, I let the spell fizzle out.

Our captors led us to the slave pens in town. Gr'ex started to gather some intel. "You said Tek'tar is asleep. He, okay?"

Gr'onk spoke up. "Terrible Tek'tar always okay. He is our chief. Most powerful one out there. He just tired from all the happenings earlier."

Gr'ex followed up on that nugget of information. "Happenings?"

"Yes, you must've sensed it. Great power washed over the whole town. We all heard a great voice speak and say they have authority. Gr'onk was so scared he soiled himself. Many of our clan do so as we are brought to our knees. Then we hear the voice get louder and say one word." Gr'onk shivered.

"What did the voice say?" Gr'ex asked.

"It was like a roar from a great dragon. It roared '**PURITY!!!**' then Gr'onk go blind from bright golden white light. When stars from eyes cleared, all the goblins helping rituals were knocked out, including Terrible Tek'tar. Now Gr'onk highest ranking goblin until one of the others wake up." Gr'onk declared.

At Gr'onk's words, Gr'ex just turned and glared at me. His mind clearly piecing together what caused the events Gr'onk described.

"You are not worried the one that claimed authority might return?" I curiously asked.

Gr'onk scratched his head with one of his fat fingers. "Uh, not really sure. Figure someone else wakes up first, then that their problem, not Gr'onk's. Me no want to deal with that again."

I looked back at my companion with a look I hoped conveyed, 'how about I activate my Dark Mantle ability?'

Gr'ex just stared back at me and shook his head. His signal told me to let the matter go for now. Soon we were at the slave pens and our captors were opening a cage door, pointing for us to enter. After promptly locking the door, the goblins left.

We found ourselves in a rather large cage that held about twenty humans. They looked rather healthy and clean, especially for being trapped in a dirty slave pen. The humans seemed wary of Gr'ex and myself, which is when I remembered I was still disguised as a goblin.

'Man, my bell sure got rung. I should not be this slow.' I thought before I loudly said to Gr'ex, "Buddy, I just realized I still have my disguise on, maybe you should do something about yours too."

Gr'ex caught my meaning and activated his disguise as I turned mine off. Some gasps came from the other prisoners.

"They're human!"

"Could be a trick."

An older well-built man pushed the others aside so he could walk up to us. "Let's not be rude especially after what we all just witnessed."

The man extended his hand in greeting. "I'm Mar but everyone just calls me Bunyan on account of my size and the fact I used to be a lumberjack."

I took the man's hand in greeting. His handshake was firm but surprisingly not overbearing, sign of a man who knew he was strong but also knew the importance of restraint. I instantly liked him. "I'm Shadowalker and this is my companion Gr'ex. What are you referring to witnessing?"

A young woman, maybe mid-twenties with red hair and freckles on her face spoke up. "He's talking about the miracle that just happened."

"Miracle?" Gr'ex asked in confusion.

The girl gave Gr'ex a look that screamed 'you have got to be kidding me.' "What miracle? You know the bright golden white light that healed all our wounds and somehow cleaned our clothes. You know, that one!"

Gr'ex just glared at me again.

"Don't say it. I'm not in the mood." I replied to my friend as I could feel his eyes bored into me.

Turning my attention to the pretty redhead, "Ah, yea sorry. I guess that could be seen as a miracle. Sorry, my head is still a bit fuzzy."

"Goblins hit you on your head as part of capturing you I bet." Bunyan commented.

"Oh." The redheaded woman said before speaking up further. "My name is Emily. I'd introduce you to the others, but they are a little standoffish with strangers. They mean well enough. Just give em time."

"Fair enough. Do you think if we broke them out, they would come with us?" I asked.

"Boss what are you doing?" Gr'ex questioned.

Bunyan chimed in. "I think so. They are scared but no one wants to stay here as a slave or end up as food."

Emily shuddered. "We've seen some of them eating what are clearly human body parts. Some even taunt us about it."

Hearing that, I turned to my companion. "You think we can just leave these people? With most of their higher ups out of commission, now is the time to get them out."

Gr'ex groaned. "Damn bleeding hearts. I had us get captured so we could gather information and when Tek'tar least expects it, strike. If we leave now, we won't get another chance like this."

I considered his words.

"You can't be serious. If you have a way out and can free us, how can you not take it?" Emily chastised.

"As much as I agree with you Gr'ex, Emily is right. We have to get these people out of here. If we do, we won't have to hold back for the final assault for fear of hurting innocent people." I reasoned.

"There are no innocents in the apocalypse. Do not lose sight of that." Gr'ex retorted.

"Okay, bad choice of words, but you get my meaning." I replied.

"I do... and I begrudgingly agree with you, but only because it means we can go all out when the time comes." Gr'ex answered.

"That is all well and good but how do you guys' plan to get us out?" Bunyan chimed in.

"Easy, we walk in the shadows." I deadpanned.

Gr'ex groaned. "Not again."

"What does that mean?" Emily asked.

"Before we get to that, we have to get everyone out of these cages. I'm going to form a large group." I stated.

Gr'ex spoke up. "There are too many. You will have to form a raid."

"What's the difference?" I inquired.

"Raids distribute more of the experience but as you are all new to the system and the world is still integrating it will not do much more than let you designate them as friendlies." Gr'ex explained.

"Well, that's all that matters. Can I designate sub commanders or captains?" I asked.

"Not at your level. Normally you would need a War Leader skill for such things. The most you can do is designate group leads that can invite people to their group." Gr'ex answered.

Emily spoke up this time. "How many can be in a group?"

"It depends. For now, assume ten at the most which by my count means we will need ten group leads." Gr'ex replied.

"Make Bunyan and I group leads. We will talk to the rest of the people and get people invited." Emily suggested.

"Works for me." I replied as I mentally called up the system commands.

*You have invited **Bunyan** and **Emily** to your party.*

You have converted your party into a raid group.

***Bunyan** has been designated **Group 1 Leader**.*

Emily has been designated **Group 2 Leader**.

You have granted your Group Leaders authority to invite other members to the raid.

That done. Bunyan and Emily got to work talking with the rest of the prisoners. While they were busy organizing the survivors, Gr'ex and I flagged down a squad of goblins.

We were thrilled when we found a Sleeping Willow squad moving through the town. The Bone Marrow goblins had left us alone after depositing us here. My guess was the ones that remained were busy trying to guard the ones unconscious.

"How did you get captured great Gr'ex?" One of the Sleeping Willow goblins asked.

"What a stupid question. How else? We let ourselves get captured." Gr'ex retorted.

The Sleeping Willow goblin bowed his head. "Of course. Please forgive my foolish question."

"We don't have time for that. You are going to help us free the other humans." I ordered.

"As you command dark one!" The whole squad said as then bowed their heads.

"Pay deference later. Release us now!" Gr'ex grumbled.

One of the goblins rushed to the cage and unlocked it.

Emily had heard the conversation as she was wondering why we would intentionally call over goblins. "What are you doing? Why are those goblins following your commands? Is this a trap?"

I pointed to the different colors on their leathers. "See those colors. That identifies them as Sleeping Willow clan. Their clan is our allies. It's a long story but their chief works for me."

Emily looked unsure.

"Look you can all stay here if you want, but now is the time to get you people out of here. So, what's it going to be?"

"Fine. I'll tell the others. I was coming over here to tell you to invite the eight people raising their hands to the raid." Emily said as she pointed in the direction of the other survivors and eight people raised their arms.

I quickly invited and promoted those eight people and refocused on the goblins.

"Tell me. How goes the evacuation of your clan?" I asked while waiting for Bunyan and Emily to get everyone invited and organized.

"The evacuation is going well, master. We believe we should be done sometime tomorrow." The Sleeping Willow goblin answered.

"That is far ahead of schedule." I commented.

"Rumors of your horrific power has spread quickly among my clan. No one wishes to anger you, master. Among the goblin people, there are legends and stories about the one who gains the Dark Mantle. This has only further fueled our zealous commitment to serving you!" The goblins kneeled and bowed their heads to me again.

"Ugh. I really am not very comfortable with this." I commented under my breath to Gr'ex.

My goblin companion cut me off. "Don't complain. Suck it up. Embrace it! You are the luckiest person I know. I'm already jealous of you. Don't make me hate you because you do something stupid like not own your responsibility or try to ignore the mantle of authority placed on your shoulders. Still can't believe of all the..." the rest of Gr'ex's grumblings were under his breath, and I had long learned to tune him out.

Emily, Bunyan, and the other eight group leaders came over. Sure, I could've tried to learn their names, but my mind was still distracted. I had notifications that called for my attention that I was actively suppressing. I did not want to get distracted while in enemy territory. For that matter, over the last couple days I have been so busy that I still haven't distributed my stat points.

'Worry about that stuff later. Focus.' I mentally told myself before giving out instructions.

I waved to the goblins. "Release the others."

The squad jumped up and ran to execute my orders.

Turning my attention to all the humans looking at me with a mix of shock and trepidation at seeing the goblins follow my orders, I began to explain my plan. "I have a spell that I can cast on myself and party members. It allows all of us to be hidden by the shadows. Once hidden, I can make a series of jumps or teleports through shadows until we are far enough that I can drop the spell."

Some seemed very uncomfortable with this statement. Several expressed their concerns.

"Is it safe?"

"How do we know it's not some trick?"

"Where can we go?"

"Nowhere is safe."

I raised my hand to get their attention. "I understand you are all scared. I have a compound not too far from here that has plenty of space underground. This place is probably the most secure area in the whole state. It's your best chance for survival until we can resolve this conflict with the goblins."

I heard the voice of what sounded like a young man speak up. "But the goblins listen to you."

"There are two goblin clans in the area. I have command over the ones called Sleeping Willow. The others, the Bone Marrow clan, are the ones that have imprisoned you. That is why we need to get you out of here now, while they are distracted and weakened. We must go now. I've never tried this on so many people at once, so everyone group up close."

The crowd did as instructed and moved closer to one another. They didn't seem pleased, but they at least knew they didn't want to be stuck in cages anymore.

I cast my spell, Shadow of Death. The shadows began to move and warp around the crowd of prisoners. Some were about to scream but clamped their hands over their mouths. More started to do the same thing when they started to see things moving in the shadows.

Not wasting any time, I started to teleport us through the shadows. Luckily the town had plenty of tall trees providing a plethora of shadows to choose from. Each teleport sucked away a good chunk of my mana pool. So much so, that after five jumps, I had to take a break to let my mana slowly recharge.

After each jump, more and more denizens of shadow could be seen. There were already a significant number of shadow creatures even on the first jump, but each time more and more showed up. They appeared to want to approach our group but remained just out of reach. Several of them hissed or growled at the humans, but one look from me, and they fell silent.

'This is so weird. Man, I will have to find time to explore this more too.'

Mana somewhat recharged, I completed two more teleports before I dropped the spell all together. I was already exhausted and that just took more out of me.

"We should be far enough away from town now. Gr'ex lead them to the compound. I'll catch up in a minute after I give myself a moment to recharge." I instructed.

"Alright everyone. Follow me. We don't have time to dally." Gr'ex ordered.

Emily stayed by me. As I leaned up against a tree and watched my mana bar increase, she spoke up. "No offense, but I don't trust you, so I'm just going to stay by you to make sure you aren't trying to pull something."

"Not a problem. I always appreciate the company of a pretty lady." I replied.

This statement seemed to make her blush as her cheeks turned red. "Don't try to distract me."

"I wouldn't think of it, cutie." I responded.

"I'm being serious, it won't work!" She retorted and almost pouted.

I stood up from leaning on the tree. "Oh, you look so cute when you pout."

"Ah!!You!" Was all Emily said before she stormed off to catch up to Bunyan.

I just chuckled to myself. 'No one tells me what to do. She is kind of fun to mess with. I'll have to let Gr'ex know, he seems to take special pleasure in messing with people.'

Catching up to Gr'ex I was in front as we approached the cabin. Suzie and Alice were sitting on the porch. The moment Alice saw me she made a beeline for me and jumped up into my arms. She gave me a big hug. "I missed you, new daddy!"

Suzie chuckled as she approached the group. "She has been going on and on for the last several hours. Something about you playing without her and she wanted to go join in the fun. I had to pull out all the stops to get her to just wait on the porch for you. She has really gotten attached to you quickly."

"Yea, she has grown on me too. Now let me put you down and I'll tell you all the gruesome details later." I told Alice.

"Okay, but don't leave anything out." Alice said.

"Such a weird huemon." Gr'ex commented.

Alice just turned to the goblin and with her finger, bopped him on the nose. "Silly Gr'exy."

She then giggled and ran into the cabin with Gr'ex chasing after her.

"I see you picked up more stragglers. I thought you were only going to go scout?" Suzie commented.

I rubbed the back of my neck. "Well, you see what happened was..."

Emily's voice interrupted me. "Suzie-cue?"

Suzie turned to the voice. "Emily? You're alive!"

The two girls embraced each other in a hug.

"It is good to see you again my friend." Suzie said as tears started to form on her face.

"I didn't know you were back in town. Last we talked; you were in LA." Emily replied. She too was crying.

I coughed. "I take it you two know each other."

"Emily was my best friend since second grade." Suzie replied as she wiped away her tears.

Smiling, I replied, "Glad you two could be reunited in such circumstances. I do not mean to interrupt your reunion, but can you work with Jebediah to get these people settled down below."

"You follow him too Suzie-cue?" Emily asked.

"Who? Shadowalker? Yea, he's been a great host. Your group is actually the second group he rescued from goblins. Come on inside and I can tell you everything as we help get everyone safe down on one of the sub-levels." Suzie stated.

I called out to everyone in the back. "Alright everyone! Head on in and down the elevators to the sub-levels! Suzie and Jebediah will help you get situated!"

With Emily's help, Suzie guided everyone inside without any problems.

I had notifications to see to and wanted to lay down in my room so as to not be disturbed. As I got into my room, I took off my shoes and plopped on the bed. Just as I was about to pull up the first notification Alice jumped on me.

"You promised stories. I want to hear what I missed." The little girl said as she stared at me with those big eyes. 'Man, her eyes look cool.' I thought before I asked, "Where is Gr'ex? Wasn't he chasing you?"

"Oh, he got tired and was all huffing and puffing after a few minutes. So, I got bored and came to find you." She replied innocently.

"Alright, alright. I will tell you all about my scouting mission." I replied.

"Including any gory or scary parts. Don't leave anything out." Alice retorted.

"Fine, fine. It all started when I used the Minor Illusion ring Gr'ex gave me…"

Chapter 23 – Travel Plans

Laraaq was itching to get back on the road. Their teams of rescuers recovered over 50 people in just a day. More were being identified as others they could rescue along the way to their destination. Carol had asked for another day to get as many locations mapped out so their people could plan effective routes.

"Carol, I respect what you are trying to do, but we can't stay here forever." Laraaq lamented.

"Didn't you say we should try to save as many people as possible?" Carol argued back.

"Yes, I did but we have to be realistic. We can do more once we get to our finals destination than remaining here. Weren't you the one who told me about the large antenna at the radio station in that town? Something about redundancies and both modern and ancient equipment making it more likely we can reach even more people."

Carol frowned at Laraaq. "I don't like you using my own logic against me. Fine, give me a few hours to finish mapping out what I got, and we can discuss our plans to leave."

"Deal. Why you're doing that I'm going to go check on Jennifer and her parents." Laraaq said.

"Sure, you are." Carol teased.

"Nah, it's nothing like that. She's cool and all but not my type." Laraaq fired back.

"Okay dearie. As long as you don't tell me Sharon is your type, we'll be good." Carol retorted.

"Yuck! Don't get me started on that piece of trash! I really regret saving her." Laraaq commented.

"Poor Simon. He's so determined, he's blind to the truth." Carol replied.

"Infatuation makes you blind. It's why I'm focused on getting everyone to Shadowalker. I plan to dump all this responsibility on him. Then I can worry about trying to date in the apocalypse." Laraaq half joked.

"You're doing well keeping everyone in line." Carol commented.

"That's because I delegate. Between you, your son, and Jacob I don't have much to worry about. Besides the rules have changed, heck in some ways maybe they were always about competency and courage to do what's right. Screw the idiots who can't understand that." Laraaq said.

"It was always about those things. The problem was all the lies being told to people saying competency didn't matter. Then we go and create incentives for us to ignore the problems and just go about our day. I can't stand incompetence; it sticks in my craw!" Carol shared her own perspective.

"Yea, you've said as much multiple times." Laraaq replied.

"Well, it's important. Don't you know when a woman repeats herself about something that means it matters to her. Come now you've got to pay attention to these things if you ever hope to find and more importantly keep a good woman, or women, or men. I don't judge." Carol teased again.

"Well, that goes both ways. I figure if we can't both put each other first then what's the point. Both have to matter or neither matter." Laraaq fired back.

"Right you are. That was how it was with Carl's father. He was a good man. I miss him terribly. But enough of that sad stuff you can't change. Go talk to Jennifer while I finish up here." Carol said as she waved her hand in clear dismissal.

Laraaq shook his head at the nosy woman. She was invaluable but man did she love to meddle in people's love lives. It was like it was part of her mission in life since the apocalypse to rescue people and then get them married off.

It didn't take Laraaq long to find Jennifer. Her dad had a welding torch and was working on the power suit. Her mom was busy reviewing what looked like binders and drawings, as she made notes in her own journal.

"Hey Jennifer, I see your parents are hard at work."

Jennifer smiled at Laraaq. "Oh yea. They are always like this. Why do you think I took up healing? See that welder. Well, let's just say he accidentally welded a part of himself to that suit, when mom initiated a startup protocol that made the suit jerk around."

Laraaq chuckled. "Ha! Sounds painful."

Her dad called out without stopping what it was doing. "Very painful!"

Her mom, not taking her eyes off the documents she was reviewing replied. "Sorry honey. I'm just glad our Jennifer was able to heal you. We may be too old to have more kids but that doesn't mean I want to stop trying."

"Mom! I don't need to hear that!" Jennifer complained.

"It's completely natural for parents to show our love for each other. You have to make time for such things if you expect a relationship to last!" Her mom quipped back.

Jennifer turned to Laraaq who was doing his best trying to hold in his laughter and failing miserably. "I doubt you came over to hear about my parents' love life. What's up?"

Chuckling Laraaq replied, "Ha! No, I didn't but it's still hilarious. I came over to let you know Carol is finishing up mapping out the rest of the possible rescue locations. She said she needed a few hours. I was wondering if you'd be down to go with us. You're one of the few healers we have."

Jennifer nodded. "Sure, sounds fun. Can't do too much at the moment anyway. Aren't you chomping at the bit to get to our destination? I know I am."

Laraaq nodded too. "Oh yea. I was just complaining about how I wanted to get on the road already. Carol reminded me I also wanted to save as many people for our new community as possible so I'm giving her the few hours she needs to help map all that out."

"It's a worthy goal to save and help people. Just don't let it result in your downfall. We can only do so much, and people forget being too nice or helpful can actually be a detriment in the long run. You don't seem like the type, I'm just saying." Jennifer commented.

Laraaq waved her comment off. "No worries. That kind of stuff frustrates me too. People think they're helping when they aren't. No place for that here. Everyone must contribute for all of us to survive. Hey, I was going to see if Christy and Mack wanted to join us for some experience gains. Want to tag along and meet them?"

"Yea go on honey. We will be busy for hours." Her mom called out without looking up once.

"Yea get out of here pumpkin. Oh, and Laraaq if you hurt my daughter, remember I own a power suit." Her dad teased.

Jennifer shook her head at her parents, then turned to Laraaq. "Sure, why not."

Laraaq and Jennifer found the family next to the moving truck with all the food. Mack was checking the truck to make sure no one messed with it. Christy and Sarah were sitting next to a makeshift fire pit. Colin was checking on the truck he drove.

"Hey guys how have you been holding up?" Laraaq asked.

Mack grunted out a response as he kept working. "Fine."

Colin came over as did Christy and Sarah.

"Hey Mr. Laraaq. Who's your friend?" Colin asked.

Sarah commented. "Wow, she's pretty."

Jennifer smiled and blushed at the random compliment.

Christy introduced herself directly. "Don't mind them. They get all tongue tied around new people. I'm Christy. That's my best friend Colin. And this is my younger sister Sarah."

"I'm Jennifer. I've joined Laraaq's team to help rescue more people. One of the things I am now is a healer. Keep that in mind in case something happens okay."

"Wow a healer. You mean you can heal people with magic like Mr. Laraaq uses fires to kill bad guys? I so want to learn magic." Colin said in excitement.

Jennifer laughed at the young man's enthusiasm.

Christy for some reason got a bit jealous at the byplay and muttered under her breath, "It's not that impressive."

Susan spoke up again. "Does that mean you can heal internal wounds or bruises too?"

Jennifer turned to Sarah. "Sure sweetie. Do you have any injuries? I have a medical scan spell that can tell me everything that's wrong. If you like I can use it on you now."

Christy pulled her sister in close. "No that's fine. She was just curious is all."

Mack finished his routine and spoke up. "We don't need anything. If you don't mind, we'd prefer to keep to ourselves."

Laraaq thought it was an odd reaction to an offer of healing. Then he remembered Mack and his group seemed to keep to themselves. They pitched in and helped wherever asked but beyond that they preferred to be left alone.

"No worries, Mack. Introducing Jennifer was only part of why we came. Carol is mapping out the remainder of the people within range we could rescue. I was coming to see if any of you wanted to go with us. Great opportunity to help people and gains some levels." Laraaq replied.

"I'd like to go if Mack and Christy are okay with it." Colin chimed in.

Mack nodded. "Go kid. It would do you some good to gain some levels and bulk up some."

Colin smiled and turned to Laraaq. "Okay, I'm in."

Christy spoke up. "I'd go but someone has to stay behind with my sister."

Mack shook his head. "Go ahead Christy. I'll stay with Sarah."

Christy seemed hesitant. She turned to Mack and offered an alternative. "What if we trade off on the missions or ask Mrs. Burns to watch her?"

Mack growled. "Family looks after family."

Laraaq spoke up. "Every able fighter is expected to participate in the battle for our new home. Good to get as strong as possible before then."

"We will rotate watching Sarah. When we get to our destination, I will allow Carol to watch her but not until then. Family looks after family."

"Your call Mack. See you in a few hours at the radio station." Laraaq replied before he and Jennifer walked away.

After they got outside hearing distance Jennifer spoke up. "Man, that guy is intense."

"Yea, he and his family keep to themselves, but they have never shirked their duties or failed to help out. I think the man just likes to be left alone. I can understand that."

Jennifer shrugged. "I guess. Just something about the man, I wouldn't want him as an enemy."

"Yea, I'm glad he's on our side. Let's go find Jacob and Carl to see how they are doing." Laraaq stated.

"Look, I'm telling you Carl, learn to harness your chi and you will be able to do some amazing things. That's how I'm able to do what I can." Jacob encouraged.

"Hey guys, what are you talking about?" Laraaq asked.

Jacob turned to Laraaq and Jennifer. "Hey Laraaq. Hey Jennifer, how are your parents settling in?"

"You should know. You and Carl have been a huge help." Jennifer replied.

'They have? Man, I'm glad I delegated. Too much to juggle. I'd rather go burn stuff to the ground.' Laraaq thought.

"Yea, well... that's our role. Laraaq here is focused on rescuing people and getting us to our final destination. We can handle some of the logistics." Carl answered as he saw Laraaq's confusion.

"I appreciate that, guys. I really do. Can't wait to turn this over to Shadowalker. He can get saddled with all the resource management while I get to defend our people." Laraaq stated.

"A protector is an admirable role and very much needed in this post apocalypse world." Jennifer commented.

"Thanks Jennifer. Now Jacob what was this talk about chi?" Laraaq asked.

"Ah, this." Jacob said as he lifted his arm and made a fist. The fist then started to glow and harden. "I call it Stone Fist technique."

"Ah cool, you're using mana to coat your fist in stone. That's cool. I can do something similar." Laraaq said.

"No, not mana. I'm using chi or Qi depending on what you practice." Jacob answered.

"What now?"

Query Accepted

Chi or Qi, as the target Jacob has mentioned, is the ability to harness and circulate life force instead of mana.

Laraaq spoke his question out loud. "So, you're telling me there is an option to harness life force too?"

"See Laraaq gets it!" Jacob said excitedly.

Query Accepted

No, you are not paying attention again. The word used was instead. Once you develop your pathways and form a core you have already chosen a path. The way you form your core, spiral, and pathways dictate whether you can use mana or chi.

"So, if you start to use chi, you can't use mana?" Laraaq replied out loud again.

"Yes, that is a problem but only once you form a core. I don't think any of us are there yet. Until then you can dabble with both, it's just harder." Jacob commented.

Query Accepted

The meat bag is correct. Mana is usually used to affect the outside world and can also enhance yourself. Chi is used to affect your body and spirit. This has the added benefit of making someone effectively immortal as long as they continue to cultivate life force. It can affect the outside world, but it is not as effective as mana.

"So, mana is better at affecting the outside world and others, while chi is better at enhancing yourself and making you immortal. Both can in a sense simulate what the other can but not as efficiently." Laraaq replied out loud again.

"Yea, which means we can live forever as cultivators and become extremely hard to kill. I'd say very important in the apocalypse." Jacob answered, still not realizing that Laraaq wasn't even talking to him.

Query Accepted

That is mostly correct. It is a moot point as you formed a core made out of mana. That is a must if you want to be any kind of spellcaster.

"That gives us all something to think about." Laraaq said, finally joining the external conversation. "We should spread the word that people will have to choose one or the other and to give it some serious thought. As it sounds like once you form your core there is no going back."

"That is important information to share. My understanding is Laraaq you've already formed your core based on mana." Carl stated.

"Oh! I hadn't heard, congratulations! I already formed my core, but it's based on chi." Jacob shared.

"Perhaps each of you could help the others once they decide the path they want to go down. They can go see Laraaq for advice on forming the mana core and see Jacob on advice forming a chi core." Carl suggested.

"I think that's a great idea." Jennifer chimed in.

"Of course, you would, you don't have to deal with the people and their incessant questions." Laraaq grumbled.

"Fine how about this. I've already decided to form a mana core for healing. Once I do, I'll take on the responsibility until we can find someone else. Sounds good?" Jennifer proposed.

"I'll take it. With one caveat. If someone else forms a core in the meantime, they can start coaching people, as I imagine you'll be busy with city planning once we get to our destination." Laraaq answered.

"I think that's fair. What do you think Carl? Jennifer?" Jacob asked.

"Agreed." Jennifer answered.

"Agreed." Carl replied.

Jacob steered the conversation forward. "Good. Now why did you two come seek us out?"

Laraaq shared his thoughts. "We came to talk about battle rotations. Carl, I'd like you, Jerome, and Mario to add a few people when we aren't on missions together."

"That's easy enough. Several of the survivors have volunteered to help. I think many of them just want to get stronger." Carl replied.

Laraaq continued. "That's good to hear. I was worried we were going to end up with more dead weight like Sharon."

"Yuck! What a toxic woman. If I have to hear her complain one more time..." Jacob chimed in.

Laraaq chuckled. "Ha! Tell me about it. Anyway, talking about more productive things, I want to take Mack's group out on some rescue missions. I was wondering if you'd like to come with us Jacob. It would be good to see those chi techniques in action."

Jacob smiled. "Sure. I'd be more than happy to fight side by side with you. I was feeling a bit behind in levels lately, so this would be great. Just let me know when."

"Awesome. Carol is marking up the maps now. We were about to head back and check on her progress. Feel free to come with."

"I probably should go too. Mom's been a bit clingy since the apocalypse. I think she just worries. I appreciate it, but it can get to be a bit much." Carl commented.

"Ha! I don't envy you. Your mother scares me." Jacob replied.

As Laraaq, Jennifer, Carl, and Jacob walked in to see Carol, Colin and Christy were already there.

"Oh good, you brought my son too. I have so much to cover." Carol said excitedly as she waved towards the giant map.

"That's a lot of dots Carol." Laraaq replied as he saw a plethora of dots on the map.

"I know! Isn't it exciting!" Carol said oblivious to Laraaq's concerns.

Chapter 24 – Sure, We Have Plenty of Room

As I awoke, I found Alice sleeping on my chest. She looked adorable, sleeping there so peacefully. I must've fallen asleep recounting my day yesterday. That artifact kicked my butt. Trying to absorb and transform it into something I could use. Going to have to be even more cautious when dealing with such energies.

'I must be more prepared to confront things like that. Heck that goblin chief looked like a nightmare waiting to happen. The guy looked ripped and clearly knows some high-level magic too.' I thought to myself as I slowly slipped out of bed and went into the master bathroom to shower and change.

I locked the door as I did not need Alice walking in and seeing something she shouldn't. After smelling myself, I immediately jumped into the shower. I just stood there for several minutes letting the hot water flow over my body.

As I cleaned myself thoroughly, I thought about that goblin chief and the upcoming battle. Up until now I was planning on a pure magic caster build for my stat point distribution, but now I was not so sure. There was no doubt in my mind that I wanted to be a mage, that was a given. The problem with most pure casters is they are glass cannons. They can dish out the magical damage, but a few hits and they are dead, or won't last long in close quarters combat. If I kept to that pure build, sure I would have plenty of mana to use, but I did not think I would live very long.

If living long was the plan, which it was, then I needed to change my thinking. Long term, my build was going to be focused on casting. Short term, I needed to survive to get to the long term. That meant I had to take a hit and be able to survive in close quarters combat.

I gained the skill **Weapons Mastery** at **Master rank**, which meant I had a plethora of weapons to choose from. It also meant I had the knowledge, and some baked in muscle memory. It was still a good idea to actually practice so as to smooth out any rough edges. The problem was I lacked the Strength and Dexterity levels to be able to stand up in melee combat.

Another consideration was all the people I was now in charge of. I could not ignore my **Charisma** stat if I wanted to avoid riots and other issues. So high enough **Charisma** could not be ignored.

My titles, perks from absorbing the **Primordial Celestial Dragon Core**, and becoming a Primordial Celestial Dragon, had given me a rather large stat boost. I still had to determine where to distribute my 117 stat points for reaching level 10.

"System, I remembered I gained a few stat points for reaching the first threshold. What is the stat point benefit for reaching the second threshold?" I asked out loud.

Query Accepted

Any who reaches the second threshold gains +13 stat points in all attributes.

"Wow, that's a nice perk! What is the requirement for reaching the second threshold?" I asked.

Query Accepted

For the +13-stat perk, they must have a minimum of 100 points in the six primary attributes.

I looked at my current stats, did some mental math, and figured out I had enough points to make that happen. I even had some to spare. Making the mental selections I confirmed my stat distribution.

Then the pain hit me. I allocated more than 40 points each to **Strength** and **Dexterity**. That much of an increase meant my body was undergoing drastic changes all at once.

I collapsed to the shower floor. My bones felt like they were stretching. If that wasn't bad enough, my muscles rapidly grew huge, then stretched and tightened, causing my body to go from a massive bodybuilder physique to a well-built runner or triathlon athlete. The whole process took maybe an hour, but it felt like I was lying there for days. I felt stiffer than when I woke up this morning.

Finally able to stand, I realized I was a few inches taller. I let the shower continue to work my new and very upset muscles. While I stood there, I looked at my updated stats.

Name: Shadowwalker	Race: Primordial Celestial Dragon	Level: 10
Strength: 117	Dexterity: 117	Constitution: 117
Intelligence: 117	Wisdom: 130	Charisma:117
Spiritual Attunement: Omni	Core Stage: Divine Infinitum	Spiral Stage: Divine Infinitum
Health, Mana, Stamina Values & Regen Rates per hour (pH)		
HP: 2,282	MP: 2,347	SP: 4,628
HP/pH: 13	MP/pH: 1,128.4	SP/pH: 1,027
Core Capacity: 65	Special: Core Generation	Core Generation: 13

"Now that is more like it!" I said as I dismissed my stats and pulled up the waiting notifications.

*Congratulations! You have taken the first step in seeking balance within your mind, body, and spirit. Very few cultivators reach this critical threshold. +13 to all stats. You have reached the second threshold: **Balanced Spiritual Signature**.*

Balanced Spiritual Signature
Description: *This threshold allows a caster or cultivator to gain greater control over their aura and overall spiritual signature. Increased core capacity and efficiency. This allows the user to have great control over how much of their presence they wish to reveal. At any time, they can mask their presence, both in mind, body functions, and soul. Additional benefit provides increased control over aura projection and suppression. Open your remaining meridians and continue to periodically remove blockages and impurities to reach future thresholds.*

'Being able to have greater control of my aura would have been super helpful yesterday! More reason to not horde my stat points for too long.

Also distribute gradually next time. Now I know what my uncle felt like when he grew several inches in height his senior year of high school.'

I reached to grab the towel and ripped the bar the towel was hanging-on right off the wall. "Crap! Okay, reminder, way more strength than before. I have to be super gentle until I get the hang of this." I told myself out loud.

I very slowly and carefully turned the nozzle controlling the water for the shower. I managed to not break it, so I claimed that was significant progress.

It was interesting that I grew a few inches, and it made me think. 'I wonder if that also affected my dragon form. Which I still haven't been able to check. Another thing to add to my list of things to do. Get some alone time away from everyone to get a feel for my dragon form. I think it would have to be after I have a better handle on my **Gravity Momentum Manipulation** ability. That way I could fly away fast enough to give me the time and distance to check myself out. I have to remind myself these are awesome problems to have. My clothes are going to be a bit tight. I wonder if we have any tailors or leatherworkers that could help.'

I grabbed some sweatpants that used to be long on me that now were a little short but still worked. Pants on, I felt comfortable leaving the bathroom to grab a shirt. As I exited the bathroom, I saw Alice sitting up wide-awake staring at me.

"You got taller new daddy. Oooo, and more muscles. Neat trick!" Alice commented as she held on to her doll and watched me like a hawk.

I quickly grabbed what used to be a loose-fitting t-shirt that was much tighter with the increased muscle mass I had. "This shirt will have to do for now. Luckily, I always bought one larger size in everything, don't know why, just did." I said more to myself than Alice.

"You got even more handsome, new daddy. The girls are going to be even more interested now, but don't worry new daddy, I won't let them hurt you." Alice said the last part with a rather scary look in her eyes for such a sweet little girl.

The look was gone in a flash, to the point I thought I might've imagined it. Shaking it off, I refocused on my plans for the day. "Want to come with me downstairs for some breakfast?"

Alice jumped up faster than I could blink. "Oooo. That sounds yummy. I am hungry and meat sounds yummy, not as yummy as playing, but still good."

Before I knew it, I was carrying her downstairs in my arms. I plopped her down gently into a seat by the kitchen as I started pulling out ingredients.

"What kind of food do you like, Alice? I heard you mention meat, which is good as that is all I seem to want to eat now a days." I said as I kept pulling food out.

"I only eat meat. Prey eats foliage. I don't want to be prey, so I eat any kind of meat." Alice replied.

"Huh. You know I feel like I said that very thing at some point in my life." I said before shaking my head. "Oh well, doesn't matter. If you like meat Alice, then you came to the right place. We have plenty of meat here."

"Oh, I know that new daddy, but let's focus on breakfast. I'm almost ravenous." Alice stated.

I cocked my head to the side in confusion, but then just dismissed it as she just smiled cutely at me. She was adorable and so reminded me of my daughter. I shifted my focus to preparing the meal. By the time I have everything cooking, the smell must've woken up Gr'ex. I saw him sitting at the table with Jek'jon and Jebediah.

Jeb leaned over to talk to Jek'jon. "You came at the perfect time. The best meals I ever have come from Shadowalker. The man is a genius chef."

"Jek'jon never smells something so good. Is all huemon food smell like this?"

"Not even close. Trust me, I tried some of the food the huemons fixed down below, horrible stuff in comparison." Gr'ex commented.

I served everyone and set plates for Suzie and her friend Emily. As they sat down to eat, I greeted them. "Good morning, ladies. No Duncan this morning? Again."

"Food smells yummy as always Shadowalker. And no. Donut hardly leaves the Communications room. He does an evening debrief with Carol on progress and situation on both sides." Suzie paused as she looked at me before continuing. "You know, you look taller and in really good shape."

"Awe, it's nothing. I just finally distributed my stat points. Figured I should do it before we deal with Tek'tar and his clan." I replied as I took my own seat at the head of the table.

That is when I noticed something was different about Emily, she had pointy Elf ears. "Race Change?" I asked just as Emily was about to take a bite of her food.

Her face turned a shade of pink. "I hadn't chosen my system perk, but after talking it over with Suzie-cue and seeing her changes as a wood elf, I decided I wanted the same benefits."

"Looks good on you. Now we have two elves in our group." I commented.

"Great, elves." Gr'ex grumbled in between bites.

Emily couldn't wait another minute and started to inhale her food. She looked up and swallowed before speaking. "This food is delicious!" She turned to her friend. "Do we get to eat like this every day?"

"Only when Shadowalker cooks and he only cooks for his party." Suzie said in between bites.

"I have never been treated so good, even as a goblin chief." Jek'jon said, glad he pledged himself to Shadowalker.

"You do have a gift my boy. I'll give ya that." Jebediah commented.

I looked over at Alice to see her rubbing her tummy, a clear smile on her face.

Deciding to get things moving I started with my team. "I'd like us to consider some hit and run tactics to start testing their defenses. I was hoping we could pull Duncan away for a few hours to join us."

"Should be doable as long as we are back in time for the evening brief. You know, about that. I'm surprised you don't want to talk to your buddy each day." Jebediah replied.

"Good to hear Duncan can join us. As for your implied question. I see no need. He will be here soon enough, and we both have plenty to get done in the meantime. He and I will swap survival stories once he is here. Laraaq is a capable man and I trust him, but I won't get my hopes up until he is here. Until then, I can push to deal with more pressing issues." I answered.

"Kind of heartless, don't you think?" Emily asked.

"Not at all. I'm just compartmentalizing and focusing on what is in front of me. Speaking of that..." I turned to Jek'jon. "What about your evacuation?"

Jek'jon finished the last bit of food on his plate before replying. "It goes too well."

"What does that mean?" Gr'ex asked before I could.

Jek'jon sighed. "My people are almost all the way through and should be ready to move out later this evening."

"Sounds good. What is the problem?" I inquired.

"Several of our neighboring clans have taken notice of our evacuation. Normally they would use this as the perfect time to move in and expand." Jek'jon began to explain.

"That is the goblin way." Gr'ex chimed in.

Jek'jon nodded. "Yes, the great Gr'ex is correct. The problem is that my people said they were leaving to come serve the one with the authority of the Dark Mantle."

"The damn blabber mouths!" Gr'ex hit his fist on the table.

The sudden move startled Jeb, Suzie, and Emily. Alice just giggled at their reaction while she listened intently.

"What are you two going on about?" Suzie asked.

I cut in. "She means about your neighbors."

Suzie frowned at me. I smiled back, and her frown melted away. "Well, that was part of it, but I also was asking about this Dark Mantle business."

Gr'ex clarified the issue. "Goblins have a history of following the strong and powerful. They also go where they think they will prosper. If Sleeping Willow's neighbors think they are coming to a lush new land to serve a powerful master..."

Jek'jon stepped in to continue his explanation. "They have entreated us to join the evacuation. Our homeland is swamps and decrepit. Resources are scarce. It is no surprise they wish to leave."

Jebediah asked the question in our minds. "How many green skins we are talking here?"

Jek'jon winced as he answered. "Over a thousand."

I groaned. "How many clans?"

"In addition to my clan, another three clans." Jek'jon replied.

"How many Bone Marrow goblins are here?" I asked.

"They exceed 1,000 now. Most of those coming are crafters, women, children. Each clan specializes in some way even if they have warriors and casters. Bone Marrow specialization is war. Though Gr'ex's clan the Death Weavers are one of the three coming through."

"My people?" Gr'ex said in surprise.

Jek'jon smiled at his friend. "Yes. I did not tell them you survived so as to ensure Kit'erak does not take his wraith from your betrayal out on your people."

Gr'ex turned to me. "The Death Weavers specialize in necromancy and curses. They will be great assets to our fight."

"Fine. They can all come, we will find somewhere to put them. However, I expect their oaths of fealty when they arrive." I answered.

"Of course, of course!" Gr'ex said excitedly.

I turned to look at Alice. "Would you go tell Melody that Jebediah needs to speak with her."

Alice smiled. "Okay!" She immediately got up and skipped to the elevator.

"Why me?" Jebediah asked.

"She likes you better. Plus, you've been helping to coordinate with her in regard to the survivors. Plus, and far more importantly, I think you're sweet on her."

Jebediah's face turned red. "I have no idea what you're talking about my boy. Though I will be glad to talk to her."

Turning to Suzie and Emily. "I still would like to go do some grinding with my party members; you are welcome to join us, Emily."

"Umm, maybe next time. I think I'll help out around here." Emily said shyly.

"Oh, come on. Join us. You need the levels." Suzie encouraged.

Emily sighed. "Fine, but I'm not a front-line fighter."

"Not a problem. Just stick by me and Donut." Suzie replied.

I shared my plan. "With that settled, new plan. We will start testing out how many Bone Marrow we can pick off. Afterwards, we split up. Gr'ex and I will rendezvous with Jek'jon and the other goblin clans while you guys get cleaned up and make sure Duncan gets back in time to give the evening report."

Jebediah left to speak with Melody and Ann who wanted to help with the coordination and overall health of the survivors. Suzie took Emily to find some weapons, preferably a gun, and gear. That left me with Gr'ex and Jek'jon.

Gr'ex spoke up. "I figured you would want to discuss this without any of the other huemons around."

"Discuss what?" I inquired.

"Discuss what he asked." Gr'ex grumbled.

"That is what he said my friend." Jek'jon chimed in.

Gr'ex sighed. "You do not yet understand my friend. You have not been around him enough. Just watch." He said to Jek'jon before turning to me and continuing. "Your increased muscle mass and height, you had a threshold breakthrough, didn't you?"

"Yes, I did. You could tell that just from my muscles and height?" I asked.

Gr'ex shook his head. "Your presence actually. You are both more commanding of attention and in better control of your aura. Such things can usually be traced back to a threshold breakthrough. Such things are more common with pure cultivators, but I know you use mana."

"In the short term I'm going with a more balanced distribution of my stat points. The different perks and titles I've gotten have allowed me to barely pass the second threshold." I explained.

"What?! Th-that requires a hundred points in all primary stats! You are only level 10!" Jek'jon exclaimed.

Gr'ex looked at his friend. "Do you see what I'm talking about now? I have never heard of anyone having those kinds of stats at level ten. He doesn't even have a class yet! This is what I have been dealing with! He defies all logic."

Jek'jon nodded. "It is most impressive. I must tell our people as it will only further rally our kind to his banner. Speaking about that, you really should consider designing a banner."

"Hold on a minute! You just accept all of this my friend? How are you not upset? I know for a fact huemons only get 5 points per level, that is 50 points maximum. I know he possesses the **World's Champion** title..." Gr'ex chimed in before Jek'jon interrupted him.

"There you have it. That is said to bestow massive increases not only when receiving the title, but it gives slight boosts to other titles. I do not see the problem, my friend. Our way is to follow the strong and powerful. If Shadowalker is this strong at level 10, just imagine what he will be able to do once he has a class."

Gr'ex spoke in frustration. "But goblins only get 4 points per level! Our class and core bonuses cannot even..."

Jek'jon put his hand on Gr'ex's shoulder. "You were the first goblin to pledge fealty to our master. I have heard several among my people call you wise for doing so, do not let your pride and ego cloud your judgement now my friend. The clans will need guidance and I have little interest beyond farming. You know that is my dream. I will fight and do as commanded, but my love is to grow things. Our people will need your guidance."

I watched the interplay. I knew I drove Gr'ex nuts at time with my defiance of the status quo. I would have to be mindful that jealousy did not fester and poison our friendship.

Gr'ex looked at his friend. "You are right. I gladly welcome the chance to guide our people to glory, even if it is in service of others."

Jek'jon clapped his friend's back. "That's the spirit. Now I must return to prepare for our arrival. I will see you both later tonight."

Jek'jon bowed to me and then left the cabin.

I turned to my friend. "Do not worry Gr'ex. I need you. I hope you understand I appreciate your help more than you may know."

Gr'ex smiled and nodded. "Okay, okay. Enough of this sappy emotional stuff. Let's go kill some people and gain some levels."

I chuckled. "Ha! Sounds good to me."

It did not take our party long to get ready and head out. Duncan had a Kevlar vest and some heavily padded clothing, with a metal baseball bat as his weapon. Jebediah had his guns, some blades, and even a few grenades. Suzie wore some yoga outfit that I imagine was for speed of movement. Emily was wearing something similar. Suzie had her guns and a long bow she found in Paul's arsenal. Emily had a few guns strapped to her, she also found a compound bow and a quiver full of arrows. Gr'ex had his staff and grabbed one of my short swords just in case.

"System, make a reminder for me to teach Gr'ex how to handle a firearm."

Reminder Added

As for me, sure I had a few pistols equipped. I also grabbed a sword from my personal collection. Yes, I collected a few. I even tried my hands at learning smithing, which Paul had encouraged me to pursue. I figured I should try to synergize what knowledge was in my head with what I thought I knew.

I repeated the plan as we got closer to enemy territory. "Alright everyone, group up. Donuts I want you and I in front. Suzie and Emily in the middle. Jebediah and Gr'ex in the back. We prioritize speed over damage. Hit em, kill what you can then fall back. Then we loop around to another area. Rinse and repeat. Any questions?"

"What if we can't outrun them?" Emily asked as she looked at Jebediah and Gr'ex.

"Don't worry about me darling. I put plenty of points into **Dexterity** and **Constitution**." Jebediah commented.

Gr'ex looked at Emily and smiled wickedly before summoning a **Dark Bolt**. "Any that get to close get one of these or one of the many curses I know."

Emily took a step closer to Suzie. "Got it. Sorry I asked."

"No need to apologize Emily. You were just concerned for the team. That is an admirable quality. Look alive everyone goblin patrol incoming." I said before catching up to Duncan as he charged the patrol to get all their attention on him.

There were six goblins.

Goblin Scout Level 20

Goblin Warrior Level 19

Goblin Scout Level 21

Goblin Archer Level 16

Goblin Warrior Level 18

Goblin Warrior Level 17

"Donut taunt as many as you can. Girls, target priority: kill any archers, then scouts. Guys scouts, then warriors." I ordered as I charged the level 19 goblin warrior.

My target had a shield and sword. The goblin warrior blocked my first swing, but I didn't realize how much strength I put behind the blow and it caught the goblin off guard causing him to stagger back. His shield was Now off center leaving him open for a follow up attack. I took the opening with a quick riposte. The move allowed me to slide just out of the way from an axe swing from one of the goblin scouts.

As I ripped out my blade, I backhanded the goblin scout who stood in temporary shock at the speed in which I dodged his attack as my combo move finished off his friend. Again, I didn't realize my own strength and my simple backhand lifted the goblin off the ground as he spun back, crashing headfirst into a nearby tree. I heard an audible snap as his head turned an angle it wasn't meant to.

I did a quick scan of the fight. Duncan had picked up the fallen shield and was easily keeping the two goblin warriors at bay. The archer was already dead, an arrow in one eye socket and a bullet hole where the other eye used to be. The girls were already taking aim at the two warriors Duncan was tanking.

Jebediah took one of the scouts with a shot in the heart, he was dead on the forest floor. The last scout was squirming on the ground, clearly in agony before a Dark Bolt ended his life.

By the time I turned to help Duncan, the girls took out the remaining warriors.

"Great job guys. No issues. Girls, great shift to the warriors." I said as I walked over to the goblin I backhanded into the tree and confirmed he was dead.

"What the hell was that?" Jebediah asked.

"Huh? What was what?" I replied.

"These guys may be smaller than us but that hit had enough force to snap its neck on impact. I've never seen you move like that in all the years I have known you. How high is your **Strength**?" Jebediah said as he looked at me.

Gr'ex growled. "That is not something you can ask! It is considered insulting to ask a stranger, let alone an ally such a question!"

I raised my hand to Gr'ex. "I put a good number of points in **Strength** and **Dexterity**. I also gained a perk that imparted knowledge of weapons."

"You can gain perks like that?" Duncan asked.

Gr'ex was the one to answer. "Of course, the capabilities of the system are vast and rather impressive."

"That's cool." Suzie commented.

"Agreed." Emily said.

Jebediah visibly calmed down. "I did not realize you would put all your points into **Strength** and **Dexterity**. When we would all discuss what we wanted in life you always talked about being a mage. I thought you wasted your chance to be one."

"That is still the long-term goal, but right now we have to survive." I replied.

"I just hope you didn't cripple your chances." Jebediah said as he put his hand on my shoulder.

"Not a chance buddy. I appreciate the concern that I blew my chance by spending all my points but don't worry. I have a plan." I said as I tapped the man's arm in acknowledgment he was just looking out for my future and not rushing into something that could be an issue later.

'Here I thought he wanted to know how I could generate that much force. Guess he hasn't figured out it takes over 100 points in **Strength** to do that kind of move. Well, I'm not going to tell him.' I thought as Jebediah nodded at me.

"Very well."

"So now that you two are done with whatever that was. Can I start raising the dead, master?" Gr'ex asked.

"Sure. Makes sense. A necromancer needs undead minions." I answered.

"He's doing what now?!" Emily asked in disgust.

"Gr'ex is an Apprentice Necromancer. Did we not mention that?" I replied.

"No, you most certainly did not!" Suzie said in agreement with her friend.

"Sounds cool." Duncan commented as he offered me a donut.

I gladly took the donut and passed one to Jebediah. The three of us watched Gr'ex work and ate our donuts in rapt attention.

Suzie and Emily volunteered to go scouting to make sure we weren't disturbed. In truth, they just wanted to be anywhere else.

Gr'ex cast **Raise Undead Minion** six times. Each time grayish-black energy would rush out and surround the corpse. Then it would delve deep into the body, filling and closing some wounds. The arrow in the goblin's eye was slowly pushed out as the Undead Zombie rose to its feet.

Duncan raised his hand to get Gr'ex's attention. I put his hand down. "This isn't school man, just ask your question." I told the excited man.

"Oh, okay. So, Mr. Gr'ex do they always get raised as an Undead Zombie?"

Gr'ex stood a bit straighter. He liked being the center of attention when he knew things others did not, especially about his craft. "No, not at all. Undead Zombies are the most efficient and easiest to produce. There are other spells that can raise skeletons or make them more sentient. If they were a caster, there are spells that can turn them into Undead Mage able to use their magic. Those are the most used variations when working with bones or a recently deceased corpse."

"Man, that is convenient. Instant army." Jebediah commented.

Gr'ex sighed. "There are limits. Level, affinity, class, stats, titles, perks, known spells, etc. all play a hand in how many undead you can control. My clan grants me a title that helps with the number of undead I can control. Kit'erak, my old master, also helped my clan gain perks to increase our Death magic capabilities. All of these guys are trash, but their bodies aren't too mutilated, which reduces the mana point or MP cost to raise them."

"Can you keep them up indefinitely?" Jebediah asked.

"That's what she said." Duncan joked.

After a few chuckles later, a confused Gr'ex answered. "That is one of the benefits of Necromancers. If you are raising existing corpses or using them as fuel it can last indefinitely. There is a very small mana drain but it's negligible. That is what makes necromancers more appealing to summoners. Well unless you are talking about a Dark Summoner but those are legends so not much point discussing."

"What's a Dark Summoner?" I asked.

Gr'ex sighed. "Fine, I'll answer your question. They are the pinnacle of both necromancer and summoner. They do not require materials to create their minions, though they still benefit from raising corpses. The major difference is they can summon permanent undead and other typically dark-aligned minions to do their bidding and then store them in their own pocket dimension. It makes them a one man or woman, army. They are the most feared weapon of the Dark, or so that is the legend. I know of no Dark Summoners in existence."

"Wow, sounds really cool." Duncan commented.

"I totally agree. Now that would be an awesome class to be able to pick." I commented.

"Agreed. Though I'd still prefer something where I can use explosives to blow up bad guys." Jebediah chimed in.

"Well, it looks like you're done raising your new minions. We should probably find the girls so we can keep repeating this process." I said as I headed in the direction, we saw them going off to scout in.

We found them about ten minutes later. The two ranged fighters had taken out a scouting group of four goblins.

"We hit them from two sides. They were dead before they even realized what had happened." Suzie explained.

"These goblins don't seem very smart. One ran right into a tree branch knocking it out. The other ran right at Suzie without trying to take any cover. Just dumb." Emily chimed in. As she turned to see Gr'ex, she was worried she might've just insulted him. "Sorry. I didn't mean anything by it."

Gr'ex looked at her confused for a minute before it dawned on him. "Why would I be insulted? These are Bone Marrow goblins; they are not exactly known for their intelligence. All huemons are not the same, are they?"

"Well, no..." Emily answered.

"Then why would I take insult when you speak about other goblins, especially ones from a different clan. Silly huemon, I mean silly elf." Gr'ex said as he walked past her to begin raising these goblins too.

"Ugh, not this again." Suzie complained.

"Eh, leave the green skin alone. We would be fools to ignore the tactical advantage his class can give us." Jebediah chimed in.

Gr'ex looked back at the trigger-happy man and gave the man the briefest of nods in acknowledgment of respect before going back to raising his minions.

'Hmmm it seems even across species, men can convey similar ways of communicating.' I thought as I watched the byplay.

After Gr'ex raised the now tenth undead minion, he smiled. "I just leveled up!"

"Really? You can level up from raising undead?" Jebediah asked.

"Of course! It's a core aspect of my class. How do you think blacksmiths and other crafters level up?" Gr'ex answered.

"I hadn't really thought about it. I just figured you kill stuff, you level." Jebediah replied.

"Well, yes. That is one of the fastest and most reliable ways to level but by far not the most common." Gr'ex stated.

"Huh? What do you mean?" Emily asked.

Gr'ex switched into his mentor mode. "Most people are non-combatants. Sure, plenty still do some level of fighting or militia work, but usually they rely on their class and professions to help them level. Sometimes the system will provide quests related to your profession for added experience. Like right now I have a quest to raise 50 undead minions. As I plan on doing such a thing anyway it is a nice benefit that helps push you closer to your next level and embrace the path you have chosen to go down."

"That's good to know and something to consider." I commented.

"I have a quest like that. It says to feed 50 people one of my donuts. I got it after I made my hundredth donut." Duncan shared.

"Huh? That seems a bit random." Suzie said.

"Not really if you think about it. Donut here loves em, it is no surprise that the system would encourage him to do what he loves." I hypothesized.

"Exactly! That is at the very core and nature of the system. Good, bad, or indifferent, it does not matter. It helps facilitate our focus which helps figure out our purpose." Gr'ex explained.

"So why haven't we gotten anything like that?" Suzie asked.

"Simple. You haven't been focusing. When you are all over the place and distracted, the system has a harder time helping you on a course of action. Start intentionally doing specific things that matter to you consistently and see what the system does in response." Gr'ex further explained.

"Worth a shot." Emily chimed in.

Suzie nodded in agreement. "Alright. Why not. Well to start I want to kill some more goblins for invading our home."

"Lead the way." Jebediah replied.

"Sure thing. I'm going to..." Suzie stopped mid-stride. "Son of a..."

"What's up?" Duncan asked his friend.

Suzie turned to Duncan with a smile on her face. "I just got a quest to kill 25 Bone Marrow clan goblin invaders. That little pompous goblin was right."

"Pompous. I'll show you pompous you ungrateful..." Gr'ex raised hand and started to summon a Dark Bolt. He was interrupted by my hand on his arm.

As he looked at me, I shook my head. "Fine, but I'm not saving her if she gets in trouble." Gr'ex said as he dropped his spell and sent his minions ahead of him as he further walked towards enemy territory.

I turned to the party. "He may be harsh in his communication, but this is the apocalypse. Being nice and fake will get you killed. Don't take for granted the knowledge he freely shares, or the kindness I share." I said the last bit as I let go of the tiniest bit of my Dark Mantle ability for the briefest of moments before turning my back on them and heading after Gr'ex.

Chapter 26 – Meeting the Clans

As the sun began to set, our party split up. Gr'ex and I making our roundabout route to meet the other goblin clans while the rest of the party head back to the compound.

It had been a very productive day. All of us leveled, some several times. Once I reached level 11, I shifted to playing a backup and support role, giving the rest of my team the opportunity to catch up in levels. And catch up they did.

Duncan and Jebediah reached level 11. Emily hit level 10. Suzie was the elf rockstar of the group, switching between her bow and her rifle. Her quick reflexes and rapid fire netted her to level 12.

The one who really reaped the rewards was Gr'ex. His Undead Zombies were beyond just back up support. In some fights, they were the perfect meat shields, soaking up damage or dog piling enemies. Sure, several were destroyed and unrecoverable, but it mattered little, as after each fight Gr'ex's zombie horde grew. He currently had 45 Undead Zombie minions. The goblin even gained three additional levels and was now sitting at level 22.

Gr'ex sent his minions out ahead of us, ensuring we would not be blindsided on our way to the rendezvous. While the goblin and his minions were keeping watch, I reviewed my notification.

Level Up! Congratulations! You are now level 11. You gain +26 stat points per level...

I just couldn't understand how so I asked my system mentally.

"System can you explain this whole +26 stat points per level? For the first ten levels I didn't get this many so I'm trying to wrap my head around this."

Query Accepted

You are seeing an increase in stat points per level due to two primary reasons. First, your Divine Infinitum originally granted you an additional +8 stat points per level. Since then, your Divine Infinitum has increased efficiency and capacity five times. This means every level you now gain +13 stat points per level from your Divine Infinitum.

"Wow! Gr'ex would lose his mind on this. Okay where are the other 13 points coming from."

Query Accepted

When you were human, you gained the standard +5 stat points per level. Your race has since changed to Primordial Celestial Dragon. This means your +5 for being human is replaced with your new racial value. Primordial Celestial Dragons are intrinsically tied to the cosmos and gain +13 stat points per level.

"That's insane. How common is it to have stat growth like that from your race?"

Query Accepted

Practically nonexistent. Primordial Celestial Dragons have one of the highest racial bonuses per level. Other dragons do not receive such bonuses. Only Ancient Omni-Dragons are your equal in stat bonuses per level.

"What is an Ancient Omni-Dragon? My Divine Infinitum references my type of affinity as Omni."

Query Partially Accepted

Ancient Omni-Dragons are the royalty of dragon kind and seen as their natural sovereigns. It is unknown why you possess Omni as your type of affinity. Currently, not available to be able to answer your question.

"Well, this is the first time you've partially been able to accept my query. Guess it is better than not being able to answer my question."

Such a situation is uncomfortable. Your Divine Infinitum is a danger to many, Omni is beyond limitless. Please refrain from further inquiries in this subject area.

Then I heard a screech in my head that made me stop dead in my tracks. It was like a computer was overheating or a fan was dying. It made me instantly decide at least for now to be careful with this Omni subject especially as it related to my **Divine Infinitum**.

Something was not comfortable with my line of questions, and it was powerful enough to interfere with my system. Last time that happened was the remnants of the Primordial Celestial Dragon in the core I absorbed, and he had apparently been around since the beginning of time. Yep, best for me to change subjects... oh look we are here at the Sleeping Willow camp.

"Welcome master!" Jek'jon greeted us as we entered the camp. He was surrounded by a few goblins in robes that looked older than dirt.

That was when I took the time to do a quick scan of the rest of the camp. There were goblins everywhere. And I do mean everywhere. Some were in the trees, some on the fort walls... 'hey how did that many goblins fit in that hut, are they part clown?' My mind caught at the absurdity of so many goblins in such a small space.

An older goblin woman in black robes who was leaning on her staff squinted at me. Her nose was huge and what hair she had was white as snow. She was sitting on some kind of skeleton amalgamation that had four legs and a crook that she could sit in. "Is this the one you claim is the one who bears the mantle."

The larger goblin man in leather armor next to her scrutinized me. He was bigger than Tek'tar but had kind eyes behind his gruff expression. "Looks a little small to me Jek'jon."

I had to blink a few times at the third elder when I noticed what he was sitting on moved. Eight stubby legs popped out from underneath. He was sitting on the biggest spider I have ever seen. It was easily his height and three times his width.

'Man, so many people are going to lose their minds when they find out there are giant spiders in the apocalypse.' I thought as I stared at the thing.

The third elder spoke. "There, there Lucile. We will see if Jek'jon is in error."

Gr'ex was standing behind me and whispered so only I could hear. "You must show my people strength, power, and wisdom. If you can show all three, they will follow you anywhere."

'Strength, power, and wisdom huh?' I thought as I released the tight control over my **Dark Mantle** ability. I then activated the Active ability and pushed more mana and stamina into it to amplify my aura across the whole camp.

Most cowered in fear. Many dropped to their knees and bowed so low their hands and heads touched the ground. The giant spider literally squealed, chittered, and then proceeded to try to dig itself into the dirt and hide. The elder who was sitting on his spider was thrown off, but he was too busy relieving himself to care. The old woman fell on her butt and the look on her face was one of fear and awe. The final elder grabbed a vial from a pouch, downed in and instantly turned invisible.

"Ooo. That guy has an invisibility potion I'm guessing. Very cool. I wonder if he has any more?" I commented on what I was seeing.

I felt a tug on my pant leg. I turned to see Gr'ex on his knees. "Dial it back... please."

"Oh, sorry about that. It just felt so nice to let go for a moment." I commented as I reapplied my tight control to reign my aura back in.

Gr'ex audibly sighed as he stood back up. "Ahhhh. So much better. Your use of your aura feels even more deadly and terrifying than before."

Gr'ex stepped around me to see the aftermath. He shook his head as more were still prostrating themselves in front of him.

The old woman seemed to regain her faculties first. She took one look at Gr'ex. "Gr'exy? I thought you died!"

"Grandma Hal'ex?" Gr'ex said in reply as he started to make his way to his grandmother.

"Gr'exy? Grandma?" I asked in shock.

The skeleton chair monster moved in Gr'ex's direction. A few moments later, grandmother and grandson were hugging and crying.

"I'll leave them to their reunion." I said to myself as I made my way to Jek'jon.

"Hey Jek'jon. I hope that removed any doubt they may have had." I commented.

Jek'jon nodded profusely. "Yes. That was most helpful to remove their doubts. Come let me introduce you to the Crawlers chief Tan'don. I'm not exactly sure where the Boom chief Mek'mar has disappeared to." Jek'jon pointed to Gr'ex. "The old crone over there hugging Gr'ex is the Death Weavers chief and Gr'ex's grandmother Hal'ex."

We walked up to Tan'don as he was using a staff to help him get to his feet. I cast **PURITY!!!** on the goblin chief to remove the smell that was already starting to waft off him.

"Oh, that feels so much better. Thank you, your dark eminence. I was a bit embarrassed that happened." Chief Tan'don replied in thanks.

"Same thing happened to me the first time I beheld Shadowalker's power. Since then, his mantle has grown more intense that I still get weak in the knees, but once you recognize him as your sovereign it changes." Jek'jon explained.

"I will keep that in mind. Come let me see if Lucile has calmed down enough for me to introduce you." Tan'don replied as he led us over to the giant spider that had buried half her body in dirt.

Tan'don tried to coax his spider mount out. "Come now Lucile, you can come out now."

The giant spider poked its head out of the dirt, took one look at me, shook its head, and proceeded to try to dig deeper into the ground.

Tan'don looked back at us. "She's usually much friendlier than this. Give me a few minutes."

Jek'jon and I backed away. As we turned in the direction of Gr'ex and his grandmother, the large goblin popped into existence a few feet in front of us.

"Ah you're back Mek'mar. Good, good. Let me introduce you to my master." Jek'jon greeted.

Mek'mar cowered. "Uh-uh, I need a few moments to... uh clean up."

I cast my **PURITY!!!** ability on the large goblin. After a flash he was clean and that is when I noticed he had different gadgets and vials attached to belts and coming out of different pockets. He reminded me of what you would get if you took a mad scientist and a goblin and mashed them together.

Mek'mar quickly ran his fingers over his gear checking everything before he audibly sighed in relief. "Whew! I was worried whatever you did might have destroyed something or ruined one of my experiments."

'He is a mad scientist!' I thought.

Just as I was about to say something Mek'mar's eyes widened, and he dropped to his knees. "Uh-Uh. I just realized you might have taken offense to my words your dark eminence. I assure you that I was more worried a chain reaction could occur, some of my items are very sensitive to magic. Please forgive me if..."

I raised my hand to stop his rambling. "Please take a breath man. And get up." That was when I realized all the goblins in the camp minus the chiefs were still bowing in supplication. I let my voice echo. "That goes for the rest of you, get up. I appreciate the sign of deference, but I need followers who will look up, otherwise you will forever be bumping into things."

The last of my words got a few chuckles from some of the braver goblins. Th crowd slowly got up and after looking my way multiple times they returned to their duties.

"You know the Sleeping Willow clan will be even more devote after today's display, master." Jek'jon whispered so only I could hear.

I nodded in acknowledgment before turning my attention back to Mek'mar. "So, I take it you're some kind of scientist?"

"Sci-en-tist?" Mek'mar sounded out the word. "I am not familiar with that word. My Boom clan specializes in Goblin Engineering. Many of our clan are Artificers and crafters. We create many different experiments and gadgets from potent alcohol to big bombs. Sure, we have many other, shall we say, less explosive items, but our clan has a strong fascination with fire and blowing things up."

"Ha!" I patted the now excited goblin engineer on the shoulder. "Jebediah is going to love you, as is my friend Laraaq!"

"I appreciate the offer your dark eminence, but I am happily married." Mek'mar replied hesitantly as it appeared earlier still feared offending me.

I shook my head and chuckled. "Ha! No, no. Not like that. They both love blowing things up. My comment was more that I'm sure they are going to love your gadgets and want to test them."

Mek'mar seemed relieved and then brightened. "Ooo, maybe they will want to test some of my more delicate experiments, after some in my clan repeatedly lost their eyebrows, they stopped offering to help their chief."

I laughed a good hearty laugh. "Ha, ha, ha, ha, ha! Now I'm certain you guys are going to get along. That is if your clan is still interested in pledging their fealty."

Mek'mar's eyes widened. "Oh, forgive me your dark eminence! In my fear and then excitement I failed to make our intentions clear and pledge my fealty. All my clan will do so."

Mek'mar got on his knees and recited the sacred words of fealty and gave his oath both for himself and his clan.

I received the notification confirmation.

Congratulations! The Boom clan goblin chief Mek'mar has pledged both his fealty and the fealty of his clan to you. They have promised to serve you in any way you require and defend your interests. You have promised them a place in your lands and holdings.

*Congratulations! As two different goblin clans have pledged fealty to you and your cause, other goblins will recognize your authority and have an increased desire to join your banner. Increased relations with any of the goblin race. This bonus increases as more clans pledge their loyalty. You have gained the title **War Chief**.*

Title: War Chief
<u>Description</u>: *Many of the more brutal and aggressive races such as goblins, Orcs, ogres, trolls, Minotaurs recognize the importance of strength and how conflict may be needed to grow and prosper. Due to the savagery such a mindset may create, these races tend to align to Dark's goals of conquest and power. Only the strongest of leaders can rally such factions in both times of war and peace. Those that can are called War Chief. This title grants +13 to all stats. +25% effectiveness of your forces in battle. In addition, grants you the **Right of Mok'Tai**.*

I didn't even have to ask as my system immediately knew what I wanted.

Query Accepted

Right of Mok'Tai
<u>Description</u>: *This is the right for one **War Chief** to challenge a clan chief or another **War Chief**. This right is to the death, but not necessarily the final death. The winner keeps what they kill, granting them authority over the other clan or war band. Please Note: Many of the Dark have used this right*

to seize control of some of the weaker races and use them for their own wicked purposes.

I finished reading and became aware of my surroundings again. 'Man, I really have to be careful about that.' I thought as I saw both Jek'jon and Mek'mar bowing. "Command us our War Chief."

"Get up, get up. What did I say about looking up. I wholeheartedly welcome the Boom clan into our ranks. I will want a full accounting of what sorts of gadgets and weapons you can make for us."

"Yes, my War Chief." Mek'mar replied.

The old woman finally walked over with Gr'ex. "Well, I guess my pledge may not be as interesting. I am Hal'ex, your dark eminence. I am the chief of the Death Weavers clan and the grandmother of my Gr'exy."

"It is a pleasure to meet you chief Hal'ex. I welcome any family of my new friend Gr'ex." I replied.

I saw Gr'ex gain a look of surprise. "You consider me your friend?!"

"Of course, Gr'ex. In such a short time, we have already been through so much. You may need some work, but we all do." I said as I put my hand on Gr'ex's shoulder.

I thought I saw tears forming in Gr'ex's eyes, but the goblin just nodded and looked away.

Hal'ex spoke up. "Well, I still want to thank you for sparing him. He said you spared him, and he has pledged his fealty and loyalty to you. It is clear you value my grandson which makes me think you will value the rest of my Death Weavers. My clan specializes in Death magic and curses, that is what we are most known for, but what many do not know is we have long worked with the Crawlers clan to gain access to their spider silk and are excellent tailors and decent enchanters if I do say so myself."

"Wow, very impressive." I acknowledged.

Hal'ex continued. "If you will accept our fealty, all that we have is yours, your dark eminence."

"You are more than welcome among my people. Besides, how could I separate family again." I replied.

Hal'ex smiled as she gave her hand to Gr'ex so he could help her to kneel. "I Hal'ex, goblin chief of the Death Weavers clan hereby, on my power, give my oath of loyalty and fealty to War Chief Shadowalker. His enemies are our enemies, his allies shall have sanctuary among our people. I pledge this with my authority as chief for myself and all of my clan, now and forever!"

"I accept the oath of loyalty and fealty from Hal'ex and the Death Weavers clan. I offer them sanctuary in my lands and to do what I can to help them prosper and grow as long as they keep true to their oath." I replied almost unbidden as the words flowed out of me.

There was a thrumming of power as she finished. "What was that?" I asked as I felt that in my bones.

Gr'ex spoke as he helped his grandmother up. "My grandmother is a powerful spellcaster. When a powerful magic user gives an oath with and on their power, it carries more weight. It is not required, but by doing so, if she ever broke her oath, she would lose all her power and the impact would cripple her if not outright kill her."

"Why?" I asked the old woman.

"Because I see something special in your eyes. You have suffered much in your life, yet you do not see it that way. Something within you holds true to hope and it is that shared hope that I have for my people. Many of my clan are casters and crafters, we have little else. We even train our young at a very early age to harness their gifts. This will show my people how important this oath is for all of us." Hal'ex explained.

I quickly reviewed and dismissed the confirmation notification.

I bowed my head in acknowledgment. "I am honored."

Hal'ex gave a wicked smile. "You should be you young one. If I was a few decades younger, no make that a few years younger I'd be chasing after you as a mate. We are hardwired to desire powerful mates and produce strong offspring. In fact, I warn you now, what some of my clan members may attempt to gain your favor."

"Umm, good to know. Oh look, Tan'don has finally coaxed Lucile out of her hiding spot." I quickly said to change the subject as I noticed a few female goblins in dark robes literally drooling and licking their lips.

I said a silent prayer. 'Oh, please let me survive the apocalypse and not have to deal with a bunch of crazy goblins in heat.'

Tan'don was leading Lucile over with her reins as he talked to her sweetly. "See Lucile, he likes us goblins. Three clans have already pledged themselves to him."

Tan'don bowed his head. "My apologies your dark eminence, spiders have a natural inclining to the dark as their sanctuary. But when they feel that very dark brings terror down on them, it is a horror unlike any other for their kind. Go ahead and slowly try to pet her, she likes to be scratched just behind the eye cluster."

I hesitantly walked over to Lucile. The giant spider was the size of a large dog. I have friends who would've already been miles away by now at the first sight of this thing. Luckily it wasn't one of my fears, but it is not like I could ignore its giant mandibles.

Once I got close enough, I slowly lowered my hand and started to first stroke Lucile's carapace before scratching at the spot Tan'don indicated. Lucile literally started to purr. Don't ask me how a giant spider can purr, but it was. Then she leaned into me like it was giving me a hug.

Tan'don clapped his hands in excitement, and I almost crapped my pants. I was so focused on the spider it completely caught me off guard.

"Excellent. As you can see your dark eminence, my clan, the Crawlers, get our name from the spider mounts we raise. They make amazing pets, loyal as long as you keep them fed that is, and as you can imagine are very capable in battle. Most spiders can lose multiple limbs and still be almost fully battle capable. We also have many beast tamers, skilled archers, and scouts."

"Most impressive, chief Tan'don." I replied.

The old goblin reminded me of a sweet old man who loved his family and was proud of them.

"I am an Earth mage and have beast tamer skills. If it will please you, your dark eminence, I will give my oath on my power and use a skill that allows our bonded spiders pledge their line to you as well." Tan'don explained.

"Please do. I might actually feel better having the spiders bound in that way." I said honestly.

Tan'don nodded before both him and Lucile bowed. The weirdest thing happened. As Tan'don spoke, it was like I could hear Lucile's chittering as a voice that overlaid or echoed after the old goblin. "I Tan'don... I Lucile... give our oaths of loyalty and fealty for both us and our brood for all eternity!"

I accepted their oaths. "I Shadowalker, accept your oaths of loyalty and fealty in the same gravity they were given. As long as you remain true to your oaths I shall stand with your people and help you grow and prosper."

This time it felt like two thrumming notes of power echoed as if singing a song of unity.

I received the confirmation notification and after reviewing and dismissing it, I saw another notification. This one had a gold border that seemed to glow.

*Congratulations! More than one faction and race previously following the Dark have joined your cause in loyalty and fealty. As you already hold the titles of **World's Champion** and **War Chief**, this grants you two additional benefits. You are now considered your own Faction. You gained the title: **Dark Eminence**.*

My system once again knew what I wanted to know.

Query Accepted

Faction: Dark Eminence *(Default Name)*
Faction Leader: *Shadowalker*
Description: *Like the **Right of Mok'Tai**, Factions have authority to parlay, conduct negotiations, form alliances, and enter into trade deals with other factions. Once your Faction territory is officially established, Contested Portals cannot be opened in your domain. This does not prevent other portals but as **Faction Leader** who possesses **Space** magic affinity, you will be notified should another portal open in your **Faction territory**.*

Title: Dark Eminence
Description: *Your Dark Mantle is recognized as the authority of power that can strike fear into your enemies and inspire your allies. Many races known to typically align with the Dark have legends of a sovereign who shall wield such power. This title acknowledges the truth in what others see within you.*

+13 to All Stats. +10% increased chance of successful negotiations. *Increased chance to cause **Horrified** status effect on enemies when you release your **Dark Mantle** aura. +25% chance to rally your forces when you are personally on the battlefield. In addition, grants you authority over your own Faction.*

As I finished reading all of that, my mind was reeling.

'So many things to consider. I was not expecting taking in what in a sense is a bunch of goblin refugees would net me so many benefits. The stat bumps alone are huge.' That train of thought was interrupted when words appeared in my vision.

Please Note: System has temporarily delayed integration of stat bonuses to allow for time to prepare for large influx of stats. Remaining time: 60 seconds.

"I have so many questions, but they will have to wait. My system delayed my stat gains from my titles to allow us to finish the oaths. Too many stat changes at once. So, I will need a few moments to acclimate." I said as I dropped to the ground, already feeling it start.

"Normally I would ask but I got to know. How many stats?" Gr'ex inquired.

I gritted my teeth as I spoke. "26 in All Attributes."

Just as the pain took me to sweet bliss and I passed out, again, I hear Gr'ex.

"You see what I have been dealing with?! What person do you know gets 26 stats in all attributes, at once! Luckiest son of a..."

I passed out before I heard him finish his rant, a smile on my face despite the pain of my bones and muscles growing and reshaping all at the same time.

Interlude- Alice

Alice finally got away from those incessant women, Melody and Ann. They would just not leave her alone to explore. It was so infuriating, so much so, that she wanted to play her fun games with the old woman. But no, Alice was a good girl, and every game had its rules.

She had snuck out of the compound to go explore. The people inside the compound were boring, no quiet dark place to play in, everything was far too well-lit, and all she could sense was the constant feeling of confusion and loss, not fun emotions at all.

That is why she was in this forest. She overheard her new daddy saying he would go meet with the new goblins. She found those creatures far more entertaining than the boring adults back at the compound.

That was when she encountered two goblins out on patrol. "Hey, look a huemon that is more our size." The one on the left said as he pointed his spear at Alice.

The goblin on the right smiled wickedly as he spoke. "Let's have some fun with her before we bring her back. She's no goblin woman but she will do!"

Alice smiled. "Are you two saying you want to play with me?"

The goblin on the left dropped his spear and drew his small dagger and gave his own evil smile. "Yes, we are going to play with you plenty. If you get out of line, I'll use my knife here to teach you a lesson."

Alice giggled. "He, he, he, he, he. That's not a knife. This is a knife." As Alice said the last part, she drew one of her special soul blades which was clearly longer and glowing a mix of spectral blue and ethereal green.

"Uhhh, maybe we should run." The goblin on the right said as he started to back away.

"So, what if she has a weapon. She is a little girl. Let's have some fun. I get first..." the goblin on the left didn't get a chance to finish his words as he was lifted by the head and slammed against a tree.

The goblin on the right startled at the sudden appearance of a giant monster of a man in some tall hat and long coat, tried to make a run for it. As he took a step, he found his legs giving out for some reason, then felt immense pain, and he flopped to the ground.

Alice knelt as she stabbed her blade into the goblin's shoulder. "Silly goblin. My friend distracted you, but I'm the one you both wanted to play with."

"Please, please..." the goblin begged.

Blade still imbedded in the goblin's shoulder; Alice clapped. "Oh goodie! I do love it when they beg to join me for all eternity, so we can all play together forever. He, he, he."

In one swift motion Alice withdrew her blade and slit it across the goblin's throat. She stood and walked over to the other goblin who interrupted her exploration. It was clear the goblin was still dazed from having its head slammed into a tree.

The dazed goblin was sitting up against the tree he had been slammed into.

"I know just what to do to help you wake up." Alice said as she materialized a second blade and stabbed both blades into the goblin's shoulders, pinned the goblin to the tree.

The mind fog of his head getting slammed into a tree cleared instantly, replaced by searing pain that he felt down into his very soul.

"AAAHHHHH!!!!"

"Now you were being very bad. Your screams are an improvement, but I'm not sure you're really getting into the game." Alice lamented.

The goblin pinned to the tree started to sob. "I-I am, am, so, so, sorry. Please it hurts!"

Alice clapped. "Now that's better. You're starting to get into it now. Don't worry, it'll be over soon, and then you can join the others."

Another quick motion and Alice removed the blades and sliced the goblin's legs, preventing him from running away. She then cut the goblin's armor and began to carve runes into his flesh. After she was done, she repeated the process on the other goblin corpse.

After two casts of her magic, Alice had two new Soul-Forged Minions. She sent them into her soul-space and continued her trek through the forest. As she walked, Alice cast her magic to remove any blood splatter on her clothes.

Several minutes later Alice reached the Sleeping Willow camp. She hid in the bushes and watched.

'Oh goodie, new daddy has just arrived.' Alice thought.

Then Shadowalker activated his Dark Mantle ability and Alice became extremely excited. She loved every moment of it washing over her. The pure joy she felt made her lean against a tree as she took it all in.

Then the aura was reined in, and Alice immediately felt the absence of the warm sensation. She had to have more. A part of her wanted to run out and ask Shadowalker to let go, but she was too weak in the knees to move.

As Alice looked out on the camp, she saw every goblin cowering in fear and utter horror. It made no sense to her why anyone would react that way. Then most of the goblins got on their hands and knees in supplication, and Alice agreed that such a response was appropriate, far better than their initial reaction.

With Shadowalker once again holding back his power, Alice felt it was time to go. "They are just going to do a bunch of boring talking. I saw what I came to see. Time to go back before those two annoying adults get too worried and cause a fuss. Soon I won't have to care about such adults, it's just not time yet my friend, but soon. I can feel it." Alice said to her dolly.

Alice cocked her head to the side like she was listening to something. "What was that? Oh, you think we should find some more naughty goblins on the way back. Yes, that's a great idea." Alice said as she held her dolly.

Chapter 27 – Progress

"This is Donut. How are you doing on your side Carol?" Duncan said.

He and the others returned to the compound just barely in time. Duncan did not like cutting it so close. He was the lifeline for these survivors and did not want to let them down. Duncan had already lost so many and had zero interest in losing more.

Carol's voice came over the air waves. "Good to hear from you. I almost thought you might miss our call." Carol said over the radio.

"I'd never do that Mrs. Burns." Duncan replied.

"How many times do I have to tell you to call me Carol?"

"Sorry, old habits." Duncan answered.

"It's fine. So, what caused you to be almost late for our evening call?" Carol asked.

"I was out leveling with Shadowalker, Gr'ex, Jebediah, Suzie-cue, and Emily. I'm level 11 now! And Suzie-cue is level 12!" Duncan reported excitedly.

"Wow, that is impressive. I'm still only level 6. What were you guys doing that earned you so many levels?" Carol replied.

"Killing Bone Marrow goblins." Duncan answered.

"Bone Marrow? Like are they made of bone?" Carol asked in confusion.

"Ha! No, no. That is just the name of their clan. They do wear a lot of bones on their person, but I think that is more decorative and I'm sure must have meaning to them, I just don't care. We killed a bunch of them." Duncan explained.

"Huh. Those are the ones occupying our town. Well at least you guys killed some of them. Wait, you mentioned Gr'ex. Isn't he a goblin? Doesn't he have a problem killing his own kind?" Carol said.

"Nah, He said, 'if they aren't part of his clan, why would he care.' The goblin seems very pragmatic. Suzie-cue says he's heartless and pompous, but I like em." Duncan relayed.

Carol shared her thoughts. "You seem to like everyone dearie. I'm sure his mindset works well in the apocalypse, but it does come off a bit cold, so I can see Suzie-cue's point. You mentioned Emily, so she survived too?"

"Yes ma'am. She and Suzie-cue both used their system perks to race change. Both are now Wood Elves. They have pointy ears and everything. I noticed how they seem more agile now. Both are wicked with a bow and a gun." Duncan answered.

"Race change?! Interesting. I hadn't realized that was an option. We will spread the word about that. Many of the people we have rescued so far have not selected their system perk. Me, I went with Soothing Voice. It adds appeal to my voice. Also helps give bonuses to people remembering what I said and helps in negotiations. But the coolest benefit was how overtime it can help heal people with wounded psyches." Carol explained.

Duncan nodded along before speaking up. "That is useful. Maybe it can help the Lost."

"The Lost?" Carol asked, having not heard that reference before.

"It is what we have started to call the people who seem to have mentally checked out. They sit there doing nothing. Our nurse Ann has been trying to help them, but Jebediah says we can only use so many of our resources on people who are lost and aren't contributing. I think that's harsh. I mean I understand, but it's hard for me to not want to help these people, so maybe that is something you can do with your Soothing Voice." Duncan explained.

Carol appreciated Duncan's commitment to helping others. She knew some would consider him a bleeding heart, but she had known the boy since he was young. He was a big ole teddy bear who genuinely would protect those weaker than him. That was his nature, and it appeared the apocalypse wasn't going to change that about him.

"It's worth a try. I do have to agree with Jebediah though. It's a harsh world out there. Far more brutal. Being blunt seems to be a saving grace, as harsh as that may sound. We cannot deny the truth, this world is not as it was, heck Mayberry never was like we thought it was. So much has already changed. Have you noticed how most cell phones aren't working anymore. That was one of the first things to stop functioning."

"Yea I asked Gr'ex about that." Duncan chimed in.

"What did he tell you?" Carol asked.

Duncan relayed what Gr'ex told him. "He said that the more fragile technology would be the first to go. Something about the mana in the environment creates a natural interface. Depending on the type of mana it could be problematic. Gr'ex has seen how effective our guns are, but he is convinced that it is only a matter of time before they start blowing up in our faces. He also mentioned the risk of encountering monsters whose skin are so tough the bullets will just bounce off them."

"Those are both scary thoughts." Carol commented.

Duncan continued. "Big time. Most of our initial successes have come from the fact that most people in our town were proud members of the NRA and always had a rifle or gun on hand."

"Yes, that proved true with Carl's group too. Their guns truly were the great equalizers." Carol chimed in.

Duncan nodded along to Carol's words even if she couldn't see him. "Gr'ex did mention that it's possible to start combining magic and tech to create items that can function in a mana rich environment."

"Oh yes. We have a couple of inventors that created a power suit, they said that combined both magic and technology. It's quite an impressive piece of hardware." Carol shared.

"Wow! That sounds super cool. I can't wait to see it! Gr'ex made mention of a goblin clan that specializes in such tech. He did caution us that some of the radio towers would be next depending on the type of technology used." Duncan replied.

"Does he have any idea how long we might have? By our estimate we are still about a day and a half from reaching you guys. It would be bad to lose our best mode of communication." Carol asked.

"He figures after the first initialization phase is complete. According to Gr'ex, something happened during the first part of initialization that delayed the mana saturation. If that hadn't occurred, we would already have lost our radio and weapons advantages." Duncan explained.

"Really? Does he know more about what happened that gave us all that much needed advantage?" Carol inquired.

"No. He just said that somehow the initial release of mana was absorbed somehow causing the reintegration process to take longer. That's all I could get out of him before he had to go organize some of the goblins." Duncan shared.

"Huh. Well, whatever it was, it has made all the difference in the world for us. Most of the survivors we have found survived because of the guns they had or found. Plus, we wouldn't even know they were there if we hadn't been able to communicate." Carol said before taking a moment to say a silent prayer before changing subjects. "Anything we should know before signing off for the evening?"

"Yes. Jek'jon told us this morning that other goblin clans want to join Shadowalker's banner. He should be meeting with them as we speak. If all goes well, we will have more allies for the upcoming battle." Duncan replied.

"Oh, that is good news. Though I still am uncertain about these goblins. But we will take all the help we can get. This will be our last communication before we head out. As I mentioned, give us about a day and a half. We will use the two-way radios on the frequency we discussed when we get within range." Carol replied.

"Roger that! Travel safe and good journey!" Duncan replied as he signed off.

Carol made her notes and waited for her son and Laraaq to return. They were due any minute. This was their last communication for the next day and a half, and wanted to make sure she didn't miss anything to report.

It took Carl about half an hour before he walked through the door. "Hey mom. No Laraaq?"

"What? No how are you doing? Just where is the boss." Carol teased her son. She knew he worked hard and seemed to put the weight of the world on his shoulders.

"Mom. You know I didn't mean anything by it. I'm just exhausted." Carl complained.

"I know, but if I don't tease you, who will. How did it go today? How was it without Laraaq there with you?" Carol asked.

"All in all, it went well. Mario and Jerome are professionals. We rescued 53 people. Most of them were in their mid to late twenties. Only a handful of those are combat ready. The rest really struggled but they managed to hold on until we got there. Very few with stockpiles of food and supplies so that will put further strain on our supplies. Most important thing, no one seemed to be a Sharon, so that was a positive." Carl reported.

"Well at least that is good. Still, you should be proud son, to have saved so many today. Our supplies are still in good order. Several of the supply teams brought back some decent hauls today." Carol encouraged.

"That's good. The last thing we want right now is people rioting out of hunger or toilet paper." Carl commented.

Carol nodded. "Most definitely. Any of them have any skills that stand out?"

Carl smiled. "I'm going to leave that in your very capable hands. Laraaq and I rescue them, you and Jacob sort em out."

"You know you maybe taller than me, but I brought you into this world, and I can take you out of it." Carol stated.

Carl raised his hands in surrender. "Okay, okay. If you need me to help you and Jacob sort people let me know."

Carol smiled. "That's better. I think we are fine; I just have to keep you on your toes, so you don't take your mom for granted."

Carl chuckled. "Ha! Fair enough mom, fair enough. Any word from Laraaq's team?"

"No, nothing. Last Jennifer radioed in; they rescued some older teenagers from a high school a few hours from here." Carol explained.

Just as she finished Laraaq and Jennifer walked through the door.

"Speak of the devil." Carol commented.

"So not a fan of that saying after the day we had." Laraaq said as he plopped down into a chair.

"That bad?" Carl asked.

"Yes and No. we had to kill some kids." Jennifer answered.

Carol's face took on a look of horror. "What do you mean you had to kill some kids?!"

"It was right after Jennifer radioed in about the high school. For the most part, they are a great bunch of people for teenagers. Their fencing team paired up with their football team to create an effective defense against the zombies. They even had a few teachers, parents, and locals who made it to the high school. The building was made of solid brick, great place to defend from." Laraaq started to explain.

"Some of the people had minor wounds, nothing too bad, that was until we came upon one of the locals. He was sick. At first, I thought he might be infected and turning into a zombie, but the truth was worse." Jennifer stated.

"Worse? How was it worse?" Carl asked.

"There were three kids about 10 years old. Two boys and one girl. They were all level 14 and had a class called **Dark Cannibal**. My system informed me that in order to get that class you have to have killed and eaten at least 20 of your own race!" Laraaq continued to explain.

Carol brought her hand to her mouth in shock. "They were so young to do such horrible things!"

"The girl had an ability called **Life Leech**. She used it to slowly weaken people, most would just think they were tired or didn't sleep well, but it progressively got worse. They would get people to isolate them out of fear of the person being infected, and then one or more would kill and eat them." Jennifer gritted her teeth as she said the last part.

"Monsters!" Carl commented.

"Exactly! So, we executed them. Sad thing is if people had just bothered to interact with their system and ask the right questions they would know to be on guard when it comes to anyone under the age of 15. Jennifer and I both went off on the adults who should've never let it get that far. We need to institute some kind of instruction for things people should be doing with their system." Laraaq sighed, letting out his frustration.

"I'll talk to Jacob about putting something together." Carol replied.

Jennifer spoke up after a moment. "Other than that, the only other issue was Mack."

Carl perked up at the mention of the man's name. He did not care for the surly trucker. "What did Mack do?"

Laraaq started to explain. "Nothing specific, other than just be obstinate and hog the kills. It was hard to reprimand him for killing monsters with his makeshift club, but he just was completely overbearing. He never dared to cross the line with me..."

Jennifer cut him off. "He crossed the line with me. He flatly ignored any orders I gave to protect people or fall back. And when I confronted him, he claimed ignorance or that he didn't hear me, 'too focused on the battle' he said. Total crap!"

"We will need to keep an eye on him. I don't trust him to watch our backs, but we need every able fighter in the upcoming battle." Laraaq chimed in.

"I'll keep his youngest with me during the battle. That way he will be less likely to do something stupid during the fight." Carol suggested.

"Not a bad idea. Family seems to be the only thing the man cares about." Carl commented.

"Now enough of that sad business. How many were you able to rescue?" Carol asked.

Laraaq smiled. "We saved 78 people and recovered several stashes of food and supplies. The high school alone had a fully stocked emergency rations kit for all their students. The fencers and football kids already wanted to join the ranks of our fighters. We dropped them off with Jacob."

Jennifer chimed in. "And we leveled. Laraaq and I are now level 12. Colin and Christy are level 11. And Mack is level 14, he gained a class called **Bruiser**." Jennifer said the last part with an annoyed look on her face.

"Well yea, easy to level when you're stealing all the kills. Jerk!" Laraaq said in frustration.

"Well, us having someone in the group with a class can only help us in the upcoming conflict." Carol said in the hopes of encouraging everyone.

Laraaq nodded. "I know you're right Carol, it just annoys me."

Carol nodded. "That is understandable. I do have some good news from Duncan. Your friend was on his way to recruit some of the goblin clans to our side. Duncan seemed excited about it."

"That is good news. If anyone can convince a group to join our cause it's Shadowalker." Laraaq stated.

Carol smiled. "Good to hear as we will need a leader who can rally people behind a common cause. Now let me tell you everything else I found out."

Interlude- Tek'tar

SMASH!

CLANG!

Gr'onk and the other Bone Marrow goblins trembled at their clan chief's fury. He was not happy when he woke up.

Tek'tar continued to rage in his throne room as he threw things about and smashed things against the walls.

After suffering great pain from the ritual backlash, he had collapsed unconscious as had many of his men that were participating in the ritual. This had left the remaining men only a small force in comparison.

When Tek'tar had awoken that idiot Gr'onk had informed him all the remaining huemon prisoners had escaped. Worse still, Gr'onk had no clue how. He thought about killing Gr'onk but he was one of the higher level men he had left.

"I will put the bastard on night soil duty for his failure!" Tek'tar exclaimed.

That thought seemed to calm Tek'tar and he collapsed into his makeshift throne.

"It was my own hubris attempting so many rituals at once. To lose that artifact now..." Tek'tar could feel his rage returning but he did his best to clamp it down.

Tek'tar had to make plans and quickly. If he wanted to claim that leyline node for himself, he would need a plan. The original plan was to sacrifice the remaining huemons to create more abominations.

There was no way Tek'tar planned to summon his master, he owed him no loyalty.

No, Kit'erak did not believe in using oaths of fealty as it bound both the liege and the supplicant. Tek'tar did not believe in using such things either. The only way to ensure loyalty was with pure strength. Excessive use of force and brutality to ensure fear kept them in line. Tek'tar had learned that much from the Orcs.

"If I claim the leyline node there is little Kit'erak can do. I know of his secret dealings with the eldritch, he will not want the Dark to become aware of such things. No, if I can claim it and have enough power to keep it then Kit'erak will be forced to back off. But what can I use to help ensure my success?" Tek'tar said to himself.

Then it hit him. Tek'tar was just talking about Kit'erak seeking power from the Eldritch. He could use that power for himself. Kit'erak, the fool, had taught Tek'tar several spells and rituals to channel Eldritch power.

"Why bother with and Undead Abomination when I can create a far more powerful Eldritch Abomination! I will only have time to create one. Without the artifact it will be tricky, and I will have to sacrifice some of my men and undead minions, but I will not make the mistake of being too greedy and attempt more than one, for now."

Tek'tar stormed out of the town hall. "Gr'onk!"

The large goblin prostrated himself before his chief. "Yes, Terrible one! What can I do to serve?"

Tek'tar kicked Gr'onk. "You have failed me. Your punishment shall be night soil duty for a week. Before you start that duty, you will rally my necromancers and other casters. We will be preparing one final ritual. Now go!"

"Yes, your Terrible one!" Gr'onk said as he bowed multiple times as he backed away to carry out his orders.

Tek'tar smiled evilly. He took true joy in watching others grovel before him. Even as a youngling, he dreamed of being the wielder of the Dark Mantle, like the legends of old. He would make people cower, with or without some aura of authority.

Returning to his throne room, Tek'tar decided to get the conversation with Kit'erak over and done with. At least now he had a valid excuse for why he didn't have the resources to summon Kit'erak.

Walking over to the communication orb, Tek'tar activated it. A moment later he saw the visage of Kit'erak the arch-lich in the orb.

Kit'erak's voice could be heard echoing across the room. "Report, you worthless servant. I grow tired of waiting. Be quick with your report, I must speak with the demons of the poisoned wood. They are sacrificing many that had pledged themselves. Fools if they thought they would gain power or matter in any way to a demon and not just being used as a pawn. Now report!"

"Huemons are very dumb, master. They are most likely north from here, if they fled to the south, Jek'jon would have them recaptured already." Tek'tar began to explain.

"That is true. The Sleeping Willow clan are excellent spies and scouts. Knowing their direction is not the same as recovering them." Kit'erak chided.

"With your permission master I plan on creating and Eldritch Abomination. It will be the perfect weapon to strike fear into the huemons!" Tek'tar stated.

"Bold plan. It is risky, which is why we discussed Undead Abominations. How many of your people will you sacrifice?" Kit'erak inquired.

Tek'tar knew his master must be desperate to agree with such a plan. The creature would be a dead giveaway of Outsider influence. That meant Tek'tar had him right where he needed him. "I was planning of sacrificing 50 of my men along with some of our Undead Zombies and Skeletons."

"Do not waste too many of your Undead Minions. We want the level of ambience Death magic to be high in the area. Use more of your underlings instead." Kit'erak ordered.

Tek'tar couldn't help but smile. "As you command, master."

"I release the hold of the large mana core and mana crystals you have." Kit'erak's voice held a command that seemed to dissolve whatever bindings were over the items.

Tek'tar felt the magical lock on them fall away. He inwardly smiled. This was why he even bothered with telling his old master his plan to begin with. He needed access to a powerful core and potent mana crystals to complete this ritual in such a short time. "Thank you, master. It shall be done."

Kit'erak glared at the large goblin. "It better or I shall see you suffer upon my arrival."

Kit'erak cut off the connection and the orb dimmed.

Tek'tar rose from his kneeling position. "Soon I will never kneel again. I will be the master soon enough."

Smiling as he exited the building, Tek'tar took the final pieces he needed to the ritual site, so he could gain his prize. "Time for some blood sacrifices."

Chapter 28 – Well, That Happened

I once again came to the floor. The goblins were kind enough to fetch a pillow from somewhere and put it under me. As I sat up, I realized that was all they did.

"Do not move too quickly. That many stats all at once takes a moment to adjust to." Hal'ex said as she sat next to me on the ground, her special undead chair creature nearby.

"How long was I out?" I asked.

"About a span or what I believe huemons call an hour. Your body was twitching violently for a while there, so we feared to do more than give you a pillow for your head."

"No wonder my whole body feels sore and wait a minute..." I started to say as I realized I ripped my shirt to shreds.

"Damn! Another shirt gone!" I lamented.

"Yes, you seem to have grown a few inches as well as increased muscle density. You are lucky your trousers are made of some kind of stretching substance, otherwise the females of my clan would be even more aggressive in their pursuits." Hal'ex explained.

"Yea they are called sweatpants with an elastic band. I figured it was a safe bet as most of my other clothes don't really fit me anymore. I appreciate you keeping the vultures at bay." I commented.

"A very apt description, my boy. I can see why my grandson likes you so much. Don't let him fool you, he feels like he has a new life filled with possibilities." Hal'ex replied.

"I'm rather fond of the guy too. Again, thank you for watching over me." I stated.

"I am a **Dark Shaman**, that means I still can heal even if I use curses and other magics to inflict suffering on my enemies. I was one of the best healers in the camp, so it made sense for me to examine you. There are some anomalies I cannot quite understand but you seem fine." Hal'ex further explained.

"Well, I appreciate that even more. I'm not ready to share all my secrets, so I ask that we leave it there for now., to be discussed at some later date." I answered.

"Done. You are not the first person to keep closely guarded secrets, in fact, that is common among the Dark." Hal'ex agreed.

"I'm not aligned with the Dark!" I protested.

Hal'ex raised her hand. "I never said you were. It is clear in how you treat my grandson and Jek'jon that you are different. I merely was stating the fact that our people are rarely treated with kindness or respect. Usually, we are told what to do and when. Not knowing those in power's secrets is commonplace for us."

Sighing, I nodded. "That is good to know about your people. I do plan to lead differently, but some secrets must be kept."

"Of course, your Dark Eminence." Hal'ex bowed her head.

Grumbling at my new title, I decided to check the notifications that awaited me.

Congratulations! You are awarded enough experience points to reach the next level!

Level Up! *Congratulations! You are now level 12! You have +26 stat points to distribute.*

Congratulations! You have once again singlehandedly defeated a Contested Portal within the first re-integration of your world. Two in the first week is an exceptionally rare achievement! Available rewards have increased the bonus from your **World's Champion** *title.*

Please choose three from the following rewards:
• *Magic Weapon*   • *Combat Skill to Adept rank*   • *Utility spell*   • *Offensive spell*   • *One random monster core*

'Well, that is pretty much the same. So, now what do I choose this time?' As my thoughts went back to last time, I was given this choice.

I started from the bottom of the options and worked my way to the top. Last time the random core was one of the best choices he ever made, granting him multiple boons. The problem was the time. It took roughly a day to absorb the core, and that was far faster than expected according to his conversation with Gr'ex afterwards. In other words, if I didn't have a giant battle looming over my head, this option would be a no brainer, this time however I may have to pass on this option.

Moving to the next option, an offensive spell could really be handy in a battle. There were still risks, it was completely random. If the spell had a long cast time, it may not be as useful as I'd like it to be. Still a contender.

Next was a Utility spell. This one is almost a must. Utility meant versatility. Now sure, it could be a niche situation, but I knew myself. It would be impossible for me to pass up on this one.

That led me to think about the last combat skill I received. I was beyond lucky to get **Weapons Mastery** at **Master** rank. That instant knowledge download nearly killed me, or at least that is what it felt like, but is has been the most versatile and useful survival skill I had. Even if I did not get something as wide a range as **Weapons Mastery**, this was another one I couldn't pass up, especially with an upcoming battle.

That left me the last option, a magic weapon. I would've dismissed this one instantly, if not for the fact the notification said the rewards would be upgraded. An upgraded weapon could make all the difference in the upcoming fight.

Choices, choices, choices. Life is all about the choices we make and what we do with the results. I had picked two of my options already, that left me to decide between magic weapon, offensive spell, or random monster core.

I wanted the core, but I couldn't be out of commission for the next day or so, that left that option sadly out. That left me with a weapon or spell. Who was I kidding, if I wanted to be a mage I was going to require as many spells as possible.

Selections made; I excitedly awaited the results. It did not take long for three new notifications to pop up in my view.

*Congratulations! You have gained the combat skill: **Unarmed Combat Mastery**. This skill has been upgraded to **Master** rank.*

Combat skill: Unarmed Combat Mastery
<u>Description</u>: *only true masters of combat know that the true weapon in battle is yourself. This combat skill can only be granted after learning and mastering multiple hand-to-hand and martial art techniques.*

A new notification immediately popped up.

*Congratulations! You have mastered two combat skills that have high synergy granting you the additional combination combat skill: **Makeshift Weaponry**. This skill mastery rank is based on the average between the two skills. Rank imparted: **Master**.*

Combat Skill: Makeshift Weaponry
<u>Description</u>: *Those rare individuals who can master martial arts and weapons mastery allows one to see everything and anything around them as a weapon.*

"Oh yea!" I said in excitement as images of Keanu Reeves using a pencil to kill someone or using a spoon as a weapon.

Oh, the ideas started to flood my mind. Then more ways to adjust my body, the names of the combat techniques. On and on, more information poured into my mind. I recognized the signs all too late. I was just able to get the words out to Hal'ex. "I did it again. Going to need a few..."

Pain and the worst splitting headache hit me. It felt like millions of pins the size of jack hammers were slamming into my skull. Each hit was a new move or form. On it went, for what felt like days but was most likely only a few hours. Then I blacked out, again!

As I awoke, it was pitch black out, the only light the stars in the sky and torches throughout camp. I held my head as I sat up.

A panting Hal'ex spoke to my side. "C-Careful... mantle."

That was when I realized in my mental overload, I stopped my tight control over my Dark Mantle, and it had flooded the entire camp. Hal'ex and many others were on their hands and knees, panting in a weird mix of fear and... hunger or joy? I couldn't quite figure out the last part of the expression. As my headache started to subside, I reined in my ability, and I saw everyone's breathing calm down.

Hal'ex leaned against her undead chair creature for support. "Thank you, your Dark Eminence. I do not know what happened to you but when you released your power it hit us all in waves. As we have pledged our fealty, the effects hit us differently than the first time. The horrific terror is still there but now there is a feeling that could be very intoxicating. The more I embraced my oath the terror lessened and was replaced with a level of empowerment I could not imagine possible for a goblin such as myself. I fear my people will want to be around you even more now."

"That is good to know. My mind was overloaded with two new combat skills. It was a lot of information and I lost control for a time. How long was I out?" I replied.

"I would say several spans, or hours I believe the term is. It was difficult to be stuck like that for such an extended period of time. Knowing my people and what I just went through, many will be fanatics from this point forward." Hal'ex answered.

"Well, that just happened. Fanatics are not something I wanted. I'll be leaning on you to help with this Hal'ex." I stated.

I decided to review the remaining notifications. This time my Utility Spell selection had multiple prompts.

Congratulations! Your granted utility spell has been randomly selected from types of magic you have high affinity with. Please wait while Magic time is chosen...

*Magic type chosen: **Time**! Please wait while the spell tier is determined...*

*The random utility **Time** magic spell has been upgraded to the maximum possible value due to the way you obtained this spell. You have learned the new utility spell: **Time Armor**. This spell is a tier 10 spell.*

Spell: Time Armor (Tier 10)
<u>Description</u>: *Surround you and your allies within the area with a layer of Time Armor. Time Armor will negate one unfavorable event that would cripple or kill the target it surrounds by negating the moment between the layer of armor and target. Once the event is prevented the Time Armor disperses. Due to the nature and power level of this spell, only magic*

equivalent to 10th tier or above can dispel this effect. Please Note: Duration lasts until used or 24 hours passes. Casting cost varies by number of people selected.

"Okay that has got to be the coolest utility spell I've ever heard of system! This will save so many lives, most likely even my own!" I said as a mental thank you to my system and whoever gave me access to it.

'Hmmm. I can't exactly let people know I have **Time** magic and I doubt any other level 12 has access to 10th tier magic. The spell description did say the cost was variable based on targets I wonder if I can figure out the scaling.' I thought just before I decided to test the new spell.

Focusing on the spell in my mind, I selected myself first and the spell took half my entire mana pool. Trying to select Hal'ex took the other half. 'So much for trying to protect my entire army. I guess that is why it's 10th tier. The mana required to cast the spell is absorbent. The fact that it lasted a day means I could probably cast it twice and my mana could recharge enough to still have mana for the fight.'

At that point the worry about people finding out about my **Time** magic seemed a moot point. If I could only cast the spell on two people in a reasonable time period, it would be a no brainer on who I would choose. I would cast the spell on myself, and when I saw Laraaq, I would make sure he had a cast of Time Armor.

Was I being selfish, absolutely. Did I care at the moment, not at all. I came back to make sure my best friend and others were saved. If this spell could save his life you bet, I was using it on him. Sure, I didn't want to die either and I used the old airplane rule to go by as it was a very important one.

The rule goes like this: In an emergency, air masks drop from the ceiling. Parents are told as part of the safety procedure to put your mask on first. Most parents are appalled at such a notion, until they are told, if you pass out from lack of oxygen there is no way you can ensure your child gets a mask or keeps a mask on. In short, you can't help others if you don't first see to your own safety.

Knowing that I had a limited mana pool currently and also knowing I would need my magic for the upcoming battle meant I had to be realistic and not be some bleeding heart. Bleeding hearts ended up bleeding all over the place until they ended up dead and usually also got others killed along the way. Nope, not my style. I was here to save the lives I could and that required me to make the tough choices and live with the consequences. Some would die because of this choice and so would have to live with that fact.

My mind resolute, I turned my attention to the final prompt.

*Congratulations! You have learned the 6th tier offensive spell: **Chain Lightning**!*

Spell: Chain Lightning (Tier 6)
Description: Shoot lightning at a target. The lightning can then arc to hit up to four additional targets. Distance and affinity determine the caster's level of control in directing the lightning arc's path.

I mean don't get me wrong, a 6th tier lightning spell that can hit multiple targets is awesome. It's just after getting the 10th tier Time Armor, in comparison it just felt lack luster. Shame on me for not appreciating the fact that I got a powerful offensive spell.

Just as I was about to dismiss the spell description, a new notification popped into my view.

*Congratulations! The additional bonus from completing two Contested Portals solo within the first week of reintegration has been applied to your Chain Lightning spell. This spell has been upgraded to **Dark Chain Lightning**!*

Dark Chain Lightning (Tier 9)
Description: This is a celestial spell and requires multiple affinities to be learned. Dark Lightning is one of the most dangerous cosmic phenomena in terrestrial form. This type of lightning contains cosmic gamma rays that arc out and travel. This changes the color from a bright light to a vibrant black that seems to spread darkness as it streaks out. Dark and Death magics are also applied to strike both body and soul in the attack. The number of targets increased based on mana expenditure. Please Note: Mana cost varies based on distance, affinities, and number of targets.

I immediately said thank you to whomever was watching over me and my system for applying that last little push. Now this was an offensive spell! I knew of dark lightning being an actual thing in nature, to have additional magics applied to harness that power and amplify its effects, made this even sweeter. The mana cost was once again rather high, so I'd once again have to be selective about when and how I used it.

Shooting lightning like that could be an effective intimidation tactic if used correctly. I wasn't opposed to such approaches if it could act as a deterrent and save lives. The real concern was how many of my abilities were dark in nature, not all, my Time Armor and regular Lightning spell were great examples of non-Dark related, but the rest had a certain feel. 'Fight fire with fire' was the saying. I would just have to be careful of the path I was walking.

Enough of those melancholy thoughts. I returned my focus outward.

"Hal'ex, are your clan and the others ready to make a long roundabout journey to the compound?" I asked as I stood up.

"Yes, your Dark Eminence. We have been preparing for the last several hours in anticipation you would want us to head out once you are ready. Jek'jon has already seen to his own patrols. They will be a buffer between our people and the Bone Marrow patrols accidentally stumbling upon us."

"Excellent! I appreciate competence and those that think ahead. That means far less for me to do. He, he, he, he!" I chuckled.

"We are used to it. If you don't think to anticipate your leaders' needs, a lowly goblin can suffer for it." Hal'ex commented.

I shook my head. "That is not my way. Sure, incompetence must be addressed and rooted out, but I am no tyrant, I appreciate those that make the effort to understand and anticipate things. I want people who think for themselves, not mindless robots."

Hal'ex smiled. "I do not know what a row-bot is, but I get the gist of your statement. You will find out clans far more cleaver than some of the other larger clans who can afford to tolerate more incompetence."

As I dusted myself off, Hal'ex handed me a dark tunic with a color mix of muted greens and blacks. "Here. Our tailors did a rough sizing and made this from some flexible spider silk. It should stretch and provide decent protection. We can discuss the enchantments for it once we get settled in. I just thought it would be best for you to not walk around bare chested all night."

I took the tunic and noticed some of the goblin females staring at me. I quickly put it on and felt at least a bit better. I was still getting looks periodically but they seemed less intense. "Thank you Hal'ex. Let's get our people moving. I'd like to get you settled into the compound before sunrise."

Chapter 29- We Are All Friends Here

For a band of over a thousand goblins they sure kept quiet. Sure, there was some noise and rustling, but that was nothing compared to what I was expecting. Communication was mostly done through hand signals.

Jek'jon traveled with us. Scouts would randomly approach him to deliver some kind of status report through quick hand and body motions. Gr'ex approached me as he could see the confusion on my face.

"Goblin sign language or Gutterspeech as it is commonly called."

"Why is it called that?" I asked.

"Simple, goblins are the bottom rungs of society. Many races consider us only fit for the gutters and latrines. As we have a decent birth rate, most Dark forces use us as fodder for their armies." Gr'ex explained.

Jek'jon approached as he heard our conversation. "They throw our race in large numbers at their enemies, if thousands die, they do not care, as long as it weakens or breaks the enemy lines. It is a rather miserable life."

"We have discussed some of this before." I commented.

"Yes, it is just important you understand our four clans are some of the smaller of the goblin race. Some clans have spent generations under one Dark Lord only to be traded like some commodity for some political favor or dark machination." Hal'ex chimed in.

"How many clans are there? Oh, and can someone teach me the language?" I asked.

"There are hundreds of clans at least. We do not know all of them, only the ones in our world or are known through stories and legends. And to answer your other question, we would be more than happy to teach you the language, you would be one of the few non-goblin leaders who bothered to attempt such a thing." Jek'jon answered.

"New world, new leadership. I welcome the chance to learn something new from my allies." I stated.

The goblin chiefs all looked at each other and smiled. Gr'ex was the one to speak up. "I can start to show you. See the angle and position of the scout's fingers? That is telling us low risk, no one spotted for one span. Then..."

Gr'ex explained as Jek'jon chimed in periodically as a new scout would return to report status and they would use that as a chance to learn more. We continued on that way for a few more hours until we finally arrived at the cabin.

Two men I recognized from the groups we had saved were on duty and very cautiously pointing their rifles our way. I believe Ann and Melody told me their names were Mitch and Gio. They were in their early twenties or very late teens and had been friends since grade school, according to Melody who was one of their teachers.

"Halt! Don't you move goblins!" Mitch called out.

Friends since grade school I could respect. Getting a weapon pointed at me, most likely one of Paul's stash, therefore one of my own guns pointed at me did not sit well with me.

"Put the guns down boys!" I replied as I approached.

It was dark out with only the stars and limited lighting from the compound to illuminate the area.

"Who goes there?" Gio said as he squinted in the dark.

"It's Shadowalker, you know, the one that owns this place!" I said with a hint of irritation creeping into my voice.

Mitch spoke up. "Step into the light, but don't you try anything funny! We already radioed for backup."

I took a long audible sigh as I tried to remind myself these were just people who were scared at a giant goblin force at their doorstep. "Ugh."

I slowly took a few steps forward. Gio shined the flashlight he had on me. The thing nearly blinded me. "Ahh!" I raised my hand up to block the light in my eyes.

The quick motion seemed to startle Gio, and he shot his rifle. I could try to dodge out of the way, but I had droves of goblins behind me. If the goblins got injured, even by accident, could end very badly and put a strain on the fragile alliance I was trying to build.

That left me the only option, I had to take this shot. Of course, that didn't mean I had to take it at full velocity. I moved just enough to take it in the shoulder, but I also used Gravity Momentum Manipulation to slow the piercing round as much as I could. It still punctured my shoulder but missed bone and more importantly didn't hit anything vital.

Still hurt like hell. "You son of a... you shot me!"

Jebediah came out just as I was taking the hit. He looked disheveled, most likely having been woken up when they radioed for back up.

"What the hell are you doing shooting at Shadowalker you idiot boy!" Jebediah said as he bopped Gio on the head.

"Owe! That hurt!" Gio complained.

It had the effect though of easing tensions of the two men. However, it did not settle the goblins down.

Different goblins cried out in anger. Several drew weapons and nocked arrows.

"How dare he attack his Dark Eminence!"

"Kill the traitorous huemons!"

"Yes, kill the traitors!"

I raised my uninjured arm. "Enough! It was an accident. The boy will be disciplined won't he Jebediah!"

'I should've cast my new spell to get some practice with it and the fact it would've avoided this situation. Going to have to turn that spell into a new habit to keep it active at least once a day.' I thought as I grimaced.

Jebediah nodded. "Yea it's clear these two aren't ready for prime time. I take responsibility on this one Shadowalker."

Then he turned to Mitch. "Go fetch Ann quick! We need her healing fast!"

Mitch didn't hesitate. Anywhere was better than here, especially as he drew a weapon on the owner of this compound, the very same man who saved his life. He worried about his best friend and knew he had to hurry and get Ann.

"Get inside and make yourself scarce. By the looks of those angry goblins, I'd keep your distance too." Jebediah ordered.

Gio turned in my direction. "I'm so sorry sir! Please forgive me!"

"I said get boy!" Jebediah said as he kicked Gio in the rear to get him moving.

Jebediah sighed. "Sorry son, I thought they might at least be ready for night duty."

I held my bleeding shoulder. I could feel my minor healing effect slowly and painstakingly push the bullet. By my guess in a few hours, it would be moved enough that I could probably pull it out myself. "It's fine, but I suggest we establish better protocols so as to not get our allies accidentally killed."

Jebediah nodded. "That's fair. I see you have made a lot of new friends. Might be a bit tight. I imagine several will be a bit unnerved too."

I turned to Gr'ex. "Get them settled on the second sub-level. Most of the humans are on the first level and the goblins being near the crafting areas would probably be more beneficial for them anyway."

"Agreed." Gr'ex said before turning to face the rest of the goblins. "Follow me inside. Stay together and do not touch anything unless instructed to do so!"

Ann came rushing out with a look of concern on her face.

"They said you were shot!" Ann said as she rushed to my side.

Some of the goblins instinctively moved to intercept her.

"She is our healer. Let her through." Gr'ex commanded.

This seemed to cause the goblins to hesitate enough for Ann to get through to me.

"At least they are protective of you." Ann commented as she examined my wound.

"They have committed themselves to help us in the upcoming battle against Bone Mar... OWE!" I started to say before she stuck her fingers into my wound.

"Oh, quit being a baby. Ah, there... got it!" Ann said as she pulled out the slug from my shoulder.

Ann looked at the porch then back at me. "That bullet should've done far more damage. You or one of the goblins must've done something to reduce the impact. The velocity alone should've shattered your shoulder bone at a minimum. Plus, the wound seemed to be healing quite fast."

I stared at her. Ann stared back. I just smiled.

"Fine! Keep your secrets. Let me heal this so you can stop bleeding on me." Ann said in frustration as she cast healing magic on my shoulder.

Ann's hands started to glow as she held the wound together. Light filled the area as I felt warmth across the shoulder and arm. When she pulled her hands away, the wound was gone.

"Ahhh! That feels great. Thank you." I said in relief as I rotated my shoulder and not feeling any pain.

"I still can't believe I can do that. So many emergency room surgeries I assisted to be able to heal wounds in seconds that normal wound take weeks." Ann commented.

"It is pretty impressive. How do you feel about being a battle medic? We don't have many healers and it could mean the difference between life and death for more than one person trying to get them back here in time." I replied.

Ann looked uncomfortable. "You make a good point. I can't deny what I can do could make all the difference. Give me some time to think about it."

"Of course. I understand the fear. You would have dedicated guards to protect you as best they could. According to Donut, my friend Laraaq found another healer that is willing to join the fight. Worst case we try to make do with one if that is your decision." I commented.

"I'll let you know beforehand. I should go see to my other duties. Melody is doing a lot with our survivors, but I think they are getting restless." Ann said before she headed back inside.

Rather than immediately go inside I took a seat on the porch. Jek'jon came out shortly after. "I figured you would be resting, your Dark Eminence."

I turned to the upbeat goblin chief. "I will in a moment. I just wanted to enjoy the relative peace of the outdoors for a bit. I was planning on grabbing a few hours' sleep at some point. Are you heading back to your camp?"

Jek'jon nodded. "Yes. We still have to keep up the ruse until you are ready or us to attack."

"Tomorrow will be our last day, I think. My friend should arrive late tomorrow or early the following day. We will attack once they arrive." I stated.

"I will inform my clan. We will be ready when you give the signal." Jek'jon bowed and left.

As I watched Jek'jon disappear into the brush, I reflected on how crazy my life was. I'm in the actual apocalypse or at least the clear start of it. I live in a compound that doubles as a fortress. I've befriended a goblin which led me to now have four goblin clans under my banner. For that matter, I needed to design a banner. Several hundred survivors were rescued. And most importantly, my best friend should be here in a day, give or take a few hours.

After that moment of self-reflection, I stood and headed inside, locking the door behind me. I took the elevator down to the lowest sub level. I didn't want to disturb Alice and I found the place oddly comforting. I was so tired I almost forgot to distribute my stat points. Luckily, this wasn't 26 stat points in all attributes but just 26 points to put somewhere. I put all 26 points into Intelligence as I knew growing my mana pool was critical. Feeling a rather impressive migraine coming on, I let the bliss of sleep take me.

I awoke a few hours later. With just a few hours of sleep I felt much better. It made me wonder if my high Constitution had anything to do with it.

It didn't take me long to head over to the second sub-level to check-in on the goblins. I swear that goblins are part clown. I had no idea how they figured out where to put everyone. The second sub-level was rather large, and it did have some areas for storage that the goblins converted into living quarters as best they could. Somehow over a thousand goblins were in this sub level. They were everywhere but they kept to the second level.

I found Gr'ex and Hal'ex talking with a few of their clansmen when I approached. "How is everyone settling in?"

The two goblin leaders gave me a hesitant look. "What's the problem?"

Hal'ex spoke first. "It is not a problem per say. Most of the Crawler clan had to set up topside. The giant spiders were not as comfortable in such a small space."

"That's not a big deal. We just have to know the area and tell the human survivors where to avoid." I replied. I could not see the issue.

Gr'ex spoke next. "My grandmother is only telling part of the story. Some of our people, specifically the Crawler clan went to explore the first sub level..."

"And? Out with-it man!" I ordered.

Gr'ex looked at his grandmother and shrugged his shoulders. Hal'ex chimed in. "The huemons got a bit startled at the sight of goblins and may have panicked a bit."

"A bit? They lost their damn minds when they saw a few of the giant spiders... and..." Gr'ex interrupted.

"Again, let me ask, and what? Just cut to the chase!" I said in frustration. 'I mean how bad could it be.' I thought.

"The giant spiders may have taken their loud gestures and quick movements as aggressive... so they started shooting their webbing at several. The goblin riders had to do everything they could to prevent their mounts from sinking their fangs into them once their prey was bound. It's instinctual." Hal'ex explained.

Gr'ex spoke up. "The huemons are still working to cut their people free. The spiders mucked up the passageway between sub floor two and sub floor one as a precaution. Last I saw Jebediah threatening to shoot anyone who tried to retaliate."

I face palmed. "Well, that's going to set us back on getting everyone working together when the fighting starts. I best take my elevator upstairs and come back down that way if the passage is clogged."

I started to walk away before turning back. "Get the passage cleared out and I expect to see Tan'don, the Crawler chief, without Lucile by my side to sort this out in an hour."

I did not wait for a response and just turned and walked to my special elevator entrance.

I entered the first level to a cacophony of voices.

"How can we sleep or rest when we know spiders the size of horses are just below us!

"They were going to eat me!"

"I still have spider webbing in my hair!"

"Burn this whole unholy place down! It's the only way to ensure the spiders are killed!"

"Yes, cleanse it with fire!"

Then I heard Melody's voice. "Hold on everyone! I share your sentiments about spiders, but freaking out won't help anyone!"

And then I heard Jebediah's sound voice of reason. "Anyone who tries to burn this place or pull anything like that will get shot... period!"

As I turned the corner, I saw at least fifty people all huddled together. Some had bits of what I assumed was spiderwebs in their hair or on their clothes. Some people were still being cut out of their bindings.

Those that could stand were. I even saw a few people I knew were 'numb' or 'lost', whatever my people were calling them. Apparently, the spider 'attack' as they were calling it had woken some of them up.

'Silver lining? Guess we will see.' I thought before I interjected myself.

When Jebediah noticed me, I saw a look of relief on his face. It was clear the man wasn't bluffing about shooting some people.

"What seems to be the problem?" I asked.

Everyone turned to me. Many had looks of anger and frustration, but I could feel the undercurrent of fear that was driving it.

"What seems to be the problem?! This is the problem!" A lady in her early twenties said as she pulled at the spiderwebbing in her hair before she continued. "I and many more of us were nearly eaten by giant spiders! Spiders, we were told, you let in here! How dare you!"

And that's when I lost it! Losing my temper, not the best approach to defuse a tense situation, I'll admit that. Also, not too proud of what I did, but at that moment, I didn't care. What can I say, I'm a work in progress. I let go of my hold of my Dark Mantle.

"HOW DARE I? HOW DARE YOU SPEAK TO ME THAT WAY! I DARE WHATEVER I WISH! DO NOT FORGET YOU ARE IN MY HOME! YOU THINK YOU CAN SPEAK TO ME LIKE THAT!" I practically roared.

Those looks of rage turned to looks of utter horror. People collapsed to their knees. Some people started to weep. I even smelled the telltale signs that several had soiled themselves.

Not gonna lie, it felt nice to bring such arrogance to a grinding halt, but I also knew it was a slippery slope, and not one I wanted to go down. I reined in my emotions and clamped down once again on my Dark Mantle ability.

The pressure on everyone vanished in an instant. Clear looks of relief were on people's faces. I still saw some lingering looks of fear too.

I spoke calmly but held firm on my stance. "Now that everyone has calmed down, we can have a civil conversation. I understand how jarring it was to know giant spiders exist let alone come face to face with some. The Crawler clan has relocated their spiders topside, taking a spot further north for now. It is not ideal, but it is apparently necessary for now. So, you do not have to worry about seeing one of the giant spiders in the underground part of the compound, but you will have to avoid a certain section of the forest."

I paused and let them collect themselves. Melody spoke up first. "That ability you have is terrifying!"

Jebediah was helping her to her feet. "Aye, son. I didn't know you had something like that. Most impressive, but scarier than a hornets' nest in your trousers!"

I smiled at the man before I continued. This time my voice was a bit more understanding. "Look, I get you are afraid. We are in the apocalypse, being scared out of your mind is a given. BUT... that fear must be tempered into something useful. Hard times create tough people. We can let this apocalypse break us or we can cling to the hope that we can carve out a home and weather the trials we most likely will endure."

I paused and scanned my eyes over the crowd before I continued. "Anyone promising you safety with no risk of harm, or a free ride is lying to you and delusional! Without your own involvement in carving out our place we will all fall. What I can commit to all of you is as long as you don't break faith with me, I will stand alongside you to help make our new home a reality! As much as you may not like it, we need the goblins to make that happen, and they too are looking to make this place a home. Only together do we have a chance of dealing with the Bone Marrow clan!"

Jebediah chimed in. "If you think about it, is it not better we point those giant spiders towards our enemies? This town is my home, and you will always have my support Shadowalker!"

"Thank you, my friend!" I replied.

Melody was next to speak up. "I may not always agree with your methods, but I cannot argue their results. I am here and not in a cage thanks to you. I can work with the other goblins, just don't ask me to interact with the spiders."

"That's fair." I acknowledged, then turned to the crowd.

I later learned the lady that went off on me, her name was Karen, no joke. She spoke up. "I am sorry, Shadowalker. I'm just scared and an arachnophobe. The giant spiders definitely didn't help! But I can't ignore that before that I have felt more secure in the last couple days than I have since this nightmare started. That's probably why I reacted so poorly, I felt secure, and that security was threatened. Rather than complain, I need to do something productive. I will help however I can. I do know how to shoot."

Her apology was the catalyst to get others to come around and offer their support. I had to remind myself that most of these people had lived entitled and sheltered lives ignorant of what real survival was about or how quickly they fell back on their old habits and took for granted their situation.

We had enemies in the town we wanted to turn into a community. They either helped or would fall, like so many others who have already died in this madness.

Turning to Melody and Jebediah, "Please see to getting everyone cleaned up. I'm going to go meet with the Crawler goblin chief."

They both nodded in acknowledgement before I left. As I turned around, I saw Alice there leaning up against the wall. "You doing okay, Alice? You look a little flushed."

Alice just smiled at me before giving me a hug and motioning for me to pick her up. "I'm fine. I just wanted you to carry me. Is it time for breakfast?"

I nodded. Survivors somewhat mollified, I headed back upstairs, with Alice in my arms, to fix some breakfast.

Chapter 30- No Rest for The Wicked

Laraaq and Jennifer

Laraaq sat in the driver's seat of his moving truck, towing the old pickup. Jennifer sat in the passenger's seat and was on the walkie talkie having a conversation with her parents. As their magi-tech power suit, or what everyone was calling the magi-mech, moved faster than the convoy. The inventor couple took on the critical role of scout and first engagement.

Previously, the convoy were using armed people on motorcycles to speed on ahead and return with any risks or dangers. If they couldn't get away, that's what being armed was about, they defended themselves until they could get away. A risky but critical job.

The magi-mech was far more armored and shielded. It also packed way more of a punch than a rifle or handgun. They had taken out several threats along the way that posed little risk for the inventor duo.

Most of the creatures they encountered were Undead Zombies. If the zombies couldn't reach you to bite or scratch you, they weren't much a problem. The couple already were level 16 from all the zombies and other monsters they took out.

Laraaq wasn't thrilled about missing all those kills and sweet experience. It did mean when they finally reached their destination, Laraaq would be full on mana. Other than being tired of driving and being stuck behind the wheel, he was ready to go.

The convoy had continued to rescue people that were along the way. Even with rescue teams leaving the convoy on random recovery missions, they were making great time. The convoy would arrive several hours ahead of schedule, and that suited Laraaq just fine.

They had over 1,500 people in the convoy now. Most were non-combatants, but many of those that were willing to fight were seasoned hunters and ex-soldiers. Laraaq wasn't thrilled with everyone they saved. Some, like Sharon, were too entitled and stuck in their old ways of manipulating people to get what they want.

Many of those who Laraaq would prefer to keep an eye on would stay back with the convoy when the real fighting starts. He knew they were a future problem, one he hated to hand over to his friend. Laraaq knew Shadowalker was better suited for the headaches that would ensue post battle, so he would support his best friend as best he could.

"How big was the cougar? Eight feet tall? That's insane?" Jennifer had headphones plugged in, which Laraaq was grateful for.

She was getting a report about one of the 'threats' her parents just eliminated. In some way Laraaq was curious as it helped break up the monotony of the drive. In other ways, he could care less, it was all just a distraction. In the end Laraaq decided to be appreciative of the time the couple was saving them and to be grateful they would have more practice fighting in the power suit they invented.

Jennifer relayed the information. "Mom & Dad took out a giant mutated cougar. They said it should be smooth sailing to our destination. They didn't want to get too close for fear their Magi-mech would draw too much attention. However, they have been able to take out any of the threats between here and their location."

"That's good news. What level are they now?" Laraaq replied.

"They just dinged 17. I'm super jealous. I so want to pick my class already." Jennifer vented.

Laraaq chuckled. "Ha! Tell me about it. I'm so over being stuck in this truck. Give me something to light on fire and I'll take it over nonstop driving any day of the week!"

A few hours later the convoy came to a stop along the road, not too far from a forest. If they continued along the road, in a few miles they would reach the town. Laraaq turned his two-way radio to the frequency Carol had told him.

A few minutes later he got a reply. "This is Donut. Over."

"Donut. This is Laraaq. We are at the rendezvous point and awaiting confirmation." Laraaq replied.

Jennifer spoke up. "You forgot to say 'over'."

Laraaq grimaced before he quickly said into the radio, "Over."

"Glad to hear it. Shadowalker left this morning for the Sleeping Willow camp. From there he was going to head to the meet up point. Once we hear back the rest of us will begin to form up for our attack. Over." Duncan said over the radio.

"We've got incoming!" Jennifer's mom said through the magi-mech's speaker.

Twenty giant spiders broke through the clearing.

"Oh, hell no!" Laraaq said as she took aim.

"Why did it have to be spiders!" Jennifer lamented.

Then Laraaq noticed goblins were sitting in saddles and behind an older goblin he thought he saw a familiar face.

The spiders stopped and the only human on the spiders got down. Laraaq heard him mumble something. "Thank you Tan'don and Lucile for the ride. It still doesn't make up for what you did, but the look on their faces was priceless."

"You jerk! Did you get taller? And more muscular?" Laraaq blurted out.

"I figured you would freak, but I couldn't pass up the chance to scare the crap out a few of your new friends. Besides, you're one to talk, look at you! You lost some weight and got taller yourself. You look good brother!" Shadowalker said as he embraced Laraaq in a big hug.

Just then a notification popped up in Laraaq's vision.

Quest Completed! *You have reunited with your best friend and brother! You have done so prior to the week's deadline and brought with you fighting forces to help defend your new home! For going above and beyond for this quest you are granted the following rewards:*
• *Title*   • *Instantly progress to the next level*   • *Race change*

Congratulations! You have gained the title: **Reliable Ally!**

Title: Reliable Ally
Description: *When times are most dire, and you are most needed you are there! Against the odds, you stick by those you care about no matter what!* **+10 to All Stats!** *+25% to stats when fighting for or with your allies.*

You are a lucky bastard! That title is only granted to those who risk their life consistently and with all their being are loyal to someone with great authority!

"Thanks, system!" Laraaq mentally replied.

Warning: If you ever betray the one you've pledged yourself to, the penalties for losing the title are quite severe!

"Not something I ever have to worry about, system. This man is my brother, he would do the same for me!" Laraaq mentally told his system.

As if to prove his point, Laraaq receive a new notification.

Temporary Buff Received: Time Armor (10th tier spell)
Duration: *24 hours or until triggered*
Description: *Prevents one fatal attack or critical injury by nullifying the time between you and the armor. With not impede range of motion or mobility.*

Laraaq inwardly smiled. His buddy Shadowalker must've used the contact from the hug to place this buff on him. 'He probably used up most of his mana to cast this on me. Yep, that's my brother!' Laraaq thought before turning his attention back to his other notifications.

Level Up! *Congratulations! You are now* **level 13!** *You have* **+10 stat points** *to distribute! You are now eligible to choose a class.* **Warning**: *Class selection can take a long time and would potentially remove you from the upcoming battle.*

"Nice warning system! So, in other words I better wait to start my class selection process!" Laraaq lamented.

Correct!

"Well, thank you for the warning, system. That could've been disastrous." Laraaq said in appreciation.

After making sure he stroked his system's ego, Laraaq decided it was time to review the last of his notifications.

Congratulations! You are eligible for a race change. Please choose from the following races:

•   *Advanced Human*
   •   *Elf*
   •   *Dwarf*
   •   *Dark Elf*
   •   *Sea Elf*
   •   *Were-honey-badger…*

The list continued on, but Laraaq ignored the other options. Once he read the Were-honey-badger, the other options held no interest for him.

"This must be from getting bitten by that Mutated Giant Honey Badger."

Correct!

Selecting his option, Laraaq began to convulse. He felt pain greater than when he distributed 40 stat points all at once. Laraaq had made the mistake of not allocating his points from level 9 through level 12 as he leveled. He felt his friend Shadowalker helped him to the ground and the bliss of unconsciousness took him.

Several people from the convoy drew their weapons thinking this stranger just attacked their leader. The goblins drew their own weapons, and some began casting spells. For a brief moment it looked like both sides would come to blows.

Jennifer broke the tension as she rushed over to Laraaq's side. "I'm a healer!"

Shadowalker allowed her to examine his friend.

After a few moments, Jennifer stood and turned to the convoy. "My Diagnostics spell is telling me he is undergoing a race change. We just need to give him some time. I imagine it was similar to when he waited to distribute his stat points from four levels."

Shadowalker

My best friend collapsed right as a notification appeared in my vision.

*Congratulations! You have gone above and beyond in finding allies to support your upcoming battle for your new home. As a reward two additional abilities within your soul are unlocked. You have gained the abilities: **Weave Sight** and **Hunter's Sense of Smell**.*

Weave Sight
<u>Description</u>: *See the very essence of those they lay their eyes on. See auras, magical signatures, and the true self of those you gaze upon. This ability also grants you access to the Weave and the strands of Fate that tie all things together. These connections to Fate are rarely glimpsed. Please Note: Master this ability to increase your influence over Fate.*

Hunter's Sense of Smell
<u>Description</u>: *Any real hunter can smell which creatures are prey or predator. You can literally smell the nature of someone by their scent. Also grants pheromone detection and purpose.*

'Wow! Both will be very useful abilities that I will figure out how to master later.' I thought as I knelt, keeping an eye on my best friend and brother.

Laraaq's body was shifting. Fur started to grow all over his body, and he grew in size and muscle mass. Then most of fur receded and I was looking at my brother again.

"I'm Jennifer by the way." The blond woman said.

I hadn't bothered to examine her as I was a bit distracted with seeing Laraaq. That was a tactical mistake and not one I would repeat as I began identifying everyone within range. After a few moments, I realized I was being rude.

"My apologies. I'm a bit distracted. I'm Shadowalker, but I'm sure you already figured that out. The older goblin behind me is Tan'don, chief of the Crawler goblin clan. They raise the giant spiders as companions and war mounts."

Jennifer commented. "Never met a goblin before. Though, I have zero interest in meeting those giant spiders. They scared many of us near to death!"

I chuckled. "Ha! This is the apocalypse. You have to get used to uncomfortable or the unordinary if you want to survive."

Jennifer pointed to the big power suit standing close by. "My parents are inventors and made the magi-tech battle suit. I think I'm good on how I'm adapting and don't need any giant spiders in my life."

That made me laugh. "Ha! Ha, ha, ha! Fair enough. Well while my buddy is sleeping perhaps you could fill me in on the convoy's fighting prowess."

Two men stepped forward. My system identified them as Carl and Jacob. Carl was the one who spoke up first. "My name is Carl. We have over 200 fighters and hunters. All of them ready to go."

Jacob followed up. "I'm Jacob. We have over 1,500 people so most will have to stay behind, and we will want people to guard them should the enemy double back in combat."

"That's a lot of risk. I recommend only the lowest levels be chosen to remain. That is what we are doing at my compound. We picked those that weren't ready for the realities of war and were of a low enough level it wouldn't make too much difference. Typically, those from the younger generation who have yet to adapt to this game like system. Their peers who have accepted our new reality are joining the fight." I explained.

An older woman my system identified as a Carol Burns spoke up. "That's smart. I'd fight but I think I'm better served to coordinate the convoy while our main force is away."

The moment she spoke up I knew she was the lady Duncan had been speaking with over the radio. She had a calming voice and per Jebediah, had a level head on her shoulders too. I nodded in acknowledgement. "That would be most helpful Carol. How many healers do you have? Any of them willing to go into combat?"

"Besides myself?" Jennifer chimed in.

I nodded in acknowledgement. "We need as many healers as possible willing to fight."

Jacob spoke up. "There are maybe 20 people with healing magic or medical skills. Of those 20, only half have openly pledged to fight. The others have offered to do triage and first aid away from the battle."

While Jacob was talking Gr'ex had dismounted and came up alongside me.

I sighed. "That's not ideal. We only have three human healers. One will stay behind at the compound, the other two are reluctantly willing to join the fight." I turned to Gr'ex. "How many goblin healers do we have?"

Gr'ex stroked his chin with his thumb and forefinger. "As you know, master, not all healers are equal. True healers about 5, most of them are funny enough from the Boom clan. Dark Shamans and those that can leech life from one to heal another, we have over 50. Most of those are from my clan, the Dark Weavers."

"Those who can leech life would be better served in the thick of things. The true healers should be held back in reserve as much as possible. Each healer should have a squad of defenders to protect them. Rule of magic combat, protect the healer." I said the last part while looking at Jennifer.

Looking back to Jacob and Carl. "Now that the most important subject is determined, healing, let's discuss other logistics. How many fighters will you be bringing? How many ranged versus melee, etc.?"

Carl spoke first this time. "We have twenty-six squads that consist of three to six people. Most are marksmen. Several are good at hand-to-hand combat."

Jacob chimed in after that. "Carl has taken on the responsibility of our ranges and rescue teams. I have taken on the responsibility for our melee fighters and spirit warriors."

"Spirit warriors?" I asked in confusion.

"Those that focus on the internal energy and cultivation overall. They have an advantage in internal control and body enhancement. Also, the easiest path to immortality." Gr'ex explained.

I turned to Gr'ex. "Sounds pretty impressive. Why haven't we discussed it before?"

"Simple. Once you form a core based on chi you have a hard time cultivating mana. That type of spirit energy is more rigid and not as adaptable as mana. Which makes it difficult for the wielder to influence the outside world. Also, if you release your chi and it is not neutral, you can poison the environment for those that do not possess the affinities. Dangerous and limited, plus the length of time and effort to get to a point of meaningful cultivation. Mana is faster and easier when it comes to magic."

"We have been making great strides in strengthening our bodies and removing impurities. I assure you Shadowalker that this path is very lucrative. We have over two hundred cultivators at various beginning stages of body enhancement. My spirit warriors will gladly take their place on the front lines." Jacob countered.

'Would've been nice to know that was an option before I formed my core. Though mine formed pretty early in all of this.' I thought.

My system once again answered my unanswered question.

Query Accepted

Your Divine Infinitum is one of the rare cores capable of cultivating multiple spiritual energies including Chi or Qi depending on your perspective.

"Really?" I mentally asked.

Query Accepted

Yes. Such spiritual energy is a more complex form of the mana energy in the universe. Please Note: Releasing complex spiritual energy can poison those around you depending on their affinities.

Well, that was one hell of a revelation. I could cultivate other forms of spiritual energy such as chi or Qi. Then, learning it was more rigid than mana due to it being a more complex form.

"System, after this upcoming battle, set a reminder for me to experiment with different forms of spiritual cultivation." I mentally requested.

Reminder Added

"Thank you."

Turning my attention back to Jacob. "Alright Jacob. Your men shall take the front. I want several placed within the ranged units for added protection. As most of our people will be using guns it will be important to keep the enemy forces from melee range for as long as possible."

A young man I identified as Colin spoke up. "Shouldn't we wait for Mr. Laraaq to wake up? I mean isn't he in charge here."

Gr'ex chuckled.

I leered at my goblin companion. I turned to Colin. "That is a fair question. You are on my lands; I have authority here. Laraaq is my brother and right-hand man. I had no intention of starting the battle or doing final deployments without him. Right now, I am getting the overall understanding of what kind of fighting force we have to work with. Any of you have a problem with that?"

As I asked my question, the goblins riding their giant spider mounts moved forward to show their support. I imagine for an intimidation factor too; it was not required. If I needed to intimidate, I just had to let up ever slightly on my tight control over my mantle.

Colin stepped back as the giant spiders stepped forward. I could literally smell the fear coming off the young man. He was not the only one I could literally smell fear on them. 'Man, this new sense is going to take some getting used to.' I thought.

A giant of a man put his hand on Colin's shoulder stopping him in his retreat. The man had a smile on his face that didn't quite reach his eyes. I could see something coming off him, but I wasn't sure what it was as I was still getting used to the extra sensory information coming from all the smells let alone what I assumed was people's auras I was seeing.

I instantly recognized this man as a fellow predator and a hunter. His gaze was like one hunter looking at another to size up the threat. I stared the man down and smiled. He recognized I wasn't bluffing.

The scents I got from him confirmed he was a hunter. He also had other scents on him. There was definitely a female scent on him. And one other scent I couldn't quite place.

'Not quite fear like the others. Hmmm, concern maybe? Yes, he's concerned about something.' I thought as I stared back at the man.

The burly man spoke up, never taking his eyes off of me as he did. "Come now Colin. No need to run away. This man clearly has support here. Laraaq did say we were coming to his friend."

"If you say so Mr. Mack." Colin replied.

Mack waved his hand towards the goblins with me. "I hear we gonna be fighting goblins, but it looks like we have some goblins on our side. How we supposed to know which ones to kill?"

"Good question Mack. Each goblin clan has an emblem and colors they wear. The Bone Marrow clan goblins typically have brown and red over a set of bones. So just remember the phrase: 'Brown and red, make em dead!' Got it?" I explained.

Mack chuckled. "Ha! I like that! Easy to use! Brown and red, make em dead!" Mack said the last part as he slammed his fist into his other hand.

Mack turned to Jacob. "You should pass the word around..."

"I need no direction from you Mack, nor did I ask for it! You've never given a crap about anyone but yourself so why now of all times are you even bothering." Jacob fired back.

"Or don't. I don't really care. I'm going to go prepare for battle." Mack said as he turned his back on Jacob and walked away.

Colin followed close behind the brute of a man.

'Interesting. There seems to be dissent amongst the ranks. I'll have to ask Laraaq about it later.' I thought as I watched the interaction.

Gr'ex whispered to me. "I know we need warriors, but really? This group seems unbalanced."

I laughed. "Ha, ha, ha, ha! You mean like our group?"

Gr'ex winced. "Okay, that is fair. That Mack... he will be a problem. He reminds me too much of the Orcs. You never turn your back on an Orc."

I nodded. "I thought you told me to never turn my back on a goblin."

"That too. Well, you do not have to worry about that now, not with your **Dark Mantle**. Mark my words when this battle is over, that man will have to be dealt with." Gr'ex replied.

"Fair enough. But that is a problem for future me. Current me has a goblin chief to kill... speaking about Tek'tar, why is he so big?" I asked as I watched Carl and Jacob huddle for a private conversation.

"Oh, that is simple. He's half Orc. Another reason not to like him." Gr'ex answered.

"You really don't like Orcs do you buddy." I commented.

"Why would I like a race that enslaves mine or treats mine as trash." Gr'ex explained.

"I've never met an Orc, but I know you cannot judge an entire race on the actions of some." I stated.

"Perhaps. I did not like huemons until we became allies. A discussion for another day. These huemons seem to be taking the big one's advice." Gr'ex gestured to Jacob and Carl.

"I'll see the word spread to everyone. Your suggestions for group make-up and deployment are sound. We will incorporate it." Carl stated.

Gr'ex spoke up loud enough for Carl and others to hear. "I did not think my master gave a suggestion, but rather an order."

Gr'ex stepped forward as his staff began to glow. Carl flinched at the act.

Jacob stepped forward. "He meant nothing by it. Would you attack allies?"

Jennifer stepped between us. "Can we stop swinging our sticks around and focus on the task at hand?"

"I can respect a peacekeeper." I nodded to Jennifer. "Besides she is right. I have little interest in making these men pee their pants before a battle and it would not do well for my companion to cripple fighters either."

"What makes you think..." Carl began to say until he dropped to his knees as I released a fraction of my **Dark Mantle** and focused it at the man.

As quickly as I released it, I clamped back down. I moved faster than I ever had, using every point of **Dexterity**. In a second, I was at Jacob's side, dagger at his throat. To Jacob's credit I could feel spiritual energy coating the man's body.

We looked at each other in the eyes before Jacob looked down at the blade pointed at his neck. Jacob smiled. "I see I am outmatched. You are just like your friend Laraaq. He made one hell of an impression as well."

I sheathed my blade. "Ha! Knowing Laraaq I can only imagine."

"He burned my nephew alive." Jacob stated.

I winced. "That sounds like him. Your nephew must've been a right bastard."

Jacob laughed. "Ha! Laraaq brought to light how true that statement is. As a leader, as a man of honor, once I knew the truth for sure, I knew what Laraaq did, was justice. I hold no ill will towards him."

Jacob held out his hand and we shook hands.

Jennifer shook her head. "Men!"

I turned to her. "Yes? What about us? In one moment, we resolved our conflict and reached an understanding. Trust me, it is a far healthier way. Now Jacob and Carl know they can follow a man with strength and at least some level of competence. Battle prowess will matter greatly in this new reality."

I tapped my sheathed blade. "As will knowing when not to kill. I may be a monster, but I am one who will fight to protect our people."

"A bit dramatic but I get your point." Jennifer replied with a smirk on her face.

"That's Shadowalker. He can be a bit intense at times, but I could not ask for anyone better to have by my side." Laraaq said as he sat up.

Jennifer rushed to his side. "You're awake! How do you feel?"

"I feel great, actually. I'm great in fact. And based on these notifications I read while you guys were sorting everything out, I'm doing even better than I thought. Let me get to my feet." Laraaq answered.

I was by his side helping Laraaq to his feet. "Of course, you'd have me sort that out."

Laraaq chuckled. "Ha! I knew you'd handle it. If they really tried anything I would've roasted them alive."

I embraced my friend in a side hug. "So, tell me about these notifications."

"I'm a **Were-honey-badger** now!" Laraaq said excitedly.

"That's freaking awesome brother! Just in time to bring the pain!" I encouraged.

"I have three forms now and I have something called **Hunter's Sense of Smell**. I'm getting all sorts of new sensory information, it's a trip. My **Strength**, **Dexterity**, and **Constitution** went up **20 points** and it increases when I'm in my were-form! Looks like even more when I'm in my full Honey-Badger form! Man, clothing is going to be an issue if I'm reading this right. What's even better is because I have high enough **Intelligence** and **Wisdom**, I can control the natural rage that comes with these forms. I can even cast my magic while in were-form!" Laraaq explained.

"Sweet! You're going to be a wrecking ball on the battlefield." I commented.

Gr'ex approached holding out a walkie-talkie. "Umm, this crude communication device is making noise."

"Walkie-talkie." I replied as I took the device from him.

"That is a horrible name. It makes no sense! The thing does not walk at all." Gr'ex complained.

"No, no. It's because you can walk..." I started to explain but just waved him off as I heard Jebediah's voice come through.

"Shadowalker you there? Over."

I pushed the button. "Yea go ahead. Over."

"We have spotted goblins heading our way. Orders? Over." Jebediah stated.

Laraaq and I quickly nodded at each other. "Looks like it's time to rumble." Laraaq said as he shifted into his were-form ripping his shirt in the process.

Laraaq grew to over two meters tall, easily seven feet tall for us Americans. He grew fur all over his body and his muzzle elongated and sharp teeth protruded.

"You look badass brother!" I said as I looked at him. Then I clicked on the walkie-talkie. "Move out. We will hit them from behind. Classic pincer move. Do as we discussed, melee in front while you do as much damage as possible from range. Over."

Turning to Jacob, Carl, and Jennifer. "You heard Jebediah, rally our forces and let's move out."

When Carl didn't move fast enough, Laraaq roared. "YOU HEARD THE MAN, MOVE!"

Chapter 31 – Fight

Jebediah

"You heard Shadowalker, let's move out! Ann, you're with my team. Everyone else, group up!" Jebediah ordered.

As the fighters started to file out of the compound, they took defensive positions. Once a position was established another group would move a way down the trail and set up their own defensive position, until another group moved ahead of them. On and on the fighter parties advanced slowly in this way.

They were unsure how close the main force of the goblins was, and they did not want to get caught out in the open.

Jebediah did his best to train their people in different jungle and forest tactics and strategies. He wishes he had more than a few days to work with them, but he got lucky with a few ex-military men that took up squad leader positions or helped with training the others. Even the goblins that joined up with them helped offer their training in crude bows and melee weapons.

Jebediah turned to Melody. "I leave the compound in your care."

Melody just nodded, tears in her eyes. She was scared for him and others. The reports she listened to said they were outnumbered by five Bone Marrow goblins to their one fighter and that was even with many of the goblins that joined their side filling their ranks. There were just too many non-combatants or those not ready to fight like Mitch and Gio.

Jebediah stared at the two young men. "You two have guard duty. Make sure nothing enters this compound that isn't human. Remember the mantra 'Brown and red, make em dead!' You take direction from Melody and do what she says got it?"

Both men snapped at attention and in unison said, "Yes Sir!"

Jebediah took a step toward Melody and pulled the older woman into a hug and kissed her on the forehead. She in turn grabbed his face and pulled him into a kiss. After a few moments they broke their embrace.

"Bout time you made yer move! I wasn't getting any younger!" Melody commented.

"Man, that was some kiss! I should've done that days ago!" Jebediah exclaimed.

"Now you have even more reason to come back safe." Melody stated.

"Yes ma'am!" Jebediah replied before walking off to join his party.

Melody turned to the two young men on the porch. "I want this place locked down tight. No one in or out, got it?"

"Yes ma'am!" The two men said in unison.

Jebediah caught up to Ann, Duncan, and Suzie. "What'd I miss?"

Duncan replied, "Nothing. Our progress is slow but cautious as we aren't taking any chances."

Suzie spoke up. "So did you finally kiss her?"

Jebediah turned a nice shade of pink.

"Kiss who?" Duncan asked.

"Melody." Ann answered.

Everyone turned to Ann. "What? I'm the resident healer. You don't think I pay attention to things? Besides, Melody has been venting to me that she was hoping you'd finally make a move."

"A gentleman doesn't kiss and tell." Jebediah replied.

Suzie smiled. "Oh goodie, there was kissing."

"I-I didn't say..." Jebediah said before Suzie cut him off.

"It's written all over your face. Don't worry about it, I was hoping the two of you would get together. Melody was a great teacher and is an awesome woman."

"I agree with Suzie-cue. Melody was an awesome teacher; you could tell she really cared about us." Duncan chimed in.

"Can we stop this conversation and focus on the task at hand, you know, like not dying." Jebediah admonished.

"Whatever you say, lover boy." Ann teased.

Jebediah's face turned a deep shade of red, but he said nothing as he moved their party to catch up with the squads at the front.

About 15 minutes later their forces made contact with the Bone Marrow clan. A few scouts were found on the path heading their way. A few quick shots from Suzie and Emily and the four scouts were dead.

That was only the beginning though as they could hear the goblins coming long before they could see them. They were not quiet and moved through the forest without much care for their lives. Undead Zombies were out front and acted as a meat shield between the forces from the compound and the Bone Marrow goblins.

"That's a lot of zombies." Emily commented as her elven eyes allowed her to see much farther than her human counterparts.

"Even more goblins behind them. Easily a few hundred, and that's just what I can see." Suzie stated.

"Well looks like we can use the toys from the Boom clan. They would burn down this forest." Jebediah said in clear disappointment.

"Form up! Melee in front! Hold them back as long as you can! Ranged, unleash hell on the back so as to avoid friendly fire!" Jebediah yelled out.

He turned to his party. "Donuts you lead the melee. Suzie-cue and Emily, I trust your shooting better than anyone else here. You take out those closer to the line. If you see any Bone Marrow goblin wearing a robe..."

"Shoot them right between the eyes!" Emily said, trying to imitate him.

Jebediah nodded. "That's right! Ann, you stay by me, but do what you can to keep the front-line fighters up!"

"Understood." Ann acknowledged.

Jebediah could see the concern on the old nurse's face. He had seen it many times on the battlefield. She was scared and nervous about screwing up. He could hear people moving into position. Putting his hand on Ann's shoulder, "It's okay to be scared. I'd be worried if you weren't. You won't be able to save everyone, so do the best you can. That's all any of us can ask."

Ann looked like she might cry, but instead she steeled herself and nodded. Jebediah nodded back before turning his full attention back to the incoming forces.

Taking aim, Jebediah began firing off round after round. Each shot delivering a headshot to a zombie's head. No matter how many he killed, more just kept coming.

Crossbow bolts whizzed by. Some embedded themselves in the trees their people were using for cover. Sadly, even more hit makeshift shields or punctured flesh.

The squad leaders were clearly ex-military used to fire fights. They would order the wounded to fall back as a fresh unit would take their place.

Many of the injured were moved to Ann if the wound was severe, otherwise they were patched up by designated first aid units who had the barest of training. Once patched up, they were sent back into the fight.

The human defenders were larger than the goblins but many of the goblins had been using the system their whole lives and had physical attributes that allowed them to go toe-to-toe with the bigger humans and still beat several of them back.

Lucky for the human defenders they had three things going for them. The Undead Zombies weren't as strong as some of the Bone Marrow goblins, allowing the humans to take zombie blows as long as they avoided the zombie bite attacks. Second, the defenders were using tactics and ranged weapons that dealt decent damage to the enemy units. Third, the defenders had their own goblin allies, and these goblins were used to fighting adversaries much stronger than them.

The Boom goblins used strange contraptions that shot out electrical shocks that zapped multiple enemies at once, locking them in place. This allowed other defenders to deliver killing blows while zapped enemy units were incapacitated. If that wasn't enough, the Boom goblins would throw vials into the mass of enemies and watch with glee as the minor explosions that went off when the vials shattered would take out multiple units.

The Death Weavers were not sitting idle either. They flung curse after curse, crippling one goblin after the other. Their necromancers sent their own skeletons to fight the undead in the enemy ranks.

Dark Bolts were seen flying from both sides of the battlefield, as both the Death Weavers and the dark magic casters from the Bone Marrow clan cast spell after spell at each other. The Death Weavers were more skilled at wielding their magic. The Bone Marrow clan had the undead numbers, but that soon proved more a liability against true necromancers.

Hal'ex sitting on her undead mobile chair was able to wrestle control of several Undead Zombies away from their master's and turn them on the others. The combination of attacks sowed chaos into the front lines, causing some sections to become useless.

Even with these tactics the human defenders were not used to fighting undead. Several were wounded when they turned their backs on units they thought defeated, only to suffer a gash from a claw or get tripped when a half-torn zombie grabbed their legs. Their goblin allies became invaluable as many stepped in to block a fatal blow or parry a lethal strike from an undead enemy.

Jebediah knew he would have to thank Hal'ex for taking control of an Undead Zombie that broke through the lines and caught the old veteran by surprise. The zombie had knocked him over and was about to slash at his throat when it stopped, got off him and ran back into the fray, now on their side. He saw the telltale signs of Death magic around her hands as he got to his feet. "Th-thank you."

Hal'ex only spared him a single nod before her attention turned back to the larger battle and attempting to wrestle more undead minions from enemy control.

Still the invaders advanced. Their original numbers of five Bone Marrow to one defender were grossly underestimated. As goblins died, both sides would raise them as new Undead Zombies to fight for their side. It started to blur the lines of who was on what side. The defenders were being pushed back as they slowly had to give up ground.

Ann was doing everything she possibly could as she healed her allies, both human and goblin. Jebediah had pushed her away when the Undead Zombie caught them by surprise. His act saved her life but cost the veteran several deep gashes and would've cost the man his life if not for Hal'ex's quick actions.

Just when the defenders thought they would have to lose even more ground a horn could be heard in the distance. The enemy forces began to slowly fall back towards the town. They did not fully retreat but had stopped their advance.

"What was that?" Ann asked.

Hal'ex who was nearby answered. "Shadowalker and his friend must have attacked their flank. Tek'tar would recall his forces to help protect his backside. The man is a coward at heart. Many goblins are."

"Does that mean we are winning?" Emily asked as she helped Ann up after she healed a wounded soldier.

"No, not at all. Tek'tar was just caught off guard. He will compensate soon enough." Hal'ex explained.

Suzie helped Jebediah to his feet. "Then now is the time that we have to push them hard." Jebediah stated.

Suzie shot an arrow with her bow, killing a Bone Marrow goblin caster. She had long run out of bullets and switched to her bow. She was getting tired. "I-I don't... think you... realize how tired people are getting." She said with clear fatigue in her voice from her rapid-fire shooting.

"No Jebediah is right. We must push the advantage now, or we may not get another chance." Mek'mar said as he overheard the conversation. He too had not stopped attacking, flinging vial after vial into the enemy ranks.

"If he doesn't pull this off, I'm going to kick his ass." Jebediah commented as he took a well-aimed shot to save Duncan from an attack on his flank from a sneaky goblin who wasn't withdrawing with the rest of his people.

Jacob

He liked this new leader. It was clear to him that Shadowalker was strong and fast, but more importantly was quick thinking. The man instantly intuited the fact that Carl and he would not follow an untested leader. Shadowalker's quick actions were not over the top but rather just enough to quickly resolve the question of who was in charge and remove any doubt of strength. It was a good sign of competence, and Jacob knew the price all too well of an incompetent leader. His own incompetence hurt many under him due to his blind love for his nephew.

Jacob had been hesitant at first when Laraaq made it clear that he was to follow his friend's orders. At first, he could not figure out why Laraaq didn't want the job. Most men would take the role of leader without question, usually their motive was one of power and control. It was clear that Laraaq would follow Shadowalker unquestionably. He now began to understand why.

It was also clear, Shadowalker was a reluctant leader. He did it out of duty and not a thirst for power. In fact, Jacob would hazard a guess that Shadowalker was probably the strongest among them. Yet if he had not witnessed it himself, Jacob would not believe it. The man had great control over his aura. Far more control than Jacob, which was hard to believe.

Jacob learned from his system that what his system called a Spiritual Cultivator would have far more control over their energies than a Mana Cultivator. Mana was more abundant, but it took multiple units of mana to produce one unit of chi. It was why, according to his system, Spiritual Cultivators believed mana was a lower form of energy. Jacob wasn't sure he believed that, but it didn't really matter.

Jacob made his choice of path in the beginning of the apocalypse, and he had little regrets about it. He was impressed with Laraaq's command of fire, what man wouldn't want to fling fireballs everywhere. The promise of immortality was what appealed to Jacob. It meant survivability and that was most important right now as he led his spiritual warriors into battle.

He was about to fight goblins of all things. In most of the fantasy novels he read goblins were the trash mobs heroes fought at the beginning because they were weak and easy to beat. That did not seem to be the case with these goblins, especially if Shadowalker's companions were any indication.

According to Shadowalker, he split the goblin forces between the compound and their side of the battle. The casters were split between both fronts, with most of them being with the compound front. The Sleeping Willow and Crawler clans were primarily with their front. Most of the spider warriors, who Jacob learned were part of the Crawler clan, were with them and would act as calvary.

Each giant spider held two goblins, one for ranged combat and one to steer and use their spear for melee combat. There was room for a third goblin on several of the larger giant spiders, and that spot is where the casters tended to sit. It made them an armored mobile weapons platform. For if the goblins on its back didn't kill you, the spider's talons, fangs, and pointed legs would.

It made Jacob a bit jealous, except for the simple fact he had zero interest in getting anywhere near those creatures. Knowing they even exist in the apocalypse would leave Jacob with nightmares for days to come. An involuntary shiver went down Jacob's spine at the thought of them being behind him. He increased his speed.

There were no goblins guarding the southern entrance into the town. It wasn't until Jacob and his men got close to Town Hall that they encountered any resistance. Goblin warriors exited the portal and were heading north to reinforce the Bone Marrow forces engaged in battle.

Jacob saw the large goblin who stood about his height. The goblin yelled out orders.

"Finally, the stragglers have come! Your chief has relocated our clan to this world so we may plunder its riches! Now go make yourselves useful!" Tek'tar said while pointing north.

A goblin flew past Tek'tar as Jacob hit the scout with a Spirit Fist. The empowered strike hit the scout so hard their ribs cracked, and the scout was dead before he hit the ground.

"ATTACK!!! Kill every Bone Marrow you see!" Jacob roared as he and his men engaged the flank of the Bone Marrow army.

Tek'tar grabbed a nearby goblin and lifted him off the ground. "Where did these huemons come from?! Where is the Sleeping Willow clan? Are they defending our southern flank?! Do something!"

What Tek'tar did not know is the Sleeping Willow goblins had knocked out their goblins left behind at the southern entrance. Using sleep bombs and other poisons and magic, Sleeping Willow had swept through the southern part of town to ensure Tek'tar would not be alerted until it was too late.

When Tek'tar dropped the goblin, he scurried off to find a signal horn to recall their forces from the northern front. Luckily for Tek'tar, he kept several of his apprentices in reserve with his new favorite toy.

Jacob dodged shots from crossbows and magic bolts shot in his direction. He moved with grace at superhuman speeds. Jacob was impressed with himself until a horrible screeching roar was heard coming from the biggest undead, he had ever seen.

Eldritch Undead Abomination Level 35

The thing was true to its name's sake, standing six meters tall, or twenty feet for Jacob's mental calculation. 'Man, it's still hard to switch from the units of measurement I grew up with as a kid.'

Jacob knew the rational part of his mind was just trying to distract him from trying to process the horror in front of him. It was an amalgamation of bodies forming huge legs and arms. Extra limbs protruded out from all over. It had multiple mouths that made a horrible cry that almost drove one mad from hearing it.

SCREECH!!!

The image and sound were so disorienting that Jacob stopped dodging and was sent flying back when a Dark Bolt hit him in the chest.

Jennifer was by his side healing him. She had only glanced at the horror for a moment before her focus was on Jacob.

"Ugh, thank you ma'am. I don't know how we are going to stop that thing!" Jacob commented as Jennifer helped him to his feet.

She had joined their frontline assault out of concern for the casualties the initial assault might sustain. Jennifer was not expecting Magic to get flung around and she most certainly did not expect whatever that thing was!

Shadowalker roared "Magimech, take that thing down!!!"

Jennifer turned in his direction to see Laraaq right next to his best friend. She focused on the Were-Honey-Badger, as her thoughts shifted from horror to Laraaq. She looked at the man in his were-honey-badger form and realized that Laraaq kind of looked cute with all that fur, fierce, but definitely adorable. She wondered how soft his fur was. Those were the random thoughts that her mind tried to focus on to avoid processing the nightmare in flesh that had entered the battlefield.

Her mind finally caught up to the command Shadowalker gave. Jennifer turned to see her parents charge the abomination in their giant power suit. She agreed with the man that her parents' invention was probably the only thing that could go toe-to-toe with that thing, but she still held pangs of concern for their safety.

Focusing on the fighting going on, Jennifer took shots with her rifle as she could while using her mana to heal nearby injured spirit warriors.

Jacob threw himself back into the fight. His blows being matched by several higher-level goblin warriors. Jacob acknowledged that he, a level 15 Spirit Warrior, was holding off four level 25 goblins. The fact that he was able to contend with multiple people ten levels higher than him reaffirmed the path he had chosen.

A Fire Spear from Laraaq pierced one of the goblin warriors' legs. Jacob used this chance to knock the goblin out with a blow to the head. 'Okay some regrets.' Jacob thought that he still would've liked to fling magic every now and then.

Knocking out one of the goblin warriors gave Jacob more breathing room to maneuver. The goblin took a fully powered Spirit Fist to the face, which should've killed it but instead the warrior was just sent into unconsciousness. 'Okay so maybe I'm not completely at the same place as these guys are, but I am able to fight three of them at the same time.' Jacob thought as he easily dodged the haymaker one of the warriors threw in his direction.

Jacob took a moment to scan the battlefield to see his fellow spirit warriors were holding up rather well, especially when the hunters caught up and provided range support.

A loud horn could be heard.

He saw more warriors rushing into central square, creating a wall of bodies that crashed against his men in melee combat. Jacob's quick reflexes and abundant dislike of spiders allowed him to dodge back in time as one of the giant spiders jumped into the fray. One of the goblin warriors was pinned to the ground by a sharp foot that went right through his abdomen. The second goblin got a spear to the face shortly after the spider landed. The final Goblin Warrior fighting Jacob took some kind of dark spell to the chest making it fall and convulse in agony.

Jacob decided he wanted to be anywhere else but that part of the fight and chose a random section of the frontline battle and headed in that direction. He had zero interest in almost crapping his pants a second time. 'I mean come on that thing was bigger than I am!' Jacob thought as he tried to shake off his thoughts and deny his startled scream.

Carl

As Carl caught up to his former leader Jacob, he had to admit the path the man had chosen was effective. His ability to fight multiple much higher-leveled goblins was impressive. Carl just knew the path wasn't for him, he preferred ranged attacks as he was a rather good shot with his rifle.

Taking a few shots in quick succession he and the hunters Carl led immediately made their presence known on the battlefield. Several of the goblins were of higher level and therefore able to take multiple hits. Though Carl still found a well-placed shot to one of a goblin's eyes to help pierce a Goblin Warrior's thick skull. That was the part Carl still struggled to wrap his mind around, the fact that with high enough stats, someone could take a bullet and only walk away with a bruise or scratch.

Seeing such reactions from goblins taking high powered rifle shots made Carl want to level. His system had told him that the Warrior class gained certain resistance skills and additional points into Constitution per level. This was why they took non-imbued bullets like being shot by rubber instead of a metal slug. Rather than be discouraged, Carl shifted his attention to lower leveled goblins, finding them easier to take out.

As goblins rushed their frontline warriors, it was clear most of the higher leveled Bone Marrow goblins were in the back of their advancing army. That most likely meant fewer casualties for their allies in the north but also made it harder for their side of the fight once the goblin reinforcements showed up. Not all the higher leveled goblins were resistant to bullets, it just meant Carl and his hunters had to take a few extra moments to better aim before firing. Precious extra moments that gave their enemy time to begin to push back the front line.

Carl noticed when Sleeping Willow goblins attacked from building rooftops and other strategic locations hitting several groups with sleeping powder or one poison or another. Such actions seemed to be more effective than the hunters' ranged attacks. Then there was the giant spider clan that Carl learned was called the Crawlers clan. A simple but well named group that described the yuck and gagging feeling Carl felt as they crawled or jumped onto and sank their fangs into their enemies.

Their goblin allies were holding the higher leveled goblin reinforcements at bay, if barely.

Laraaq charged right into a group of goblins who had just taken down and butchered one of Jacob's Spirit Warriors. Laraaq cast fire spell after fire spell as he also would slice open goblins or gut them with a badger claw. Viscera was all around the Were-Honey-Badger as he ripped and bit into his enemies. It was like watching a force of nature.

Grappling attacks failed to find purchase as Laraaq's skin seemed to shift or move allowing him to swing around for well-placed retaliations. 'Man, now I see why they say honey badgers don't give a crap!' Carl thought as he watched in fascination.

A streak of darkness crackled as the line of pure night impacted multiple goblins leaving holes right through them as it moved to its next victim. When Carl turned toward the source of such an awesome display, he found Shadowalker standing there smiling with what Carl assumed looked like joyous surprise on his face. Carl guessed that was the first time the man had used that spell. Whatever it was it seemed to scare several goblins as they tried to distance themselves from their fallen comrades.

Carl then heard a battle cry from one of the Sleeping Willow goblins. "For Shadowalker!!!"

The goblin had a mad look of glee as he flung himself off the building. He landed blades first imbedded into the Goblin Warrior that broke his fall. The goblin that Carl identified as Goob'reks ripped his blades out and with wild abandon wreaked havoc on the enemy ranks.

Several other goblins seemed to take this as a good idea and dropped into the fray, all yelling out battle cries of, "For Shadowalker!!!"

"Okay those goblins are crazy, but effective." Carl commented as he watched the squad of goblin fanatics lay waste to the enemy forces around them.

Carl ordered some of his hunters to provide cover fire for Goob'reks and his fellow fanatics. Turning to scan the battlefield to see if any other situation required Carl's immediate attention, he saw Laraaq break through the frontline and head straight for a giant goblin yelling out orders called Tek'tar. He had never seen a goblin that tall and muscular.

Figuring if anyone could handle that beast of a goblin, Carl was about to resume scanning the battlefield when a large crack sounded as some kind of magic hit Laraaq and sent him flying back to crash into a nearby building. The force so intense it knocked him through the brick wall.

"Noooo!!!" Carl heard Jennifer as he saw her run as fast as she could towards the building Laraaq crashed into.

Tek'tar laughed. "Ha, ha, ha, ha! Foolish huemons! Nothing can stop the Terrible Tek'tar! I may have had to use one of my remaining instant kill artifacts, but that matters not. Kneel and beg for my mercy now and I may spare your lives!"

Tek'tar turned to the battling giant Eldritch Undead Abomination and the Magitech power suit. He began to cast sickly green glowing magic towards the suit of armor. "Time to end this farce!"

Chapter 32 – Showdown

Gr'ex, Jek'jon, & Tan'don

Gr'ex shook his head as he saw his master's friend crash into a building. "Well, he's dead. No one could've survived an instant kill artifact like that."

Gr'ex was on Lucile with Tan'don and Jek'jon. Lucile was towards the back of the battle as Gr'ex and Tan'don had zero interest in getting in melee range. They were both casters and were best at ranged combat.

"Agreed. Our new master is not going to be happy to lose his friend. Hopefully he doesn't take it out on us." Tan'don replied.

"No, Shadowalker is not like that. He actually cares about us. Laraaq should've known better than to charge at the boss." Gr'ex commented.

"He probably thought if he took him out it would be all over." Jek'jon theorized.

"Ha! Not likely with that abomination in the mix. That thing would go feral the moment its master is killed. It will have to be taken down first." Gr'ex stated.

Tan'don nodded in agreement. "I still cannot believe Tek'tar would be foolish enough to tangle with the Eldritch."

"Please. Tek'tar has always been a power-hungry fool." Gr'ex replied.

Tan'don looked incredulously at Gr'ex. "You are one to talk Gr'ex."

"Hey! I have grown since then! It is not all about power for me..." Gr'ex retorted.

"Now maybe, but just last week when we talked, you had that power hungry look in your eye you've had since we were little." Jek'jon fired back.

Gr'ex harrumphed.

Jek'jon decided to stop teasing his best friend. "We have more important things to worry about than Gr'ex's personal growth as a goblin."

"Agreed!" Tan'don said as he cast an **Earth** spell to subtly change the ground underneath some Bone Marrow goblins causing them to lose their balance and fall over. Goob'reks and his squad used the opportunity to kill the off-balance goblins.

"That Goob'reks is impressive." Tan'don commented.

"He took Gr'ex's recommendation to embrace the Shadow class. After meeting Shadowalker he practically jumped at the chance. He and his squad are absolute fanatics when it comes to Shadowalker. Though many of my people, myself included are as well." Jek'jon explained.

Gr'ex threw a **Death Bolt** at a Bone Marrow warrior that broke through the line. The goblin screamed before falling dead, only to rise again as one of Gr'ex's minions. The undead minion turned around and plugged the hole in the line he'd just made. "I love that spell!"

"Of course, you do, it's a classic. I still cannot believe some necromancers are unaware if you dual cast it with **Raise Dead** they comeback stronger than normal undead minions." Jek'jon commented.

"I did not know that, and I am twice both your ages combined!" Tan'don commented as he shot out an **Earth Spike** to impale another goblin who broke their attacking line.

"Yea but that is because you are and **Earth Tamer**. Strong with beasts and **Earth** magic but little to do with necromancy." Jek'jon stated.

"Grandma taught Jek'jon, and I when we were kids." Gr'ex explained.

"Hal'ex is a fine woman. Such a talented goblin female." Tan'don commented with a wistful smile on his face.

Jek'jon and Gr'ex looked at each other before Gr'ex about gagged. Jek'jon put his hand on the Crawlers chief's shoulder. "Ignore Gr'ex. I think it is sweet when older goblins can find love."

Tan'don's face turned a shade of purple. "Wait, what? No... I just..." he stuttered out before looking at Gr'ex. "Sorry my boy, your grandma and I wanted to find the right time to tell you..."

"Tell me what?" Gr'ex began to say when it clicked in his head. "Nooo..." Gr'ex said before he sent another **Death Bolt** at a charging goblin. That made him think of his grandma and how she could still whoop his behind even now, so he decided to change his tune. "You know what, never mind. You two do you... I mean, Ugh I just do not want to see it."

Jek'jon just laughed at his friend's embarrassment as he sent his own undead minions charging into the fight.

Gr'ex cast spell after spell, trying to shift his mind from the thoughts running unbidden in his mind. "Must get image of Grandma and Tan'don out of my head!"

"Well don't give them to me!" Jek'jon teased as he cast his own spells at their enemies.

After that reveal, Gr'ex stopped his musings and put all his focus on the battle. The trio of goblin casters wreaked havoc on the battlefield wherever Lucile took them. The spider was smart, and it was clear this was not her first battle either. She guided them to areas where the attacking lines were wavering so as they buckled, the trio of casters stepped in and plugged the hole and pushed on.

Laraaq

A workbench had arrested Laraaq's momentum after he crashed through the brick wall. It took him several moments to untangle himself from the rubble. Laraaq knew the **Time Armor** buff Shadowwalker placed on him saved his life. He also knew his **were-form** helped him survive going through a brick wall. There were bruises in multiple places and cuts and gashes on his arms and torso.

Just as Laraaq was standing up after extricating himself from the rubble, Jennifer burst in through the hole in the wall.

"Laraaq! Are you okay?! Wait! How are you standing?" Jennifer blurted out multiple statements and questions as her brain processed what she was seeing.

"My **were-form** makes me pretty durable." Laraaq commented as he had blood running down his left arm.

"Apparently not durable enough. Hold still and let me heal you!" Jennifer said as she cast her diagnostics and healing spells.

After a few minutes Laraaq was feeling fine. He knew he would be sore later but that was a small price to pay when surviving an instant kill artifact and crashing through a brick wall. "Come on we have to get back out there!" Laraaq said as he started to head for the same hole he made.

"You just got slammed through a wall and you want to go back out there?!" Jennifer asked incredulously.

Laraaq looked at her. Other than his best friend and some family, he wasn't used to people being concerned for his well-being. "Look I appreciate the concern, but you checked me out, I'm fine."

"Multiple lacerations and a few broken bones would not classify as fine!" Jennifer argued.

"But you healed those wounds." Laraaq retorted.

"Yes, but I'm running low on mana, what if something else happens. I may not be able to save you." Jennifer said concerned.

"I appreciate that Jennifer, but there is zero chance I'm not going back into that fight, not when my best friend and your parents are out there risking their lives! What kind of a man would I be? More importantly what kind of a friend would that make me?!" Laraaq explained.

He wanted her to know he appreciated the concern, but Laraaq could not live with himself if others he cared about were risking their lives and he did nothing.

Jennifer sighed. She knew he was right. She did not want anything to happen to her family and the friends she started to make either. "You're right. I just lost control of my emotions for a moment there. I'm fine." She loaded a round into her rifle. "Let's kill some goblins!"

"I knew I liked you!" Laraaq said as he stepped out from the hole.

Laraaq surrounded his fist in flame. Realizing it didn't burn him he got a crazy idea. Concentrating he spread the fire all over his body. Jennifer stepped back from the heat.

Laraaq was rewarded with a notification.

*Congratulations! You have unlocked the spell **Flame Armor**! This is a 5th tier spell!*

Spell: Flame Armor (5th Tier)
Description: *Surround yourself in burning flames. These flames do not harm you but can burn your enemies and counteract any Water or Ice attacks. Causes a slow but constant drain on mana. The more mana channeled into the spell the more intense the heat.*

Laraaq yelled out at Tek'tar and flipped him the bird. "Flame on, bitches!"

After shocking and insulting the goblin boss Laraaq and Jennifer witnessed the Eldritch Undead Abomination deal a devastating blow to the Magimech. The giant power suit crashed into a nearby building and did not get up.

"Go! I'll get your parents some payback!" Laraaq said as he shifted into full Battle Honey-Badger form, growing to four meters tall, still covered in flames.

Laraaq barreled into the Eldritch Abomination. The monster screamed as each blow Laraaq landed burn the abomination's flesh. The two behemoths batted at each other relentlessly as their fight moved them further west of the battle and the fallen Magimech.

Jennifer wasted no time rushing to the giant power suit. The thing had a huge dent in it and sparks were periodically coming from certain parts of the Magimech. She carefully navigated the collapsed building the suit had crushed.

Jennifer was able to reach the small emergency hatch they built just in case the main hatch was damaged, which it was. Opening the hatch, she quickly found her mom and dad both unconscious, blood and visible wounds on their faces. She immediately began to cast her diagnostics and healing spells on them, focusing on the life-threatening injuries first.

Jennifer knew she did not have enough mana to fix all of their injuries. As she cast one healing spell after the other, Jennifer just hoped it would be enough. After healing her father, who was closer, she moved to her mother, casting the last of her power in the hope it would be enough to save her life.

'Laraaq, kick that ugly monster's butt. Make it pay for what it did...' was the last thing Jennifer thought before she passed out from mana fatigue.

I had been fighting on the frontlines when Tek'tar used some kind of instant kill artifact on Laraaq. After seeing my best friend get thrown through a wall and then step out completely fine and looking like a flaming badger. 'I know there is a joke in there somewhere.' I thought before I turned my attention on dodging these Bone Marrow goblins.

Many of the goblins seemed to be moving through molasses in winter with how slow they were. I realized with my mental speed and Dexterity increases it made it easy to dodge and counterattack them with a Dark Bolt or quick slash with my blade. Only the more Dexterity based fighters proved a problem to my speed.

The combination of Master ranked **Weapons Mastery** and **Unarmed Combat Mastery** helped me quickly adapt to the fight as if I was easily recalling a memory of where I had done this exact fight in the past. I made short work of those that entered my path. Every now and then I would shoot off a **Dark Lightning** spell that would wreak havoc on the enemy, causing several to move away from my part of the battlefield.

As I made my way through the enemy forces, I saw the Eldritch Abomination batter away the Magimech. My heart swelled with concern as I saw the dented and broken power suit collapse the building it fell on. I had given them the order to fight that thing, but I had no time for guilt, I had to remain focused on the battle.

Then my best friend proved what a powerhouse he was as he shifted into his full battle form wrapped in flames as he barreled into the Eldritch Abomination. I had to trust he would handle the monster, allowing me to focus on the next biggest threat, Tek'tar. I jumped up to the platform the goblin chief stood on.

"Time to end this Tek'tar!" I roared.

Tek'tar laughed. "Puny huemon! You are no match for Tek'tar. You are only level 13 and have not even selected a class yet!"

I had to get Tek'tar to use whatever trump cards he had. I decided to taunt the goblin. "If I'm no match for you, then why did I ruin your ritual the first time you tried it?"

Rage spread over Tek'tar's face. "YOU WERE THE ONE!" He roared as he slashed out with his staff.

I parried the blow but felt some kind of magic try to flow down my blade and latch onto my hand. I quickly shook it off and whatever it was fell right off me. Tek'tar did not look pleased at that as he kept swinging. Every so often I would feel that magic attempt to again take hold, only to fall right off me.

We traded blows back and forth. One thing I could say about Tek'tar is he did not skimp on his physical attributes. The buff goblin hit like a semi-truck every time I made the mistake of blocking instead of parrying his blows.

In fury, Tek'tar reached into his battle robes. "Fine you have forced me to use this! Consider it a compliment I find you worthy!" He withdrew a small totem and snapped it in half. A sickly green erupted from the totem and struck out at me. It was too close for me to dodge fully in time.

I was hit with the energy point blank, but my partial dodge prevented me from being knocked back. Instead, I hit the ground hard, and my Time Armor activated and negated the blow. I stood back up, dusted myself off, and wiped the blood from my busted nose. "That actually hurt. In the wise words of Ben Stiller, nobody makes me bleed my own blood."

This seemed to infuriate Tek'tar even more. "Ahhh! How are you still alive!" The goblin chief charged me.

He almost knocked me off the platform we were fighting on from the sheer power of the blow I could only partially parry.

We continued to exchange blows. His staff had a sharp edge to the end, so Tek'tar was able to turn it at the last minute and cut me a few times. The goblin seemed to frown when I did not collapse in pain. My guess was he had some type of curse or poison on it.

Tek'tar withdrew another totem and immediately shattered it. "This time the magic didn't hit me but rather it surrounded Tek'tar. "STOP!" The goblin called out and I paused involuntarily.

"Ha, ha, ha, ha! I temporarily have access to the words of power! You are mine to command! Nothing will stop me from claiming the Leyline Nexus! Nothing!" Tek'tar said in triumph.

His words triggered something in me. I could feel a vision pop into my mind unbidden. The world around me faded and I was floating far above, able to see the entire planet. Then I saw lines of magical power flow over the Earth, forming a network of various kinds of magic. The lines I instinctively knew to be leylines did not flow in a straight line or in the same direction. Some bent in certain places and where certain lines crossed, I knew to be a Leyline Nexus. Some of these points seemed to glow brighter than others.

A small handful seemed to flow to somewhere else, not of this world, connecting them to another plane of existence. Of those I saw that shone brightest less than a handful seemed to touch to a place beyond my current comprehension. Those few seemed to have a magical lock that anchored them in a way I could not understand.

That was when I realized one of the brightest nodes looked familiar. As the vision zoomed in, I soon understood why I thought I recognized it. The forest, the town nearby, what I was seeing was the compound. No, it was what was underneath the compound.

I felt a backhanded slap that knocked me to the ground and brought me out of the vision. Tek'tar was standing over me, a vicious grin spread on his face. That is when I felt the pain in my side. The bastard had cut me with his staff when I was lost to my vision. I hadn't even felt it, not until I came too.

Apparently, my lack of response had pissed him off, so he used a body enhanced backhand that made my head hit the ground and bounce. That was either what brought me out of the vision, or I had understood what I was meant to. Somehow Paul found one of these special nexus points and built the compound over it. How he knew about it or figured out it was there I did not know but I knew I did not want this jerk to have it.

I winced in pain as every part of me ached or hurt. 'Man, how hard can that guy hit?'

"That's better! I want you to look me in the eyes when I kill you!" Tek'tar taunted.

A sudden commotion drew both our eyes. Laraaq was beaten and battered but he had managed to bite down on the amalgamation of heads that made up the Eldritch Abomination faces. Along with his claws, Laraaq bit down and pulled with all his might ripping the mound of flesh off and killing the Eldritch Abomination.

They both fell to the ground, abomination dead and starting to decompose as the Eldritch energy was an anathema to life in this world. Laraaq fell unconscious, flames going out has he reverted to his human form, buck naked as the day he was born.

Tek'tar turned back to me, rage in his eyes. "No matter, I will make another one from the corpses of you and your friends." Then the goblin laughed at my inability to move. "Ha, ha, ha, ha! I shall enjoy killing you huemon!"

As he was about to impale me with the pointy end of his staff, I saw Gr'ex come out of nowhere. He, Tan'don, and Jek'jon were riding Lucile. Tan'don and Jek'jon were using their magic to keep the other goblin forces at bay, which allowed Gr'ex to focus his attacks on Tek'tar.

"That's my huemon you ugly, wart-faced bastard!" Gr'ex roared as he and Lucile knocked Tek'tar off his feet.

"Ha, ha, ha! Die you good for nothing son of an Orc!" Gr'ex taunted as he cast his Curse of Agony at Tek'tar before Lucile's momentum would require her to catch herself before they both were carried over the platform.

I saw the look of shock on Gr'ex's face as the enemy chief moved his staff up as it intercepted the curse, flared a sickly green color, and flung the spell back at them. The spell magnified and hit Lucile and everyone riding her. Gr'ex, Tan'don, Jek'jon, and Lucile all howled in pain. Their bodies locked up as the momentum from the leap sent them crashing to the other side of the platform.

Tek'tar stood up and looked over at the fallen spider and my friend. "It is good you are still alive Gr'ex." Tek'tar shook his head. "A shame you decided to side with the losing side Jek'jon. I never liked you anyway. Stay there and suffer as I kill off this huemon. Then I will deal with all of you! Maybe I'll have roasted spider for dinner in celebration of my victory."

My mind scrambled to think of a solution. These words of power Tek'tar had access to seem to have some command over me. Just as my mind thought that my consciousness fell into another vision. I was back floating in space.

This vision felt different. Half the cosmos disappeared in golden white light. I floated between the stars and golden white space.

"What am I doing here?" I cried out.

I hear two distinct laughs. "This is the one you have chosen as your successor, Chronos?"

"Yes! He is worthy!" Chronos stated.

"That remains to be seen. He did choose to take on the burden of Champion of his world, but he denied his salvation." This disembodied voice said.

I recognized the voice from the weird dream I had when the apocalypse started. The voice of Chronos I instantly knew was the Primordial Celestial Dragon whose core I absorbed.

"He denied his salvation for a chance to save others." Chronos commented.

"Umm I don't mean to be rude, but I'm about to be turned into a giant kebob if we don't hurry this up." I said in a panic, knowing Tek'tar was only a few steps from me, and I hadn't felt his first attack the last time I had a vision.

"Ha, ha, ha, ha, ha! Do you think the two of us cannot pause time to have a conversation with you? I was once called the god of time and space after all. Though I never really cared for that title. Mortals don't really understand gods from God." Chronos stated.

"And I always appreciated your understanding of the truth my old friend." the disembodied voice said.

"Umm, I'm lost." I commented.

"Of course, you have felt lost since you denied your own salvation, but you have not truly been lost." The disembodied voice replied.

Chronos spoke up. "What do you know of faith?"

"That it is a power that can literally influence the world around you." I answered.

"Yes, that is part of it. When many begin to believe the same thing, they give that thing power. This can give rise to minor entities of power; some call them gods. There are other beings who rise to the height of their power that helps them transcend their mortal coils. The Greek gods were such beings. I will not bore you with the details, but Pride makes them disconnect from the one true source, God with a capital G."

"But what does that have to do with my situation right now? These words of power Tek'tar is using have commanded me to not move!" I lamented.

"It is important because there are things I can and cannot say. What I have told you so far are foundational truths you must hold on to as you will need them when the time comes." Chronos explained.

"Did you just make a pun about time? Wait, how are you even here? I thought i absorbed you." I groaned.

"Hmmm, that was not intentional. Yes, you absorbed almost all of me. I held this last spark of my existence for this exact moment. When you truly master time, you will understand more than you can imagine currently. You see I was given the **Dark Mantle** as part of my charge. It's true power is in the authority it grants you over the Dark and the creatures there." Chronos explained.

"I know that. I have used it several times before." I replied.

"No! You do not understand, it grants you authority over all that is the Dark! I can say no more until you begin to truly understand." Chronos stated.

What was he trying to tell me? A dear friend of mine wrote a book on true authority and how it comes from God. True authority cannot be taken from you by anyone other than the one who granted it to you. If God gave Chronos the **Dark Mantle** he was giving him authority over the Dark, but how did that help me now? Then the realization hit me like an explosion, and I blurted out the answer.

"No one can command me or use the Dark against me since I possess true authority over that power. I have been denying my authority out of the fear and jealousy it instills in others."

"You shall keep the authority over the Dark. As a result of this moment, you may one day come to be one with the Dark and side with those who have fallen. If you do choose that path the Light will forever be in opposition to your designs." The disembodied voice proclaimed.

There was no malice or threat, just stating a simple fact and outcome.

"Now comes the fun part!" Chronos exclaimed.

"Uh, fun part?" I hesitantly asked.

Chronos continued to explain. "To protect the authority of Time and Space, my power was split into two. Part of my power, the **Infinite Well of Time Magic** was locked in an artifact that looked like a simple magic book. I used the disguise of a wolf known as Valaxia to hide its true purpose. Someone has already claimed the **Infinite Well of Time Magic**. However, I held back this last spark of myself. You shall have authority over time, only the one with the **Infinite Well of Time Magic** will be outside your awareness. Forgive the pun, but it will take you many years to comprehend what is about to happen. If I could tell you more I would."

There was a pause and when Chronos next spoke I realized he was talking to the disembodied voice. "I chose this one to impart my authority over Time and Space that you gave me so long ago. This soul, this mind, and spirit is the one **I CHOOSE AS MY SUCCESSOR!**"

"SO AGREED!"

I felt the cosmos itself rush into me until there was only the golden light left around me.

"The path you are undertaking..." the disembodied voice paused and said nothing for a few moments. "You must use both your mind and intuition only when you are whole and are ready shall we meet again."

"But you are my intuition, aren't you? Or at least you are connected to it." I commented.

"Wise beyond your years. I weep for the hardships you and your world will endure."

There was a flash of light so bright I shut my eyes. When I opened them, I saw Tek'tar exactly the same distance from me as before. 'Good no time has passed. Time to do this.'

I released my tight hold on my **Dark Mantle** ability. The moment I did, the chains I felt wrapped around my will shattered into nothing and I stood up and took a step toward the goblin chief.

Tek'tar stopped mid-stride, horror on his face. "No! That's not possible! I command you to STOP!"

I took another step forward, not even feeling the effects. If only I had released my **Dark Mantle** earlier. Tek'tar stood there in shock unsure what to do. He had never heard of anyone not submitting to the words of power, especially one so low leveled.

"Command me? I TAKE COMMANDS FROM NO ONE! I AM THE ONE WITH THE AUTHORITY HERE!" I roared as I fully released my power.

The whole battlefield stopped. The jarring effects from my **Dark Mantle** woke Laraaq and Jennifer from their unconsciousness. I heard Laraaq say, "Oh man, I'm naked. You there give me your pants, that's an order!"

A notification with gold bordered and bold lettering popped into my vision. I instantly read the information.

Congratulations! The Primordial Celestial Dragon Chronos, also known as the god of Time and Space, has named you, their Successor! Your Dark Mantle ability is fully unlocked. You have received part of the Mantle of Time and Space. As this is incomplete you are not granted an ability but your control over Time and Space Magic has greatly increased. Please Note: You may want to kill the one that holds the Infinite Well of Time Magic to fully gain this authority.

Another prompt appeared in front of my vision.

In order to receive the full inheritance from Chronos you must be in your true dragon form. Do you wish to shift back into your dragon form? Yes, or No?

"You know what, yes!" I said out loud as I accepted the prompt.

My clothes ripped and I instantly grew almost twelve meters tall. This was the first time I was finally able to see myself in my dragon form. I glistened golden white with wing membranes that looked like star filled night.

I began to feel energy pour into me. Before my body could lock up, I reached down, picked up Tek'tar and bit his head off.

Then I felt power flood into me and my Divine Infinitum. I dropped the corpse as my body began to freeze and lost all focus of the outside world. I instantly understood why I had to be in this form. The influx of power was so intense I feared it might burn out my channels. My eyes began to glow, and I roared so loud it echoed for miles.

RROOAARRR!!!!!

Every single living being for miles stopped and turned in my direction. Little did I know this caused quite a stir at the compound. Every goblin regardless of what side they were on immediately dropped to their knees in supplication.

Laraaq finished putting on pants he had taken from one of the soldiers who was too shocked to move or respond. "Of course, he's a dragon. If anyone would become a dragon it's Shadowalker." Laraaq just chuckled, happy for his brother as he knew how much Shadowalker loved dragons. "Huh? Now we both have an awesome form to wreak havoc with."

Once the wave of power had passed and I had control over my body again I looked around. I realized I had grown larger or everything else shrunk. Seeing everyone stunned completing unmoving, all the goblins bowing in supplication, I realized I couldn't remain in this form. I shifted back into human form.

I too was completely naked. Luckily, Laraaq had acquired another pair of pants for me to put on. "Thanks, brother!"

"Of course, looks like you and I are going to have to keep extra pairs of pants on hand for when we go full beast mode." Laraaq commented.

"Good point! We should talk to Hal'ex about seeing what her Death Weavers can make." I replied when I heard Gr'ex coming to the platform.

"YOU ARE AN ANCIENT DRAGON!" Gr'ex said in exasperation.

"Yep." I answered.

"This whole time... wait that's the core you got?!" Gr'ex said as he realized how I ended up as a dragon.

"Yep. Pretty cool race change, huh?" I said with a huge smile on my face.

"Luckiest son of..." Gr'ex started to say before Hal'ex was there on her undead mobile chair creature. She popped Gr'ex on the head. "Do not be rude to someone who could've just eaten me or still might."

"Gr'ex rubbed his head. "Sorry grandmother."

Mek'mar bowed in front of me. "Ancient one. What are your orders regarding the Bone Marrow clan?"

Gr'ex clarified for my understanding. "You killed their chief, by rights you are their new **Warchief**."

"Not sure I can trust them after..." I started to say before Jek'jon politely spoke up. "My apologies for interrupting you Dark One, but after your display..." Jek'jon waved to the still bowing goblins. "They will follow you unto death as many of us will."

"They will need a new chief to handle things and coordinate with." I smiled at Gr'ex. It was time to reward his loyalty for stepping in to save me at the last minute. "Gr'ex, you decide on who their new chief will be. Regardless of who it is, they work through you as my right hand in all things related to our goblin people."

Gr'ex's grind was practically ear to ear as he rubbed his hands together in glee. "I know just the goblin for the job."

Chapter 33 – One, Two, Someone Touched You

Melody

Even though Melody was still at the compound and nowhere near the battle, she could still hear the fighting and explosions from here. Then she heard that awful roar that rattled the very walls.

Melody was pacing back and forth before she turned to Mitch who was keeping his eyes on the outside. "I better go check on Alice. I don't want her to be scared."

Mitch just nodded at Melody before he turned his attention back to the makeshift murder hole he was using to spot any enemy units. He didn't want any goblins sneaking by and attacking the compound when there were so few fighters present.

Though Mitch wanted to be out there, he knew how important it was to protect the civilians. Plus, deep down Mitch knew he wasn't ready. Besides the fact he was still too low a level to tangle with most of the goblin enemies. He still couldn't believe they had goblin clans fighting alongside them.

A few minutes later Mitch heard Melody scream in panic. He turned to see her running down the stairs. "What's wrong ma'am?!"

"It's Alice! She's gone!" Melody exclaimed.

Mitch tried to calm the older woman down. "I'm sure she is around here somewhere. It's not like she could've gotten very far. Everything is locked up tight."

Just as Mitch said those words, they heard Alice's voice coming from outside. "One, two, someone touched you. Three, four, make them hit the floor. Five, six, daddy says cut off their..."

Both Mitch and Melody looked at each other before they both turned their heads to look outside. Alice turned and waved at them before she went skipping into the bushes.

"How did she get out? I checked all the exits; they were locked up tight. Gio even doublechecked them just to be sure!" Mitch asked in confusion.

"I don't care. I'm going after her! Open the door!" Melody said in a clear panic.

"I can't do that Ma'am. It's not safe out there right now." Mitch replied as he stood in front of the door blocking her way.

"And is it any safer for a little helpless girl?! I'm going! So, you better open this door or so help me!" Melody exclaimed.

"Alright will you at least give me a second and I'll see if Gio can take my place." Mitch replied as he turned to leave.

"No time!" Melody said as she unlocked the door and took off after Alice.

"Crap! I'm gonna get in so much trouble for this! Jebediah is gonna kill me!" Mitch said as he locked the door and went to go find Gio.

Mack and Sarah

"Come on! Move faster Sarah! We just won and daddy wants to celebrate in a way only you know how to do!" Mack said excitedly as he dragged Sarah further into the woods.

They had beaten those short green skinned monsters and he had gained a few levels from all those kills. The aftermath of the battle was still being sorted out. Mack had enough after he saw Laraaq turn into a giant flaming badger and take out a giant abomination. If that wasn't bad enough, he saw that Shadowalker guy turn into a freaking dragon! No way did he want to be anywhere near those two while they sorted out the loot. He used the chaos of everything to sneak off the battlefield and go get Sarah.

Mack felt great and he wanted to celebrate. He reached the convoy without anyone stopping him. The vehicles were still lined up in rows. All the non-combatants were staying put, they were waiting for an all-clear signal.

Mack walked right up to the truck and grabbed his daughter. She was with Carol who gave him a puzzled look. "Is the fighting over? I haven't received the all-clear signal from my son."

They are wrapping up the battle, but I wanted to keep my daughter safe." Mack explained.

When Carol protested, "We should wait for the all-clear signal if you are worried about your daughter." Mack backhanded the old woman.

"Stupid old crone. Don't get in my way when it comes to my kid!" Mack said before he took off with Sarah in tow.

Mack knew it was only a matter of time before that goody two-shoes Laraaq would start dictating how they were going to live.

"I thought I would play nice until I could take over this place. That was my original plan, but now that I know they are monsters, I am taking you away from here!" Mack explained to Sarah as he continued to pull her along.

"I don't want to leave my sister. I want to see Christy!" Sarah said as she tried to pull her hand away. "Owe! Daddy, you're hurting me." Sarah winced in pain as Mack's vice grip pulled her along.

"Come on. Keep up. Just a bit farther. We are going to celebrate my level gains and I want to make sure we aren't interrupted." Mack said as his heart raced.

———

Christy

Christy was chasing after a few goblins that had run away at the roar of the giant dragon that showed up out of nowhere. Her biggest concern was the fact the goblins were heading to the convoy where her little sister was. "You bastards aren't getting my little sister!" Christy yelled as she chased after them.

She was catching up to the three goblins left. Pulling out one of her throwing knives, Christy chucked it at the goblin farthest from her. The blade flew true.

THUNK!

Was the only sound that was heard as the blade sunk into the back of the goblin's neck killing it instantly and dropping it to the forest floor.

Christy could see they were almost to the road where the rest of the convoy was stationed. She chucked another throwing knife at one of the two remaining goblins. The blade sliced open the goblin's calf and it stumbled. Christy took the goblin's head with her sword as she ran by.

"One of you monsters left. You can't get away from me!" Christy roared as she gained on the last goblin.

Christy and the remaining goblin left the canopy of trees only a few seconds apart. When the goblin saw all the vehicles and humans, he realized he had made an error and was trapped. He dropped to his knees and prostrated himself. "I surrender. I surrender!"

As much as Christy wanted to kill the goblin, she flipped her blade around and smacked the goblin in the head with the hilt of her sword making the little goblin crumble the rest of the way to the ground unconscious.

Christy caught one of the young guys who were left as a feeble defense for the convoy. "Hey you. Grab some zip ties and bind this goblin until we can figure out what to do with him. I'm going to check on my sister."

"Uh I think your dad already came and picked her up." The guy said.

Those words drove a chill of terror down her spine.

"What?!" Christy exclaimed.

Just then Carol Burns stumbled as she tried to get up. "Mrs. Burns!" Christy cried out as she rushed over.

"What happened?! Are you okay?! Where is Sarah?!" Christy asked.

"I'll be fine dearie. This old lady is a survivor." Carol said.

Christy helped her back into the jeep seat. "Your father came running. He said the battle was wrapping up and he wanted to get his daughter. He had a weird look in his eyes, so it made me speak up. I told him we should wait. He backhanded me for my trouble and told me to mind my own business." Carol explained.

Christy clinched her sword until her knuckles were white. 'No more! I've stood by too long! This ends tonight, I don't care if he is my father!'

"Are you okay dearie? What's wrong?" Carol asked.

Christy ignored Carol and took off into the woods in pursuit of her sister and the man she once called father.

Carol saw her go and called out to the young man who was tying up the unconscious goblin. "Hand me the walkie talkie will you, dearie."

The guy winced as the old woman scared him and he was trying to go unnoticed as he was tying up the unconscious goblin.

"Here you go." The guy said as he handed her his walkie talkie.

"Laraaq. Come in Laraaq. This is Carol! Got an urgent S.O.S for you! Over!" Carol called through the radio.

Shadowalker, Laraaq, and Carl

"Laraaq! Come in Laraaq. This is Carol! Got an urgent S.O.S for you! Over!" Laraaq heard Carol's voice call for him just as he gave his best friend a hug. The battle was over, and my best friend and I finally had a chance to greet each other properly, especially now that we both had pants on.

Carl had jumped up onto the platform. Carol's voice was coming from the walkie-talkie in Carl's hand.

Just then I received a call over my walkie talkie that was lying on the platform floor next to my ripped pants. "Umm. Mr. Shadowalker. This is Mitch. I'm chasing after Melody. Over." The man sounded out of breath.

"Ha, ha, ha. Looks like we are both being called. No rest for the wicked." I joked with Laraaq.

Laraaq grabbed the walkie talkie from Carl and replied. "Go ahead Carol. What's up? Over."

"Something is up with Mack. He seemed crazed. He took Sarah and hit me when I tried to stop him. I told Christy and she took off after them. Over."

Carl, having overheard what Mack did, was instantly furious. "I'm going to kill that scum for hitting my mom!"

Laraaq nodded to Carl as he replied on the radio. "We will handle it, Carol. Over."

While Laraaq was getting his call I was replying to mine. "What's going on Mitch? Melody wouldn't just take off. Over."

"It-its Alice sir. She somehow got outside and took off into the woods. In a panic, Melody chased after her. I had to grab Gio to take my post before I followed in pursuit. Over." Mitch explained.

"Whose Alice?" Laraaq asked.

"Long story." I replied quickly before responding to Mitch.

"You did the right thing Mitch. I'll find them. Call me if you find them before I do. Over." I ordered.

Laraaq and I looked at each other. Then I noticed the girl I thought I heard was named Christy. "Hey isn't that her?" I said as I pointed.

"You go deal with that, while I go find Alice and Melody. Call me over the radio if you need any help. Good journey my friend." I said as I latched my walkie-talkie onto my pants.

Laraaq nodded. "Same. Call me if you need anything. We can rendezvous at the compound. Good journey."

"Good journey!" I replied before taking off.

Laraaq, Christy, & Carl

It didn't take Laraaq and Carl long to catch up with Christy. "Christy stop!"

She halted for only a moment. "What?! No time. I have to find Mack and my sister!"

Laraaq noticed the panic in her voice. Rather than stop her Laraaq ran alongside her. "Why would that be problem? Isn't he, her father?" As he said it, everything seemed to click.

Laraaq grabbed Christy and brought her up short. "Is he molesting you two?! Tell me!"

Tears started to flow down Christy's face as she finally brought the truth to the forefront of her mind. She could barely get out the words. "He stopped a few years back with me... but Sarah..."

Christy cried into Laraaq's chest, having finally told her dark secret. The rage that burned inside Laraaq ignited his core and his eyes started to glow as he lifted Christy's chin. "If I had known earlier, I would've killed him already. He dies tonight! Understood!" Laraaq said the last part as he looked at Carl.

"Hey no argument here. I already planned on it after I heard he hit my mom." Carl agreed.

Laraaq turned back to Christy. "You ready to save your sister?"

Christy nodded and the three of them took off in hot pursuit. If Laraaq found him he would make him suffer.

Mack & Sarah Meet Alice

Mack found a secluded enough spot. "This will do. Now let's celebrate." The mask Mack wore around others fell away, and the depraved scum of the earth showed his true self.

Sarah shivered as she began to undress. She was not moving fast enough for him, so he backhanded her. "Look what you made me do to you! You know better than to keep me waiting!"

Mack pinned her down just as he heard some leaves rustling. He drew his blade and turned to see the cutest, most innocent little girl standing there. She was the most adorable thing he had ever seen. She wore a dress that made Mack's mouth water at the thought of taking her innocence.

Alice smiled, waved, and asked, "Hi! I'm Alice. Do you want to play with me?"

Mack licked his lips. "Definitely. You both can play with me."

Alice frowned. "I thought you wanted to play with me. I don't want to play with her."

Mack looked back at Sarah, then back to Alice. He stood up. "You're right. She is getting a little too old for my tastes anyway. I'm sure you'll be plenty fun on your own."

Alice smiled again and clapped her hands. "Oh goodie!"

She then skipped over to Sarah and bent down to whisper in her ear. "Daddy says little girls like yourself shouldn't watch or hear what happens next. Close your eyes and cover your ears okay."

Alice then patted Sarah on the head and rustled her hair. "My new daddy gives me head pats and I love them. Don't they feel great?"

Sarah nodded before she closed her eyes and covered her ears. For some reason this girl, Alice, made Sarah feel safe and that she could trust her.

"I'll show you more than some pathetic head pats little girl. I'll show you what only a man can show you." Mack said as he reached for her.

Alice scowled. "Why did you have to go and insult my new daddy like that?"

A flash of moonlight flew between them before Mack lost complete control of his hands. He looked down to see what had happened to them. To his horror he watched as they separated from his body and slowly fell to the ground, blood started gushing out.

Mack screamed. "AHHHHHAAAA!!!!"

"You bitch! I'm going to make you pay!" Mack roared.

"Tsk, tsk. My imaginary friend doesn't like bad language." Alice said as a giant fist punched Mack in the face sending him sprawling.

Alice tapped the bloody blade to her chin as if she was contemplating something. "What game shall we play? You are an exceptionally bad one, soul as black as night."

"Uh." Mack said groggily. "I'm not playing with you, you're a crazy bitch!"

Next thing Mack knew he was lifted off the ground and went flying into a tree so hard, it was knocked down.

"Tsk, tsk. I told you; my friend doesn't like bad language. Besides you can't back out once you say you want to play. Those are the rules of the game. Something tells me you have been exceptionally bad at following the rules."

Alice snapped her fingers. "I know! We will play the gobble, gobble game! That's a special one. I save that for the truly naughty ones."

Mack tried to get up and run away but Alice moved quick like lightning and slashed the tendons in his legs. He collapsed and twitched.

Alice giggled. "He, he, he! Oh goodie, it looks like you at least know how to play the 'fish' game. That is always a fun one to start with."

She then made several slashes, cutting away his clothes and digging her blades into his flesh.

Mack screamed again. "AHHHHH!"

"Don't worry we will get to play forever and ever. You see my daddy taught me a spell that is so much fun to use. It makes it so we can play forever and ever, but first the gobble, gobble game!"

With a thought two giant hands grabbed Mack's head and jaw. Both hands pulled, dislocating Mack's jaw and causing the man to scream a primal guttural scream of pure agony and terror that could be heard throughout the forest.

"AHHHAAA!!!!!"

Alice then used her blades to separate the man's genitalia from his body and shove them into his mouth.

"Eat up!" With that command the brute's giant hands began to work Mack's head and jaw to make the man chew and swallow.

The entire time Alice cut symbols into his flesh as she sang. "One, two, someone touched you. Three, four, make them hit the floor. Five, six, daddy says cut off their..."

She just finished cutting all the symbols into his flesh. Alcie stood over the now almost dead and mutilated body. She began to cast her **Create Soul-Forged Minion** spell when multiple people entered the clearing at almost the exact same time.

Shadowalker

I was the first to arrive a fraction before everyone else. I immediately took in the horrific scene before me.

A little girl, I assumed was Sarah from what he overheard from Laraaq's radio call. Her lip was busted open, and it was clear she would have bruises. Sarah had her eyes closed and hands over her ears.

There was a giant brute of a man or skeleton in a large, brimmed hat and trench coat. As I tried to use my inspect ability, it glitched and all I got back was the word 'golem'. 'Huh? That was weird.' I thought as I looked the brute of a man over.

He kind of reminded me of the creepy doll Alice carried around. He had positioned himself between Sarah and what I assumed was what was left of Mack. I say what was left as the body was rather mutilated. Based on positioning, my guess was the brute was either trying to shield her from the gruesome sight or protect her from Mack, probably a bit of both.

Alice had two blades that glowed ethereal green in the moonlight as they dripped with blood. Her hands, dress, and part of her face were covered in blood. Whatever spell she had just cast was making the symbols she had carved into Mack's flesh glow a combination of ethereal green I somehow instinctually knew was **Soul** magic and black that reminded me of the **Death** magic spells Gr'ex taught me.

What was left of Mack continued to glow. He was missing his hands and genitalia, which sent a shiver down my spine.

My mind reeled as I processed what Alice had done.

I felt Gr'ex and Jek'jon both step into the small clearing right next to me. Their eyes practically bulged out of their sockets as they took it all in.

Laraaq, Christy, and Carl all stepped into view.

As everyone was taking in what they were seeing, Alice's spell completed, and the body morphed and stretched until it was covered in some sort of skintight suit of armor. That was the trigger that made the rest of the scene register for Laraaq. The moment that happened, Laraaq summoned two **Flame Spears**.

Laraaq yelled, "KILL IT WITH FIRE!!!" As he threw the two **Flame Spears** right at Alice.

I immediately cast my **Time Armor** spell around Alice as I cried out. "WAIT!"

I shouldn't have bothered. The giant golem stepped in front of Alice and lifted his trench coat which seemed to absorb the flame spears as they hit him.

Laraaq shouted. "You don't understand! The system told me that any child under 15 should've been taken by the rapture. They only remain if they're a monster! We have to kill it!"

Christy rushed over to her sister Sarah. Checking that Sarah was for the most part okay, Christy spoke up. "My sister is 13."

This statement brought Laraaq up short. He had not seen anything bad with Sarah, but he knew what the system told him, and he would never forget those three evil kids that had murdered all those people.

Sarah jumped out of Christy's arms and went to Alice. "Thank you for saving me."

Christy walked slowly in front of the two girls. She could see Laraaq and Carl's uncertainty. Both men wanted to bring as much firepower as they could to nuke this little area.

Christy spoke to Laraaq. "When this first all happened, I tried to find out why we were left to suffer after..." she looked at the now Soul-Forged minion that used to be her father. "After what he did to both of us."

She sighed as tears started to form in her eyes. "You're right that the system said there is a high chance they could be too far gone, but some are here because they don't think they are worthy to be saved, or they just refused to go. I know I was angry, confused, and... and so much more."

Christy bent down so she was eye level with Alice. "Thank you for doing what I couldn't to save my sister and me." She choked out the last part as tears ran down her face.

Sarah hugged her big sister and they both had a good cry.

Alice waved her hands, and the blades were gone along with all the blood on her. She put her hands on both their shoulders. "It's okay. Daddy made me this way. He said I had to be a good girl and hunt down all those who hurt children so that one day there would be a world without such horrors in them."

Alice then gave them both a big hug. Then she looked back at me. "My daddy sent me here to this time and place... I now know he wanted me to help him, and his friends make the world a better place."

As she finished, she walked up to me, and I knelt to be at her eye level. "You remember don't you daddy? The pain you felt when you were a child, what they did to you."

I don't know what came over me as I got a bit choked up as if the dam broke on the memories I suppressed for so long.

In that moment, I lost all care for Mack and what was done to him. If what she said was true, then I knew exactly how she felt about people like Mack. I felt it too, the raw anger at wanting to punish those who would dare to hurt children. It may not be the kind thing to do, or turning the other cheek, but this was the apocalypse, and I wasn't going to play nice with scum like that.

"There he is." Alice said as she looked into my eyes. I hadn't realized it, but I had let go of my hold over my **Dark Mantle** ability. Laraaq thought it was cool and oddly enough so did Christy and Sarah.

Alice smiled. "Yep, there he is."

Laraaq asked Alice, "There who is?"

Alice turned to him. "My daddy." She said as she pointed to me. "He is my daddy. At first, I wasn't sure it was him, as his power feels different, like he's not whole."

At that moment a memory came rushing to the forefront of my mind unbidden. It felt clearer than what I remembered when I went through it.

I was floating in an endless space of golden white. "You are not whole. You are fractured. I have set in motion what shall heal you and make you whole again. This I can do for the one who stands in between us all!"

When I came to the present Alice was smiling back at me only a few inches from me. "Yes, daddy you are not whole yet, but you will be. I wasn't sure it was you at first, as you are so fractured now and missing much of yourself. However, I knew once you stopped holding back your power that it was you."

Alice wrapped her arms around herself. "I love the feeling of your unleashed power, it's like a warm blanket that wraps you up and comforts you."

Gr'ex chuckled. "Ha! More like wraps you around and chokes you!"

I glared at Gr'ex and slightly focused my **Dark Mantle** in his direction. He whimpered.

Alice spoke up. "Don't worry Uncle Gr'ex, I remember you too." She then turned to Laraaq. "And you too Uncle Laraaq."

Both Gr'ex and Laraaq looked confused.

Alice continued. "You both don't exactly feel the same either, but I can tell it's you. Daddy created me, forged me with the power to take the souls that should go to the Dark, and instead turn them into something we can use."

"Are you saying I turned you into this?" I asked incredulously and about to kick my own butt if I had corrupted an innocent girl in such a way.

Alice laughed. "He, he, he, he! Silly daddy. No, you 'Created' me using **Creation** magic mixed with **Soul**, **Mind**, and **Death** magic. There are some others in there that you said I would learn eventually. You made me in this form to look this old so as to draw out the monsters hiding in plain sight."

She put her hand on my shoulder. "You said you became the bridge to bring those back from oblivion, all those who lost all hope or had been corrupted by the Dark. You came back to save them and to give them a new path to walk."

Alice then pointed to herself. "Those that refused salvation, or an alternative path, were left to me to reap. You told me when you created me that you and your friends had come upon a horrible scene where children had been brutally raped and murdered. It made you remember what was done to you when you were a child. In your sorrow and rage you brought me into being."

Gr'ex couldn't help it. "Of course! He would learn **Creation** magic at some point! **Soul** and **Mind** magic, why not. Unbelievable the luck and talent... can't a goblin catch a break!"

Alice giggled. "He, he, he! Silly uncle. You said something similar many times on our adventures."

Alice smiled as she turned her attention back to me. "You sent me back to this time and place."

"Back?" I asked.

"**Time** magic silly daddy. I already sense it in your core."

Gr'ex threw up his arms. "That's it I quit! I'm going to become a farmer like Jek'jon wants!"

Jek'jon had a look of joy on his face. "Truly my friend? Oh, think of the wonders we will grow."

Gr'ex grew more frustrated as his friend clearly didn't pick up on his sarcasm. "Ahhhh! No, you idiot! I just meant..."

Alice leaned over and with her index finger bopped Gr'ex's nose. "Silly uncle. You know you love daddy and that you are proud to stand beside him and Uncle Laraaq."

"That's ridiculous." Gr'ex protested.

"You told me yourself." Alice stated.

Gr'ex seemed flustered. "Well-well, maybe in the future, but not now, got it!" He said the last part as he crossed his arms.

Jek'jon spoke up as he patted his friend on the shoulder. "It's okay my friend. You told me the same thing the other night. Over a jug of the Boom clan's special brew."

Gr'ex just pouted more.

Both Laraaq and I laughed at his antics. "Ha, ha, ha, ha! Leave it to Gr'ex to provide comic relief! It's okay buddy I love you too." I commented.

"Oh, is that why you keep him around?" Laraaq teased.

Alice laughed again. "He, he, he, he, he! Feels just like old times, like we are a family again."

I wrapped the little girl in a hug as I picked her up. I don't know what would've driven me to such a state in the future to create a being who was literally made to hunt down rapists and child molesters and take their souls from the Dark, but I would not deny that it was in my nature to do so. It was a fine line between justice and being a monster, but one that I would walk as long as I had my best friend, apparent daughter, and now new friends.

Turning to my allies, new friends, and family. "Come, it is time for us to go to our new home and celebrate!"

End of Apocalypse Unleashed-Book 1: And, So, It Begins

Epilogue

Outside the Newly Named Hope's Defiance

Gr'ex stood before the remaining Bone Marrow goblins. "Gr'onk, our master has chosen you to lead the remaining Bone Marrow clan goblins. Do you accept the position as chief of the Bone Marrow clan and pledge your fealty to our master Shadowalker? He who by right of combat killed Tek'tar and must now decide the fate of your clan."

"Gr'onk, accepts position of chief of Bone Marrow clan goblins and pledges fealty to the one who wears the Dark Mantle, my master Shadowalker and will follow the wisdom of the great Gr'ex!"

Gr'ex smiled. "Excellent! Now who disagrees with this decision and wishes to challenge it?"

Three large muscular goblins with axes stood up.

"Ah, perfect. **Curse of Agony, Curse of Agony, Curse of Agony**!" Gr'ex cast three curses, one for each challenger.

All three goblins fell to the ground screaming in pain that went down to their very souls.

Gr'ex looked out at the rest of the goblins who cowered in fear. "Let this be a lesson. You should never dare challenge my words or the commands of our master. Gr'onk has been chosen to lead. Should he fail, Shadowalker, or I will decide who shall succeed him. Is that understood?!"

Like a chorus the goblins replied. "Yes, Great Gr'ex, we shall serve and obey!"

Gr'ex smiled wickedly. 'Yes! This is how it is supposed to be! As much as I hate to admit it, giving my oath to Shadowalker has grown my own influence and power. He is the one with the **Dark Mantle**. Fine! That man just keeps getting more blessed as he has gained my loyalty damn it!'

Kit'erak raged. The lich knew the moment the portal was closed. In his fury, he shot one of his slaves with a spell that caused their flesh to decay as they slowly died, only to later be raised as another undead minion. "That worthless Tek'tar! I knew I should not have sent such morons! If only Gr'ex had not died so early in my campaign."

Kit'erak left the throne room and went into his private laboratory.

Slamming the door shut with magic, he approached the old tomes he had discovered. Rechecking his notes he exclaimed, "I am certain it is there! I may not be able to obtain it prior to the first phase of the integration, but that just means more undead minions when I pry it from their dead bodies."

Kit'erak chuckled. He, he, he, he, he. Yes, I will need to grow my army if I intend to keep it. I'll make the demons think I am just reallocating my forces to wipe out any resistance from the Light. They are so blinded by their hatred; they will not care. By the time they do, it will be too late, and my master will break into this reality and lay waste to our enemies!"

"First I will contact the demons that poisonous woods, Holly Woods I believe the demons called it." Kit'erak said as he launched a special Orb of Communication, he kept behind anti-scrying enchantments to ensure his plans could not be overheard.

The face of a horned demon came into clear view inside the orb. "What do you want lich?"

"Where is Abaddon?" Kit'erak asked as he ignored the disrespectful tone of the demon.

"It is none of your concern. Why have you called us?" the demon replied.

Kit'erak decided to gamble. "I must speak with Abaddon. I require more forces to quell an uprising of the Light."

"The Light in the apocalypse! Unacceptable!" The demon roared before he calmed down and continued. "Abaddon is checking in on his latest pet, a possible Dark Summoner. What do you require to deal with the blight that is the Light?"

"I will have to bring some of my forces through your Lost Angels territory. Supplies and weapons, perhaps some human slaves I can use as fodder or make undead minions out of." Kit'erak replied.

"Very well you will have what you require. Do not fail us Kit'erak, the Light is not allowed to remain in this world, it belongs to the Dark." The demon said before cutting off the connection.

After putting the orb away behind the anti-scrying enchantments, Kit'erak picked up a different orb.

Kit'erak activated his Orb of Communication to contact one of his apprentices. "They should be in a land with many ports, or something like that. Yes, he must move southeast and claim my prize."

Somewhere Dark and Dreary

'What am I doing here in frigid cold? Doing what I must, that's what.' Lilandra thought as she glided about the snow, that by her estimate was several feet deep.

The former queen of the djinn used her control over the elements to surround her with warm air as she glided along. No matter how hot she made the layer of air, the snow beneath her never melted and Lilandra still couldn't completely shake off the bone weary cold.

She finally spotted her destination. "That log cabin looks like something out of a horror movie. Ah human entertainment, what nightmares they conjure for themselves. When will they learn." Lilandra said to herself more as a distraction for her mind than anything.

As she approached the door, Lilandra hesitated. Was she truly ready to do this? No, but she knew she had to. The Light and the Dark were making moves, she had too as well. Mind made up; Lilandra opened the cabin door.

Upon entering she saw no fire in the hearth, no candle, only a dull glow that seemed to radiate all around the interior. Lilandra's eye took in the array of animal skins hanging on a few racks, clearly in the middle of the tanning process. Blood was on the floor in some places, mostly near a table that looked to be used for skinning animals.

A voice spoke in the darkness. "I see you are free from your prison. Why have you come to my home uninvited, dearie?"

Lilandra could not pinpoint the direction the voice was coming from, so she just spoke as she turned in the hopes of catching a glimpse of the owner of this place. "I have come seeking your aid."

Lightning quick, a blade flashed, pointed up towards her throat. As Lilandra looked down to the wielder, she saw an old crone of a woman in old, ratted robes, slender to the point of bony. Her skin was white as snow, as was the color of her hair tied in a bun. She had one hand on the long skinning knife and the other on a cane that she was leaning on. What caught Lilandra's attention the most though was the old woman's cold piercing blue eyes.

The old crone spoke. "You come seeking my help?! You may be my daughter's sister, but you are no child of mine! The nerve you have for even daring to enter my home! I should gut you, here and now! Skin you alive for even daring to intrude on my domain!"

Every one of the old woman's words felt like the cold slap of sleet from a raging blizzard. Lilandra took it all. She knew why the old crone was angry and she agreed with her completely. But she was here not for herself but her master. "I wish to talk. Allow us a chance to speak and I will go after, never to return if you so wish it."

"Careful dearie, a wish from a djinn offered cannot be undone." The old crone retorted before continuing. "Why would I bother to deal with the djinn? Your children were part of why I lost my son-in-law, and I actually truly liked him. Your people's actions broke my daughter's heart and left my granddaughter without a father! Again, why should I not unmake you where you stand?"

Lilandra knew such words were not an idle threat. This woman was known as the unmaker and could easily end her if Lilandra did not put up a fight.

"Because I need to speak with your daughter regarding the one, I serve. The Light and Dark are on the move again."

"They are always on the move. Damn them and their constant war!" The old crone retorted.

Lilandra ignored the outburst and continued. "The apocalypse has been unleashed, you must've felt it, even from here." Lilandra answered.

A large black crow cawed in the corner.

CAW! CAW!

The old woman went completely still for a moment, looked back at the crow then back at Lilandra. A second later she withdrew her blade and hid it in her robes just as lightning quick as before. "Very well. I will listen, but only for a moment. Come, have a seat."

"Thank you. How do you wish me to address you, Morta, Atropos, Unmaker?" Lilandra replied unsure how to proceed.

"Please you can call me Mother Winter here. I have no need to hide what I am in my place of power." Mother Winter said as she sat down on one of the two remaining wooden chairs and motioned to the wooden chair in front of Lilandra.

"Thank you." Lilandra said as she took her seat.

Lilandra took a breath to gather her thoughts before speaking. "The one that I serve is the one that freed me from my prison. I have become his first disciple. He is why I have come. I believe the Light doesn't trust him and may move against him. The Dark has already made moves against him by taking a man he calls brother and twisting him to their purposes."

"Careful dearie. Winter is all too familiar with the Dark, we must keep it and other things far worse at bay now, thanks to your failures. Now, tell me, what makes this one so special, beyond freeing you that is." Mother Winter asked.

"He has claimed ownership of the Hidden Infinite Nexus Realm." Lilandra replied.

Ice immediately formed on the tip of Mother Winter's cane before she slammed it into the floor causing the ice to shatter. "WHAT?! IMPOSSIBLE!!! NO ONE CAN CLAIM THE INFINITE NEXUS!"

The crow cried out again and Mother Winter settled down.

CAW! CAW!

Lilandra took the opening. "Only one such as him could have done it. He possesses complete affinity for all magics, such a thing is exceptionally rare but not unheard of."

"Yes, but that is only found in the royal bloodline of those dragons, and they are all gone!" Mother Winter protested.

"As you know, my prison and penance were to be the arbiter for the Hidden Infinite Nexus Realm. A place that no one could find, trapping me forever." Lilandra replied.

Mother Winter growled. "You'll get no sympathy from me or my family."

Lilandra held up her hands. "I am not seeking any. I would have paid the price over and over again for the part my kind had in so many deaths. What resulted..."

"Enough! Get to the point child! Winter is direct and bites down to the bone. Logic is our way, not flowery words." Mother Winter scolded.

Lilandra knew this would not be easy. Sighing, she continued. "I come to you for more than one reason. First, I ask that you tell your daughter, my once sister in arms, all that we discuss on this day, so she may decide for herself what to do. Second, know that I came to Winter first."

Mother Winter waved her hand in dismissal. "Please, you and I both know Summer's hot rage would result in their instant attack. You came to Winter because as cold and harsh we may be, our logic can temper our fury. My daughter and I are the only ones who can stand against Summer when they discover you have been released from your prison..."

CAW! CAW!

Mother Winter paused as she heard the crow calls. "Well perhaps we are not the only ones, but it matters not. I see through you child. You were always the youngest of us."

Lilandra nodded. She knew she could not fool the Old Crone. "True. I want Winter to meet the man I call Master and decide on whether to align with the Master of the Hidden Infinite Nexus Realm. He will need powerful allies now that that realm has been discovered."

Lilandra held up her hand to forestall Mother Winter's retort. "Plus, the apocalypse being unleashed on Earth will cause realms to merge back creating a possible connection with the Hidden Realm. If a connection is made, and the Dark or something worse gets their hands on it, we all could be in grave danger."

"That I can agree with you on. Is that all you have to say? I grow tired of this conversation." Mother Winter replied.

Lilandra took another breath. This next part had to be handled with the utmost care. One wrong move could spell the end for her new master. "There is one last thing. I believe, but am not sure, that I have encountered the reincarnation of the Huntsman."

Mother Winter rose from her seat as ice began to form everywhere. Spikes of ice jutted from every direction inching ever closer to Lilandra, but before Mother Winter could say anything the crow cawed again.

CAW! CAW!

Mother Winter sat back down but did not dismiss the ice. "Explain... now!"

Lilandra did as she was asked. "As you know, many fell in the Great War so long ago. The Huntsman's loss left nature in turmoil. No one to call for the Great Hunt means no one to rally others to cull those monsters who seek to upend the balance. The magic that is the Great Hunt is part of Winter's domain as it is typically conducted during the height of Winter."

Mother Winter growled. "I was there at the first hunt! I need no history lesson child! Now quit stalling and tell me where a most precious child of Winter is!"

Lilandra knew this situation was precarious at best. She risked the Old Crone's wraith but had to stick with the plan. "The Huntsman is a child of spring, born between the seasons and you know that..." she held up her hands as she saw Mother Winter reach inside her robe.

"I am merely being precise. Do not worry, I acknowledge Winter's claim. The Wild Hunt is always conducted at the height of Winter's power." Lilandra quickly added.

That seemed to mollify Mother Winter, as she withdrew her hand from her robe.

Lilandra pushed on. "Now as I said, I cannot be sure. Animals and creatures of nature seemed to recognize his authority and either wish to serve him or flee from his presence. The man is a natural hunter, like he was born to it. These are just some of my observations, there is more, but still, I am unsure. So, my suspicion is only that, a suspicion. Should that prove not valid, I ask you not take out your disappointment on the man. Can I have Winter's agreement on this?"

Mother Winter sighed. "You have my agreement on it, but I will not speak for my daughter. But I will share your words with her. Knowing this is only a chance and perhaps a slim one at that, will temper her fury at not regaining some of Winter's former power. Why do you care though? You ask for much for some random creature. Why would you be so careful as to gain agreements before revealing their name and location, it makes no sense."

Lilandra knew this was it. She mentally crossed her fingers. "His name is Deathwalker. He is the one that freed me and is the Master of the Hidden Infinite Nexus Realm."

Mother Winter dropped her cane. After a moment composing herself, the cane flew into her hand, and she leaned on it once again. "No wonder you were so careful. You know if it turns out he is the Huntsman it will give Winter a claim on that most sacred realm and more importantly a new home for our people. My daughter..."

Mother Winter paused for a moment to find the right words. "She would not like the outcome should this suspicion prove false. Too much would ride on it. My daughter may take matters in her own hands to bring this Deathwalker to our side. Go now. I must consider the words you have shared."

The spikes of ice receded and dissolved into nothing.

Lilandra bowed her head in acknowledgment before standing. "If you do decide to tell her, he is exploring the land of Timberfall. When you talk to Mab, would you include one last thing?"

Mother Winter looked up from her contemplation and stared at Lilandra but did not speak. Lilandra took that as opening enough.

"Tell her that I miss my dear friend and sister. We once were the closest of friends, like sisters. She may never be able to forgive me, but I still miss her and Tatania both. The three of us were to be your successors, but the results of the war changed so much."

Lilandra quickly left before she made a fool of herself. For millennia she had watched Deathwalker's home reality and his world. She had found great entertainment in watching them grow and invent new things. Which is why she could not reveal the one thing she witnessed, not even with her new master. The fact that in his act of claiming the Infinite Nexus, it became the catalyst that caused all of this, including the very apocalypse on his world.

She observed a new player on the stage, this Shadowalker, and worried for when he crossed paths with Deathwalker. Shadowalker had to many attributes of the Dark. Should he learn Deathwalker was the cause of so much suffering, Lilandra was concerned what would happen. No, she would not reveal that until she absolutely had to.

— — — —-

Once Mother Winter felt Lilandra leave her realm she turned to the giant crow. It took to the air and started to shimmer as it transformed. In its place was an Irish looking woman with red hair in robes fit for any battle mage.

The Morrigan took the seat Lilandra was just sitting in and smiled at her longtime friend.

Mother Winter looked at the Morrigan. "Well, what do you think my old friend?"

"Fate twists and turns around this master of hers as does it twist around others. It clouds my vision of her and most definitely of him. Whomever he is, I can tell you three things..." Morrigan paused and collected her thoughts.

Morrigan held up a finger. "One, a war greater than any before is coming, I can feel it in my very being."

She held up a second finger. "Two, Fate twists and turns around him. It calls to him and is a part of him like no other I have witnessed in the weave before. Time is both a part of him and his ally or it will soon be, Time is funny like that. It is hazy but I can sense that much." The Morrigan explained.

"That is not very helpful. We have known it was only a matter of time, Winter has been fighting back the Dark and worse things beyond the realms for millennia. There is a reason my daughter is called the Queen of Air and Darkness. But a war for the Infinite Nexus, that is worse than even the last Great War of the heavens." Mother Winter lamented.

"Yes, it will be. As I said that much I can see clearly. And if I can see that in the weave, so can the others." Morrigan commented as she thought of the spider goddesses that seemed to be rather active lately.

Turning to Mother Winter, Morrigan spoke up "We both must choose sides soon enough. I warn you, my friend. Do not be on the wrong side of this conflict. Every fiber in my being says Winter must join with this Deathwalker."

Mother Winter sat silently for a minute before speaking up. "You said you had three things to tell me. What was the third?"

Morrigan cast a complex weave of magic to further surround her and Mother Winter.

Mother Winter raised an eyebrow.

Morrigan sighed as she spoke. "Ahhh. One cannot be too careful. This last part is why every fiber in my being says join him. You may only speak of this to Mother Summer should Queen Tatiana find her Oberon. For the Dark has designs on him."

Mother Winter's other eyebrow went up.

Morrigan continued. "The Master of the Infinite Nexus is a Nexus himself. I do not speak of just some spark who can act as a knot in the Weave, and influence fate. When I say this, I mean the Nexus of Nexus's. Only the Creator is greater in this way. Which means God had a hand in this. Imagine it sister, a Nexus like no other Master of the Infinite Nexus! A spark that can influence fate and reality itself in control of a place that is connected to all realities! This will be a war for stakes higher than anything we have encountered before."

Mother Winter spoke up. "Finding a nexus is difficult at best. Some show themselves as Namers or become lesser gods themselves. How can you be so certain? Even we, the Sisters of Fate, have difficulties finding such beings."

"My gift is to find them, both on the battlefield and before they come into their true power. I am certain the Light gave me this glimpse. For when I check the Weave to find this Deathwalker, he cannot be found. The strand is hidden now." Morrigan explained.

"That would be the influence of the Hidden Realm. For you to have glimpsed it says much, but it does not prove anything to me, nor will it matter to my daughter. If he is the Huntsman, Winter will make their claim." Mother Winter commented.

"Then you will join this upcoming war? I thought you and Mother Summer were not involved in such matters any longer. You told me that falls to the current queens." Morrigan replied.

"Neither my daughter, nor I will remain neutral again, but we must be certain before choosing a side." Mother Winter answered.

"Then know this. I also sense other sparks of Fate, knots in the Weave are emerging. All are either tied to this Deathwalker or have some connection with him. Some may be a brother in arms others could be something else altogether, even an enemy. Either way they have a part to play in this upcoming conflict." Morrigan explained.

"If there are more knots in Weave why this one? Why not one of the others?" Mother Winter asked.

"When I try to look at the other knots, I feel an echo that traces back to either Deathwalker himself or something he does. That many knots tied to one being..." Morrigan shook her head before continuing. "No, I will make myself known to this Deathwalker when the time comes." Morrigan replied.

Mother Winter sighed. She was too old for all this. "Very well my old friend, I think I will join you. If he is the Huntsman, Winter must have him again. This Deathwalker must be assessed and only a queen can do so. As a queen of

Winter, I should have enough of Winter in me to see if he truly is the one, we seek."

Morrigan nodded in agreement.

"Though, from what you tell me, I should side with him regardless. As you know, my old friend, that is not Winter's way." Mother Winter commented.

Morrigan chuckled. "Ha! No, it is not, but my advice still stands. I will welcome the company on the journey regardless."

Mother Winter nodded. "I will inform my daughter of what I have learned. I do not expect her to rush if I inform her of my intentions to meet the man..."

Morrigan finished her statement. "But she may not be fully rational in such matters. These things bring up old wounds that have never fully healed. Our decisions are our fate unless we make different decisions to offset the outcome."

Mother Winter smiled at her oldest friend. "Come let us plan our trip to Timberfall and go before Mother Summer returns."

Somewhere in a Lush Forest

A small fairy flew as fast as their wings could carry them. They entered the royal hall of the Summer Court like lightning, only stopping in front of Queen Titania.

The fairy bowed. "M-my Queen!"

"What is so important you break with protocol and risk incurring my wraith?!" Queen Titania inquired.

The little fairy trembled. They had definitely drawn the short straw. "M-Mother Summer is..."

"What about my mother?!" Queen Titania interrupted as her red hair began to glow like fire.

The double doors swung open and an older woman with a cane strode in with confidence. She may be a crone but still held a vibrancy of life to her that age could not seem to take. "The fairy is trying to tell you I am here my daughter!"

"Mother? You are here! W-what? W-why?" Queen Titania stammered out in shock as her mind tried to wrestle with the situation.

She could count on one hand the number of times she had seen her mother outside her shared realm with Mother Winter.

Mother Summer walked halfway through the hall when she stopped and slammed the end of her cane on the hall floor.

THUD! THUD! THUD!

"LEAVE US! NOW!" Mother Summer commanded.

There were various fey nobles and attendants present. They all vanished, moving as quickly as possible to not incur either queen's wraith. As they all were making a quick exit, Mother Summer continued to approach her daughter.

Once they were alone, Mother Summer erected multiple anti-scrying and spying barriers. Queen Titania had a look of shock on her face. This was most unusual for her mother.

'What is going on?' Queen Titania thought.

Mother Summer embraced her daughter in a hug. "It is good to see you, my daughter."

Queen Titania just sat there in confusion. Her mother hadn't been very affectionate, or understanding for that matter, for thousands of years. Ever since Titania made the mistake of joining the Dark in the last war to show her support to her people, her mother had become distant.

When they lost the war, Titania's love, her soulmate, and King of the Fae, Oberon gave up his life to save her and the remaining fey who survived the war. This more than anything had driven a wedge between Titania and her mother so large you could fit star systems in between them. So, receiving a hug from her mother was the most baffling of events for Titania.

Mother Summer spoke up as Tatiana remained frozen in utter confusion. "Has it been so long that you don't remember how to hug your mother?"

"Uh! No... it is just..." Tatania began to say but decided to go with it. 'When might I ever get another one of these?' Queen Titania thought as she returned her mother's hug.

The two remained that way for a few moments until Mother Summer broke the embrace. She stepped back to get a better look at her daughter. "We have much to discuss. I do not have as much time as I would like before I must return to my sister, Mother Winter."

"What is with all this secrecy, mother? What would you hide from Winter or the Summer court for that matter?" Titania asked.

Mother Summer smiled. "Sharp as ever my daughter."

"Physical affection and now a compliment. You have hardly even spoken to me directly in thousands of years, usually choosing intermediaries, now this. I just... Why?" Titania settled on the question she really wanted answered.

Mother Summer knew her own pain and loss caused her to shun her own daughter for far too long. "I have left you alone in your grief, due to my own feelings of loss. For that I am sorry."

Queen Titania was even more floored by those simple words. In her entire life, this was the second time her mother said sorry. The first being when Titania took up the burden as queen. If she did not know for a fact the person in front of her was her mother, Tatiana would think she was speaking to an imposter.

Mother Summer sighed. "I still do not fully trust your decisions daughter, which is why I have come."

"There is the heart of it. But why now? I have been Queen of Summer for thousands of years and you have rarely interfered with any of my decisions, even when I chose to side with the Dark in the last Great War. What has you so concerned, mother?" Titania challenged.

Mother Summer sighed again. "No, I have only offered council when you asked for it. Perhaps that is part of my failing, but life finds a way and I felt so must you."

She paused before continuing. "My sister is focused on the ending or unmaking of things, that has always been her domain. Mine has always been in birth and rebirth, life itself. As that is my dominion, I have been given a glimpse of fate, a vision that I have come to share with you daughter, but only you. Our court must not yet know. I fear not all of them can be trusted, and Winter must not be told until we have no choice."

Queen Titania stood up straighter in her throne made of elegantly shaped wood. It was clear what her mother was about to share held great importance.

"The Light promised Oberon would one day be reborn. That was their only concession for us. The only glimmer of hope to regain our king. I have witnessed a knot in the Weave. One that tells me in my bones Oberon is in the world you now reside in. But I see a darkness that creeps ever closer to turn this hopeful future king to their side."

"My husband lives?! I have heard of no new fey born. Do not toy with my heart mother, I cannot bear any more suffering to it. Far too many pretenders have come and failed, burned to ash for their transgressions!" Queen Titania's eyes flared with power as flames erupted from her hand.

"Calm yourself, my daughter. Fate is a difficult thing to read. What I know is he was not born to the fey, but he is one of us. Much has been set in motion and caution is required. Now is when you must be patient..." Mother Summer was interrupted by her daughter.

"I have been patient long enough! Where is this hopeful Oberon?! I will test him!"

Mother Summer put her hand on her daughter's shoulder and the fires died out instantly. "No daughter. You cannot be the first to test him. What I have glimpsed says he must be tested by others first."

Mother Summer could see the pain in her daughter's eyes. "I know you have waited and your heart aches for your mate, I miss him too. But you must wait a bit longer. There are other sparks that have ignited recently. They are all knots in the Weave. So many, in such a short timeframe, speak of a new age of great change coming. We cannot afford to be on the wrong side of this inevitable conflict again."

Titania stared into her mother's eyes. The resolute look in her mother's eyes made her hold in her retort.

Mother Summer, seeing her daughter's fire tempered yet waiting to lash out at a moment's notice, nodded in acknowledgement. "Very well daughter. I will be the one to test this would-be-king. I ask you to wait until I am certain. I ask this as one of the Parcae. This is a matter for the Fates."

Queen Titania was now shocked for an additional time. Her mother never asked her anything. She told, but never asked.

'This is her olive branch.' Titania thought before speaking up.

Queen Tatania's voice took on a formal tone. "I will do this out of respect for the Queen that Was and for one of the Fates. Is there anything else one of the Parcae has need of?"

Mother Summer withdrew her hand from her daughter's shoulder. Sadness filled her eyes. This was not how she had hoped the reunion would go, but she had one more issue to address.

Mother Summer's voice took on an equal formality. "Yes, I have one more request for the Queen of the Summer Court. The spider goddesses are attempting to manipulate the Weave. A Dark Summoner has been brought to the underground lands of the Dark Elves. The Dark with the help from Winter has laid claim over this knot in the Weave. I do not know if the Winter Queen is involved, but a Dark Summoner is an army unto themselves, they are beyond dangerous. If they were to become a general in the Dark's army..."

Mother Summer shook her head. "No! Summer must not join the Dark, you must intercede, Queen of Summer!"

"A Dark Summoner is a being of legend! You say the Dark has already laid claim to this creature! And you just told me the Dark has machinations on the man who might be the reincarnation of my lost love! And you want me to not align with a force that could deliver me both!" Queen Titania said in frustration.

Mother Summer's voice took on a tenderness Titania had not heard for thousands of years. "Yes, my daughter. Summer must learn its lesson from the last war. If we can save our hopeful king, we will, but everything I have seen in the Weave says if we join the Dark, all of Summer, all of life and nature is lost."

Titania took on an equal tone of tenderness and concern. "What of your grandchild? If she were to find out Oberon is reborn, not even I could stop her machinations."

Mother Summer nodded. "That is why she must not know. If you must reveal anything about this day, let it be of the danger of the Dark Summoner and our pledge to the Light to fight the Dark alongside Winter. If Winter has gone back on their word, we will fight them alongside the Light."

"Very well mother. I will do as you ask, but not right away." Queen Tatania raised her hand this time to forestall her mother.

"I agree a Dark Summoner is one of the deadliest threats the Dark can wield, but there is rumor of a powerful prophecy being fulfilled on this world. Summer must see its outcome as well. This world is the closest thing we have to a home since our exile from Avalon. I will ask your granddaughter to intercede on this prophecy. Only then will I address this Dark Summoner." Queen Titania explained.

Mother Summer nodded. "Very well. I will abide by this decision. Give my granddaughter my love. I must return to my realm. I must find a way to distract my sister long enough to test this would-be-king."

Afterword

I wanted to thank you, fellow Travelers, for reading my third book. This series is a bit on the darker side, exploring the monster in all of us, it is the apocalypse after all. Even at the end of the world, some humor, even dark humor is needed to survive.

I started writing out of love for fantasy and science fiction but that has grown into a joy of finding ways to remind all of us that we matter and are here for a reason. Hopefully you will continue this journey with me. The Apocalypse Unleashed series is part of a larger universe called the Omniverse. The universe I am creating will span several stories and take us all on a journey of adventure and discovery.

I also wanted to take this time to thank my family and friends who have been supportive through the good and rough times. My family came here with nothing, they talked funny and prayed differently than others, but they came together and helped each other rise. Their stories have inspired me to create and pursue my own calling.

"We are not meant to live this life alone. We are more alike than different; we just have to look past the surface." That fundamental truth has always stuck with me and is a part of my writing. My hope is you will enjoy these stories and find something in them that speaks to you.

If you like these words or enjoy these stories, please leave a positive five-star review, it does make all the difference.

About the Author

ItalianDragon has a love for all things creative from art to fantasy, science fiction, and anime. Writing with a belief we are all more similar than different and just have to look for the similarities. Coming from an immigrant family who taught him the importance of self-accountability, critical thinking, and looking out for one another. You are bound to find such relatable reminders in his writing. ItalianDragon enjoys including cultural, popular, and nerd references to add to the humor and fun easter eggs we can all relate to.

Please click the link to follow the author on Amazon.
https://www.amazon.com/author/italiandragon

www.ingramcontent.com/pod-product-compliance
Lightning Source LLC
Chambersburg PA
CBHW050915030726
47503CB00007BB/2301